PENGUIN CLASSIC CRIME

THE FACE ON THE CUTTING-ROOM FLOOR

CAMERON McCABE

The Face on the Cutting-Room Floor

PENGUIN BOOKS

Penguin Books Ltd, Harmondsworth, Middlesex, England
Viking Penguin Inc., 40 West 23rd Street, New York, New York 10010, U.S.A.
Penguin Books Australia Ltd, Ringwood, Victoria, Australia
Penguin Books Canada Limited, 2801 John Street, Markham, Ontario, Canada L3R 1B4
Penguin Books (N.Z.) Ltd, 182–190 Wairau Road, Auckland 10, New Zealand

First published by Gollancz 1937
Published in Penguin Books 1986

Made and printed in Great Britain by
Richard Clay (The Chaucer Press) Ltd, Bungay, Suffolk
Typeset in 9½/11 pt. Monophoto Plantin

To pay back a debt to
Jim Harris and his camp
in Archirondel Bay,
for the long nights of that
summer of 1935 when
Mr McCabe's story broke

Contents

WARNING TO DÉBUTANTS
IN THE LIBEL BUSINESS

Any person wishing to identify himself, or herself, or any other person, dead or alive, with any character in this book, may do so at his, or her, own discretion. It shall be explicitly stated, however, that no such identification was intended, or called for, by the author. Any person who doubts the author's word for this, and accuses him – in spite of the above explicit statement to the contrary – of having committed a libel by portraying any actual person, alive or dead, will therefore himself commit a libel, namely, that of accusing the author of telling lies, and will thus himself be sued for libelling the author instead of the author being sued for libelling him.

SENTIMENTAL EXEGESIS

There is an expression in filmland which is genuinely tragic. It is 'the face on the cutting-room floor'. It refers to those actors and actresses who are cut right out of pictures. For one reason or another, it is found, after a picture has been completed, that their part is unnecessary. Thus are dreams and hopes felled with one snip of the scissors.

OTTO LUDWIG in *The World Film Encyclopedia*

The Face on the
Cutting-Room Floor

One

He walked in without knocking and began to talk before the door had closed behind him.

'You have to re-edit the junk,' he said. Then he coughed and wiped the sweat off his neck. Sweat always showed on his neck, never on his forehead. He was too fat. He loved French pastries and Viennese strudel. It was an unhappy love. You could see him growing fatter and he didn't like it.

'Yes, sir,' I said, 'and what can I do for your personal comfort?'

He smiled – rather reluctantly – and after a little while he said, still breathing in an unpleasant way: 'No kidding, Mac. Cut it out. Cut out the girl.'

'Sir,' I said, 'my client's reputation is spotless. He is happily married and there is no other woman in his life.'

He interrupted, somewhat too quickly, shouting: 'Stop it.'

Then he looked round, vaguely and without aim, and when he continued speaking his voice was tired.

'All right,' he said, 'check that witty brain of yours, it's running away with you. Now listen: you must cut out that Estella girl, every scene with her, I can't have her, the picture's too long. You cut it down to seven thousand feet. I'll send Robertson to help, and between the two of you you can do some juggling with your scissors and celluloid. You like it, don't you? What you say?'

'It smells,' I said.

He frowned. The skin of his forehead moved like skin on boiling milk. Then he smiled again.

'You're right,' he said, 'it smells. I should describe it as a singularly ripe piece of cheese.'

'The girl's got looks –' I said.

'– like a show-window dummy in a beauty parlour,' he said.

'She's all right,' I said. 'You wait and see. She's nineteen.'

'She's a wow!' he shouted. 'Bottle it.' Then, quietly and almost apologetically, a quick association of word and meaning: 'You got a drink?'

I quoted: 'Studio Regulations, Number Seven, Paragraph Four: "It is strictly requested that the –" '

'Go on,' he said, 'say some more. Your brain's sparkling today. Give me some Scotch.'

I took the bottle and the syphon from under the table.

'Soda?' I asked.

'Straight.'

We sat down and drank.

'A foul business,' he said.

After a while he got up and walked about.

'Right,' I said, 'it's so foul it smells like your singularly ripe cheese. You can't catch rats with that. But I'm smelling a rat. Why do you want to cut her out?'

'None of your business,' he said.

I stood up and walked over to him.

He did not turn to face me.

I had to address his back.

'Now listen, Mr Bloom,' I said to his back. 'Let's get this straight. You are the boss of this pot-house. You are the producer and I'm the chief cutter, and if you say, "Cut," I cut. But if you ask me to cut the other woman out of a triangle story and make it a straight honeymoon for two, then I'm just itching to hand you the scissors and let you try it for yourself.'

He looked at me over his shoulder with a tension in the muscles of his jaw. It was interesting to watch the movements which happened on his face.

'Because you see,' I said, 'what you want isn't cutting: it's a jigsaw puzzle. Robertson is a fine cutter, but if you cut out the point of a story there won't be a story left, and no Robertson and no McCabe's going to get you out of that rat-trap.'

He smiled. Then he said: 'Yes, sir, and what can I do for your personal comfort? Something is wrong with you. Sounds pretty serious. Must be the nerves. You'd better see a specialist.'

'I'll have to,' I said.

'Ring up Robertson,' he said, turned and went out.

Two

I tried to ring Robertson but there was no reply. It was twenty-five past six and I was certain that he was still in his office; I rang again but the line was engaged.

'Blast those switchboard fumblers,' I said.

Dinah Lee smiled behind her typewriter.

I looked at her and she started to hammer away on the keys.

'What are you playing, my sunshine?' I asked her.

'Tiger Rag,' she said and rattled on.

'Hell,' I said. 'This is no Gin Mill Upright, it's a typewriter.'

'Robertson's in the cutting-room,' she said.

'Which one?'

She said something but I couldn't understand her with the noise of the Remington going on all the time.

I thought he would be in Number Two and I went out. When I passed Bloom's office I heard people shouting inside. There were two voices. One of them, I thought, was Estella's. But I wasn't sure whether it was a rehearsal or some real quarrel.

The lift was not working so I had to walk down all the stairs to the studio. They had *Conversation after Midnight* on Stage A, and on Stage B they were shooting the night-club sequence for *Black and White Blues*. Outside in the yard they were trying some extra scenes for *Peep and Judy Show*, the Inigo Ransom comedy which was long over schedule time. I met the continuity girl from the new studio and I asked her whether she had seen anything of Robertson lately. She was tired and said no she had not and asked me how I was getting on with the cutting of *The Waning Moon*. She was interested in it because she had been floor secretary for the production.

I said I was getting on all right and she said: 'That's good, but now I must go over to the canteen to get a bite of something, I'm starving.'

I walked across the yard to the new buildings and asked for the Special Effects Department. They were still working there, putting furniture in the offices and wiring the studios for the new high-voltage lamps. The girl in the box was new, I had never seen her before. She was very polite and asked me to sit down while she was trying to find Robertson somewhere. She rang through to Robertson's office but again there was no reply. I said I would walk right up and she showed me the way.

She was pretty and she smelled good.

'What's your name?' I asked her.

She said 'Robertson, May – May Robertson' and smiled.

I looked at her but before I could say anything she said: 'Right. You are a detective: I'm John's sister.'

I thought I ought to be polite too. So I said 'I'm awfully glad' and went upstairs.

The walls smelled of paint and lime and mortar. There was a glass plate on the door:

JOHN ROBERTSON, M.SC., A.R.C.S.
SPECIAL EFFECTS DEPARTMENT
BRITISH AND ALLIED FILM PRODUCTIONS

I knocked. There was no reply. I knocked again and tried the handle. The door opened. I walked in.

It was a large white room, a sort of miniature studio. There were all sorts of lamps: arcs, inkies, jupiter lamps, babies and broads and spots; two cameras, tripods, trolleys, a small truck, and a great collection of screens; niggers, gobos, dollies; focusing boards, number boards, clappers; a cutting-bench with spools, winders, grease pencils, scissors, film cement on it, a film bin with a bin stick on the left hand and a film horse on the right. There was a new moviola of a very handsome type. There was a new sound-booth with recorder, mike and amplifier complete, and there was the most marvellous gadget-box I had ever seen. It had absolutely everything in it, masks and vignettes and diffusers, apparatus for dunning and back projection, changing bags and tools and everything.

Everybody was talking about Robertson's new Silent-Automatic-Infra. They called it the pride of the Special Effects

Department. It was Robertson's own construction, designed and built in the studio, an automatic camera for infra-red light. The thing was miraculous. It was smooth and absolutely noiseless. It worked in light and darkness equally well. There had been a story going round the studio that Robertson had once fixed the camera in the dark-room without the people knowing it and next morning he had shown them the film in his little private theatre. That was the first film anyone had ever taken of work in the dark-room. The studio technicians went mad. For some weeks even the trade journals talked about Robertson.

We didn't like him at first. He was a college boy. So we watched him. But he was all right.

And there was the camera. I went over and looked at it. When I touched the gear it was warm. He must have been working it a short time ago.

I went out to look for him. I tried the cutting-rooms and the head offices, even Bloom's office. He was nowhere.

Then I thought I had better have another look in his room. I knocked and of course there was no reply. Then I banged my head against the door because quite automatically I had tried to open it. But the door had not given way. It was locked.

I was fed up like hell. I had spent twenty-odd minutes trying to see that man Robertson. It was now a quarter to seven and he had left. I had missed him at least three times.

He had been there directly after my first call: I remembered distinctly having heard the *engaged* signal. He had been in his room shortly before I had first entered: I had found the camera gear still warm. And he had been there again after I had left and now he had locked the shop and gone home.

I cursed him and went out.

Three

I walked across the street to the garage. Most of the cars were still there but I could not find mine. I asked Max.

'You never brought her in this morning, sir,' he said with reproof in his voice.

Then I remembered that I had left her at Lewis's to have the brakes overhauled.

I mooched about for some time.

I looked at the sky and it was red in the west.

Then I was suddenly in the crowd of clerks and typists rushing towards King's Cross Met station and was dragged with them and swept away and did not resist.

In the air there was the smell of too many things. But I didn't mind. The smoke of the chimneys went with the exhaust from the cars, and the girls smelled of powder and lipstick and perfume, and that went with the smoke and the fumes and the sweat of men, and that was all right with me and I liked it.

It was a warm evening, much too warm really, one of those last evenings in November with the feel of July or August and the sky orange and heavy.

At King's Cross tube station I bought some evening papers and a pink-faced old man came up to me and said: 'You are studying politics too.'

I said: 'Now how did you know that?'

He said: 'You bought three papers at the same time.'

He had brownish-grey hair like gunmetal.

I said: 'How clever. There are still some geniuses left over.'

He said: 'Yes. Have you followed the Johnson-Myers trial?'

I said: 'I thought you were studying politics.'

He said: 'Yes. Politics too. Everything. But what do you think about murders?'

I said: 'Nothing. I never think about murders. I don't even read about them.'

He laughed. He had good white teeth. He did not smoke. There was no yellow between the teeth.

He said: 'Listen to this: Myers is having an affair with Johnson's wife. Johnson makes a plan to pay them back, both of them. He starts by pinching Myers's gun. Then he puts some sort of sleeping draught in her tea and puts Myers's gun in her hand. Then he phones Myers and tells him he has just found his wife dead, killed with Myers's gun.'

He looked at me.

His eyes were brown and friendly.

'What do you think?' he asked.

'Silly,' I said. 'It's damned silly.'

'Listen now,' he said. 'It goes on. Myers doesn't react the way Johnson has expected. Instead of clearing out, as he should have done, he drives straight over to Johnson's who doesn't want him there at all. He certainly does not want him so close. But when he tells him to get out, the good old mess begins. Johnson tries to keep Myers away from the woman and in the hubbub the gun goes off and kills her. Now she's really dead and neither of the two men knows who's responsible for the shot and each one blames himself.'

He paused again. Then he said: 'Glorious, what?'

I said: 'She must have been the kind of woman I should like to have known better.'

He laughed. 'Which way are you going?' he asked.

'I'm going the other way,' I said.

He called me back. 'Wait,' he said. 'What about the Grainger-Bennett fight?'

I turned round and he came over to me again.

'Who won?' I asked him.

He took up his paper and read out: 'Kid Grainger gained a fine fast victory when in the eighth round he knocked out Ginger Bennett at the new Empress Ring at Earl's Court . . .'

I said: 'I can read. You may not believe it.'

He said: 'Ginger boxed brainily, although mostly on the defensive. The Kid's all-action close-quarter work was the predominating feature of the early rounds.'

I asked him: 'Did you learn that by heart?'

He said: 'No, I wrote it. Listen: the Kid was at a physical disadvantage, yet he made the running, never giving Ginger a chance to settle down and box, and his two-handed tearaway fighting had Ginger perpetually nonplussed. Bennett certainly made use of his straight left but was only allowed to do so at infrequent intervals. He did better in the sixth round, when he scored with a well-timed right to the jaw. The side of his face, however, had become considerably swollen and the referee paid a visit to his corner at the end of the seventh round. But Ginger decided to continue.'

I said: 'Jesus Christ! You know the business. Are you a pro?'

'I used to be.'

'What are you now?'

He didn't reply. He said: 'The contest was scheduled for twelve rounds but in the eighth round the Kid belted Ginger about the body relentlessly and hooked well-judged blows to the chin which brought Bennett down for the second time. He got up at seven but the Kid punched so hard with his right that after a couple of blows he had his opponent on the boards for the full count.'

I said: 'Now let me have a look at your paper.'

He said 'With pleasure' and gave me the paper.

There it was, exactly as he said it.

'It was unquestionably one of the best heavyweight fights we have watched for a long time. Never a dull moment and very little clinching. Kid Grainger was the more aggressive boxer, and scored cleverly with his heavy left lead. Ginger Bennett endeavoured to bring his old cleverness into action but Grainger was too smart for him.'

I said: 'Now I can read it alone.'

He said: 'Trouble was that the promoters were left with little scope for filling the remainder of the programme. Quite frankly the rest of the bill was cheap . . .'

'Why do you say "quite frankly"?' I asked him.

He stopped, looked at me, grew thoughtful. Then he said: 'Yes. You're quite right. It's this damned journalese. But listen to this: there is some news from the Ogaden front. The Italians have bombed some hundred Abyssinian villages and Ras Seyoum is still hiding.'

'Those sons of bitches,' I said.

'Yes,' he said, 'you're right there. "I will have peace; I need peace; we must have peace," said Mussolini in a *New York Times* interview, 14th April 1934.'

'Do you know all these dates by heart?' I asked.

'Yes,' he said, 'Good night.'

He went towards the Angel.

I waited for a bus. The bus came but as it was one of the jolting type I could not read any more. The headlines were the only things I could read. '2,000,000 Russian Loan Talks in London,' 'Oil Search Will Start in 12 Counties,' 'Police Seek Man with 50 Aliases,' 'Gold Coins Stored by Road Sweeper in Old Safe' they said, and other nice things.

By the time we passed Tottenham Court Road my eyes were tired and I started looking out into the street. There were restaurants and snack bars on the right and shops with second-hand cars on the left. I thought that it was not really worth leaving the car at Mike Lewis's for such a long time. She was three years old now and I could just as well give her to one of those car-exchange people here in Euston Road and get a new one. The 1935 Riley two-seater perhaps, or a little green M.G. No, green was no good. Everybody nowadays had one of these green two-seaters. Probably they were given away as an advertisement for some manufacturers of green motor-car paint – yes, given away to customers who didn't object to the colour. I wouldn't do that. I would have grey so that the dirt wouldn't show. I would talk to Lewis about it –

The conductor called 'Great Portland Steet' and I got off.

In Lewis's shop there was still a light. I had been afraid that I would be late. They usually closed quite early. He did repairs for me more or less out of friendship. We had been at Douaumont together. He was a Frenchman. A French Jew from Lyons. A good salesman. A bad driver.

But there was nobody in the shop. I went over to the office at the back and knocked at the door. Dinah Lee came out.

'Hallo, Mac, I didn't hear you. I've switched off the bell.'

'What are you doing here?' I asked her.

'Dodging a divorcée,' she said. 'Come inside. Shortly after you had left, Lewis rang up for you and when I told him that you were most probably on your way to Great Portland Street he said that he had to leave at once and asked me to come over to his place and wait for you here. I was here before you, and here we are.'

'Where's Mike?'

'Oh, he's gone to feed. You are to ring him tomorrow morning.'

'Thanks. Where's he gone to?'

'The little Chop Suey in Buckingham Street.'

'What are you doing tonight, Dinah?'

'I have to close the shop. Then I'll have some grub too.'

'I mean: are you free tonight?'

'Yes, certainly. Why?'

'Let's go together.'

'Fine. Where shall we go? Chop Suey?'

'Hell, no. I hate Chinese food. Let's try the Turkish place in Greek Street. It's different.'

'No wonder. Like the Hotel Swastika in Rue de Palestine. But I like it. Don't you like the big doorman with the little kilt?'

'It isn't a kilt, damn you!'

'Oh, I'm sorry, Mac. I always forget you're Scotch. What is it really?'

'It is some Turkish skirt which looks like a kilt.'

'It isn't Turkish, it's Greek.'

'Anyway, it's not a kilt.'

She began powdering her face.

'Don't put white on your nose,' I said, 'it stands out like a traffic sign.'

'You're an old Scotch warrior,' she said. 'What do you know about tender English ladies?'

'*Ladies –*' I said.

'I'll tell you,' she said. 'I'll explain it to you. It is a special favour. You must promise to keep it from your girl friends.'

'Sure.'

'You see,' she said, 'you see, when I am excited I get a little perspiration here . . .' With the little finger of her left hand she touched the little dale between nostril and cheek, first on the left side, then on the right.

I thought: 'Narcissus seeing himself in the mirror of the lake.' And I said: 'You're sweet, may I kiss you?'

'No,' she said, stretched on tiptoe, threw her arms around my neck and kissed me on the mouth.

I looked at her. She was tiny, less than medium height, slender and soft-fleshed, the way a woman should be built.

'Now I have to start all over again,' she said, tracing her lips with a dark carmine. 'But what does the male know about make-up . . .' Then, interrupting herself: '. . . oh, but I was going to tell you, I *must* use white for my nose – I cannot possibly use a dark shade – when I perspire here . . .' The same gentle gesture: '. . . it will make dark patches – the powder will get moist – I shall look old – and you won't love me any more.'

'To hell with you,' I thought.

She put the mirror and the lipstick in the bag and closed it.

'Finished?' I asked her. 'Work is done?'

'No work is ever finished. But some work is done. That's the difference. I'm ready. Let's go.'

'Has Mike got the car here?' I asked her.

'She's in the garage. I'll get her for you.'

She came back in the car. 'Let me drive,' she begged.

'Have you got a licence?'

'For everything,' she said.

I sat down in the front seat.

She pressed the starter.

The car started lightly and swiftly.

You could feel it had a fine acceleration now. So the repair had been worth it after all.

We went down Great Portland Street, turned left into Oxford Street and via Soho Square to Greek Street, leaving the car in a little back street behind the restaurant.

Dinah lifted the doorman's skirt and slapped him on the back.

'You mustn't do that,' I said. 'It isn't done in this country.'

'But you do it in Scotland, don't you?'

She smiled and her lips puckered.

'I don't like you like that,' I said.

We went in.

It was warm and lovely inside. We both liked it because it was so un-English. They had carpets and glass cases with oriental necklaces and cigarettes and a fine carved sideboard. There were funny coloured Greek plates on a little frieze and carpets on the floor and over the door and between the tables, but not where they had the carved Spanish walls separating the tables so that they formed niches.

We ordered peperoni and mousaka aubergine and pilaff and bamia ragout and petits pois ragout and lobia ragout and shared the lot.

Dinah asked: 'Why do they always have French names for the dishes even in Greek restaurants?' and I didn't answer because I didn't feel like answering but I ordered a bottle of that dark yellow Greek wine and I told her it grew on the slopes of the Acropolis and she said she knew that there were no vineyards in

Athens and I laughed because I knew that she was lying and I felt happy knowing it.

She had discovered something and read it out aloud:

'The management of this restaurant has the pleasure to inform his clientele that Mr Papaioannou . . . I can't read it, what a name . . . to inform his clientele that Mr Fantastic-Greek-Name has been awarded the Grand Prix with Gold Medal at the International Exhibition in Paris 15th December 1930 . . .' She read it from a poster on the wall.

I said: '. . . for the excellence and purity of his food. Do you like the mirror with the carved frame?'

She said: 'Yes, what about the glass flowers?'

'No.'

A fat woman with too much *décolletée* entered left and disappeared right.

Dinah frowned and said: 'And this is where you spend your time.'

I said: 'Yes, and you yours.'

She said: 'There are no men in *décolletée* here. So why shouldn't I spend my time here?'

I said: 'All right.'

The fat woman came and offered us long Turkish cigarettes and little red cubes of a sweet stuff that smelled like soap and tasted like hell. Dinah said it was rose water.

We smoked the cigarettes and drank thick black coffee with much sugar. It was so thick that the spoon didn't touch the cup when you put it in the coffee. Then we left.

'What now?' I asked her.

'Let's dance!'

'Where?'

'You know the little Negro club in Kingly Street?'

'You mean the "Haunt"? I knew it when it was still in Little Pulteney Street.'

'Right. Let's go there.'

She put her arms round my neck again and kissed me.

'Not yet.'

'Why not?'

'It's too early. Besides, you behave too badly. You must never kiss a man in the street.'

'*Not* in the street – but *where*?' she asked looking straight into my eyes with that curious upward look that has become one of the female standard gestures since Theda Bara started it round about 1915 in one of her early screen vamping parts.

'Drop it,' I said.

'But what shall we do?'

'Have you been to see the French show at the Casino?'

'Yes. And I don't like it. I cannot imagine anybody liking it. I am surprised at you. I never thought you cared for that sort of thing.'

'I don't. But I thought you maybe would like it.'

'Don't talk Americanese. It don't suit you.'

She was seriously annoyed.

'Don't say "it don't".'

'Hell!'

We walked silently to the car and got in.

'Well?' I asked.

'Well?'

'Listen, my darling,' I said. 'If you do not care for "that sort of thing" – why do you go to see it?'

'I didn't go. Somebody took me.'

'So that's it. People take you. Who was it?'

'Bloom.'

I said nothing. She said: 'Mac – you disappoint me more and more.'

'The one thing important is not to disappoint oneself,' I said.

She said nothing.

There we were sitting in this lonely two-seater car with nothing but the nightfall of the darkly-lit back street around us and here we were behaving like a dead-alive married couple in bed at night after too many years of connubial bliss and mixed pickles gone by. Late Night Final Blues. And yet had only begun tonight . . .

Suddenly she looked at me and laughed. I looked at her and laughed too.

'Do you like Mickey Mouse?' I asked her.

'Yes, darling,' she said and kissed me. That was the third time. But before I could say anything she said: 'You mustn't kiss a man in the street, not even in a car, especially not in a car. Oh, darling, let's go to a News Theatre and see Walt Disney's latest epics.'

'Right,' I said and started the car.

We drove to the Tatler in Charing Cross Road and saw a very good programme. We enjoyed it and afterwards we went to a little French restaurant in Frith Street and had a *café noir* and cream and croissants with butter, that was like first breakfast, and when it was half past twelve we went back to the Lex Garage and fetched the car and drove up Regent Street and turned right into Kingly Street, just past Liberty's Swiss chalets, and stopped at the club.

I signed her in the book and she left her coat to the attendant and we went in.

Music came softly from downstairs and there was the sound of dancing feet and of somebody tapping and it smelled thick and warm and in the air there was that curious mixture of French perfume and American cigarettes.

Mrs Levy was sitting at a little table at the left with a lot of photographs of coloured artists hanging on the wall at her side. She was the boss of the club but she always had a coloured manager to entertain people and to produce the authentic Harlem atmosphere. The coloured managers changed, came and went, and some of them opened clubs of their own, but Mrs Levy stayed, and with her stayed a small gang of faithful ones and I didn't feel sorry that I was one of them.

We went downstairs to the little dark-green room with lamps hidden behind green silk and sat down and listened to the band playing blues and watched the hips and breasts of the women dancing and drank and smoked those sweet American cigarettes which taste as if they are drugged.

We danced and I felt her body moving against mine and I thought I was in love with her.

She was a fine dancer and I enjoyed the night with the white teeth of the Negroes and their fine and graceful bodies and the band playing blues and rumbas in turns.

I looked at her face and I saw that she was looking at me with her eyes big and dark and shiny and her mouth dark too but red and moist and weak and twisted in a way a woman's mouth should never be in public.

She was not beautiful but a hell of a lot of those things a man wants were in her face, but then they played 'St Louis Blues' and I saw Ian Jensen coming down the stairs with Maria Ray on his arm and I felt sick, ashamed of getting sentimental, but I knew that I didn't care a damn for Dinah Lee and I knew that there was Maria Ray and I knew that I would never be able to get away from Maria Ray and now I knew it for certain and I looked at Dinah and Dinah looked at me and then at Ian and Maria and I saw that Dinah had seen everything and understood everything and I saw that she was weary and tired.

They played 'St Louis Blues' and a little Negro girl sang:

> I hate to see
> That evenin' sun go down.
> Oh, I hate to see
> That evenin' sun go down,
> 'Cause my baby
> She done left this town.

And there was Maria with that man Jensen with his face like a Copenhagen hairdresser. Couldn't she have found anybody else to take her out? Just that pink-faced dummy. God, his hair was even whiter than it had been yesterday. In the studio they called him Black and White because of those black eyebrows and that platinum hair of his. They called him a genius of acting but he couldn't speak a line without the director dictating word by word and gesture by gesture. And so he was the Great Man. The New and Greater Rudolph Valentino. The Mystery Man from the North. Scandinavia's Challenge to the Film World. Hell Scandinavia. And Maria on his arm. Go over and punch him in that sweet pinkish face of his. Knock it to pieces. Knock it flat. Bed Bug. Getting some thousand quid for nothing. Ruddocks for riff-raff. And now with Maria on his arm. Just that dirty brick-presser.

> Got the St Louis Blues
> Just as blue as I can be.
> Got the St Louis Blues
> Just as blue as I can be.
> That man's got a heart
> Like a rock cast in the sea.

– and Maria with him. What did she do with him? Hell, what a question –

> For else she wouldn't have gone
> So far from me.

If it had even been Bloom. Yes, Bloom. Bloom was a man. He was fat and oily and suave, quite, but he was a man. He knew what he was talking about. He could read and write and he knew how to make three grand out of three pence. But that's what that man could do too. Make money. Hell, money –

> Gipsy done told me,
> Says don't you wear no black.
> Yes she done told me,
> Says don't you wear no black.
> Go to St Louis,
> See that you can win her back.

Yes, that's what you would do. Go to St Louis and win her back. What do you mean, win her back? As if you'd ever lost her. Go to St Louis. Christ! Go over to her table and ask her to dance. Show her Dinah's rumba step.

> A red-headed woman
> Loves to keep a good man down;
> A blond-headed lady
> Sends the good man out of town.

But that's what he could do just as well. Dance. Those gloomy-eyed pansies could always dance. Don't ask her to dance. Talk to her. Talk like hell. Talk about what? Talk about books, films, theatre, anything. But does she care? Like hell she does. She don't. Ask her about her make-up. That's what she likes to hear.

> If I'm feelin' tomorrow
> Like I'm feelin' today,
> If I'm feelin' tomorrow
> Just like I feel today,
> I'm gonna pack my troubles
> And make my get-away.

Make your get-away. That's what you would do. That's what he would do. Make his get-away. That harmless baby face of his. Smash it.

> I love my honey
> Until the day I die.

Oh Christ. You could sit down and cry. It won't help. Nothing would help. Eat it up. The man is all right. He earns his living like you and me. Right. Let him have his fun. Maybe she likes him. Why shouldn't she? Sure she likes him. Right. Give him a chance.

'Let's dance, Dinah. Let's do the St Louis Blues. Get up. Come on, swing it. Yeah man. That's the stuff. Shake it.'

'You're drunk.'

'I'm not. Come on, darling. Let's show them a number. Come on.'

'Sit down, Mac.' Low, harsh, sullen voice: 'Shut up. Leave me alone.'

Well so she's doing that too. Gone. Going, going, gone. A Harlem torch song.

'There's Robertson. He's looking at you. Pull yourself together.'

Robertson? That meant business. Excellent. No talk. No Maria. No Jensen. No St Louis Blues.

Business, no rumba.

'Hallo, Mac.'

'Hallo, John.'

'How you keeping?'

'Keeping fit. And you?'

'Could be worse.'

'Well, sit down.'

'Thanks.'

'Cigarette?'

'Virginia?'

'Yes.'

'No thanks. I only smoke Turkish. Sorry.'

'Right.'

Silence. They've finished 'St Louis Blues'. Now they're playing 'Clarinet Marmalade'. The cornet's good. They should play 'Cornet Chop Suey'. King Oliver did it back in the 'twenties. About the time they made 'Cushion Foot Stomp' and Papa Handy was still playing blues in Memphis.

'I say, Mac, has Bloom talked to you?'

'About the Estella girl? Re-editing the whole stuff?'

'That's it.'

'Well?'

'Lousy.'

'Quite.'

The trumpet is out of tune. If these guys could only stop imitating Armstrong. They should learn to play a straight chorus from a printed headline before they start trying to hit high ones.

'Where've you been today? I've been trying to get you on the phone all the afternoon, and Mac's got flat-footed trying to find you,' Dinah said.

I had quite forgotten that she was there.

'Yes,' I said. 'I've been looking for you – wait a minute – Bloom left at twenty past six – yes, from twenty-five past six till a quarter to seven. First your number was engaged, then you had suddenly disappeared, then you went back and played with your Automatic-Infra and then you locked your shop and disappeared for good.'

Robertson looked at me and then at Dinah, questioningly.

'What's it?' she asked him.

He looked at her, then back at me. Then he started chewing his upper lip. Then he got up and said: 'Well, I better be going.'

'What's the matter?' I asked him. 'You got a date?'

He looked at me again and said nothing.

'Well?' I said.

'Goodbye,' he said.

'Sit down,' Dinah said.

'Just a moment,' I said.

I got up and walked over to Maria's table.

'Hallo, Mac,' she said. 'How d'you do? You know Mr Jensen?'

'And how,' I said.

'Let's dance,' she said.

She smiled.

We danced. As soon as we had got far enough away from Jensen her face changed. She looked at me, annoyed and irritated. 'What the hell's the matter with you tonight?' she asked. 'Why do you treat everybody like poison?'

'I don't like that young man of yours.'

She let my shoulder go and for a moment it looked as if she was going to leave me standing in the middle of the floor.

Then she went on dancing.

She smiled again.

'Jealous, Mac?' she asked.

I thought 'I've no reason to be jealous –' and I said it.

But after some time I added: '– unfortunately.'

When it was out I could have killed myself. I was fed up with all I had said and done that night.

'Let's stop dancing, if you don't mind,' I said.

I saw her back to her table. Robertson had left our table. He was now sitting with Jensen, talking to him. Both remained seated when we came. Neither of them looked at me. Maria sat down and I went back to my table.

'Listen, Mac, this is curious,' Dinah said. 'Robertson says he left the studio at a quarter past four and he never went back. He says he locked his room and he showed me the key.'

I sat down and closed my eyes. They pressed from inside against the lids. I could not get my thoughts together. My throat felt like emery paper. And there was the blood knocking against the carotid. It was a hell of a night. That was what happened to you when you enjoyed yourself. Had some drinks and some cigarettes and some music and then you went home with a head like an ant-hill.

Then suddenly I had it.

'Jesus Christ,' I said. 'The face on the cutting-room floor.'

Dinah rose with me.

'What's up?' she asked.

'Sit down,' I said. 'Listen carefully. You must keep

Robertson here for at least two hours. Do what you can. Talk, dance, do anything you like. Be nice to him.'

'That's simple,' she said. 'What are you doing?'

'I'm leaving.'

'Going home?'

'Oh, no,' I said.

I went out. In the late evening there had been a thunderstorm. Now it was cool and clear and nice to drive with the sound of the tyres on the wet street.

Four

The next morning when I arrived at the studio the crowds were already there. The garage was crammed full with cars which did not belong to the studio gang. In the small lane behind the dubbing-stage there was an ambulance car and behind it one of those small black Hillman four-seaters, the police type of quick-runner.

At the front entrance a crowd of news-hawks and picture-snatchers had a row with the doorman. I made three efforts to force my way through. But when I had finally got through and I saw there was a new doorman and when that doorman asked me whether I had a studio-pass I shook my head sadly and said: 'I was just trying to trespass, so sorry, but you were too smart for me.'

He smiled proudly and said: 'Out you go.'

'Certainly,' I said and went to the back entrance of the new studio.

Macauley was at the door and let me in.

'What are you guys trying to do?' I asked him. 'Lock out your staff?'

'Haven't you heard?' he asked, angry that I had not heard and anxious to tell me all about it.

'Spill it,' I said.

'Well, you see, Mr McCabe,' he said, and he had the air of a man who is prepared to talk for some time, 'you see, when Mr Robertson opened the door of his room this morning –'

'Cut it down,' I said, 'make it snappy.'

He was disappointed. He looked like a bitch in heat who had missed her opportunity.

'Well, she's dead,' he said.

'Hell,' I said, 'who?'

'The new girl. Estella.'

'Lord in heaven,' I said. 'Where is she?'

'In his room. In Mr Robertson's room.'

I ran down the passage. The lift was still out of order. On the staircase I ran myself out of breath. I met nobody in the upper passage but there was a crowd at the entrance to Robertson's room on the third floor.

'You can't go in,' said the bobby who stood guard. 'Keep off the door.'

'Let me have a look,' I said.

'You can't –' he said.

'Get out,' I said and walked in.

But there was not much to see. She was lying there with her face on the floor and both her shoulders and her breasts covering the ground but the hips were turned to the left so that only the right leg and the right foot were on the floor but the left leg and the left knee, bent by the rigor, were resting on the right leg, both knee and foot hanging in the air, the knee some inches to the front, the foot some inches to the back. There were those two small wounds on her left arm between hand and forearm, two inches above the wrist. She had lost much blood, almost all her blood, the floor was covered with it, and she was dead and cold and pale. I had never known that a human being could look so pale. But she was young and very beautiful and there was nothing bad and disgusting about that dead body, except the paleness, of course, and the blood sprinkles all over the creamy white dress. But that looked almost like some curiously modernistic sort of design. Worth or Patou could show it in their summer collection. '*Rhapsodie en Rouge et Crème.*' But Worth was too English, no, Patou would be better, Patou or Saint Simon, that great new designer Bloom had engaged for our new production. He paid him a ridiculous salary, but the man was worth his money.

And there was that girl in her strange red and white gown, lovely and young and beautiful to look at, except for that blood on the floor and the wounds on her wrist.

I left the bobby and went out and walked across the yard to my room and looked at Dinah typing, looked at her strained face for a moment and went out again to the cutting-room and the first thing I saw was Estella's face on the floor, her face on the cutting-room floor, and I looked at the little piece of celluloid, held it up against the light and compared it with the face I had seen in Robertson's room.

But it was no good comparing, I had to go on with the job, I rang up Dinah and asked her to send the script over to the cutting-room, I sat down at the one cutting-desk which was empty and switched the light on, I looked at the continuity notes and then back at the script and then at the last rushes they had put on the desk.

It was no good. There you had those twenty thousand feet of film suddenly dumped on you, twenty thousand feet costing £60,000, £3 a foot, and then you were asked to cut that down to seven thousand feet, still costing £60,000, but now one foot costing £8 10s.

There you had a nice story of a boy and a girl and another girl coming between and he double-crossing both of them but finally returning to the first girl. It was a nice story, quite conventional but not too hackneyed; interesting situations, good scenery, clever machine-gun dialogue, lifelike acting, really good acting from the two girls, particularly from Estella, the second girl. Maria Ray as the first girl was not so good in her part but then she was just Maria and that was enough. And Jensen as the man – well, it was a shock to see him working on the floor but he was good enough on the screen and people liked him.

But the acting honours really went to Estella. It was her first big part and she played it as only first big parts are played: bad and enthusiastic and without any discipline, but better than she would play in ten years' time when routine and technique would have made her smart and polished and uneasy to look at. And then this idiot Bloom came in and asked you to cut her out.

I felt sore like hell.

Then I got up and went over to Bloom's office. I knocked and walked in without waiting for a reply.

There were four people inside. Bloom behind his desk, in the club-chairs two guys who looked like coppers, and the doctor, a white-haired old man, at the window, standing with his back to the street.

Bloom did not get up. He looked at me and said: 'Would you mind knocking before you come in, Mr McCabe?'

'Sure,' I said, 'I mean, not at all, Mr Bloom. Besides, I did knock, didn't I, Dr French?'

The white-haired old man smiled and said: 'Yes, Mr McCabe. You did knock but you didn't wait for the come in.'

'There was no come in,' I said. 'Bloom, did you say come in? You didn't. Well, gentlemen, so I walked right in.'

There was silence for a while. Then Bloom said: 'What's the matter with you, Mac?'

'Why did you want to blot out the Estella girl?' I asked.

Bloom said 'What do you mean?' in a voice which was rough with hoarseness. Then suddenly he went so pale that it looked like a badly faked trick of the Special Effects Department.

'I mean, why did you want to cut Estella out of her picture? Why did you want to cut her out of the chance of her lifetime? But I must not put it like that. You're a businessman. Then why did you ask me to cut your picture to pieces? That picture must have cost you about sixty thousand. Not much, of course. But I mean what was the exact reason for killing Estella Lamare?'

Nobody spoke. I did not even hear their breathing.

There was a pause. I heard the street cars outside in King's Cross Street and a funny klaxon of a bus passing by and a heavy lorry shaking the walls of the house. Then there was a faint sound of music coming from Stage B. They were still shooting for the nightclub sequence of *Black and White Blues*. Now I heard the sound from Stage A too. Robert Seaman was directing *Conversation after Midnight*. I heard him shouting commands and I laughed because his voice was so much like that of my first schoolteacher. His name was Buttersoft and we used to tease him a lot.

Then Bloom's voice again: 'Get out.' And his breathing again and the other people's breathing too.

I turned round and went out. I heard no word, not even after I was already three steps away in the passage, and the door did not open for me.

Five

I worked all day in the cutting-room, did not pause for lunch and not even for tea and at about six o'clock the door opened and Robertson came in. He sat down and smoked his pathetic little menthol cigarette. I heard the sucking, it was not a pleasant sound, but he did not speak and I did not speak, only the unpleasant sound of the cigarette between his teeth and the clapping of the scissors and the rustle of the celluloid and the rotating of the winder.

Then a girl from the joining-room came in and asked me something about the order of the rushes from *Peep and Judy Show* and I told her and she left and then Robertson stood up and said: 'It must have happened between a quarter past four and a quarter to seven.'

'Yes,' I said.

'When did you first try to ring me?'

'After Bloom had left. That means twenty-five past six.'

'And when did you find the line engaged?'

'About five minutes later. Half past.'

'And then you went straight over to my room?'

'I didn't know the way. I had to ask your sister. And I talked to the continuity girl in the yard for a moment. I believe it must have been between six thirty-five and six forty –'

'And you found the camera still warm?'

'Yes. And I returned at a quarter to seven and found the door locked.'

There was another pause. Then, reluctantly, he said: 'Last night I thought you were drunk, both of you.'

'I was drunk all right,' I said, 'but I knew that somebody

had been in your room between twenty-five past six and a quarter to seven.'

Then he said: 'The door was connected with the camera. If anybody has been in the room there must be a film. But there is no film. Somebody has emptied the camera. There is not one inch of film left.'

'You mean it was not suicide? She has not done it herself?'

'I don't know. Maybe she has. But somebody else has been in there. Either together with her or before or afterwards.'

So that was it. I looked at the film on the floor, then out of the window. It was raining. Autumn had begun. The soft summer air had gone. I saw the navvies asphalting the street, the black hole in the middle of the street with the gas pipes passing under the ground; in the bottom of the hole water had collected and there was the rain falling and drawing expanding circles into the surface.

Two children digging in the mud. Playing underground trains.

So that was all there was left. Dig up the mud and play underground trains. And the rain falling with the roofs wet and the streets wet and the water dripping from the edges of the windows.

I sat down again; then he sat down too.

'What about Bloom?' he asked.

'Well?' I asked back.

'I don't know,' he said. 'Has he been cross-questioning you yet?'

'Who?' I asked.

'His name is Smith. Plain Mr Smith. Detective Inspector Smith from Scotland Yard.'

'No,' I said, 'what does he look like?'

'Like Mr Smith. Like Detective Inspector Smith from Scotland Yard. He says that you were the first one to give him an idea what this is all about. You bumped straight into his examination. You did not even knock before you came in. You walked straight into Bloom and accused him of killing Estella Lamare. He always thought there was something fishy about Bloom.'

'Always?'

'That's what he said.'

'You really think he's got a hunch?'

'He says he has.'

'And what's your guess?'

'I don't guess. I know. I know somebody has pinched one reel of film showing every detail of the little musical comedy which was played last night without my consent in my room. And I'm going to find that film.'

'If it still exists,' I said. 'If it was murder and if I'd done it I would get rid of the stuff before I'd do anything else. What do you think, why does he pinch it?'

'There are various possibilities. To start with, you don't know who pinched it. If it was murder and if the murderer's taken it, he has most probably got rid of it. That's plain. But you're not sure it wasn't somebody else. You know, even if it was murder somebody else may have got hold of the film. For instance, a friend of the murderer trying to cover him – what do you say?'

'But you're not sure it wasn't suicide. You know she had the best reason in the world. Bloom diddled her out of the chance of a lifetime.'

'Yes. That was a dirty trick. I can't see the point at all.'

I laughed.

He asked: 'What?'

He didn't fall in on that.

He said: 'If she, I mean Estella, if she'd done it herself, he must be having a hell of a time. Bloom, I mean.'

He said that and went to the door. To prevent blocking in fire emergencies, all doors in the studio opened outwards. So he bumped straight into a big fair-haired man who was standing outside.

'Hallo, Inspector,' Robertson said. 'But you mustn't listen at doors. Only stage detectives do.'

The man said nothing. He walked in and closed the door leaving Robertson outside.

Then he looked at me and smiled.

'Mr McCabe, if I'm not mistaken?' he asked.

'The same,' I said.

'Well, as Mr Robertson has been kind enough to spare me the bother of having to introduce myself, we could just as well plunge right into the subject. May I take a seat?'

I pulled out a chair from under the cutting-desk.

He said: 'Thanks, I'll sit on the table.'

He leaned against the desk, half sitting, one foot resting on the floor, the other one crossed over somewhat undecidedly, half pending in the air like a question.

'You smoke?' he asked.

'Thanks,' I said. 'Not in a cutting-room.'

'Well, Mr McCabe,' he said putting back his cigarette case,

'will you allow me to put some questions before you? Merely informal, of course. Just for the inquest.'

'Sure,' I said, 'do your duty. I'm glad if I can help you in any way.'

'You can,' he said, 'you have already.'

'That's news,' I said.

'You walked into Mr Bloom's office and asked him some very pointed questions. May I ask you now what sort of reason you had for questioning Mr Bloom in this – may I say – rather peremptory way?'

'Certainly you may. But I would like to ask you a question too. Do you happen to know anything about film production?'

'Not much.'

He smiled, but without embarrassment.

'I go to the pictures once or twice a week –'

I interrupted him: '– have you ever heard that a film is sometimes changed after it is finished? You find for instance that a certain actor or actress does not fit into the cast. But you discover that only after the production has left the floor, that means after you have the whole stuff fixed on celluloid. Well, what would you do in that case?'

'I would choose my actors from the beginning so that they fit into the cast. I wouldn't risk any such unpleasant surprise results.'

'Yes, one would think so. But things look different on celluloid. It is by no means unusual to change the stars round after a film has been produced. By careful adjustment the second lead can be changed into the hero, mainly by cutting short the original hero's scenes and giving fuller length to the sequences played by the second lead –'

He stood up and said: 'I appreciate your opinions, Mr McCabe, but –'

'– they are not my opinions, or at least not exclusively my opinions. I am sorry to interrupt you.'

'Not at all,' he said. '*I* am sorry. I interrupted first. Go on.'

'These things are plain facts. A man called Otto Ludwig, who is one of our finest cutters, once wrote the story of a film editor who made a complete film without the hero acting a single scene for it. What the cutter did was to dig out all the star's old pictures and from them he obtained sufficient situations to enable him to work his hero into the leading part.'

'Come to the point,' he said without annoyance.

'Sometimes a girl – or a man – will "steal" a picture from

the star. Her acting will be so good that she stands out, over-shadowing the heroine completely. So her part has to be toned down in the cutting-room for the benefit of the star and the story.'

'And that is what had happened in the case of Estella Lamare?'

'Not exactly. Bloom wanted me to cut her out of the picture completely.'

'Would that be possible?'

'Certainly. But only at the cost of the story. And of course we would have to do a lot of re-takes.'

'A curious waste of money.'

'Yes,' I said. 'And now we agree, Inspector. A very curious waste of money indeed: particularly since the girl turned out perfectly, in the studio as well as on the screen. And that, Inspector, is the exact reason for my pointed question to Mr Bloom.'

He said 'Thank you' and stood up. Then he added: 'And now you shall have the answer to your question.'

'Just a moment,' I said. 'Would you mind if I ask my secretary to take some shorthand notes of your statement?'

'A novelty,' he said. 'Reversal of the judicial process. Are you interested in criminology?'

'Never mind,' I said, 'would you take objection to my request?'

'Not at all.'

'Thank you. Then I shall call my secretary.'

I rang and Dinah came in with her notebook and sat down.

'Take a statement,' I said.

'An interview,' he corrected. 'Do you happen to know that Mr Bloom was on rather intimate terms with Miss Lamare?'

'You mean whether he had an affair with her?'

'Exactly.'

'I know nothing about it. But if you ask me what I believe I'll tell you.'

'Well –?' he asked.

'Bloom would pay you a dividend for that joke,' I said. 'That's more than a joke: it's a crystal ball!'

'Meaning –'

'Bloom isn't that type of man. He is not the type of film producer you see in film productions of the type.'

'I like your juggling with words –'

'So do I. Bloom is no sugar-daddy. He never was a casting director.'

'Maybe he wasn't. I'm rather inclined to believe you. But

this is where you're getting off. Bloom *did* make advances. He even proposed to her.'

'Proposed what? You don't mean marriage?'

'Not exactly marriage. But something like it. You could call it the simpler pleasures of married life.'

'Ah. And she turned him down?'

'Yes.'

'And he turned yellow and let her take the fall?'

'Yes, letting you drop on her.'

'Hallo, Dinah,' I said. 'You can go. You can burn the statement. You can enrich your waste-paper basket.'

I could not help laughing.

Smith smiled back and said nothing.

What a nice man he was. So utterly unlike a copper. Nice and quiet and gentlemanly. Very much like Oscar Wilde's idea of a gentleman. What a pleasant lack of pedantry. A good man.

He had an agreeable gesture of patting his hair above the temples. Rather effeminate. He caressed the light-blue veins which showed on the white skin over his temporal bone and said with a friendly motion of his shoulders: 'Well, that's all, Mr McCabe. That's all we know at present.'

He took his coat and went to the door. There he turned round slowly and said: 'I almost forgot. Isador Bloom says it was he who killed Estella. He is pleading guilty.'

Then he went out, bowing first to Dinah and then to me.

'Why did he bow to me first?' she asked. 'It isn't done to bow to typists, is it?'

'I don't know, darling,' I said. 'I would rather bow to you than to him.'

Six

That night I met Christensen in Guilford Street, not far from Jensen's flat.

'Hallo, Chris,' I said. 'How are things? How is Jensen? I haven't seen him since last night.'

'Hallo, Mac,' he said.

'What's on?' I asked him. 'You got the blues?'

'No,' he said. 'Can I talk to you for a moment?'

'Sure,' I said. 'Let's go to Cookie's.'

We sat at a little table close to the wall which was yellow and plain. But the other wall opposite had a fantastic design representing some people at a round table. One of the figures wore a top hat which showed that it was a man. That indication was necessary because the men looked like women and the women looked like men. The colours were too glaring. They were like the music white guys play when they are copying coloured folks – not hot by nature but by lack of harmony.

He looked at the painting and said: 'I killed Estella Lamare.'

'Another one,' I said.

For a moment he looked at me blankly, then he cracked up and his expression changed to wonder and then to intense amazement. He still looked at me and now it was a questioning look.

'You are the second murderer,' I explained.

'I do not understand,' he said.

'Neither do I,' I said.

'I killed Estella Lamare,' he said again.

'You said that before,' I said.

'I killed her by accident yesterday at about half past seven,' he said. Then he got up and said: 'And now I am going to phone the police.'

'Wait a minute,' I said. 'Why did you kill her? Besides, there is no telephone in this place.'

He went to the door and said: 'Then I shall go to the nearest telephone box.'

I stood up and seized him by the collar of his shirt. It was a shirt with an attached collar. I wrested the collar round my hand until he choked and got white in the face. I said 'Sit down!' and forced him down on his chair. Then he spoke and his voice was quiet and normal and clear except for that slow and curious intonation, his Scandinavian accent and his all too correct construction of the phrases.

'It is very simple. I loved Estella and when she told me the day before yesterday that Bloom had proposed to her and that she was going to accept – well – I just could not stand it. So I followed her to the studio. But she asked me to leave her alone. I implored her to grant me an interview but she said there was no place where we could talk. So I left her. But going out I saw the keys of all the rooms hanging on the back wall in the janitor's box and when he looked away for a moment I took one and went back again. Alone in the corridor I looked at it and it was Number 126, that is Robertson's door number. So I went back to her dressing-room and asked her to meet me in Robertson's studio.

'And then everything happened very quickly. I said I would kill myself if she married Bloom. She said she loved me but she had to think of her career and she would rather kill herself. And before she had finished the words she took the scraping knife from the cutting-desk. I tried to take it from her and we struggled and suddenly the blood was spurting from her wrist and I was frightened and I ran out of the room and locked the door behind me and ran downstairs. The doorman was not in his office so I had time to hang the key on its hook in the box and I went out and nobody saw me.'

It was a long speech, without intervals, and all too fluently to be convincing.

'A nice story,' I said. 'A very good story indeed. And now tell me what happened to the film.'

He looked at me blankly.

'Do you happen to know anything about the film which

showed the death of Estella Lamare and which disappeared after the death of Estella Lamare?'

'No,' he said slowly. 'I know nothing about it.'

'Good,' I said, 'then you'd better phone the police.'

Seven

I stood in one corner of the studio gallery and looked down on Stage B where Victor Rosenzweig was directing the last street scene of *Black and White Blues*. Yesterday they had finished the night-club sequence. And now Vic was talking to the funny, explaining the next scene. I heard the two voices rising faintly from the floor below. I heard the commands and signals of the scene shifters who moved some heavy floats across the floor. It was early morning and there were not many people in the studio. The crowd had not yet arrived, only Vic and the old funny were talking in this corner underneath the gallery and in another corner the assistant director, a new man, was shouting at the top of his voice. At first I could not hear what it was all about but when I heard William's voice I knew that something was wrong with the props.

Something was always wrong with the props in this studio though Bill was really the most efficient prop man I had met in any studio. He had a nice deep voice very much like the bass of a Negro glee club and this voice seemed to annoy everybody in a curiously unreasonable and quite incomprehensible way.

'All right, slave driver,' said the voice, 'I get them flowers and put some aspirin in the water and you'll have your little birthday present for sweetie pie.'

But then the slave driver shouting again and Bill replying without emotion: 'All right, all right, pipe down, ol' man.'

Somebody strolled across the floor and I asked one of the grips who the man was. 'Don't yer knaw?' he said. 'Why, man, that's Vic's new heavy. Can't yer see the boot-polish on that lady-killin' moustache of 'is?'

He felt flattered that I had asked him for information.

'You seen Maria anywhere?' I asked.

'Not yet, sir,' he said.

I thought he said sir because he did not know my name.

'I'm McCabe,' I said. 'Cutting –'

'I know,' he said. '*Do* I know you! You're the cutting chief, you're the man what made the boss own up –'

'Just a moment,' I said. 'You'd better clean your teeth before you start talking. That dirty talk is going to do us a lot of good.'

'Well,' he said. 'What's the good word? Ain't yer got enough on that guy to make sure of nailin' 'im all right?'

He turned round to go away without haste.

I caught him by the lapel of his overall.

'You stay here,' I told him. 'What are you getting at?'

'No good talkin' this close to the mike,' he said and walked off.

I looked round and I saw the boom being lowered from the crane on to the floor. The pole with the microphone on it passed less than six feet from us. If they had it switched on they must have caught that blabber in the sound-booth, possibly they had even recorded it. But that was rather improbable.

Looking down, I saw they were already rehearsing on the floor.

Vic took the meg and shouted something at the camera people. They were changing the set-up. He shouted: 'What are we waiting for?' Somebody said: 'Waiting for sound.'

The second assistant shouted: 'Quiet on the floor please.'

The camera man focused on Jim's stand-in.

The second assistant said, quite unnecessarily, 'Ready to shoot.' Then he skipped out of sight, the first camera man shouted 'Line up OK' and Vic shouted 'Turn 'em over' and I heard the camera motor behind the padding getting up speed. The padding was too thin. The lights were not fully turned on and Vic shouted: 'Christ! Light 'em up! Flash 'em!' Then the lights flashing on and the soundboom operator's voice 'OK for sound.' Then Vic's voice again shouting 'Quiet please, action' and the number boy jumping from the side of the set with the clapperboard in his hand. I could not read the letters in the ridiculous glare of the arclight, but I heard the boy's voice reading it out for the sound track:

BLACK AND WHITE BLUES
VICTOR ROSENZWEIG
JIM JEFFERSON
I. 412, TAKE I

Then he jumped out of sight and the funny and Jim did their turn. The scene did not last longer than half a minute, then the clapper boy jumped in front of the camera and hit the boards together to synchronize the sound and action and then that seemed to be finished. But Vic was not satisfied. They had to do it all over again.

I. 412, TAKE 2

shouted the number boy, but half-way through the scene Vic shouted 'Cut! For Christ's sake, cut! Save 'em!' So they switched the lights off and I walked down the stairs to talk to Vic. He shouted 'Circle it!' but when I passed the a.d. he grumbled 'That meg wielder's mad. Such a nice getover.'

'Hallo, Vic,' I said.

'Hallo, Mac,' he growled. 'That dirty ham with his dump pan –'

Then he turned round and looked at the crowd. He picked out the still photographer. He winked to him and said: 'Take some stills.' Then in a lower voice: 'Keep them busy for a minute.' Then loud again: 'OK?'

'That's OK with me,' said the stillman and bowed from the waist.

When he had gone Vic turned to me and said: 'Hell, Mac, what's it all about? You're supposed to know something. Let's have the dirt.'

Some of the extras came nearer and waited for me to finish so that they could talk to Vic.

Vic turned round and shouted 'Get out, you bloody lens lizards!' and his face was exaggeratedly furious which made it funny.

'The studio's going nuts,' I said. 'I just want to know one thing: who's that grips over there?'

'Going nuts all right,' he said and looked at the man in the overall. 'They call him Happy. That's all I know. But now' – he was white and his face had red spots – 'now, Mac, tell me, what's it all about Bloom and Chris and the whole Estella business –?'

'Give me Happy for a moment,' I said, 'then I'll tell you all about it.'

'But who –?'

I had to interrupt him. 'Can I take Happy up to my room for a moment?'

'Yes, sure. But tell me, Mac, what –'

'Cut it out,' I said. 'Happy first.'

'All right, Mr Holmes,' he said, 'and how's our friend Dr Watson?'

'Dusty,' I said and went over to Happy.

'Hallo,' he said, 'here we are again.'

'Happy, this is Mr McCabe, our Supervising Film Editor. He wants to have a chat with you,' said Vic.

'That's another department, I'm a scene shifter,' said Happy.

'Come on, Happy,' I said.

We went up to my room. Happy rolled himself a cigarette and lit it. He smoked and hummed a little twelve-bar blues tune to himself. But his eyes smiled.

'I like your singing,' I said.

'Pity I ain't got a voice,' he said, 'gosh, what a great singer I'd be if I'd got a voice.'

He kept on humming.

Then he suddenly said: 'Bloom's in a tough spot right now, ain't he?'

'I'm glad you've started the game,' I said.

'Yes,' he said, 'why not? There ain't no harm in talking.'

'You should know,' I said to encourage him.

He hummed again. Between two notes he said 'Sock 'im on the boko' – and three bars later – 'or you'll be sunk.'

'Make yourself plain,' I said.

'The thing's no good. Chris is wriggling out from under,' he said joyfully. 'You gotta give 'im the works.'

His eyes showed nothing beyond the smile which was friendly.

I looked at him.

'It's all up with your case against Bloom if you don't keep that fella Chris from stirring things up.'

He beamed with delight.

'What you say?' he asked.

'I just wonder what you're getting at,' I said.

'You don't have to worry none about that. You'd better let me have the lowdown on something I wanna know.'

'Sure,' I said, 'spill it.'

'Right,' he said.

Then he smiled again and asked cheerfully: 'What kind o' job did you put up on rosy-cheeked friend Bloom?'

'Ah!' I said. 'Now I get you. Little Happy's collected detective stories, bound in pigskin, with a frontispiece showing the eminent author at work, thirty-two fine mounted collotype plates, ten in colour and six monochrome. It's all a big frame up and I'm the one that's spilling the dirt on Bloom. But you won't hand me over, Mr Happy, will you? I hate crossed bars from the inside.'

'The day before yesterday, sometime after seven fifteen, the Estella girl was pooped. It's a pipe somebody knows something about that afternoon,' he said.

I said: 'You forgot to put the plug in. The whole bath is running out.'

'It's gonna raise a stink,' he said.

'Have it your way,' I said.

'You're smoked,' he said.

'I'll recommend you to my superiors at Scotland Yard,' I said.

'Lay low,' he said, 'you ain't got the right temper. You'll fly off the handle.'

I stood up and said: 'The flesh is willing but the spirit is weak.'

He got up and went out. I heard his humming fading out in the distance together with his footsteps. Then it got lost in the staircase.

Eight

At six o'clock when I was leaving the studio I met Dick Flaherty
and some other people from the studio orchestra. They were going
to the Gramo Studio to make some records of our latest tunes and
they were one man short in the rhythm section. They asked me
whether I wouldn't like to hit a suitcase and I said yes, so we took a
tube up to Hampstead.

We made a couple of hot ones for Parlotone release and I
enjoyed it but when they started recording the waltz from
Conversation after Midnight I stepped out and went back to King's
Cross Street to fetch the car.

I had dinner at Simpson's and then some coffee at the Café
Royal and when it was ten o'clock I left and rang Bloomsbury 6364
and asked for Miss Ray. The maid said Miss Ray was in her bath
and I said thank you no message, and rang off.

It was still raining when I came out, so I put the hood up
and drove through Wardour Street and turned right into Oxford
Street and then down New Oxford Street and Holborn and left into
some small street I did not know until I came through Lamb's
Conduit Street to the Foundling Estate.

It was cool and quiet here, the trees smelled fresh and dewy.
It was lovely to have this big open space with Brunswick Square
on the left and the children's playground in the middle and
Mecklenburg Square on the right. I took the right turning into the
Square and then the left one into the dead-end which has still kept
the curiously haughty mood of eighteenth-century Bloomsbury,
feudally dignified and aristocratically secluded, but all this in a
strangely ludicrous way because this was London with tubes
running underneath and the streetcars rattling along Gray's Inn

Road and sometimes from above the sound of the mail planes going south in the night.

I rang the bell and the maid opened the door. 'Miss Ray is not at home,' she said and I said 'Thank you, she is expecting me' and the maid said 'I'm sorry' and I said 'Don't be sorry, be careful' and by the time we had walked up to the top where Maria lived the maid had told me everything I wanted to know so that I could have turned back to go home again. But then I heard Maria's voice and I knew that I would not go home. Yet it was not a good feeling to know it.

She was not in the dining-room and not in the lounge and I followed the voice till I found her in the bedroom, lying on the couch, crying and talking to herself. I sat down by her side and bent down to kiss her neck which was strong and still brown from the summer and when I felt her neck there was suddenly all that summer again, the evenings on the lake with the pale light of the stars coming through the cover of the canoe and the sound of the water rushing along underneath. Those evenings, still warm from the sun in the genial water but slowly getting cooler with the night falling and the moon waning and the shadows in your eyes darkening. And you could feel the wind getting strong and cool over the water but inside it was warm with you and the shadows in your eyes darkening. Times long past and gone, summer bygone, long-forgotten day – I felt it all again but then suddenly I smelled the salt of her tears, here, in her room in Mecklenburg Square, now, in November, and I pulled her body back until her head was in my lap and when I kissed her I felt her tears running hot over my mouth and I felt the salt on my lips and outside the brown leaves falling and the air dark and heavy with the autumn and the streets wet in the rain.

I heard the rain for a long time afterwards. The noise on roof and window and the streetcars rolling over the points – hard, rattling sound in the still of the night. Then, some hours later, the milk wagon, clatter of brass knockers against doors, and the 'oo-oo' of the milkman, 'war-cry of the union of milk traders', Bill called it. Then the morning papers and the early post and when I heard a clock sound from somewhere and then another one and still a third one it was eight o'clock and I got up and went into the bathroom and had a hot bath and a cold shower. I found the razor and shaved without a mirror, lying in the warm water and afterwards washing the lather off with the cold shower. The window was sweating, steamed with a white London dew, and when I wiped a little peephole I saw that the rain was still falling.

I went into the kitchen. The maid was not there. I switched on the electric stove and started water for tea and milk for porridge. I sliced some bread and put it on the griller and whilst it was being toasted I rummaged the pantry for butter and orange marmalade. I could not find either. I was on the verge of despair when I finally discovered both on the dresser directly behind the toast griller where I should have looked at the beginning. The water boiled and the porridge was ready and I dished it up and set it on a tray and carried it over to the bedroom.

Maria was awake and lay there on the bed with open eyes. She was lying on her back, looking up to the ceiling, aimless and empty-faced, in the mild light of the morning which came in thin lines through the window shutters. Her shoulders were broad and straight and brown but just above the breasts the skin was white and pale where the sun had not penetrated the bathing suit.

I set the tray down on the bedside table and said: 'Tea for two.'

I had to say something cliché to keep myself under control.

But Maria looked at the tray, then at my face and then she smiled, and the smile brought me down on my knees and made me kiss her against my will. Through the roughness of the sheets I felt the softness of her body on my lips and the touch, even more against my will than the kiss, made me faint with love. Then I looked up and I saw that she was crying.

'Love,' I said but she did not hear me because my throat was too dry to speak but she felt my eyes on her face and she said: 'Why didn't you tell them that Jensen killed Estella?'

I felt the blood rushing out of my veins, first from the head and then from the fingertips and then from the toes. I felt the cold creeping up from below and sinking down from above and all the time rising in my arms up to my shoulders, realizing how I was slowly losing the feeling of all my limbs which was a curious sensation with my heart beating in my ears and in my temples and in my neck and then finally the blood rushing back and I feeling my limbs again and breathing deeply and quickly and then slower and then everything was all right again and now standing upright at the left side of Maria's bed and looking down at her face which is weak now and wet with tears and not beautiful for fear and anger are too big in her eyes.

And her voice again, now hoarse and sore, 'If you don't tell them I shall have to do it. Why don't you do it?'

'I thought they would believe it was suicide,' I said. 'But what do you know about it?'

I said that and I felt my limbs dying again and my eyes

heavy with my lids pressing down from above and my tongue dry and heavy too.

'I know he did it. I saw it.'

'What did you see?'

Heart beating. Pulse and arteries and temples and throat.

'I saw how he killed her.'

'Were you in Robertson's studio?'

Hot, sore throat. Tired, burning eyes. And the blood hammering louder in the ears.

'Oh, no. I saw the film. I was with him. I was in the bedroom and the door was ajar and I saw it through the crack from the bedroom.'

I stood up and went out. It was hard to walk down all those stairs. But then it was good to feel the cool air in the morning.

A man and a woman were standing in the middle of the street. They were quarrelling. It was no good quarrelling. It wouldn't help. It wasn't worth it. It wasn't worth quarrelling. It was no use quarrelling. Those two people there could just as well finish their quarrel in the middle of the road.

I started the car and made the klaxon sound so that the two jumped aside, he to the left, she to the right, and I drove through between them, right in the middle between them, but finally there was nothing but the cool morning air and the wind and the monotony of the motor in my ears.

Nine

I asked for Detective Inspector Smith and the man behind the counter pressed a button and there was a buzzing sound and he took off the receiver and said something but I could not understand what, then he slammed the receiver on the prong and said: 'Room 213, second floor. Inspector Smith will see you now.'

I found the door and knocked and entered.

'Hallo, Mr McCabe,' he said, 'good to see you, sit down, have a cigarette,' all in one breath and at the same pitch.

I said 'Thanks, I'll have one of my own' and sat down.

'I got the third murderer,' I said.

'Who's it?' he asked without astonishment.

'A man called Jensen, one of our stars, the man who played opposite Estella Lamare.'

'I know, I know,' he said, 'and there was another girl in it, Maria Beam or Maria Flash or something like that.'

'Leave out the other girl,' I said, 'let's talk business.'

'Please yourself,' he said, 'where did you find number three?'

'Has Robertson told you of his hunch?'

'Yes, he told me all about it. He had an automatic camera connected with the door, a thing which would automatically follow anyone who entered the room. That correct?'

'Yes. And the spool of that camera is missing. Probably with a film in it. Somebody has pinched it. There were three possible reasons for doing that. Can you make them out?'

'Number One: the murderer realized that he was being photographed. So he stopped the camera and destroyed the film. Number Two: another person entered the room after the murderer and took the film. There is an infinite number of reasons for Number Two. Maybe it's a veil and maybe it's a gum shoe. Maybe it's blackmail. Kind of hard to pick the right one. And Number Three: it was not murder at all but just a plain and simple case of suicide. Then you have the same infinite number of possible reasons for having your film pinched. I've not the faintest idea who is who and which is which.'

'I never heard a sleuth saying that,' I said.

'You're mistaken,' he said, 'you heard it once. Just now.'

'I found the film,' I said.

'Where did you find it?'

'Why don't you ask what you want to know? You meant to ask "How did you know there was something wrong with Jensen?" Isn't that a much better question?'

He smiled. He said: 'All right, Dr Freud. I've asked you once before if you were interested in criminology. You said "Never mind".'

'I say it again; never mind.'

'If you don't mind I'd rather advise you: *do* mind it sometimes.'

'I do. Sometimes. And I *do* mind your advice.'

'You'd make a good bully in the C.I.D. Where's the film?'

'I've got it here.'

'Can I see it?'

'Certainly. You got a projector?'

'Yes. I got an audience too. But the show is not on yet. Let's say: doors open at seven o'clock tonight. Can you manage?'

'I guess I'll have to.'

'Right. Can you leave me the film?'

'I'd rather not.'

He chewed the sides of his lower lip. Then he got up and said: 'Well, that'll do. Seven p.m.'

'I'll be there,' I said, and went out. He *would* say pee emm. I wondered why he hadn't said pip emma.

When I drove to the studio I felt somebody was following me. It was a small black Hillman, the police type of quick-runner.

Ten

The first face I saw when I entered was Bloom's. Then I saw Christensen and then Maria and Robertson. I only missed Happy. Otherwise the party was complete.

In one corner of the room was a 35-mm projector which made me laugh because it looked so like a Heath Robinson cartoon. On the wall opposite they had put up a white bed-sheet as a screen. Underneath the sheet, on the floor, two small electro-dynamic loudspeakers were fixed with cordage.

Smith, standing in the middle of the room, had lost the nonchalant air of the morning. I expected him to say something like 'Gentlemen, I have the honour of introducing to you Mr McCabe, our new cinema expert, who will show you his latest production, *The Death of Estella Lamare*,' but he simply said: 'Thank you, Mr McCabe, let's start as soon as possible.'

I inserted the film into the projector and asked Smith to switch off the light. In the dark I could see only the figures of a huge clock which was standing left of the screen in one corner. It had luminous figures.

Then I started the projector.

I knew the film.

The reactions of the others interested me.

I wanted to study Bloom's face, I wanted to see Maria's movements, I wanted to watch Christensen's actions, I wanted to keep my eyes on Robertson.

While the projector was gathering speed I went across to the front so that I could see their faces. The faces were white and distorted in the glare of the light which was reflected by the screen. The light was bright and unmoving, for I had put twenty feet of blank film as a leader at the beginning of the picture and while the leader was running my eyes got used to the light.

Bloom's face was green and wet. His eyes lay deep in the shadow of his projecting frontal bone for he kept head and shoulders bent so that the light from the screen fell straight on his frontal arch and aslant on forehead and face. On the wide cheek-bones there lay white spots of light with dark shadows underneath in the hollows which gave the face a consumptive expression. The broad lips were tightly closed. The head sat deep in the shoulders, the neck was too short, the shoulders stood out on both sides of the face at the level of the ears.

Maria's face was white and hard and nervous. Her eyes twitched.

Christensen was quiet, blond, callous, cold, expectant.

Robertson showed nothing beyond technical interest. He smoked for he knew that he had loaded the camera with non-flam film.

Suddenly the light grew darker and began to flicker and I knew that the leader was finished and that the film had now started. I heard Jensen's voice and Estella's voice and it was not astonishing to hear their voices now. I heard the two voices quarrelling with each other, Jensen saying, 'I can't, I'm sick like hell, let me go, I don't want you, why don't you go?' and Estella's voice only whimpering and both sounded ridiculous like a badly overacted scene from a cheap love-story picture.

I heard the voices from the screen but I saw the people here in the room. I saw Maria's face, how her lids got slowly weary and sank down and how the lips grew flaccid and how all features gave way until she suddenly pulled herself together and how now weakness and disappointment changed slowly into something I didn't like to watch.

Christensen's countenance, tense and stirred but without astonishment, and Estella's voice saying slowly and desperately 'I love you, Ian, and if you keep on running after Maria Ray I shall kill myself. There is nothing left but that' and again that sounded cheap and ridiculous and unreal.

Bloom's face then, green, wet, sick, strained with disgust and fatigue.

Only Robertson and Smith without emotion, the expression of their faces and limbs holding nothing beyond concentration and intense watchfulness.

And the voices of Jensen and Estella slowly dying and only the sounds of their breathing left and I knew that he was trying to take that knife from her and I knew that suddenly a small black spot would show on her white dress and I knew that spot would grow bigger and darker and Jensen's face would grow white and pallid and wet like Bloom's face was now and the dread expression of that face slowly changing to fright and then to fear and then to deadly panic, his eyes looking for the door and his hands hanging white and heavy from his wrists, those white hands, but the finger-tips dark and wet and dripping with blood, and I smiled because all that was too badly overacted and I could not force myself to believe that it was genuine.

Then Christensen's face sombre and almost annoyed and Maria's face no longer angry but now twisted with jealousy which had no sense in it and Bloom's face tired and hopeless and weak from sadness and Robertson quiet and eager and Smith taciturn and without expression.

That was the last of it, then darkness for a moment and light again. These people seemed curiously little changed in the daylight and the expression of those faces barely altered with the end of the screening. They all looked as if they were still watching the film. When Smith stood up their eyes followed him for a very short time but merely to fall back soon into their old expression.

Smith wandered awhile to and fro between the projector and the screen and at each turn from the screen to the projector he looked up to throw a glance at his audience. Then he cast down his eyes again and stopped at the projector. From a distance it seemed as if he was studying the mechanism but I felt certain that his eyes looked quite blankly at the part of machinery on which they were resting.

Then he suddenly turned round and said something which hit everybody in the room with a highly unexpected blow in the back.

'Gentlemen,' he said, 'you are at liberty to leave this room. Thank you, gentlemen!'

Of course they were at liberty. No one had ever doubted that.

There was a short interlude of silence.

Then Maria stood up and grinned. Then she burst into laughter and said 'Do I look like a les? Here, I ask you, *gentlemen*' – she accentuated the word in a way which made it a parody on Smith's diction – 'I ask you why is that dirty little copper insulting me? Gentlemen! Are there no gentlemen in this room to defend a lady?'

And into the tensely painful silence which followed there

burst Bloom's voice, slow and deep in his chest at first and then exploding between tight lips. But what he said nobody could hear.

Smith, standing at the projector, watched him, his eyes only slits with the lids heavy and low. Robertson leaned back in his chair and blew clouds of smoke in a strictly vertical direction towards the ceiling.

Maria's hands gripped the backs of two chairs on either side of her.

They waited for Bloom's voice to become understandable.

There was a sort of passionate patience in Smith's waiting.

But when Bloom's voice became clear it was a disappointment. He merely said 'Shut up Ma . . . you don't understand . . . you never do' with long intervals of silence between the words.

'But she does. She understands perfectly. I want to have a talk with her. Alone, if you don't mind, gentlemen.'

That was Smith. They had completely forgotten him.

Bloom was the first to get up, wearily. Robertson followed. Then Christensen. They went out.

Smith looked at me.

I said: 'I'm staying.'

Smith said: 'I want to talk to you too.'

I said: 'Why don't you?'

He said: 'Afterwards.'

I said: 'Now.'

He said: 'All right.'

We sat down. Smith got up and went to the door and closed it and sat down too.

Eleven

Maria wept silently and steadily. Smith looked at her, looked down at his feet, then turned to me and asked: 'How much does she know?'

He spoke as if she was not in the room.

I said: 'Ask her.'

He looked at her for a second, then turned back to me and asked: 'How much do *you* know?'

He put an accent on 'you'.

I said: 'They put in too many ingredients. It's turbid now. But if you put some more in, it may get clear again.'

He smiled and asked: 'What do you want to know?'

I said: 'I want to know what *you* think.'

He said: 'There's nothing to think. The thing is finished. You saw it. You found it yourself. Pity they didn't put up a reward. Otherwise you would get it.'

I asked him: 'Why did you want to talk to me? And what about?'

'I asked you before,' he said, 'but you didn't reply. How did you find the film?'

I looked at Maria. She had stopped crying. Her eyes were big, open, aimless, blank. I looked at her, trying to force her eyes towards me. I looked at her, forgetting everything else until I felt I was weakening and sweat broke out and I felt wet all over. I saw green rings dancing in the air. Green, then red, then purple turning into violet. It was like that game you used to play as a kid in bed when mother had switched out the light but you couldn't sleep yet and the darkness was so sweet and comforting. You pressed your hands on your eyes until those green and red figures came up dancing in the night. You couldn't do that very long. It hurt too much. But still for some time after you had taken your hands away the coloured things kept on dancing in the dark until the dimness of the light from the window broke through, and the thing faded out slowly with the outlines of the room fading in at the same time. That was what dissolves in colour would look like one day when they would have learned how to mix colours for films.

And like that it was now, when Maria's head slowly turned and her eyes looked at me, first through the motley veil, then the veil fading out and her eyes clearly looking at me. She shook her head, slowly, almost imperceptibly.

I felt faint when I breathed again. I looked at Smith. He did not seem to have seen anything. The whole had not lasted longer than a fraction of a second. There had been no hesitation when I answered Smith's question now.

'I found the film in Jensen's flat in Guilford Street,' I said.

'Where was he? Was he there?' Smith asked.

'That's the point,' I said. 'He was not there. And he won't be there now. And I don't think you'll find him anywhere in this United Kingdom of ours.'

'What's the point?' he asked.

'The point is that he should have been there. He is on today's schedule. He should be in the studio. But he isn't. That means he is breaking a contract which brought him fifteen thousand and which will cost him twice that if he jumps out. Now he did jump out and he must have had some very reasonable reasons for doing that.'

'Ah! That's the way the wind blows.'

'It's the way I caught the wind. I rang him at eight in the morning –'

'Whom? Jensen?'

'Yes.'

'Today?'

'Yes. And there was no reply. I rang again and spoke to the housekeeper and the housekeeper said Mr Jensen had left three days ago. I asked whether he knew anything about Mr Jensen's return and he replied: "No, Mr Jensen has left for good. He's gone home to see his dear old mother. I think he must have been fed up with pitchers and movies and the lot of it. And he has settled all his bills, Mr Jensen has. He was a very nice gentleman, Mr Jensen was." That's the housekeeper speaking his mind. I'm giving you his exact words.'

'And then you went up to the flat, told the housekeeper a nice story, or bribed him, searched every corner of the place, and finally found the one piece of incriminating evidence which the perpetrator had fortunately left behind at the free disposal of the police.'

He smiled in a deliberately crooked way.

'There's something wrong with coppers,' I said. 'You can't punch them in the jaw when you want to.'

He smiled and looked at Maria.

Maria said: 'You are mistaken, Inspector. *I* had the film. Mr McCabe took it from me.'

Smith smiled with his eyes only and said: 'Now we're getting somewhere. Go on.'

'No need to go on. We have arrived,' I said.

'Is that so? Well then, will you kindly let me have the exact timetable, Mr McCabe?' he said. 'Ladies first,' I said.

Maria said: 'You saw the last of Ian when' – stopped, corrected herself – 'you saw the last of Mr Jensen when he ran out of Robertson's room, leaving Estella behind. You don't know what happened afterwards –'

'Well!' asked Smith.

'Don't say "well",' said Maria, 'it wasn't well at all. As a matter of fact it was rather badly done. He came straight over to my dressing-room and told me he had killed Estella Lamare and left her in Robertson's room. I asked him "Intention or accident?" and he said "Self-defence". I knew that Robertson had the automatic camera connected with the door. So I went over to Room 126 and found Estella on the floor. She was cold and dead. There was no doubt about that. So there was nothing to do but to take the film and to go back to my room.'

Smith looked at her with an amused smile in the outer corners of his eyes. He hummed a little melody, throwing here and there some words into the tune.

'You-told-me-but-half-of-the-story,' he hummed.

Then he asked: 'Why didn't you notify the police? What did you do with the film? How did Mr McCabe take it from you?'

Then he continued his musical pastime.

Maria said: 'There we have three questions. Your singing, Smith, comes at a most inappropriate moment. When you stop it I shall answer your questions.'

Smith stopped abruptly and said: 'I beg your pardon.'

Maria grinned at him and said: 'Well, if you beg me, you shall have me.'

Smith bowed and said: 'Thank you.'

Maria closed her eyes with a painful smile and said: 'Don't mention it.'

Smith glanced at her with a cheerful gesture and said: 'Would you mind if I *do* mention it?'

Maria opened her eyes and said: 'I did not think it safe to notify the police until I had viewed the film myself. When I ran the film through my projector at home I found that Jensen had told me the truth. It was self-defence, but for you it would have been murder. So that film was not evidence; it was counter-evidence.'

I stood up and said: 'Thank you. The witness Maria Ray may go. The next witness is Mr McCabe. Yes, your Lordship. Right here, your Lordship.'

Smith said: 'What a nice cross-examination. It goes all by itself. A perpetuum mobile. You *are* interested in criminology, Mr McCabe, aren't you?'

He was tiresome.

I didn't reply.

I said: 'After I had spoken to Jensen's housekeeper I rang Maria.'

'Miss Ray,' he corrected.

'I asked her whether she knew anything of Jensen's whereabouts. She said no, she did not, and asked whether I knew anything. I said no, but I had something to tell her and she said come along at once. So I mounted my tin lizzie and drove her to Mecklenburg Square. And Miss Ray was terribly pleased to see me and gave me the film as a wedding present and I said thank you very much, many happy returns of the day, and kissed her goodbye and drove back to see you, my dear Smith. And you were very pleased to see me, too.'

'He walked in without even saying good morning,' said Maria. 'He said point blank that he knew Jensen had killed Estella, and he blackmailed me into surrendering the film to him. He threatened to get me prosecuted for being an accessory after the fact, for deliberate suppression of the fact, and for the holding back of important evidence. He got me into the wildest hysterics and finally forced me into delivering him the film. And that's the end of the story.'

Smith stood up and said: 'Thank you. I wish to inform you that we have taken the liberty of recording your statements on the dictaphone. I take it that you realize the importance of your depositions.'

I said, 'Certainly.'

Maria said: 'Perfectly.'

When we went out I said to Maria: 'Few of God's chillun have got wings.'

She looked at her fingertips and said: 'There are still too many that have.'

Twelve

I could not sleep that night. I had a letter from Maria to meet her Monday night at twelve o'clock at a new address. I didn't like the idea of it. I turned from one side to the other and back again with the sheets wrinkled on the mattress, feeling hot and cold in turns and finally trying to think things without sense in order to make myself believe I was dreaming. Sometimes it worked. Tonight it did not work.

I lay on my back and looked up at the ceiling where the light from the street made shadows and reflections.

I heard a car passing outside and I followed its course through Bennett Street and up to St James's Street and then already lost in the noise of Piccadilly. Curious how many movements there were going on all through the night. So many movements of things and men. I tried to see the things which were going on now side by side. I kept on following the car though I could not hear it any more. I thought it would probably go through Piccadilly to Piccadilly Circus and then it would turn left into Regent Street and up to Oxford Street but it could also go on straight across Leicester Square to Charing Cross Road and then up to Tottenham Court Road and into Bloomsbury where Maria lived.

When I realized where I had arrived I felt annoyed and began to think of a new course for the car. It was a nice game. Something like playing trains. Playing cars now. But then for some reason I suddenly could not remember any streets and I went back to the sounds I heard and the lights I saw on the ceiling. I heard footsteps, two voices, a key, a door being opened and closed with the syncopic afterbeat of the door-knocker which fell back on the brass plate. Other footsteps passed and a girl laughed and three howling men wandered along Bennett Street. You could hear the tune they sang and it was all wrong because they were drunk but you could also hear the echo and it was like long shadows thrown against the cold walls of the houses.

Then suddenly I remembered the streets again. And the first thing I remembered were the arches under Adelphi, now broken up; the dark gangways underground and the old woman there sleeping on rags and yesterday's news with the water dripping from above and the cats hunting rats in the wine cellars and on top of the arches at the front entrance of the Savoy tails and evening gowns were leaving for some late club in Greek Street or Frith Street or Soho Square and I knew that I remembered it quite clearly now and I followed those tails and gowns on their way where they would never meet the navvies working all night nor the London Transport repair gang hammering on the rails of the trams in the light of their acetylene flares and I thought that all over London in the cold coffee stalls they were drinking their teas and oxos and bovrils and eating steak and kidney pies now in the night which is always wet in London in the autumn so that your coat feels damp and awkward when you see the sun coming up red over Whitechapel.

There was no hope of sleep now and I got up and put on my dressing-gown. Then I heard the telephone ringing and I took some ice out of the Frigidaire and put the plug in the sink and turned the water on and put my head into it and with the water running from my face and down along the folds of the dressing-gown and dropping from there down to the floor I walked to the telephone and said 'Hallo.'

It was Robertson's voice and it was harsh and rasping.

'Hallo, Mac, this is John,' he said, 'forgive me. But this is important. Have you been asleep?'

I said: 'No, I couldn't. What's the news?'

'I couldn't either,' he said. 'Now listen. Did you find the film loose or wound up on the spool?'

I felt sick. I said: 'Loose. And it was in a lousy state. I had to wind it up on my own spool.'

'Yes, I thought it was yours.'

'Go on,' I said, 'what's the important news?'

'I only wanted to make sure –' he said warily.

'– sure of what?'

He hesitated and then he said in a different voice: 'Are you very sleepy, Mac?'

'You asked me that before. I wish I was.'

'All right, then,' he said quickly, 'let's run over to Maria and find out about the spool.'

'Not now,' I said. 'It's four o'clock.'

'I can't wait,' he said.

'Learn to,' I said.

He hesitated again and continued after a second in the same quick and somewhat irritated way. 'I cannot tell you, Mac, because I know nothing definite yet. But I assure you it is very important and I must see Maria at once.'

I said 'Some stars rise at night. Maria doesn't' and rang off and went to bed and fell asleep at once and slept for five hours until nine o'clock when the maid knocked and came in with a tray and a telegram which said:

Two timer caught tripping. Wait and see.

A fake name of sender was given. But the address was *Aardals, Norway.*

I burned the telegram in the fireplace, washed, dressed, had breakfast and went to the studio.

Thirteen

I was cutting the last sequences of *The Waning Moon* when Robertson came in and sat down. He wanted to ask me something but he did not know how to start his question. He looked at my scissors and said: 'I often wonder why you people always cut on the *end* of a movement instead of cutting right *on* the movement.'

I answered and he said something else about cutting and editing. We talked about the montage of the Russian films, about the French avant-garde, about the photography of the early Swedish silents and the sets of the German film classics. We talked about everything but the thing we wanted to talk about. He did not know how to shift the theme and I did not want to start the shifting.

Shortly after one I said that I felt hungry and we went down to the canteen. Just as we were ordering the soup Vic came in from the other side and said 'Hallo, can I join you?' and we said 'Certainly, it's a pleasure, sit down' and he sat down and ordered soup too.

'I hear that Bloom is not going back to his office,' he said after we had finished with the most important studio gossip.

Robertson looked up and said nothing.

Vic looked at me. He smiled in a provocative and tactless way.

I said: 'The soup is lousy. I wish they would get a cook. This one hates cooking. He should be drowned in his soup.'

Vic said: 'I haven't seen him yet. I mean Bloom, not the cook. Have you seen him, Mac?'

I said: 'This soup must be infectious. People get such a bad taste from it.'

Robertson ladled his soup.

After he had finished he said: 'This girl Estella who is dead has a greater success now than she would ever have had alive.'

When he said that I remembered that he was a college boy. He had an Oxford attitude towards things. That attitude was sometimes in his voice. It was there now.

He said: 'The reaction of the studio is particularly interesting. Everybody shows a certain reflex of the events which have passed and it is surprising to see that those reflexes are so much more striking than the events which they reflect. Everywhere I perceive people who want to make certain remarks but do not dare to do so. Others are annoyed without reason, again others are sulky, wary, irritable or provocative, suggestive, derisive – a veritably curious reaction.'

Vic, imitating Robertson, said: 'A strangely inappropriate relation between cause and effect.'

I thought that he was more intelligent than I had hitherto believed.

Robertson ordered roast beef and Yorkshire pudding.

I ordered chicken fricassee.

Vic ordered sausage and mashed.

Then he said: 'Now listen, people, John is right. The other day Mac said the same, only in simpler language: the whole studio is going nuts. Now let's talk turkey. Jensen killed Estella. That's plain. But what about Chris? Why did he say he did it? And what about Bloom? You accused him of murder, Mac, and you must know why. It isn't my business to ask you what reasons you had to suspect him. But I want to know why Bloom admitted something he had never done. That's what I want to know and that's what everybody here wants to know. No wonder they are all getting screwy with you guys stalling all the time and keeping the lights in the dark.'

There was a silence.

Then he continued in the same irritated and reproachful tone: 'Let me get in on it, whatever it is, you hear me? Let me get in on it!'

Robertson said: 'Much ado about nothing.'

I said: 'A tragedy of errors.'

And another voice shouted with a derisive sort of pathos: 'We want Shakespeare – dead or alive!' and added explanatorily: 'Old Vic Audience on First Night after Curtain Has Dropped.'

It sounded like a newspaper headline.

I said: 'Hallo, Smith. Vic wants to get in on it. Do you think you could help him in any way possible?'

Smith laughed and said 'I'll take you in on it, son' with the face of a good-natured tough. 'I'll take you in, all right.'

He sat down on a chair I pushed over to him.

Then his face changed and his voice meant business when he asked: 'Tell me something about Estella Lamare. Where did she come from? What sort of people? Who did she play around with?'

He did not address anybody in particular.

Vic, still imitating Robertson, said: 'Estella Lamare was a nonentity. She never existed. The body deceased before the spirit could manifest itself.'

Then he continued in his normal voice: 'Her real name was Esther Lammer. I believe she came from somewhere in the East End, Whitechapel or Stepney Green or Limehouse or the docks. Somewhere round about there.'

Robertson said: 'West India Dock Road.'

I looked up.

Vic stared at him.

Smith asked: 'How do you know?'

Robertson said: 'She told me.'

Smith kept his eyes fixed on Robertson's face.

Vic said: 'She never told anybody.'

Robertson said: 'She told *me*.'

Vic said: 'She must have had some sort of reason.'

Robertson said: ' "It isn't my business to ask you what reasons you had to suspect him." '

He was quoting Vic's own words.

Smith looked questioningly at me.

But he said nothing.

I told him.

'Vic has just been asking me questions. He wants to know why I charged Bloom with Estella's murder, why Bloom admitted the charge, why Christensen charged himself with the same killing, and why I'm keeping it all to myself.'

Smith said: 'I wish *I* knew.'

Vic said: 'I thought you *did* know.'

He was genuinely disappointed.

John smiled complacently.

'I wish I were a detective. I would clear up crimes all day.'

Smith smiled back.

'*To clear up a murder you must do your own killing.*'

He said that in a curious matter-of-fact voice. It was a statement, not a joke.

John threw a fit and leaned forward.

Smith's right hand gripped John's left wrist.

Smith's left hand took a glass and forced some water between John's tight lips.

John gulped, opened his eyes and said nothing.

Vic looked reflectively at John, then questioningly at Smith and blankly at me.

Smith said: 'I want to know more about Estella Lamare, alias Esther Lammer, alias Edna Lenore.'

Robertson lowered one eyebrow and lifted the other.

He did not move.

Vic put his elbows on the table and looked around searchingly.

He made no effort to feign disinterestedness.

He brought his eyes to Smith and asked: '*Edna?* Edna *What –?*'

Smith interrupted him.

He spoke without sympathy.

He was continuing his explanations.

He was not replying to Vic's question.

He said: 'She used that name before she took up films. That was at time when she lived at Pembroke Street, St Aldate's, Oxford. Mr Robertson could tell us more about that epoch in the deceased lady's life.'

Robertson sat firmly in his chair with the weight of his shoulders against the back of the chair.

When he spoke he did not turn his head.

But he spoke politely.

He looked straight in front of himself without particular aim and said: 'You, Mr Smith, appear to know so much more about Miss Lamare than anybody else present at this table. It would be really impudence on my side if I were to bore you with the telling of stories which you will certainly know already.'

Smith laughed in a friendly manner and said acknowledgingly: 'You have missed your career, Robertson. You are a diplomat.'

Robertson grinned and said nothing.

Vic had been sitting with his mouth open.

Now he closed it and made a face which was hopeless and desperate with not understanding.

Smith turned to him.

He had the voice of a music-hall conjuror.

He explained: 'Now, ladies and gentlemen, is the appropriate moment to show the cards. It is now the time when no secret can remain concealed. Gentlemen, Mr John Robertson will tell us now the story of the once so glamorous Miss Estella Lamare.'

Robertson stood up and spat out.

His eyes and the corners of his mouth danced with disgust.

He turned round and went out.

'. . . and then there were only three,' Smith hummed to himself.

Vic stood up and said reproachfully: 'Didn't I say the studio is going nuts?'

He turned and went out to follow John.

Smith leaned back in his chair and said: 'His vocabulary is very poor.'

I hummed: '. . . and then there were only two.'

Smith said: 'I like your friend Robertson. His manners are so captivating.'

I stood up and went out.

Smith called after me: '. . . and finally there was only one.'

Fourteen

About five minutes later when I was in the cutting-room the telephone rang and when I took the receiver the operator said: 'Detective Inspector Smith to see Mr McCabe.'

I said: 'Send him up.'

He came in and said: 'Sorry to pop in on you again. But the scene was really much too short. As a matter of fact your exit was premature.'

I said: 'I never had enough experience for that type of Punch and Judy show.'

He said: 'Yes. What you want is a good rehearsal.'

I said: 'If you give me a chance I'll try my best to get some outside experience.'

He said: 'You shall have it. I'm going to pay a visit to Messrs Lammer senior.'

'To West India Dock Road?'

'The same. Let's have a look at the family. Come on. A family party.'

I said: 'It's nothing in my life.'

He said: 'Come on. Cut the phlegm.'

He kept on talking in that pleasant way until Dinah came in to get my signature for some letters. When she saw Smith she flinched and said: 'Oh, I'm so sorry. I thought Mr McCabe was alone. Sorry to disturb you.'

Smith did not turn round.

He looked at me and smiled complacently.

He said: 'I do not feel disturbed in the least. Here, Mr McCabe, do I look disturbed?'

Then he looked at her and said: 'You did not disturb us at

all. Not me. Though of course I cannot guarantee for Mr McCabe. But who in heaven or on earth could guarantee for Mr McCabe? Could you?'

He lifted his brows and twisted the corners of his mouth in that artificial way which I knew by now.

Dinah, with helpless and bewildered eyes, searched my face for some sort of support.

But I could not help her, not even with my eyes, because Smith was watching me.

He kept on talking to Dinah, answering his own question: 'You couldn't guarantee for Mr McCabe. Not even you. No.'

He got up and snapped his fingers at her.

'I'll tell you why I got that idea. It was like this. Mr McCabe here tells me you are his secretary. All right, I'm saying to myself, nice kid, his secretary. Good. Then one evening I'm seeing Mr McCabe here and Miss Dinah kissing in the street. Well, I'm saying to myself, so she's his girl too. And he never told me about that. Well, well, you can't guarantee for Mr McCabe. You really can't.'

Dinah's confused face became annoyed.

Smith said: 'Yes and then one night when I'm keeping company with an old friend walking his beat on the Gray's Inn Road–Theobald's Road line we hear a sound coming from Heathcote Street and we turn left and then right again and there we see two dogs fighting.'

He stopped speaking and after a while he said: 'Well.'

Dinah made a deliberately perplexed face.

She put her lips to my ear and asked me in a low voice but so that Smith could still hear it: 'Is he – I mean, I'm sorry for him – but is he quite . . . well, you know what I mean. You see, I can't make head or tail of what he is talking about, can you?'

I said: 'Wait.'

Smith said: 'But then we see a car behind those dogs. The car is there and nobody to be seen anywhere near it. We ring the bell of the last house in that dead end of Mecklenburg Square – no reply – and no light. Well, we can figure to ourselves what's going on upstairs. So we just make a note of the car and the number and the street and later on forget all about it 'cause I was the one who did the scribbling and he was the one to do the reporting but when he is thinking of it next morning he finds that he ain't got the notes and then he remembers I got them but then he's forgetting all about it and that's how we'd been kind of passing it on.'

'So what?' I asked him: 'Are you going to prefer charges against me?'

He said: 'Oh, I see. You mean to say that it was your car? Yes, I thought so too. Very, very interesting.'

I said: 'Very, very funny. Present your bill any time you like. At your earliest convenience. I'm at your disposal.'

He grinned tolerantly and turned to Dinah. 'Well, my dear young lady,' he said in an exaggeratedly polite voice, 'well, you see my point, don't you?'

Dinah said: 'That's a laugh.'

But it really did not matter what she said.

She did not understand Smith.

Her face showed that plainly.

She could have said 'Swim, swan, over the sea, swim, swan, swim. Swim, swan, back again, well swum, swan' and it would still have meant 'I have not the faintest idea what you're talking about.'

But Smith continued, either because he did not care whether she understood him, or because he was sure she would understand him soon enough if he would only keep on talking.

'Now one evening, some few days ago, just after I'd left this place here, I was walking down Gray's Inn Road again and when I got to Heathcote Street I suddenly remembered that night and seeing the car here which was really Mr McCabe's car, and so I take heart and walk over to that last house in the dead end of Mecklenburg Square figuring that I'm about to meet Miss Lee here 'cause you see I'm still thinking all the time that she's Mr McCabe's girl or something and that she's the most likely one he'd be spending his nights with, see, but then somebody else comes out, a maid in a nice black and white uniform, and I ask her about Miss Lee and she says there's no Miss Lee in the house and there's never been any, not that she knows, anyway. So I ask her about Mr McCabe and she hears the name and pulls a face and bangs the door in my face. And there am I standing out in the cold all alone.'

He had spoken the last words without directly addressing either of us.

Now he turned to Dinah again.

He said: 'Yes, so that wasn't your house at all – but whose house was it, do you have any idea, Miss Lee? Who was Mr McCabe spending the night with, leaving his car outside all night and not even turning the lights on, which is really very thoughtless of Mr McCabe, considering what an intelligent and thoughtful man he is otherwise. What you say, Miss Lee?'

Dinah's face was white and disgusted.

She tried to make it look casual but she did not succeed.

Her eyes looked about without finding a place to rest on and she did not know what to do with her hands.

I looked at Smith and I saw that he watched her with intense attention.

I struck a match and brought it down to a piece of waste film which was hanging over the edge of the cutting-desk.

At first Smith did not look because he thought I was lighting a cigarette.

But when the film caught fire he turned quickly round to see.

Dinah relaxed for a second when she felt that the tension of Smith's eyes had left her but at once her face grew tense again when she saw the film burning.

I threw some cushions on the blaze and said it was nothing, just a minor accident.

Smith threw a very circumspect glance around.

His eyes looked reflectively at me, rested for a moment on the little pile of cushions, followed the thin line of smoke which rose from it and came to rest on Dinah's face which had lost every strain and was now again pink and lovely like a colour-photo advertising face-cream or some kind of beauty skin-lotion.

She looked obligingly at me and said: 'Will you sign the letters now, Mr McCabe?'

I said 'Certainly, thank you' and put my signature on the dotted line Dinah always liked to type out.

Dinah leaned forward, took the letters, said 'Thank you,' bowed to Smith, said 'Goodbye, Mr Smith, pleased to have met you' and went out.

Smith said 'Goodbye, goodbye, thank you, pleased to have met you,' sat down and said 'So that's that.'

I said: 'Are you sure that that's really that?'

He leaned back in his chair, leaving a cloud of smoke over his head.

I went on, saying: 'If I were you, I wouldn't be too sure.'

He said: 'If I were you I wouldn't be either.'

I said: 'Gosh, the things you would do if you were I.'

He said solemnly 'You're right' as if that meant anything.

I said: 'Nobody is so right that he wasn't wrong at the same time.'

He said: 'Oh, I see, yes. I get you now.'

I said: 'Don't be rash. You wait and see who's getting whom.'

He grinned approvingly and said: 'This is a very thrilling game. You could play it for hours if you like it.'

I said: 'Yes, but I don't like it.'

I went over to the cutting-bench and took the cushions away. The film was still smouldering but the cushions had not suffered much.

Then Smith's voice, coming from behind, asked in his usual abominably cheerful way: 'Well, Mr McCabe, are we going to West India Dock Road?'

I turned on my heels to see his face.

It was calm, serious and pleasant.

I said: 'I like bulls. They are so big and friendly. But they are out of place in a china shop, they muddle up things in a terrible way. And afterwards you can't even hold them responsible for the damage they've done.'

He grinned again.

He looked very pleased.

He said: 'Yes, but who is the bull? That's the question. And besides – whoever he may be, I don't think he likes the china shop. That's the answer. I didn't like muddling up things. I suppose you didn't either. I guess nobody really wanted it. But here we are, right in the china shop. It's a mess.'

I told him what I thought.

'I think your method of questioning people is very interest-ing – both the quality and the quantity of it. I mean both the numbers of people you ask questions – just for the inquest, of course! – and the way you do it. And then the stories you tell people. Did you have to tell Dinah that story about my car and Maria's house? I ask you merely because I'm interested in the methods detectives use to clear up crimes.'

He said: 'You are interested in criminology, aren't you? I asked you that before, didn't I?'

I said: 'That is one of the questions I was referring to.'

His face changed and he said seriously: 'I have to question everybody. That's my job. And I have to use every method to get the answer. Every method which seems fair to me.'

I said: 'Different people have different ideas of what is fair and what not.'

He said: 'Yes, I know you are one of those who have different ideas.'

I asked him: 'In that case why did you pick me of all guys to make that Whitechapel excursion with you?'

He said: 'West India Dock Road.'

I said: 'What?'

He explained it.

'West India Dock Road, not Whitechapel.'

Then: 'I didn't pick you, I asked you to help me.'

Then: 'I asked you because I thought you got the right sort of eyes to look at things and see what is behind them. I still think I'm right about that.'

A white darting flame flashed up behind my back.

I went down on the floor throwing my arms forward so that I could catch the cushions I had dropped there and flung them back at the cutting-desk where the film had caught fire again.

I hit the fire right in the centre.

Sparks flew up and lit the whole celluloid of the waste film bin.

Smith threw the sand bucket at me. I emptied it on the fire, the fire smoked, smouldered, stank, went out.

Smith smiled.

I chewed my lower lip.

Dinah came in, sniffed at the heap of smoking cushions, screwed up her nose and rushed out again.

Smith looked at me with a friendly sort of scoff.

He quoted: ' "Every method which seems fair to me. But different people have different ideas of what is fair and what not." '

I said: 'All right. Let's go to West India Dock Road.'

When we left there was still the smell in the air.

But it was not very bad.

Fifteen

It was about five o'clock when we came out into the street. There was a thick fog which killed the colours and made everything soft and grey. You could see only the outlines of things without their depth and distance. You lost the feeling of space, that was a very odd sensation, but then the fog hurt the throat and made breathing heavy and after some time it gave you a headache.

When we had the car out of the garage it began to rain in thin and noiseless slants. We got the hood up and put it over, then we drove down to Holborn and along Newgate Street, Cheapside, Poultry, passing the Bank, into Cornhill and up Leadenhall Street, into Aldgate, Whitechapel High Street, Commercial Road and turned right into West India Dock Road. Later we found that we could have gone a much shorter way along London Wall, but we did not know that then. The house was on the right-hand side of the street not far from the former German Sailors' Home which is a dark and seemingly disused building now. On the ground floor was an Arabian restaurant which had little dishes with curry and chutney and green tea in the window.

Smith talked to the man in the restaurant.

The man was short, broad shouldered, slim hipped, short necked.

His face was sentimental in an unpleasant manner.

The man said something and pointed upwards.

Smith nodded and the man answered with a smile that showed red teeth. He chewed betel.

Smith winked at me.

I followed.

Smith introduced me to the man, giving a wrong name which sounded like Belfry or Welfry.

The man bowed very politely and we went upstairs.

The staircase was dark and smelt of garlic. The stairs creaked and I smiled because the dirty window with the shadow of Smith passing in front of it looked so much like a scene from an underworld film of the early German school.

We went up to the top.

Smith knocked.

The door was open but we did not enter because there was no reply.

Smith knocked again.

Inside a bolt was pushed from another door and steps came nearer.

Then she opened the door without asking any questions. She was an old woman with a wrinkled face of the captivatingly ugly type without teeth but gentle and quiet as only the faces of crippled or very old people are.

Smith said: 'Good afternoon.'

The woman said: 'Eh?'

Smith said again, now in a louder voice: 'Good afternoon. Are you Mrs Lammer?'

The woman came closer and turned her left ear up to Smith's mouth. Again she asked: 'Eh?'

Smith brought his mouth as close to her ear as he could without touching it and shouted: 'What's your name? *Your name!*'

The woman smiled with a happy expression and said: 'Oh, yes, I understand you now. My name –'

Smith said desperately: 'Yes, your name! What's your name?'

The woman said 'Annamaria de la Santa Bellina Lamare' or something like that.

Smith said faintly: 'Jesus, that's no name. It's a bad reputation.'

I said: 'Don't give up hope. Everything may still turn out all right. And after every storm the sun breaks through the clouds again.'

Smith shouted into the woman's ear: 'I am a friend of your daughter's. I want you to help me. Will you tell me something?'

The old woman went inside, sat down on a plush chair and began to cry.

Smith followed her and put an arm round her shoulder.

It was very touching.

He mumbled: 'Now, now, Mrs Lammer –'

Then he corrected himself: 'Don't cry, Mrs Lamare. It's just . . . I mean it's just, well, just dispensation. Yes, that's what it is. It's just providence.'

He breathed again.

The woman sobbed.

She had not understood Smith's last words.

He had not raised his voice.

She was too deaf.

She whimpered: 'It's just . . . because . . . because I haven't seen her . . . for such a long time . . . because she never wrote . . . because I never got a line from her . . .'

Smith looked puzzled.

I said: 'Ask her whether she ever reads any newspapers.'

He asked her.

At first she did not understand.

He had to ask her twice.

Then she said: 'No . . . they are only liars . . . they are all liars . . . all men are liars . . .'

I said: 'Quite. Listen to that, Smith. Your victim shows philosophical tendencies. Rather in the Aldington line.'

Smith changed his method.

He said: 'Oh, Estella's quite all right. Don't you grieve. It's only that she's so terribly busy.'

The old woman opened her eyes and looked up at Smith.

Her face showed that she did not believe him.

But she was grateful for his words.

Smith asked her: 'When did you see her last, Mrs Lamare?'

She began to cry again.

Smith asked her once more: 'When was she here last time?'

She wiped her tears with her skirt and said: 'That's almost two years now . . . I mean, since she married and went to America . . . two years . . .'

She cried.

Smith sat down on the floor and said: 'That's news. I wish we'd get some more like that.'

I said: 'You always get news from people who don't read newspapers.'

Smith seemed all right again.

He had given up glaring at the woman.

He smiled and said: 'Oh, yes, how is he? I mean her husband. I always forget his name. What was it? And how is he, tell me?'

She did not look up. But she smiled into her lap. She smiled gently and happily.

She said: 'Robert . . . he was such a nice man . . . Robert was . . . He was a good son-in-law . . . he was.'

I said: 'Let's get out. It's too touching. I can't stand it. Let's have a little walk.'

Smith said nothing.

I said: 'Ask her if she has a photo of her good son-in-law.'

He asked her. She got up and opened a drawer. She gave him the photo. He took it.

I looked at his eyes. They leered at the photo.

I looked over his shoulder at the photo.

It showed two people, Estella and a man.

I knew the man.

It was Robertson.

I said: 'How nice. A family party. Bring your own tea, we provide crockery and hot water.'

He said: 'All right. Let's have a walk now.'

We said goodbye to Mrs Lammer and Smith had to promise that he would come back soon and tell her more about Estella, all about her and how she was getting on in the States . . .

Sixteen

'Now we've got to stick like a leech to our friend Jensen,' said Smith, settled down on the right-hand side of my car and took the wheel.

'Interpretation by contraries – an effective technique of deduction,' I suggested and looked appreciatively at his eyes which were green and without expression.

He started the car. We turned. The turning circle was not more than thirty-five feet.

He jumped the car into second gear and burst the speedometer. It was a nice way of driving.

We went up West India Dock Road and turned left into Commercial Road.

He said, without looking at me: 'Yes, don't I interpret by contraries . . . I find the nicest sort of evidence against Mr Jensen . . . and then I let Mr Jensen run away . . . Instead of trying some ketchup with Mr Jensen, I am . . . asking you questions . . . and asking Miss Ray questions . . . and asking Mr Robertson questions. Yes, and then I find the nicest sort of evidence against Mr Robertson . . . and instead of asking him questions . . . I am beginning to run after Mr Jensen . . . Always doing the other thing . . .'

I said: 'All great detectives are strange and mysterious.'

He turned to face me for a moment. But he had to turn back quickly because we were in Aldgate in a traffic block which suddenly started to move.

When we passed the Bank he said something I didn't understand at first. He spoke over his left shoulder. He asked: 'Do you know Norway?'

85

I said: 'Aardals. Southern Norway, Df, page 80.'

He stopped the car so abruptly that my head was slung forward against the dashboard.

His face had lost its calm acuteness. It was shapeless with rage and it was without character. This was the first time I had seen him cracking up like that. I felt disappointed and somewhat ashamed for his sake.

His eyes wide open, with the whites bulging out at the edges, frowned at me. His mouth was slack. Then he tried to make it tense again and said: 'If you keep on keeping things back I can't do my job.'

I said: 'Keep-keep.'

He asked: 'What?' Then: 'Oh, I see. Hell. I shall have to lock you up –'

I said: '– so that I won't be able to find any more pieces of evidence for you?'

'– so that you won't be able to interfere with my business.'

Then he suddenly shouted at me: 'Why don't *you* do the job? Go to Scotland Yard and tell them Smith is not the right man to handle it: *you* are the one they are looking for!'

He dropped back, relapsing into reproachful silence.

After some time he tried another one. This time he was polite. He said: 'I appreciate you a lot, Mr McCabe. I think you are the only one who is seeing straight through this mess. But I wish you'd tell me something about the things you see there.'

I was tired of him saying the same things again and again. I said: 'Yes, yes, maybe. Maybe, maybe.'

That annoyed him. He said: 'Anything *may* be, but nothing *is*. That's the hell with you people.'

He started the car. He turned left into Queen Victoria Street in order to get out of the traffic.

Then he shot his big gun.

He said: 'Jensen is back in Town. I'm getting anonymous letters. It's his handwriting.'

I said: 'Ah.'

He said: 'What did you say?'

We had gone up the Embankment. Now we turned right towards Whitehall and stopped at the Yard. Smith got out. I took the wheel and drove off towards Trafalgar Square. It was a dark night and the black block of the Home Office grew without contours into the night. There were some few lights in Downing Street and when I passed the War Office I looked up to the sky and I saw the moon red and dirty in the fog above the roof.

A cheap metaphor in the rain.

Seventeen

The rain ceased for some hours after midnight but it began again in the early dawn and it kept on raining while I washed and shaved and it was still raining when the telephone rang shortly after breakfast, that was about ten o'clock and it was still dark outside. It was Smith and his voice sounded quite different from yesterday.

He said: 'Will you please come to number sixty-nine Delilah Square at once. It's urgent.'

I said: 'Yes, if you tell me where it is.'

He said: 'Don't you know? I knew it.'

I said: 'How should I know every damned little place in London? I'm not a policeman. You are one.'

He asked: 'Did I disturb you in your precious sleep? You sound so startled.'

I said: 'God bless your precious humour. Happy in your hospitality. And grateful thanks for your friendly sympathy. I see you at Samson Square.'

He said: 'Delilah Square.'

I said: 'All right. Sixty-nine. Goodbye.'

I put the receiver down, took it up again and phoned the garage to send the car. They sent a mechanic, they were good people, it was quick service, the car was there in seven minutes. I gave the mechanic a shilling and drove out into the rain.

Delilah Square was a curious little street in the Abbey Road district. It was one of those old streets which drive you crazy because the other side of the street has another name and the street turns three times, once to the right, then to the left, and finally it leads you with an odd angle into some sort of blind alley. You pass the house three times before you know it is the one you are looking for because you keep your eyes on the other side of the street and that side has another name.

But I found the house quite quickly.

I rang.

A young woman with a frightened face opened the door.

I asked her for Smith.

She said: 'The gentleman from the police is upstairs. Are you Mr Robertson, sir?'

I said: 'Not that I know. No, really, I don't think so.'

I went up to Smith and said: 'I guess you are waiting for Robertson. Why just Robertson? Why not Christensen and Bloom too?'

'Yes,' he said, 'and why not Miss Ray and Miss Lee and our friend Happy?'

'Oh,' I said, 'so you found him at last. What's your verdict?'

'He doesn't talk to me. But I've been told he's been talking to you. Isn't that right?'

'Oh yes. He's putting the blame on me. But I don't know his background. Did you dig up anything about that?'

Smith laughed. 'You missed something. That's the best part of the story. Listen –'

But he could not tell me anything.

Robertson came in.

Smith stood up and stretched his hand out to him.

'Hallo,' he said, 'how are you? I haven't seen you for ages. Take a seat.'

Robertson sat down and said: 'You saw me yesterday if I am not mistaken.'

Smith giggled and said: 'I wanted to ask you something about your wife.'

Robertson did not appear to be moved.

He said: 'I have no wife.'

Smith said: 'I know.'

Robertson said: 'Well, what are you asking me about?'

Smith said: 'I'm sorry. I wanted to ask you something about the late Mrs Robertson.'

Robertson said: 'I am not married and I never was.'

He spoke without surprise and without anger. But there was a slight reproach in his voice.

Smith said: 'Mr McCabe and I had yesterday the great honour of meeting Mrs Annamaria de la Santa Bellina Lamare.'

Robertson said: 'What language is that? It sounds like a cocktail of Italian and Spanish with a shot of Portuguese.'

Smith seemed puzzled.

I said: 'It's contradiction which makes the work of a detective so interesting.'

Robertson said: 'Not only the work of a detective.'

Smith said: 'Mr Ian Jensen shot himself last night in the next room in this house.'

Robertson asked: 'Why? Why did he come back.'

Smith said: 'They always come back. That's an old story. Curious how these old melodramas always come true in practice.'

Robertson asked: 'But why did he ... why did he shoot himself?'

Smith asked him: 'Have you ever killed somebody?'

Robertson jerked forward.

Smith said: 'I haven't. But what I've seen of other people tells me that you generally don't have a very pleasant feeling afterwards. Sort of unhealthy after-effect. Rather uncomfortable, like feeling seedy. You know, the night after the morning before.'

Robertson asked: 'He committed suicide out of remorse?'

Smith said: 'I don't know. It looks like it. But I don't know. That's why I've asked you to come here. I want you to tell me everything which may attract your attention in any way. You both knew Mr Jensen much better than I did. Now let's have a look at him.'

He opened the door.

Robertson followed hesitatingly.

I got up and followed Robertson.

The place was indifferent. The normal furnished-house atmosphere. Victorian wallpaper, roses. Dirty red curtains. Imitation rugs. Table without polish. Chairs with red plush, slightly torn in places. Window on the left, looking on to a back yard, next house opposite, thirty feet distant. Gas fire, Mr Therm will pick you up, consult the Gas Light and Coke Company, Never Lets London Down.

Paper flowers, ash tray, bottle of ink on the mantelpiece. On the right-hand side from the door, opposite the window, a large French double bed. There was the corpse, stretched out comfortably, a gun in his right hand, small hole in right temple, big hole in left temple. The bullet had gone right through, entering right, leaving left. I could not see where it had landed.

The thing looked all right. The perfect suicide. I could not find anything unusual. There was nothing strange about Jensen and there was nothing strange about the room, but there was something very strange about Jensen's presence in this room. With his income he could have lived in the Savoy or in the Dorchester. But there he was in a cheap furnished house in Delilah Square.

Smith looked questioningly at me.

I shook my head no.

Robertson was too worn out to say anything.

I made a sign to Smith and we left, Robertson following.

I asked Smith whether I could give him a lift.

He said: 'No, thank you.'

I put Robertson in the car and drove to the studio.

The rain had become worse.

Eighteen

There was not much work to do. The laboratory sent up some rushes from *Black and White Blues* but I passed them on to the cutters to get them synced up.

I did not like the job.

They were still using clappers and I wished to God they would go over to start marks, little holes to be punched into the sound track and into the action film to put them both in sync. How much work that would save. Clappers disturbed the actors. They gave me hell. Whenever you had to synchronize sound and picture you had to go back to the beginning. You had to keep the length of all cut-out pieces in mind. You had to have a head like a calculating prodigy. I sent the rushes over to the cutters.

Afterwards when they would have joined all the shots in numerical order I would go down to the show-room with Vic and James Jefferson to have a look at the lot.

I knew it would give trouble again.

It always gave trouble with Vic. He liked his picture to look exactly as it would look on the stage. He did not like my editing.

He would say: 'Mac, stop that fancy cutting of yours. I don't want no Russian fireworks.'

And I would say: 'It's an ostrich walk. It walks. It don't stand still. I wish you wouldn't bury your head in the sand. You'd better move! This is a movie, no ham stable.'

And he would say disgustedly: 'That's just it. I wish it *was* a ham stable. I *am* an old ham, Mac. I want them to *act*. How can they act if you cut them dead after every gesture they do? Give them a chance. Let them act!'

We had the same argument every time.

That's why his pictures were always photographed theatre. They never became films.

Five-minute shots and no cuts. You can't do that.

It was much easier to work with Robert Seaman. He always approved of the kind of rough-cut I liked to do. He never made any alterations. Sometimes he made some suggestions. Generally they were good. But they were one-sided. He liked contrasts. He liked to combine dark shots with light shots, quick movement with slow movement or two movements counteracting each other.

He called that dialectic editing.

It was effective.

But Bloom did not like it so much.

I thought of that when I settled down to do the fine-cut of *Conversation after Midnight*. By tomorrow evening I had to be ready for Bloom and Seaman. They would pass it.

I hitched the reel up and worked for three hours. Then it was all right.

But I had forgotten to have lunch.

I rang for Dinah.

She did not reply.

I had another look at the fine-cut.

Five minutes later she came in.

She had black eyes and white lips. That meant trouble.

She said: 'Yes?' Her voice came from deep in her chest. I knew what that meant.

I stood up.

She stood in the door and did not close it and did not move.

I said: 'Come on, Dinah. Do something. You're getting stiff. I don't like the open-door policy. It's too draughty.'

She did not move.

I said nothing. I outwaited her. She came in and closed the door behind her.

I said: 'All right. Thank you. Sit down.'

She sat down. She looked at me. She still did not speak. I did not speak either.

I outwaited her again. She said: 'The studio is talking about Jensen's suicide.'

I could not help laughing. I said: 'Well, you surprise me. That's the last thing I would have expected.'

She kept on speaking as if I had said nothing. She said: 'It was not suicide. You know that.'

I said: 'Well, Mrs Holmes, here's to Sherlock.'

She said, in a sort of acknowledging tone: 'What a ride you gave me!'

I said: 'Lo and behold, here is another one to the old souse.'

She said: 'I fell for you headlong.'

She said that very drily, almost casually, quite without emotion.

I made no reply.

She said: 'Oh, Mr McCabe, how wonderful, how tough you are. I adore big, silent men.'

'All right,' I said, 'come on. Let's go to bed.'

Her face changed again. It became serious, almost sincere. She said: 'Mac, you better go back to Maria. I must keep aloof.'

I did not know whether she was still acting.

I said: 'Yes. Maybe you're right. Get her on the phone.'

Dinah's face became white. Black rings came out under her eyes. It was the contrast which made me see them now. I did not know whether they had been there all the time.

I knew that I had made the first mistake. I called her. I said: 'Dinah.' I said it first softly and then sharply.

She did not listen.

She went to the phone.

She dialled.

I thought she was dialling the central to make them find Maria for her.

But she phoned Maria's dressing-room direct.

She knew the number by heart.

She had called that number too often.

She got through.

I heard the clicking of the receiver being taken off at the other end.

I heard Maria's voice saying 'Hallo.'

The voice sounded hard.

I was not sure whether it was only the metal which made it sound like this.

But I heard the voice clearly.

You should not be able to hear somebody's voice so distinctly from ten feet distance.

It is indiscreet.

Dinah said: 'This is Mr McCabe's secretary speaking. Could I speak to Miss Ray, please?'

I felt Maria's hesitation.

Then Maria's voice said in another tone: 'I am sorry. Miss Ray is not in.'

I did not hear the clicking yet. She had not put the receiver down. She was listening.

I went quickly over to the phone and took the receiver from Dinah.

I said: 'Maria?'

I heard how the receiver at the other end was slowly put down.

Now I finally heard the click.

I turned round and said: 'Dinah.'

There was no reply.

There was nobody in the room.

Nineteen

East of Whitechapel over the river there was a light which turned white. Afterwards there was too much brown fog. I could not see stars. So I walked on. In these cool nights after the days which are getting shorter now it is lovely to hang about the bridges and watch the yellow river passing by underneath. Things change and it's good they change, but it's bad when you don't know what the change is for. It's also bad when they change and afterwards there's nothing left by which to remember how it was before. It's very bad when there's nothing left afterwards. It makes you think and once you start thinking you see it's all messed up. And if you try to clear up the mess you get a kick in the pants. They like to keep it muddled up as it is. It's better for them. They get more out of it. They don't like changes. They're afraid of them.

It had been a good game at the beginning but now it was just a fag-end. They did not keep to the rules and they did not even invent good bluffs. They slackened down. They did not keep watch. They put the cards on the table without thinking. They just put them down the way they came. There was no fun left. If a guy allows you to make a sap of him you'd better take your hat and go away. It's better to be welshed on and know it than to welsh on the other guy and get away with it. If there's no more need to sew your shirt on you could just as well jump in the lake. You can go places that are not on the level and do things that are off-colour when you're willing to put up a fight for the things you've done but it's not worth it when the other one is dodging instead of hitting back.

You don't know whether you'd better stick around or beat it.

You can't play with whipper-snappers.

I walked along the Embankment down with the river towards Tower Bridge. From the docks, half a mile off, came the faint sound of a boat going upstream. I was just there when the bridge opened and some time afterwards the boat came up and passed by without noise in the dark.

I went down the stairs to see the boat from under the bridge. I saw the lights in the cabins and the green light at starboard and the red at port. The red light was at lee, we had north wind and it was getting cooler at nightfall.

When the lights had fainted in the fog I heard a voice humming in the dark. I listened to it. It had a good and manly sound. I could not find out from where it came. Now there was another voice. There were four or five voices and that was a very odd tune they were humming. It was weary and it was like homesickness and it had a curious rhythm I had never heard before. It gives you a strangely sultry feeling of a sentimental kind to hear voices at night singing somewhere and you don't know where. When you were a kid long ago and mother was still there she used to give you cool wet packs round your chest often when you were sick with fever and that gave you the feeling tight and sultry and somehow pleasant in an odd way: and it was like that now.

Then I saw the men. They were sitting down to the left on a jut about three yards long and one wide and not more than two inches above the waterline. They were sitting, seven men, with their bums on the cold wet stone and their legs drawn close and their backs against the wall and their heads back over their shoulders against the wall and their caps tilted back in the neck, and singing like that, like cats up towards the sky. They could not sing. But it wouldn't have given you that odd feeling if they'd had voices like Caruso. One had a banjo but it was not a real banjo, not even a nigger banjo without bottom like they have it on the levee and in the Chicago southside dives. It was a kid's banjo made of pasteboard and cheap wood and it was glued over with glazed paper of a funny violet blue colour which reflected the light of the stars now that the fog had got thinner.

> Mary, O Mary, O Mary at home,
> Lift the sail, lift the sail,
> Ahoaho.
> Mary, O Mary, O Mary's dead;
> Stow the sail, stow the sail,
> O—A—O—A!

That was what they sang and then I knew what it was. They were singing shanties, now in this year of grace when the mechanical cranes across the river in Hay's Wharf were unloading the Soviet boats which had arrived from Leningrad that night. Now they were singing because there was nothing else to do, no lifting of sails and no stowing of sails because they had electrical winches now and no handjacks and donkey engines and mechanical capstans and there were no hands wanted and you could read that everywhere and so there was nothing to do but to sit and to sing shanties and to play a kid's banjo. And that was all there was left and you could look round where you wished and it was always the same and everywhere the same and there was nothing left but serenading the moon in the fog and seeing the water rise and the night fall and the fog thicken.

When the men had stopped singing I saw a small boat passing under the bridge and going down with the river and I heard the oars hitting the water and somebody playing a mouth organ and then the men sang 'Fag End Blues' and then 'Misty Night Blues' and 'Tenderloin Blues' and they sang softly and quite given to the singing. They had one leader of the chorus and the others followed in harmonies which came by themselves, humming to themselves and not caring. They made pauses and intervals and smoked and sang again and paused again but nobody spoke and then I walked away with the sound of 'Tenderloin Blues' in my head and the night got dark and wet.

I saw the ships in the water and the lights of the stars in the water and the reflections under the bridges. The pubs were about to close and when the doors opened there were waves of smell and light and sound floating out into the fog. There was laundry hung up on lines across the darkness in the back yards. I passed some sluices and locks and got a light from a nightwatchman in a warehouse in China Street. In the small streets there were lighted windows and one was open and you could see the warmth from inside passing out into the mist and there were whirls of smoke and fog in the light and a girl sang 'When your lover has gone,' and her voice was low and husky from too much smoking.

They did everything too much. They could not stop when they'd had enough. You must never do anything too much. Listen to people and see things and smell them and feel what they are like and then smoke your pipe and go away. Don't ever stay too long: the roof may come down. Go away before it gets dark. Leave no trace behind. The dawn is cold and there is still much wind to come before daybreak.

They got Estella and then Jensen and they will get you next. Nobody is going to get away. Fight it – and it won't fight back. Try to dodge it – and it will kill you from behind. Run away – and it won't follow you. But it will get you in the end. It gets me and you and the big ones and the tiny ones and those with good white teeth and those without. Don't sleep too long: you miss too much. The days are short and they are still getting shorter. Get your food before the other one gets it: he is also hungry. Hit him on the jaw when he tries to be quicker. Never let a bad man down: the good ones will follow you. But there are few good ones left. The penitence is long but the deed was short enough.

Jensen gave it to Estella and then he got it himself. Things run like that. It begins one morning in November and it ends one night in December. Everything passes. Sit down and do your business. Or stand up if you have to. But do your business, don't leave anything undone, and do it well. And afterwards leave your place clean and tidy. That's the one thing which matters. Do it and when you look back see that it was well done. But don't look back too much.

Bloom had never got back to his office: they had got him. Christensen had dropped out. I couldn't understand why he did that thing, charging himself with something somebody else had done. But it was the same with Bloom. I never understood why he did it. That was the second dark spot.

There were the three girls, one dead, two left over. Never have two girls: have three. Two are too much. Have one or have none. But two will always get you into trouble. There was Jensen and there were other people like that.

There were the two men left over. Robertson had got himself into trouble and Robertson would get Smith or Smith would get Robertson and finally Smith would get himself.

So there was only Happy left.

Now I had it all clear. Keep away from the two girls and set the men together by the ears. Find out the backgrounds of Bloom, Christensen, Happy. Finally Smith and Robertson: play off one against the other and make them contradict themselves and each other.

It had been a good evening, walking and seeing things, listening and thinking. Now I could go home.

I got the last train from Mile End tube station.

Twenty

When the phone rang next morning I did not answer it at first. But then it rang again and I thought I would not be able to sleep anyway so I took up the receiver. A funny little voice asked: 'Hallo, is that Mr McCabe?'

I said: 'Haven't I heard that voice before?'

The voice said: 'Oh yes. This is May Robertson, you may remember me, I showed you the way once when you were looking for my brother the night before . . . before . . .'

I said: 'All right. Let's leave it at before. What can I do for you?'

She said: 'You can't do anything for me. You can do something for yourself.'

I said: 'Good. Tell me what it is and if it's good I'll do it.'

She said: 'They got him this morning and took him away to the Yard.'

I asked: 'Who got whom?'

She said: 'Smith got John. But listen –'

I said: 'That is very sad. What has it got to do with me?'

She said: 'Listen: John said he believed they found something new about Jensen. It was not suicide. It was murder.'

I said: 'Lovely. A merry-go-round. How life repeats itself. With Estella it was also suicide at first.'

She said: 'They got something on him. They searched our place – they had done it already once before – but now it appears they have found something that got him into trouble –'

I said: 'I still can't see what that has got to do with me.'

She said hesitatingly: 'I suppose you can't help John. But you could help yourself –'

I said: 'All right. Come on. Shoot.'

She said slowly: 'John told me you were all mixed up in it –'

I said: 'Maybe he was. I was not.'

She said: 'He told me he knew you were in it and you'd better do what you can for yourself.'

I said: 'I guess he used to tell you fairy tales when you were kids? Stories with lots of ogres and witches in them?'

She said: 'You guessed right.'

I said: 'Listen: one more question. Have you phoned me once before this morning?'

She said: 'No.'

I said: 'Then I guessed wrong. They'll be here in some minutes to get me too.'

She asked: 'Why don't you beat it?'

I said: 'There's no reason why I should. Thanks for the flowers.'

She said: 'You're welcome, goodbye,' and rang off.

Robert Seaman would have called it a dialectic development of events: I had guessed right and wrong at the same time: half an hour later they knocked and the maid came to ask me whether she should let them in. I was in the bath towelling myself. I shouted: 'Let them in. Sit them down. Fill them some drinks.'

When I had my trousers on I walked over to the lounge. Smith and two plain-clothes men got up from the chairs.

I buttoned my collar on. I said: 'The great man himself. How are you, Smith?'

He said: 'Fine. But it's getting cold. I mean it's really getting cold.'

I said: 'Yes. It must be. You brought two guys with you to keep you warm.'

The plain-clothes guys couldn't take it. They made faces as if I had offered them castor oil.

Smith took it. He smiled.

He said: 'Plenty of things have happened since last night. You'll see. If you don't already know. Usually you have your own ways of snapping up news before other guys get it.'

I said. 'All right. Give me a hand. Fix that stud for me, will you. Why don't they make shirts without studs?'

Smith got up and fixed it. Then he sat down again. The plain-clothes men gaped at him.

I asked them: 'You're newly acquainted with Inspector Smith?'

They looked at Smith to ask him whether they should reply. He nodded approvingly.

The one said: 'Yes, sir. I have been in another department.'

The other one said: 'No, sir. I have known the Inspector for some time.'

I said: 'And you're still surprised at him? You should feel ashamed of yourself. There are men of the hour: he's the man of the second. He changes from second to second. He's a chameleon.' I turned quickly to the first man and shouted at him: 'Didn't he have black hair yesterday?'

The man blushed, thought a moment, swallowed and said: 'I don't think so, sir. I think he always has been fair.'

Smith laughed uproariously. He said: 'McCabe, you're sure one of the greatest bullies I've ever encountered. You should most certainly join the C.I.D. And believe me, that ain't no compliment.'

I said: 'Smith, we understand each other. I'm ready. Come on. Let's go. Where are we going?'

He said: 'You would call it a family party. The biggest gathering ever of the Dear Old Gang.'

'All of them?' I asked.

'Bloom, Christensen, Robertson, Miss Ray, Miss Lee. Someone missing?'

'Yes,' I said. 'Happy is missing.'

'Yes,' he said. 'You're right. Happy is missing.'

'Where is he?' I asked him.

'He's missing,' he said.

They had a Black Maria waiting outside. That was really funny. I laughed.

I asked: 'Is this thing generally up to the mark? I mean cowing witnesses by putting them in a tough-guys' van?'

Smith said: 'Yes, it's quite up to the mark. Sometimes we even throw them in the can. We call it detention on remand. You may have heard of it.'

The van started. Smith sat opposite me, one of the cops was on my left, the other one on Smith's right.

We had a twenty-minute ride without speaking. Then we stopped and the driver opened the door from outside. We stepped out.

This was not Scotland Yard.

It was sixty-nine Delilah Square.

We went upstairs. Smith was at my side, the one copper

walked in front of us, the other one followed behind. The first copper stopped in front of the door which led to the bedroom. Smith and I followed. The rear guard ran into me. I knocked him back. The first copper asked Smith something with his eyes. Smith nodded. The copper opened the door. Smith made a sign to me to enter. I entered. Smith followed. The other copper closed the door behind me. He remained at the door with his back resting against it.

They were sitting on a row of chairs on the left side, the window side of the room. They were all there. Bloom, Maria, Dinah, Chris and Robertson. I flirted a hand at them and saluted. Chris alone winked back. The body was not there.

I said: 'Hallo, Gang. Everybody happy?'

Nobody replied. I expected no reply.

Smith showed me a chair at the end of the row.

I sat down.

Smith remained standing.

I said: 'Sit down, Sergeant Smith. Your legs will get stiff.'

Smith, without smiling, said: 'Keep your mouth shut, Trumpeter McCabe. Your tongue will get stiff.'

I said: 'Excellent, Smith. I think you will make a great career.'

He said: 'I think so too.' Then he cleared his throat and his face changed. He addressed the crowd. They looked at him. He said: 'Ladies and gentlemen, I do not intend to waste my time and yours making flowery speeches. Mr Ian Jensen did not commit suicide. He was murdered. We had a post-mortem. The autopsy showed that there was enough poison in his stomach to kill him just as efficiently as the bullet could have done it. But the bullet has not done it. It was the sleeping draught. Though that was probably not what the murderer had intended. Let's call him, or her, Mr or Mrs or Miss X. Now, X wanted to make Mr Jensen unconscious, then he laid him down on the bed, put the gun in Jensen's hand and pulled the trigger. It was a silent gun. The housekeeper heard the shot in spite of it but she thought it was a car backfiring in the street. She found Jensen dead next morning and phoned us. That's all. You know the rest.'

Chris asked: 'Couldn't it be suicide in spite of all that? Mr Jensen could have taken the sleeping draught and fired the shot as well, couldn't he?'

Smith laughed. He said with friendly scorn: 'That is only metaphysically possible. As he didn't take the drug after the shot had killed him he must have fired the shot after the drug had killed him.'

I laughed. Nobody else laughed. I laughed because I thought it was funny that none of them was able to appreciate Smith's lovely explanations. Even if one of them was the murderer he should have been able to control himself.

Robertson asked: 'Couldn't it have happened like this: he took the sleeping draught and fired the shot shortly before the draught had its effect?'

Smith said: 'No. We found that he was already dead when the shot was fired. You, ladies and gentlemen, are here partially as witnesses – whether you know that or not – and partially as persons under suspicion of murder. We have neither cause nor intention to hide this. You are the people who are, in some way or another, concerned in this affair. You are here to see a demonstration of what we think happened. We are going to reconstruct the murder as far as we can see it. We want you to help us and support us by giving us any facts known to you, any facts or suggestions which may supplement or complete our evidence. I wish to warn you that any statement you make may be used against you. Thank you.'

He walked over to the plain-clothes man at the door and talked something over with him. He spoke too low, I could not hear what he said.

Then he came forward again and said: 'Ladies and gentlemen. We would appreciate a volunteer from your ranks to take Mr Jensen's part in the reconstruction. This is not a very pleasant business. Who is going to help us?'

Nobody got up.

Smith did not appear to have expected anything else. He said: 'I would suggest Mr McCabe!'

That got me. He knew that. I had not expected it. I thought: Christ, what is that fool getting at, this is idiotic, he behaves as if he thinks I'd done it.

I did not get up. I said: 'Sometimes a man in the winter opens the window of his room because there's a smell in the room. But he only has the heart to open the window because he doesn't know yet how cold he'll feel afterwards. Keep that in mind, Smith. Keep your window closed no matter how it smells.'

He said: 'Go to hell!'

I said: 'All right, boys, come on, let's go.'

He asked: 'Where are you going?'

I said: 'To hell. Didn't you tell me to?'

He laughed.

He said: 'McCabe, we're getting on swell. I never got on so swell with any witness before.'

I said: 'Now come on, I'm Jensen. What have I got to do?'

He laughed and said: 'So that's the solution: you are Jensen. Take off those false whiskers. What you got to do? Come to life again and tell us all about your murder.' Then, seriously: 'Sit down on that chair.'

He pointed at the chair before the table. I sat down.

He talked again to the copper at the door. The copper went out.

Then Smith said: 'Quiet, please. Listen, friends –'

I thought: The ladies and gentlemen are dropped, that's a bad sign.

Smith said: 'Jensen was expecting somebody that night. We call him or her Mr X or Miss X or Mrs X. For quite a long time before Jensen was killed he had sent us that kind of letter with no name underneath. The afternoon before the night he was shot he wrote us that the hour of decision was getting near and that he would now soon settle his account with the person who had got him into all this trouble. So he was expecting X that night. The housekeeper did not see X. Possibly Jensen opened the door himself. Anyway X got in. X may be in this room now and probably he or she could explain everything much better than we can explain it to him or her – but for all that we want him or her to listen to our explanations –'

There was a knock at the door.

Smith said: 'Come in.'

The copper came in.

Smith continued: '– X came in. Jensen and X had a short talk. Probably they tried to settle their business in peace. Anyway they settled down to drinking. That started it. We don't know whether Jensen threatened X or whether X himself took Jensen's gun from out of the bedside table. The fact is Jensen was killed by his own gun in his own hand after he had swallowed a lovely portion of his sleeping draught. It could have been like that –' He turned round and said: 'Come on.'

The copper came and sat down opposite me. The copper looked at Smith. Smith nodded. The copper poured two drinks. He shoved one over to me. Smith said to me: 'Drink that. There's no poison in it.'

I said: 'That's a mistake. There *should* be some in it.'

He said: 'Don't trouble, it's only a sleeping draught. You go on, drink it and go to sleep.'

I said: 'Yes, and wake up in heaven.'

Smith said: 'You are an optimist.'

The copper and I settled down to serious drinking.

After a minute or so Smith took up the two glasses.

I looked at Robertson.

Robertson saw my eyes and looked at the glasses. He thought a moment, then he said: 'Another question, inspector. What happened to the glasses? No fingerprints? Any traces of poison?'

Smith's eyes changed. It was as if you could hear the bolts shoot home inside him. He locked himself up. It was a fine ugly foolproof expression on his face. He should be grateful to his pro-creator for furnishing him with such a face to wear on the front side of his head, I thought.

'No,' he said to Robertson, 'no fingerprints, no traces of poison in the glasses.'

And he had a face, God! Plenty of good old poker-playing guys would have given him any game, unplayed, for that face of his.

Christensen stood up and walked across the room and stopped in front of Smith.

He had been Jensen's best friend. He was about to crack up. You could see it in his fingers, the way they twitched, and in his lids, because he tried too hard to keep them steady.

He asked again, to make sure: 'No poison in the glass?'

Smith said: 'No.'

'No fingerprints on either glass?'

'No.'

Christensen's fingers cramped and I thought: Now. But he kept himself well and without a wrong ring in his voice he asked: 'The glasses had been wiped afterwards?'

Smith did not move. He said: 'Yes.'

Christensen said: 'Which means it was not suicide.'

There was no question in his voice. He knew now.

Smith said: 'It was not suicide, it was murder.'

Chris walked over to the window and closed it and came back and said: 'What about the reconstruction of the murder?'

Smith had his head lowered and his chin stretched forward which gave him the look of a fighting bull about to charge.

But you can't fight blind bulls. It was sad. All of it was sad. The balance had gone.

At first it had been better than any game: watching the other fellow and trying to figure out what he's thinking about and what he's thinking about you and what he's about to do and whether he's going to do what he thinks, and trying to counter everything he thinks and feels and does and trying to counter even those things he thinks but doesn't dare to do. Trying to nag him by talking rubbish and juggling with words and talking about anything except those things he wants to talk about, just keeping on talking until he gets tired of it and cuts the cackle and comes to the 'osses.

And Smith was the loser. He would crack up. He would do it any minute now. I had the game in my hand and I had his number and he knew it.

Christensen said 'Smith, the reconstruction of the murder,' and Smith didn't do a thing. But Chris remembered what this was all about. That this was murder and Smith was the man to clear up the murder and find the one who had done it, and that I, McCabe, had popped in to do my own bit of stirring up the mud and seeing it get clear again.

There are always some who watch the fight and others who do the fighting and I like both of them but I don't like those who forget what they are fighting about when the fight is getting too tough.

And now Smith had forgotten what the fight was all about and it was easy for him to forget what it was about because he had nothing to fight for, nothing except his job and that was little enough for him though it might have been much for others in his place. But Christensen had something to fight for and he didn't forget in the fight what the fight was fought for.

And so he stood up against Smith and said 'I want you to give us the reconstruction of the murder' and that was as if it was Smith's cue for cracking up and Smith said 'You'd better put Mr McCabe in charge of the reconstruction. He remembers the Myers-Johnson case better than I do' and Smith took his hat and walked out.

The first thing I felt was the drink, how it had got me and how Smith had got me by giving it to me. A lousy little trick and it had got me like all lousy little tricks always get you, easier than the fine big clever well-thought-out bluffs.

Smith had gone out and they all looked at me and they looked at me so blankly that I knew none of them remembered the Myers-Johnson case and none of them had understood what Smith meant.

He had meant to scare me. He had meant to give me hell by telling me he thought I had done it. I of all people should have killed Jensen and in the same way the woman had been killed by the man in the Myers-Johnson case. He had meant to make me trap myself but what he had done was to give himself away. He couldn't wait. The pace had been too slow for him and he thought he could get there earlier by running and jumping to conclusions. Now he had told me what he thought but I hadn't told him what I thought and I wouldn't tell for I could wait and the pace was not too slow for me.

'Well, ladies and gentlemen, I guess we've done with the reconstruction of the murder. Let's go home,' I said.

'I always like to get home early,' said Robertson.

Then I remembered.

'He's forgotten you. God, that's a joke,' I said.

'Yes, that's a joke,' he admitted.

'Aren't you under arrest?' I asked.

'I was,' he said.

The others looked at me and then they went out.

When they had all left the room he said: 'Yes, I'm not under arrest any longer.'

'Fine,' I said. 'Congratulations.'

'I owe it to you,' he said.

'Don't forget to pay it back,' I said and went out.

Twenty-one

Then I thought of the old man. I suddenly remembered he had hair like gunmetal.

I went to the telephone box at the end of Delilah Square and phoned the *Evening Express* and asked for the boxing reporter.

'Mr Humphreys is out,' he said.

'When can I find him?' I asked.

'Tomorrow morning,' he said.

I said 'Thank you' and rang off.

I drove down to Lower Regent Street to have lunch at the Bulgaria Restaurant.

It was a good lunch but after the second course I remembered the old man again and I asked the waiter to have somebody phone the *Evening Express* and ask for Mr Humphreys' address.

He took a long time for that phone call and I didn't like the food. They served the fish and took it away and brought the escalope and I couldn't eat it and when he came with the trolley for sweets he brought a note which read 'Telephone Report. Table 21. The *Evening Express* cannot give the address of any member of its Editorial Staff.'

I left the sweet to the waiter and paid and went out.

I drove down to Fleet Street and gave my card to the boy in the hall of the *Evening Express* building and asked him to get me anybody from the editorial staff.

I didn't have to wait long and I was looking the other way when somebody tapped me on the right shoulder and I turned round and there was the old man smiling at me.

'Hallo, Mr Humphreys,' I said, 'I thought you were out.'

'I was out for lunch and so was Mr Humphreys,' he said.

'And how are you, both of you, I mean you and Mr Humphreys?' I asked.

'Thanks, I'm fine. But Mr Humphreys has unfortunately contracted a slight cold.'

'What's your name?' I asked him. 'I'm sorry I forgot to ask you when we met the first and last time.'

'Never mind,' he said. 'I didn't ask you either. I never ask people for their names.'

'Then you must have a good memory for people,' I said.

'Too good,' he said. 'It's bad for an old man to have a good memory.'

'Have a bad one,' I suggested.

'My name is Müller,' he said. 'Humphreys is the Chief. I'm the Second.'

'Now listen, Mr Miller –' I said.

'Müller,' he said. 'U with two dots.'

'Are you German?' I asked.

'I used to be,' he said.

'Fine,' I said. 'I used to be Scottish.'

'What are you now?' he asked.

'American,' I said. 'Glasgow born, first name Cameron.'

'When did you go to the States?' he asked.

'I didn't go. I couldn't go. My father carried me.'

'When was that?' he asked.

'Thirty-nine years ago,' I said.

'How old are you?' he said.

'Thirty-eight,' I said.

He said: 'Come on, let's have a drink on that.'

We went to the pub in Fetter Lane.

'What'll you have?' he asked.

'Pink gin,' I said.

'Two pink gins,' he said to the pubster.

'Listen, Mr Müller –' I said.

'You still remember my name?' he asked.

'I do. I've got a fine memory,' I said.

'You too?' he asked.

'Now, about your memory. Do you remember what we were talking about in front of the King's Cross tube station news stall?'

'Lovely word,' he said. 'King's Cross tube station news-stall.'

'Do you remember?' I asked him.

'I'm listening,' he said.

'A man got shot. Shot himself or was shot by another guy with his own gun. They found traces of an overdose of a sleeping draught in his stomach.'

'The Johnson-Myers trial,' he said.

'No. They say the sleeping draught killed him. The bullet came too late. It hit a dead man.'

'Lovely,' he said. 'I must make a note of that.'

'Can they really prove that the poison killed him before the bullet did?'

'That's very funny,' he said, 'you mean the poison killed him before the shot was fired?'

'Yes. Can they prove that?'

'I don't know,' he said. 'I'm not a doctor.'

'You're a nice old man. What do you think?'

'I think it's possible. There's a lot of precedents where they did prove it.'

'Looks sad,' I said. 'Cameron McCabe's dear old mother'll have to cry some buckets full of tears.'

'Why?' he asked. 'You're not mixed up in it?'

'How do you know?' I asked. 'I've done it.'

'Have you?' he asked.

'They believe I have.'

'But you haven't,' he said.

'Looks damned much as if I had.'

'Faked evidence?' he asked.

'Are you?' I asked.

'Am I what?' he asked.

'Are you faked evidence?'

He laughed. Then he said: 'You think they are going to check up on your moves and then they are going to find me and they are sure to run across some guy who has listened to what I told you about the Johnson-Myers case and so they know you know how it was done. Is that it?'

'That's it,' I said.

'That's what?' he said. 'About a million people approximately have read what I told you. About twenty million have read the Johnson-Myers trial in other papers.'

'So what?' I said.

'Twenty-one million suspects,' he said.

'Yes. Twenty-one million and one, to be exact. And I'm just the one they've chosen to pick on.'

'Did you sock a copper in the jaw or slosh his mother-in-law or what got you mixed up in it?'

'I socked a copper-in-law and sloshed his mother in the jaw.'

'Come on. Cut the big bad talk. What do they want to pocket you for?'

'Just for the ducks of it.'

'That's a sound reason,' he said.

'Here's the story,' I said. 'We made a film, the name doesn't matter, a normal average box-office proposition. Nine reels, sixty thousand quid, two stars and one newcomer in a triangular story, Maria Ray is the first girl, Ian Jensen is the man in the case and a young girl called Estella Lamare, a newcomer, is the second girl. Now one day when the film is finished and I'm almost through with the rough-cut, Bloom, the big boss, bumps into the cutting-room and tells me to cut out the Estella girl, just cut her plain out of the picture. Now I didn't know then and I still don't know what he wanted me to do that for. Maybe he had a quarrel with the girl – somebody said he tried to make her and got a cold shoulder – but that doesn't seem likely to me. There was a rumour that another company was producing a triangle story too much like ours and Bloom was afraid of losing his money if the other picture came out before his would be finished. But that doesn't seem to make sense either. I never heard of any other film so much like ours. You know, all films are more or less alike, and in the film chronicles of the future they won't record any individual pictures anyway – they'll talk only about different types of movies and talkies and weepies and laughies.'

'I hear you,' he said.

'All right,' I said. 'I'm coming to the point. Bloom said the picture was too long and when he asked me to cut out all scenes with Estella I smelled trouble coming because I knew this picture meant everything to that Estella girl. So I didn't start on the cutting; it was a difficult job anyway and I went out to look for a man called Robertson, who is the best cutter in the studio though he's constantly experimenting in what he calls his special effects department. I couldn't find him, and there was something fishy about the whole business of his whereabouts that afternoon. I found out about it all when I met him the same night at a club with Maria and Ian. Anyway next morning the Estella girl was found dead with two small wrist wounds in Robertson's room.'

'No good,' he said.

'Why?' I asked.

'Cheap,' he said. 'Bad melodrama. No invention. Babies in Gangland.'

'All right,' I said. 'First Rules of Gangfare for Beginners. It's always difficult at the beginning and it gets worse as it goes on.'

'Never mind. I've got my umbrella,' he said.

'That's good. You'll need it. It goes on. Listen: that guy Robertson had a lovely little hobby, a camera that focused automatically on a person once the motor was started by some kind of gadget. Now he had the camera connected with the door in his room and in front of the camera in that room of all places that Estella girl had got to get herself bumped off. And, of course, to make it a fine yellow mystery thriller the film had to disappear mysteriously.'

'Which film?' he asked.

'The one the camera took of the murder.'

'How do you know that the camera actually took a film?'

'We found it.'

'*We* found what?'

'We found the film.'

'The film of the murder?'

'Yes. The film of the murder. Jensen killed her either intentionally or in self-defence. She had been his girl but he had left her for Maria Ray and she threatened to kill herself and he gave her a little assistance.'

'Didn't you say it was self-defence?'

'Perhaps. You can't see it on the film. It looks as if he's trying to take the knife away from her when she threatens to kill herself. But maybe he fakes.'

'Why should he? Was there anybody else in the room?'

'I don't know. I don't think so. But perhaps he knew about the camera.'

'If he knew about the camera, and intended to make it public that he had acted in self-defence, then he wouldn't have pinched the film.'

'He didn't pinch the film. Maria Ray did. At least, that's her story. She says Jensen came to her room to see her after he'd left the Estella girl dead in Robertson's room, telling her he had killed her accidentally in self-defence.'

'And she went back to the room and pinched the film without raising an alarm and without touching the body?'

'That's her story.'

'What's yours?'

'I like this girl Maria. So I told Smith I found the film in Jensen's flat.'

'Who's Smith?'

'He's the big blue-eyed boy in the case. The official sleuth.'

'You're the unofficial one?'

'There's a lot of unofficial ones in this case and all around it.'

'Equal rights for others,' he said.

'Yes,' I said, 'and anyone can have his own sister's opinion.'

'You must have had a lovely time in your studio,' he said.

'It's no studio,' I said, 'it's a loony bin.'

'Tell me more about it. I like it very much now. It makes me feel at home,' he said.

'Take care of your umbrella,' I said, 'it's getting involved now. Any questions before the curtain goes up again?'

'Yes. What about Bloom and the first part of the story? Any connections with the rest, or just modern story-telling?'

'That's one of my questions. That's what I'm telling you the story for. Now keep that in mind: Bloom is double-crossing Estella, we don't know why, and the next morning the Estella girl is found dead and we all think it's suicide because of Bloom's damned lousy double-cross walk, but then it turns out to be murder.'

'Or perhaps manslaughter,' he said.

'Or perhaps not,' I said.

'Now what comes next?' he asked.

'Next comes a confession,' I said.

'By Jensen?'

'No, by Bloom.'

He asked. 'What?' and that was the first time he got interested. 'What did he confess, and why?'

'He confessed he had killed Estella Lamare but why he confessed – that's the next question I'm booking for me. Keep it in mind.'

'I will,' he said. 'You know I've got a fine memory.'

'You told me,' I said.

'I sure did,' he said.

'Yes,' I said.

'Now what's next after this?' he asked.

'Another confession,' I said.

'By Bloom?'

'No, by Chris.'

'Who's Chris?'

'He's Jensen's boy friend. A good fellow. Better than Jensen. Too good for Jensen. Much too good for Jensen.'

'You don't like Jensen?'

'I didn't like Jensen.'

'You like him now?'

'No. He's dead.'

'You told me.'

'Didn't you know that before?'

'Yes. I read it in the papers.'

'Now why didn't you tell me that before?'

'It's so much better the way you tell it. It's a new story.'

'That's the art of story-telling,' I admitted.

'Now what about Chris's confession?' asked Müller.

'Yes. That's another dark spot. Keep that in mind as question number three.'

'What happened?'

'He confessed and what he confessed checked up with what actually happened.'

'Well, ain't that fine!'

'Yeah. Only he didn't do it.'

'Who did do it?'

'Chris didn't do it.'

'Now this is getting somewhat loony. Didn't you say Chris's confession checked up with the actual facts?'

'Yes. I said it.'

'So what?'

'Chris told *Jensen's* story exactly as it happened. Only he said it was *his* story.'

'Well, probably he saw the film before you found it.'

'No, he didn't.'

'How do you know?'

'It doesn't check up.'

'Doesn't check up with what?'

'With what actually happened.'

'All right. Now what's next?'

'Robertson.'

'Why? What's wrong with him? Did he kill her?'

'No. Jensen did. But it happened in Robertson's room.'

'Is that all you have against him?'

'I have nothing at all against him. But here are the facts: Robertson knew Estella before she took up film work. Her real name is Esther Lammer but after she took up films she began calling herself Estella Lamare and before that there was another episode under the name of Edna Lenore. That was some years ago in Oxford where Robertson met her. There was something slightly fishy about her. Perhaps she was merely cracked, perhaps worse. It's in the family. She's got a mother who's damned downright nutty all over.'

'How do you know?'

'I met the charming lady. Big boy Smith took me out for a ride to see her in her own domestic surroundings. West India Dock Road and that's what it looks like and there's a smell of garlic about the place so it blows you out before you get in.'

'What happened in the West India Docks?'

'I told you she's nuts from top to bottom and back again the whole way from bottom to top. She doesn't know her daughter's dead and she thinks she's married in the States and Robertson's her husband and she thinks he's a good son-in-law.'

'So what are you doing about it?'

'What am I to do? That's Smith's business.'

'So what's Smith doing?'

'Talking.'

'What about?'

'About anything except the things he wants to talk about.'

'Tell me something about him. What kind of a guy is he?'

'He's got an overseas accent but he doesn't talk genuine Americanese. He's too English to be American and too American to be English. He's a Cockney, grown up in Canada. Canadian citizen, lived there until he didn't like it any longer, walked over the frontier into God's Own Country and joined the Feds. When they started the G-man-wife-and-children-business they sacked him because they didn't like his methods. He's a barking sleuth. His bark is worse than his bite and he's got ideas of his own and when they found that out they didn't like it and he didn't like it either and so they sent him back to his home-grown lumber mills. He couldn't stick it there so he blew across the ditch and somebody fixed him in the Yard and there he is now with his ideas of his own and his peculiar bark and they don't like it here better than they did yonder in the Windy City.'

'I don't believe a word,' he said.

'Neither do I,' I said.

'They wouldn't take a Canadian into the Feds unless he's something extra special and they wouldn't take an Anglo-Canadian ex-G-man into the Yard unless he's a damned big shot bigger than their biggest shot.'

'You're not so far wrong there,' I said.

'Why don't you come home with me and let us talk in comfort?' he asked.

'Sure,' I said.

So we went to his place.

It was a lovely little flat with steel chairs on a blue Chinese carpet and a steel-blue metallic wallpaper with one green Cézanne and one chrome yellow Van Gogh hanging very low, white curtains, an Empire table and three German baroque cupboards. It was a fine and fantastic mixture and if somebody had told me about it I would have laughed, but seeing it I liked it and so did the old man.

'Excuse me,' he said. 'I'm having a wash. Here's the telephone. Use it. I won't be a minute.'

He went out and I heard the water running in the bath.

I phoned the studio and told them I would be back at six. When they asked me where I had been I told them the Jensen murder investigation had kept me and they said, 'All right, but come along as soon as possible, we're waiting for you with the fine-cut of *Black and White Blues*.'

I asked them to switch me through to Maria's dressing-room.

There was no reply.

I rang Smith.

They said he was out.

I rang Chris.

His landlady said he hadn't been home since breakfast.

I rang the studio again and asked for Robertson.

He answered.

'Listen, John,' I said, 'what happened? How did you get home?'

'Nothing happened,' he said, 'I got here all right.'

'Have you heard anything from Smith?'

'Nothing at all.'

'How's Maria?'

'She's in love with you.'

'What did you say?'

'You asked "How's Maria?" I said "She's in love with you." Anything wrong with that?'

'Something is damned wrong with that,' I said. 'How do you come to know that so well, anyway?'

'You ever heard of fighting hens?' he asked.

'Fighting cocks,' I said.

'No, fighting hens.'

'What happened?' I asked.

'They fought on the way back. Dinah lost half of her left ear, Maria got a black eye and a bite in her right thumb. Perfect recreation for modern heroines.'

'All right,' I said. 'I'll be there before you ring off.'

'I'm ringing off now,' he said. 'If you want to make it you must make it quickly.'

The telephone rang. The old man came back and took off the receiver.

'It's for you,' he said.

I took the receiver.

It was Smith's voice.

He said: 'Hallo, McCabe. John talked to me. He's right. I owe you some apologies. How are you? Why don't you come over here and let's smooth it out over a couple of good old good ones?'

I was fed up and I told him how I felt.

'Listen,' he said. 'We're all waiting for you. We got to bury this morning. Throw it in the hole and dump dirt down on its coffin. I'll let you preach the funeral sermon and afterwards we'll have a whoopee party to celebrate the new morning.'

'The new morning glory,' I said.

'Come along,' he said, 'they all want to see you.'

'Yes – you, John, Maria, Dinah, Chris, Bloom, perhaps Happy too?'

The old man interrupted me. He took the receiver from my ear, slammed it on the prong and turned round to face me.

'Now, son,' he said, 'sit down. This is getting serious. I hear you talking to that guy Smith about a couple of names and if I'm not far wrong they're the names of all those guys and dames that are mixed up in your sweet little double-murder game. And I get myself boozed up 'stead of listening in to your talk about the Chinese angle. Now shoot, son, and let an old geezer help you if he can.'

I told him that it was all right now – that Smith had apologized and that they were going to have a little repentance party.

'That's just it,' he said. 'Why the hell doesn't he lock up the whole gang?'

'Me too?'

'Not you. Only those who have confessed they've killed one or the other of those who have been bumped off.'

'Nobody ever confessed to having killed Jensen.'

'No, but two confessed to having bumped off the girl.'

'Yes. Two confessed it and a third one did it.'

'Now let me see whether I've got it right by now. It begins with Estella being found shot. At first you think it's suicide, then Bloom comes along and says he killed her, and Smith, instead of locking him up, lets him go catch larks with his tale and waits for more evidence to come. But instead of getting new evidence he bumps into a second confession, this time by Jensen's friend Chris, and instead of cracking down on him he lets him run loose with the second murder confession, undisturbed by either confession and still believing it's suicide. Now –'

I had to interrupt him. 'I don't know what Smith actually believed. I don't think he ever believed for a moment it was suicide. He's not that nutty.'

'All right. Sure is anyway that he doesn't do anything about the confessions.'

'It isn't. He may have done something about them. He may have talked to Chris and Bloom. He only didn't lock them up.'

'That's the one thing he should have done.'

'Perhaps the law doesn't allow it.'

'Babe in the woods,' he said. 'You can do anything you want with the law. That's what it's there for. They can juggle with the paragraphs and what they can do they will do.'

'Anyway he didn't. I told you he's a guy with ideas of his own.'

'Friend, they won't have such things at the Yard. He's got to stick to the routine business or else they'll sack him –'

'– same as they did in the States?'

'Not the same but very much like it. Anyway, along comes the film that shows Jensen killed Estella. Perfect evidence, everything in butter, a medal for a sleuth. Then Jensen runs away, hides, and about a week later he climbs out of the cellar and shoots himself. Or at least that's what it looks like. Looks like a fine perfect case of suicide from remorse. Another medal for the sleuth.'

'Yes,' I said, 'but then he takes the medals off and tells you you're all walking the wrong street; it wasn't suicide but murder.'

'Yes,' said the old man. 'Of course. And everybody is suspected of course, just the way it should be. Everybody's looking for evidence; Smith finds some, Robertson finds some, you find some and he starts cracking down on everyone of you trying to scare you silly so you tell him everything you know. Perfectly legal, third medal for the sleuth.'

'Perfectly legal all right. The snag is only that he insists on picking me of all people to crack down on. And here I am with the cold rain on my face.'

'Run along home to mammy,' he said. 'That man Smith sure is a fine sleuth judging from how he's got you falling for that song and dance of his. You think he hasn't tried the same tricks on everybody else in the case? Well, you go on thinking what you like. I'm going out to have a drink and you go back to Big Boy Smith and bring him a bunch of flowers with congratulations from Grandfather Müller. Beat it, son.'

'Hold on a moment. There's a little incident we haven't mentioned yet. Let's bat it around first and then you tell me if you still think what you think now.'

He leaned back in his chair and smiled disgustedly.

I told him the story.

'I liked Estella, I didn't like Jensen. So when we discovered that Jensen had killed her I went off on my own, looking for brother J. There were four people I liked to know more about: Chris, Bloom, Robertson and Maria Ray. At least one of them should know something about Jensen's whereabouts. My first thought is: Babies always run home to shed tears in mammy's lap. So I step out into the rain looking for letters from, or other things about, Norway. No success. Well, I think, I'll be dirty so-and-so if I can't find that batty Mr Son-of-a-bitch. So I'm starting my career as a sleuth by pinching keys and having copies cut. Maria Ray lets me search her place without a warrant. Nothing there. The next guy I want is brother John Robertson. As to him, he doesn't like to have other guys hanging about his place. So I wait till he's gone, then I use my own key plus my own judgement and frisk the joint. And it's the way it happens only in bad detective thrillers and in real life: there sure is the thing I'm looking for, nicely packed up in the desk drawer: a map of Norway with a sweet little red ink circle round a place called Aardals in Southern Norway in the square Df. I think: I'll be damned; it's too bad to be true. And just to get me doing figure eights I hear a key in the lock and in comes friend Smith. Now this Maison Robertson has a funny ground-plan. It's a ground-floor flat and when you open the front door you walk straight into the intimate privies. Next comes the bedroom with toplight and only after that you enter the living-room where I'm crouching on my belly behind the writing-desk, feeling very funny about it all and feeding on dust and dirt from the carpet. So the first thing Smith does is having a look at the bath, in the bath, under the bath and over the bath, and thoroughly he does it too. I look at him for a while, enjoying to see another guy work, until he's finished with the bathroom and proceeds to the bedroom. Enter Smith and exit McCabe through the window.'

'It smells so much of paste and paint that you can almost believe it,' said the old man.

'Yes. The overpitched yarn; here it is again – and it's still getting worse. Did I tell you we went out to have a look at Estella's mother?'

'Smith and you? To West India Dock Road?'

'Yes. Now this is what happens on the way back: Smith is trying to catch me with a quick one. So without introduction he turns round in the car and shoots a question at me. "Do you know Norway?" he asks. "I'll get you, Mr Harmless-Babyface" I'm saying to myself. And to him I say: "Norway? Yeah, sure I know Norway. Aardals, Southern Norway, Df, page 80' which is the number of the Norway page in the atlas out of which Robertson has torn the map. And that sure gives him the business. He brakes the car so damned sudden that I hit my nose on the dashboard. He cracks up and says: "If you keep on keeping things back I can't do my job." Then he flies into a kind of puberty rage, shouting: "Why don't *you* do the job? Go to Scotland Yard and tell them Smith is not the right man to handle it; *you* are the one they are looking for." "You're sure right," I say to myself and loud I say: "Yes, yes. Maybe." And so we leave it for the moment at maybe. The catch comes in later when I discover that Smith hasn't done a damned thing about Robertson. He keeps on asking fool questions in public but he doesn't lock him up until he finds Jensen shot in Delilah Square – that's the place where they finally found him.'

'So he never left London?'

'He did. He actually went to that Aardals place in Norway. Only they didn't find out about that before there wasn't much left of him. So he doesn't lock up Robertson before he knows it's murder. Then he arranges a reconstruction of the way he thinks the murder has happened but instead of asking the others questions they all ask Smith questions and he gets confused, hits out at me with a hint about the Johnson-Myers case and runs out of the room, slams the door and beats it, leaving brother Robertson free and without obligations. Now do you see the catch?'

'A sleuth doesn't allow you to ask him questions unless he wants you to ask them. A sleuth doesn't get confused by your questions, he doesn't run out of the room, doesn't slam the door, doesn't forget to lock up a guy – unless he's playing a game. On the other hand it isn't done in the Yard to play slapstick comedies of that kind. So it's rather difficult to decide what your friend Smith is leading up to. I see the catch but I can't make sense of it.'

'All right,' I said, 'don't abuse me. It's quite in vain: I always miss the point.'

'It's a good and wholesome habit,' he said.

'I take it as a compliment,' I said.

'Now run along to your reconciliation party and enjoy yourself,' he said. 'Good night, son.'

'Good night,' I said, 'it has been a Day of Atonement.'

'Close the door when you go out, please,' he said.

'I will,' I said.

Twenty-two

I went back to Fleet Street to fetch the car from where I had left it and a bobby who was waiting there was pleased to take my number, name and address and promised to send the summons punctually with the first post the next morning. ' ''Twill be two quid for causing an obstruction on the King's highway.'

I said: 'Thanks for keeping watch so faithfully all the time. I hope I'll be able to square it one day. Let's meet again.'

'We will,' he said.

I drove to the studio and left the car in the garage.

The doorman didn't know where the gang was but I met May Robertson in the staircase and she said: 'Try the projection-room.'

I met them all in Robertson's room. They had the lights on and they were sitting there in the seats looking at the screen but the projector wasn't running.

'We were going to run the film through again,' Smith said.

'Oh,' I said, 'that's the film you are going to show us now – now I see.'

'You see what?' he asked. 'I wish somebody would finally let me know what he sees in all this muddle. It would save me a lot of trouble.'

'I thought tonight we were going to play a funeral march on top of the ruins of your murder investigation. Now you start investigating again. Don't you get fed up with yourself?'

I missed the body on the floor. Then I remembered that I had not been in here since that day with the white dress and the red spots on the floor and the bobby outside at the door and the crowd pushing in from the gangway and the police car waiting down below in the road.

'Make yourselves comfortable, friends,' said Smith.

'Damn you,' I said but I didn't want to and afterwards I was sorry about it.

'What's it, Mac?' he asked.

'Nothing,' I said.

'You could just as well run the film through the projector. You've done it once before,' he suggested.

I was tired and fed up.

I said: 'All right. Once again. I'll soon get into the habit.'

He said: 'I'm afraid you will.'

I didn't reply. The game was finished. Smith had cracked up. The fun had gone west. I wished he would stop. He had lost what he had to lose and he still kept on doing things. He should go home and cry about himself instead of playing the busybody.

I said: 'All right. Let me have the film. I'll put it in. Where is it?'

'It's all right,' said John. 'I'm doing it. Come on, let's sit down.'

He closed the film chamber and moved some chairs so that they stood in two rows facing the screen.

I wondered what he used the chairs for when he had no visitors.

Smith said: 'Come on, Mac, start. Will you please switch the light off, John.'

I said: 'Come on, John, switch the light off. Will you please start, Mac.'

Smith said: 'I'm sorry. Have I been impolite? Pardon me, Mr McCabe.'

I started the film.

I was not really interested. I had seen it all before and there was nothing new to be seen. The old story again: Eve, Lilith and Adam – now Maria, Estella and Jensen – Eve and Adam quarrelling about Lilith – now Estella and Jensen quarrelling about Maria – Estella threatening to kill herself – Jensen gripping her – they both struggling for the knife – then the dark spot on her wrist – red it should have been instead of dark but Technicolor wasn't so good yet, anyway – the dark spot growing and Jensen looking at it – the lines on his face running all through the scale of fright from faintly rising anxiety through growing anguish and fear to violent terror and deadly panic – and his eyes already searching for a way of escape before he succeeds in making his legs move – and then they start moving – but the camera moves with him – does not let him escape – pans with him when he runs to the door – and opens the door – runs away – and the door swings back – and Estella remaining alone on the floor – bleeding herself to death – too damned cheap – as if straining after some childish melodramatic effect of pity – poor little Estella's done gone.

But then she's not done gone – she gets up again – the film goes on – goes on and on and on – this isn't the same film I showed them – they've stuck another piece of film to the end of that piece I gave them – they've found the end of it – and they stuck it on to my piece – and now they make me run it through the projector to see what I'm going to do – Oh Christ, what a mess –

And in that damned second my hands stopped the projector before I could keep them from doing what they had done, before I knew what I was thinking about. The eternal story and the eternal blunder – one ephemeral story and one ephemeral blunder – eternal and ephemeral, Lord – and the projector had stopped while I was still thinking about something else – thinking about it – and then suddenly wondering what it was I was thinking about.

All the time I had been so sure that I was thinking about something – had been so sure of it that it had never occurred to me to ask myself what it actually was, this thing I was trying so hard to figure out.

And then it was Smith's voice which suddenly brought it back again to my mind.

'I knew you killed him,' said Smith. 'I knew it all the time.'

Then the old man came in and I was still standing at the projector and I was looking at him when he came in and I heard him asking something but I didn't understand it and I was looking at him all the time while Smith was saying something to the two coppers who had come in after the old man.

Then I knew what the old man had asked. 'What happened?' he had asked, and Smith said: 'There you are, we have been waiting for you. It's a fine and dramatic entry, just at the right moment. McCabe would like it if he felt better.'

I don't feel bad, I thought. I don't feel bad at all.

'You are Inspector Smith, I presume?' asked the old man.

'Yes,' said Smith, 'you met the right one this time. And your name is Müller – "u" with two dots, if I didn't misunderstand you on the telephone?'

'You didn't. Tell me what happened.'

'I will,' said Smith. 'Watch Mr McCabe,' he said to the two

coppers. And to Robertson: 'Let's run it back again. John, you better do it this time. Brother Mac is still dizzy.'

'All right,' said John, got up, went to the projector, said 'Sit down, Mac,' wound the film back, started the projector, and there it was again, the third time now.

Jensen and Estella and the quarrel and the fight and Jensen searching for the door and out he runs and it is not the end, it is not the end, on it goes, on and on.

The camera swings back to Estella, what a fine camera this is, back it swings to Estella there where she has dropped on the floor, and the floor underneath her arm already dark with blood, and her eyes closed, but the corners of her mouth still twitching, and from time to time a shudder over her nostrils. Jensen has gone, left her for dead, but she isn't dead and he didn't know it, never knew it, never learnt that he hadn't killed her, died without knowing it, the little sap. On it goes on the screen with her eyes opening and slowly searching the room, then suddenly discovering the wound on her wrist, opening her mouth to shout, too weak to shout, but still strong enough to move her right hand over to her left wrist to cover the two little wounds with her hand, covering them, stopping the haemorrhage, covering the wounds with her lips, covering the wounds, sinking back with fatigue, but soon opening her eyes again, getting up, getting up slowly, trembling, but standing upright now, standing, looking, looking at the door, remembering, remembering the man who had gone, looking, her eyes darkening, thinking, thinking hard with trembling eyelids and twitching lips, thinking hard, finding what she was looking for, finding that it wasn't worth it, she was alone now, she would be alone anyway, whatever it was that was going to happen it wasn't important any longer, had happened, was not to change, was never to change, never to be changed, wouldn't change, couldn't change, could never be changed, should never be changed, would never be changed, was gone for good and for ever and for all eternity.

Tearing off her covering hands, breaking down, dropping back again on the floor, lying there, eyes closing, closed now, face moving, convulsively, jerkily, moving, still moving, moving for ever, trembling again, trembling, quietening, resting, no longer moving, has moved enough, will never move again.

It was all as it had been. I thought it would be changed. I had been sure it would be changed. I had been so sure everything would be changed that it came to me like a blow below the belt now I saw it was all the same.

Gone she was, yes, sir.

Gone. Out. The end of it. After us the deluge.

Down with her, take earth in your hands, crumble it, crush it, grind it to dust where it came from, made of dust to go back to dust, go where you came from, go and don't show yourself, don't ever show yourself again to those who knew you before you were born, turn round, hide it, hide your face, hide your eyes, close your ears, don't look, don't listen, go.

We have seen you, we have watched you, we have looked at you at night when we did not know you were there. We have seen you, we have seen you grow, we have seen you go, we have always seen you, we will never forget you, go.

Have seen you, onward from all beginning on, still see you, will see you always and ever, will see you to the end of your days.

Go.

Some few feet of blank film, the end of it, lights on. Silence and stillness.

'It's the best picture I've seen for years,' said Müller.

'Documentary film' said John. 'Human Documentary Film – a new category.'

'And it's a fine case, too,' said Müller. 'I think it's the finest case I've ever had anything to do with.'

'That's what they say every time a case is finished. The same exaggeration over and over again,' said I.

And when I said it I listened to myself with astonishment because I didn't feel like saying anything and what I said was the last thing I wanted to say.

Smith got up and said: 'Cameron McCabe, I arrest you for the murder of Ian Jensen.'

I said: 'Go to hell.'

Smith said: 'If I wasn't what I am I'd sock you silly.'

I said: 'Cut the melodrama.'

Smith didn't reply. He couldn't. He was so surprised he couldn't find words. I had seen him crack up but I had never seen him so surprised.

I looked at his face and it was working overtime.

I felt sick but I knew I had to go through with it.

I looked at Maria. She stood upright with her eyes closed. Her body swayed a little and from time to time her hips trembled.

I said to Smith: 'You can charge me with what you damned well please. If you prove your charge we'll play balls together. If you don't you can go where I told you.'

Smith said: 'All right. Let's sit down again, friends; let's see what we can do to please Mr McCabe. Here goes.'

Maria laughed. Then she sat down.

I remained standing where I was.

Smith lit a cigarette, carefully, tilting his face slightly upwards so that the smoke wouldn't get into his eyes. He had to do that because he smoked a funny kind of cigarette, big and thick, his own figure.

He put the lighter back into his vest-pocket, spat once, nervously. It was a gesture. He just moved lips and tongue. Nothing came out.

He put his hands into his trouser pockets, marched four steps, turned round, took his right hand out of his pocket, put it up to his cigarette, took the cigarette out of his mouth, puffed out smoke, the skin above his eyebrows ruffled, put the cigarette back between his lips in the left corner, was about to say something, changed his mind, smoked with his eyes aimlessly searching the ground, and then lifted his head quickly, laughed shortly, and stagily, squinted his eyes up at me and said: 'You've just seen a film which changes our whole theory about the death of two people . . .'

I interrupted: '*Your* whole theory about the death of two people.'

He said: 'The *official* theory.'

'*Which* official theory?' I asked.

'*My* official theory,' he said.

'All right,' I said. 'That's what I wanted to point out. Now try to think clearly.'

He showed nothing, neither in his face, nor in any part of his body. No unwilling movement to betray himself.

'Mr McCabe,' he said with his eyes still squinting up at me. 'My dear Mr McCabe. We will have to encounter great difficulties if you choose to go on in this way. I suggest we try to make it easier for both parties . . .'

'What do you mean by both parties?' I asked back before he could finish his sentence. 'There are ten persons here in this room, and you talk about two parties. Don't always think of yourself. There are others present. Think of your guests.'

He chewed at his cigarette. Now I had him where I wanted him. 'Go on,' I said. 'Tell me all about your film. It was a fine show. Where did you get it and what makes you think that I killed Jensen? Where's the connection between the two? What makes you think there has to be a connection? Spit it out. I'm waiting. I've got a hell of a lot of work to do tonight. Don't keep me longer than necessary.'

Smith threw away his cigarette. Everything he did was stagy.

He said: 'Miss Lee, will you tell Mr McCabe where you found this film about which he is inquiring.'

Dinah said: 'I will.'

She got up slowly. When she stood up the light fell on her face. I saw that the rings round her eyes were still black and her lips white – the same face I had first seen that afternoon when she had come into the cutting-room, saying 'Yes?' with her voice deep in her chest, then waiting for me to say something and finally bursting out with: 'The studio is talking about Jensen's suicide.' She had still had that face when I had seen her last, that same afternoon when I had asked her to ring up Maria. And today she still had not changed. And as she stood there I knew what was coming. I saw it quite clearly and I felt dead frightened for I saw that I had been all wrong about Smith. This round went to him, no doubt. But I knew the gong hadn't rung yet. Not the final gong yet. Some more rounds to go. All right. Don't get excited. Wait what she's going to say.

She said: 'I found the film in Mr McCabe's flat when I went to see him Friday morning at four o'clock.'

Smith asked: 'What were you doing in Mr McCabe's flat at four o'clock in the morning?'

Dinah said: 'Mr McCabe and I went that night to a night-club where we met Miss Ray and Mr Jensen and Mr Robertson. Mr McCabe left at half past one. Before he left he asked me to try and keep Mr Robertson from going away before half past three. I thought Mr McCabe had some very urgent reasons for asking me to do something so unusual and I tried my best to do as he had told me. Mr Robertson and I spent two very pleasant hours together. We left the club at half past three sharp and Mr Robertson saw me home. As soon as Mr Robertson was far enough away I went out again to see Mr McCabe and to ask him why he had gone away and why he had asked me to keep Mr Robertson from leaving the club. That's what I was doing in Mr McCabe's flat at four o'clock.'

I said: 'Thank you. That was very badly done. I could drub a speech like that much better into a witness. Really, Smith, I thought better of you.'

Smith said: 'You dare to accuse me of faking evidence?'

I said: 'Not yet. I just said I could train a witness so that she would make a better impression on the Court than Miss Lee here.'

'This is no trial,' he said.

'It sounds too damned much like it was one,' I said.

By now there was a lovely marked difference between our ways of talking. While Smith normally tried to talk tough

Americanese he attempted now to talk as formally as possible. But now I talked his own language and he didn't like it a bit.

He said: 'Will you please tell us what happened at Mr McCabe's flat that night, Miss Lee?'

'I will,' she said. 'I took a taxi to Mr McCabe's flat in order to . . .'

Smith interrupted her. 'How did you happen to know Mr McCabe's address? Have you ever been to see him before?'

'No,' she said. 'But I am Mr McCabe's secretary. Sometimes I have to forward letters to Mr McCabe's private address. That is how I happened to know the address.'

'All right. Thank you. Continue, please,' said Smith.

It was so funny that I could not help laughing.

Smith looked plainly surprised.

Then I knew he wasn't so sure of his case as he pretended to be.

'So what happened at my flat Dinah?' I asked her. Then, turning to him: 'As a matter of fact, Smith, I never saw her that night after I'd left the club. I wonder whether you would believe me.'

'Not only that I *would*, but I *do*,' he said.

'You do what?' I asked him to gain time. I had not expected he would admit that.

'I believe that you didn't see her that night after you left your club.'

'Do you?' I asked.

'Yes,' he said. Then to Dinah: 'Will you tell us now what happened, Miss Lee.'

'I was just going to tell you,' she said.

'Sorry I interrupted you,' said Smith.

'I wish you would stop interrupting me now at least,' she said grimacing at him with her white lips and her black rings round her eyes.

I liked their little fight. He hadn't got her yet as far as he wanted her. She didn't like him and much as she was mad with me now he still couldn't make her like him. That gave me an advantage which I knew how to appreciate.

Dinah said: 'I took a taxi to Bennett Street. All the windows in Mr McCabe's house were dark with the exception of one on the first floor. I saw a shadow passing behind the curtain, then the front door opened and a lady came out. I told her I had forgotten my key and she let me in. She took my taxi, gave an address, and drove off. I went up to the first floor. Then, on the staircase, I suddenly realized what Mr McCabe had been doing these last two hours. I had seen the woman come out of the house, and I felt so ashamed that I turned round again without knocking at Mr McCabe's door. But turning round my feet touched something and when I bent down to pick it up from the doormat I felt it was a curiously small roll of film. Now film people are funny: once they touch celluloid they forget everything else. I picked the film up and put it in my handbag, thinking I would have to return it to Mr McCabe. I was not mad with Mac any longer. I felt just sick and fed up and tired and longing to go to bed. I turned round and went out. The light in Mac's window on the first floor was still on when I looked up from the street. I walked up to St James's Street and got a taxi at the corner of Piccadilly. I was home at a quarter past four. When I opened my bag to take out the latchkey the film fell out. That brought everything back to me. After I'd switched the light on the first thing I did was to have a look at the film. It was cut off at the beginning. I could recognize Estella with my bare eye. There was nobody else on that bit of film. I had no projector so it was difficult to recognize what was actually happening. But I studied it for quite a long time: it was the film of Estella's suicide. At the beginning she was lying on the floor like dead with the one or two little wounds dark on her wrist and the blood squirting out. Then she opened her eyes, looked at the wounds and covered them, first with her lips, then with her hands. She got up, looked around, looked at her wrist, tore her hands off again and dropped down almost the same second. Then it went on with her unmoving on the floor and the blood squirting out until the end of the reel.'

'Thank you, Miss Lee,' said Smith. 'Are you sure the film we have just shown is the same which you found in Mr McCabe's house?'

'The last part of it is the same,' said Dinah. 'The first part is the same which Mr McCabe showed us at seven o'clock on Sunday in your room, inspector.'

'But you are satisfied that the end of the film which you have been shown here is the same as the roll of film you found on Mr McCabe's doormat.'

'I am perfectly satisfied,' said Dinah.

'Right,' said Smith, 'thank you,' and beamed with delight. 'What about it, Mr McCabe,' he said, 'now what about it, Mr McCabe, put two and two together . . .'

'Yes,' I said, 'put two and two together, one 2 on top of the other 2, and it makes $\frac{2}{2}$, which is equal to 1. You thought if you put two and two together it should make four, didn't you, Smith, but it makes only one, and the other three are missing. That's where your sleuthing leads you into blind alleys. Give it up, Smith – it's an unremunerative art.'

'Look, brother McCabe, would you like to know that we are going to hang you for the murder of Mr Ian Jensen on the strength of that evidence Miss Lee has just given us?'

Dinah said 'No, no, no,' with big eyes, black pupils in white eyeballs, white eyeballs in the black-ringed oval frame of upper and lower eyelid. 'Oh no, I didn't mean to, I never, no, please, no,' she said with her body erect and stiff and unmoving.

Smith looked disappointed.

I said: 'All right, Dinah.' To Smith: 'You are going to hang me on the strength of Miss Lee's *evidence*, are you, Smith? Now did I really hear you say evidence? Allow me to tear your cobwebs to pieces. Miss Lee said she saw only one light in my house and that was in a window on the first floor. Did you, Miss Lee? Is that correct?'

'Yes,' said Dinah.

'Thank you, Dinah. Naturally you concluded that I had to be in that room on the first floor with the light on, didn't you, Dinah?'

'I did, yes.' She felt better now she saw I was not going to take it without hitting back.

I knew it was the one way of making her feel better.

'All right, Dinah. It was my room all right. But that night you had no evidence whatsoever that it was my doormat where you found the film. Either somebody told you afterwards that my flat was on the first floor, or you stated something you didn't know. Now that's the way they hang people.'

Smith snapped in. 'You admit, Mr McCabe, that it was *your* doormat. You admit that it was in front of your door that Miss Lee found the film, do you admit that, Mr McCabe?'

'I don't admit anything at all. How the hell shall I admit anything Miss Lee has done. If she admits she found that in-criminating piece of evidence – all right, then – throw her in the can, lock her up, let her swing. But for Christ's sake don't bother me.'

'Get me right, Mr McCabe,' said Smith quietly. 'You admit that it was your doormat where Miss Lee *says* she found the film, is that right?'

'It isn't right at all. I can't admit anything anybody else does, has done or will do. I can't possibly admit anything another person *states* he has done, or seen, because I can't possibly know whether it isn't a false statement. Oh no, you get it all mixed up, brother muddle-head Smith.'

'Pipedown,' said he. 'You know I can take a lot, but you just go on throwing dirt at people and wait what's going to happen to you. You call the judge a muddle-head when it comes to your trial and see what you get – a sentence for contempt of court. In the long run it won't matter anyway: *you* haven't much time left and *they* can't hang you twice. There's consolation for you. And anyway I don't care whether you do or don't admit it. We'll establish that point without you. We know which flat is yours and Miss Lee knows where she found the film. That's enough.'

I had to contradict him to get him all flushed up again. 'Did you say it's enough, Smith? It isn't. Dinah is wrong about the woman for instance. I never had a lady visitor that night. The girl Dinah met didn't come out of my place, even though my window may have been the only one with a light in it. There are more flats than one in my house, and – adopting your thesis – if a girl leaves a boy's flat at four o'clock in the morning she doesn't always switch the light on. People are tired at four o'clock in the morning, and a good girl likes to put her boy to bed before she says good night to him. It's the maternal instinct. You may never have heard of it, Smith. Besides, in my house there are rooms with windows looking out to the back. And lastly, the girl may have been just in the staircase on her way down from, let us say, the top floor when Dinah's taxi stopped in front of the house. Now, ladies and gentlemen, there's your evidence.'

I looked round and I saw they enjoyed it. So I continued before they could change their minds. 'But I don't care a damn about that evidence of yours, Dinah. I've no time to bother about anyone's petty sentiments. The whole damned lot of you. Doesn't worry me a hoot. The only thing which worries me is the thing they want to hang me for. I didn't kill Jensen, though I won't tell you, Smith, that I'm sorry he got bumped off. I never liked him and I'm glad he's gone. But if you want to nail me for killing someone I want to see why. As yet I don't see the connection between this flick here and your murder rap there, Smith. Now, you tell me how you get the clues and how you come to your conclusions and maybe I'll like it and maybe I won't but anyway I won't talk turkey before you shoot your load off. And don't strew any sugar. You won't hit me anyway. So now let's shoot.'

'That's reasonable,' said Smith. 'As a matter of fact, that's just what I was going to do.'

'Who stops you?' I asked him.

'I haven't started yet,' he said and smiled and threw the ash of his short thick cigarette into the ashtray. He had smoked it up to the last bit. It was a gold-tipped Continental make. I wondered. He'd been in America too long, I thought. And no one ever gets away from smoking American cigarettes once he's got into the habit. It's a habit that sticks unless you're highbrow and prefer to smoke long paper-mouthed Russian fags or cork-tipped French sissie brands.

The silly faces of all the others in the room were a joy to watch. If men have nothing to do they degrade to monkeys. These people here had nothing to do but to watch. And though watching they still didn't understand what it was all about, couldn't follow, could see neither Smith's point nor mine, could not follow any argument though everyone of them knew some links which his neighbour didn't know, but none of them could link all the links to make a chain that made sense.

Maria looked pale, beautiful and dumb as a film star of repute should look.

Chris understood little and was displeased with the rest. He looked it, too.

Dinah regained some of her composure by looking stubborn. My attack had forced her into the defensive and the necessity of fighting back had given her something to do. Effort had displaced fright. She looked taciturn now.

John understood more than the rest. He was the only one, except Müller, who tried seriously to combine the various contradictions and weigh one against the other to make sense of the lot. But he didn't get far.

Müller got further than John. He smiled and waited. He didn't try to hide that he knew enough facts to enable him to follow the to-and-fro of arguments with ease. He knew the basis and he saw the superstructure as it rose built up on check and counter-check.

Bloom was white, tired, disinterested. Not disinterested from lack of interest or from impartiality but from inability to cope with the growing complications of this case which he had understood at the beginning but failed to understand now as the threads ran away on their own into various directions. He could not gather them together any more.

Smith's cigarette in the ashtray smouldered. He took it out again, pressed his thumb on the stump, grinded, looked up, laughed, said: 'All right, McCabe, let's take it up exactly as you commanded: how I come to my conclusions, how I get my clues and how I work the junk out with my methods. We'll give you a chance. It's the least we can do for you.'

'It's the last you can do for me before you hang me. Now let's have the fruits of your sleuthing. Now, ladies and gentlemen, I call upon the right honourable Mr Sherlock Doyle to honour us by giving his views on the subject of picking up clues. After the right honourable gentleman's speech we will hear Mr Conan Holmes on how to indict a criminal on clues picked up by Mr Sherlock Doyle. Mr Chairman, ladies and gentlemen: the right honourable Mr Sherlock Doyle. Wild applause.'

'Look, Mr McCabe,' said Smith. 'I don't believe in the Sherlock Holmes-Conan Doyle tradition of hanging a man on the strength of detectives' clues – you know, the cigarette-ash-on-the-drawing-room-floor kind of thing. It's no good because there is always an unlimitable number of possibilities from which to make faulty deductions: either you leave out one or two clues, or you misinterpret one or two, and in any case the result is never fool-proof. The only man to clear up a crime is the criminal himself: make him do it. And I'll make you do it, McCabe, I'll make you do it sure enough.'

His knuckles were white.

'I remember, Smith, what you told me once: "If you want to clear up a murder you must do your own killing." Do I remember correctly?'

'You do,' he said, and did not show any sign that it caused him inconvenience to be quoted.

'Isn't there a slight contradiction between those two great sleuthing epigrams of yours, inspector?'

Now I had to be as polite as possible.

'Why, no,' he said with a harmless old man's baby-face – the Will Rogers kind of genuine surprise.

'Why, yes,' I told him. 'Look: your first rule for detectives, "The only man to clear up a crime is the criminal himself – make him do it", treats the task the detective sets himself to make his criminal confess. But your second rule, "If you want to clear up a murder you must do your own killing", means making the detective the murderer or the murderer the detective – and I, for one, sir, prefer the latter solution. It takes a load off my shoulders and lets it drop on yours. You can take it, can't you, inspector?'

He said: 'How to trip others on their hard and fast rules. Beating the cop at his own game. Ain't he a clever boy, Mrs McCabe's youngster, eh?'

'Now tell your story,' I said.

'As you command, Mr McCabe,' He turned to the stenographer and asked: 'You're taking notes, are you?'

'Yes, sir,' said the little man and wiped his glasses.

'All right, don't wipe your glasses, take notes,' said Smith. Then he turned round to face me and continued without interruption. 'It's really a very simple story. Jensen has an affair with Miss Lamare. When he gets tired of her he falls in love with Miss Ray. But Miss Lamare is not willing to let Jensen go. So she arranges another meeting with him – in Mr Robertson's room of all places. Neither of them knew that Mr Robertson was experimenting with an automatically focusing camera which was recording everything its lens and mike could gather. You all know the result: we have just seen it on the screen. Miss Lamare threatens to kill herself, he tries to take the knife away and in the struggle she gets her artery cut – it is not quite clear whether by accident or by intention – either his or her intention. Anyway, there she is with the blood squirting from her wrist and Jensen is so frightened that he runs out and away. Then he realizes that there is no real evidence against him – remember, ladies and gentlemen, that Jensen knows nothing about the camera. So he asks himself: What is the best thing to do? And he answers himself: The best thing to do is to appear unconcerned. So he decides to go to a night-club and make whoopee. The best person to go with him is Miss Ray – in case anybody should ever suspect him – she's the most unlikely person he would choose for company. So he asks her to go to a night-club with him. She says yes and off they go.

'This is Thursday night. Now some hours earlier the same afternoon Mr Bloom comes to see Mr McCabe about a certain technical matter. He wants Mr McCabe to cut Miss Lamare out of a film which has just been finished with Miss Ray, Mr Jensen and Miss Lamare in the leading parts. Mr McCabe being an intelligent man sees at once that this is a most unreasonable thing to ask of him. So when Mr Bloom has left him Mr McCabe goes to find his friend Robertson to ask his technical advice. This is at six twenty-five on Thursday afternoon. Mr McCabe tries to ring Mr Robertson's room but can't get any reply. He rings again and finds the line engaged. He gives up telephoning and decides to make a personal call on Mr Robertson. But when he gets to Mr Robertson's room he finds it empty. He sees, however, that somebody has just been working Mr Robertson's camera: the gear is still warm. He goes out again to look for Mr Robertson. No success. Then he thinks he'd better have another try at Mr Robertson's room. When he comes back the door is locked. This is at a quarter to seven. By this time Mr McCabe is fed up and goes to fetch his car from a repair shop in Great Portland Street where he has left it to have it over-hauled. For a certain reason which I'll explain later he takes an unusually long time to get to Great Portland Street so that when he gets there he finds his secretary, Miss Lee, guarding the shop. Mr Lewis, the shop proprietor, a friend of Mr McCabe, has rung her at the studio to warn McCabe that he had to leave in a few minutes' time. She took a taxi to Great Portland Street and now she is actually there before Mr McCabe arrives. Mr McCabe, pleased with such efficiency and moreover pleased with the general feminine appearance of this girl whom he has never considered as anything else but his efficient secretary, asks her to spend the evening with him. She accepts gladly and the two spend some very pleasant hours together, winding up at the same night-club which Miss Ray and Mr Jensen have chosen for that evening. To make the party complete Mr Robertson drops in too. This is not such a very astonishing trick of fortune. As a matter of fact it's merely a matter of probability. The night-club in question is the studio people's haunt – small wonder that they also meet there that critical night. In the course of the conversation Mr Robertson tells Miss Lee that he left the studio at a quarter past four and locked the door of his room. Mr McCabe remembers his experiences that afternoon between six twenty-five and six forty-five – the telephone engaged signal from Mr Robertson's room – the open door – the warm gearbox of the camera. He thinks: "There is something fishy about this. Why does this man Robertson tell me fibs?" Normally Mr McCabe is an unsuspecting young man without any tendency to-wards melodrama. But that night he's kind of brought up to the mark prepared to smell a rat wherever he'll find a chance to smell one – you remember the visit Mr Bloom paid Mr McCabe that afternoon and Mr Bloom's curiously unreasonable request to cut Miss Lamare out of a picture which has just been finished at enormous cost. Besides he has met Mr Müller' – pointing at Müller – 'this gentleman here – at King's Cross tube station and the talk with Mr Müller, who is a rather unusual gentleman, brought Mr McCabe into that certain state of sensibility where you put 2 and 2 together and the result – as Mr McCabe told us a minute ago – is not 4 but $\frac{2}{3}$. Mr McCabe combines all those things he has seen and heard that afternoon. He has a vague idea that there is something fishy about Mr Bloom, Miss Lamare and Mr Robertson; so he decides to pay a little night visit to the studio. As he doesn't want to be disturbed by anyone else who may have the same crack idea of looking for trouble in the B.A.F. Studio at night-time he asks Miss

Lee to keep Mr Robertson at the club for two hours – those two hours he wants to spend at the studio. This is at about half past one. Mr McCabe leaves the club and drives to the studio. All the time he is thinking: "How am I going to get in?" But now when he stops the car at the corner of King's Cross Road he realizes that he won't have any difficulties at all – there is still a light in the laboratories. So he walks straight up to the box intending to ask the janitor for the key of Mr Robertson's room. But he finds the box empty and the hook for Robertson's key on the board empty too. He thinks: "What the hell is this doorkeeper doing? He can't leave his box at this time of the night with the door wide open. Any crook can walk in without anyone seeing him." And in walks Mr McCabe without anyone seeing him. Neither does he meet anyone on his way up to room 126 and when he gets there he finds the door closed but not locked and when he opens it he jumps back for there's the body of Estella on the floor and the floor all round her covered with blood. Now there he has what he has been looking for. First he doesn't know what to do. He's a film editor and though he has often seen things like this on celluloid they've never happened to him in real life. So in his slight confusion he looks for something tangible, something he's used to, something about which he knows more than about this dirty business here in front of him. And he finds the camera, Mr Robertson's automatic camera – and there is the solution of all his troubles – there's a film camera and that's a thing he knows. He tiptoes over to the camera, carefully avoiding the blood on the floor, and only when he is about to take the film out of the camera he remembers that he'd better put his gloves on in case somebody may find his fingerprints and suspect him of having something to do with the killing. So he takes the film out – it's ready developed – that's another trick of Mr Robertson's automatic camera – he uses reversal film and an ultra-fast developer developing in a tank which is fixed to the camera as a part of it. He puts it in the projector and runs it through. It's the film you all know by now. And here the story really begins.'

He breathed, smoked, drank a glass of water, gulped down the whole contents of it and continued speaking, wiping his mouth and focusing his eyes on Maria.

Maria looked back with a dead expression on her face – pale, indifferent, non-committal. She was not trying to hide something; nothing she might have tried to hide was left in her.

Smith, without taking his eyes off her, continued: 'As Mr McCabe watched the film of Miss Lamare's suicide unroll that night in Mr Robertson's studio he had the idea of his life. He didn't like Jensen. He disliked him from the first moment and things got very bad when Jensen fell for Miss Ray. This was at the beginning of September, only two weeks after Mr McCabe's return from his holidays which he spent in the pleasant company of Miss Ray. Now there's the angle for another repetition of the old story. And here was Mr McCabe's chance to get rid of Mr Jensen. Now you must remember that Mr McCabe is a film-cutter and a very good one at that – also remember that Mr Bloom ordered Mr McCabe to *cut* Estella out of the film – therefore his interest is subconsciously centred on cutting – and he sees his chance at once when he looks at the film: there is a break in the middle after Jensen's unheroic and all too hurried departure. Up to that point it looks like murder. If the film were cut at that point he could easily have Jensen indicted for murder. Mr McCabe plays with the idea for a moment but throws it overboard soon – he is no criminal – not yet anyway – it is not until four days later that he develops into something which you could rightly call a criminal.

'So at that time he wouldn't dream of letting a man hang for a murder which the man hadn't done – not even a man he likes as little as Jensen. But he has the film and he is going to make use of it. So then he has the great idea: he cuts off the last bit of film – the suicide bit – puts it away and drives over to Jensen's house with the first part – the apparent murder part – in his pocket. There is light in Mr Jensen's room on the second floor. Mr McCabe rings the doorbell. There is no reply. Mr McCabe rings again. The light in Mr Jensen's room goes out. Mr McCabe tries his own key to open the door. By some chance the key fits. Mr McCabe goes up to the second floor. The door is open. Jensen never locked it when he was at home. Mr McCabe hesitates when he hears no sound, sees no light. He asks tentatively: "Mr Jensen?" No reply. Again: "Mr Jensen? This is McCabe." – No reply. Then he has the right idea. "Look, Mr Jensen," he says, "this is McCabe. Wherever you are, come out and let me talk to you. I have to tell you something about Estella Lamare. You better come out and talk to me before the police come along to talk to you." That has its effect. A door is opened, the light is switched on and Jensen, in a dressing-gown, without pyjama trousers, bows to Mr McCabe.

' "A late visit. To what do I owe the honour of your call, sir?" he asks. And Mr McCabe says something in reply – you know the kind of thing Mr McCabe says in reply – and finally they get down to business. Jensen, the parvenu, has his own projector, of course. And Mr McCabe asks him for the privilege of being allowed to use it. Jensen says: "Yes, do, by all means." Mr McCabe puts in the film and starts the projector. Jensen sees the most irrefutable evidence of what looks like murder. And – now this is really the decisive point – as he himself believes that he has killed Estella, he gets dead frightened and when Mr McCabe sees that he gets his effect he settles down and makes his suggestion: "If you promise to leave this country here and now and without fail I'll keep this film to myself. No one has probably seen you – so you can go home in peace and I'll send you a newspaper cutting of the coroner's verdict: 'Suicide while of unsound mind' it will be. Agreed?" "A gentleman's agreement," says Jensen and leaves his flat not more than twenty minutes after Mr McCabe has left.'

Smith stopped, took another cigarette out of his case and looked round while lighting the cigarette. He was very sure of himself now, quite sure of his effect, without a doubt of the successful outcome of the afternoon's work.

He felt proud watching the changes which had happened on his listeners' faces. The old monkey expression had disappeared: they had something to do now. But a new monkey expression had appeared in various lines of their faces: they had something to do now: they understood and they felt so proud in their new-found knowledge that they thought they had learned to understand it all through their own intelligence. Bloom looked vain, proud and ridiculous. Chris smiled to himself, with a sweet little of-course-I-knew-it-all-the-time smile. Dinah looked angry, puzzled and somewhat perturbed. John was still trying solemnly to combine clues and weigh one against the other. He looked ludicrous in a different way from Bloom. Müller was quiet. He looked more expectant than I had ever seen him before. Smith smiled and when he showed his teeth his face looked like Bloom's. Then he looked at me, put his smile away, smoked hastily, put his cigarette in the ashtray before he had half finished it, poured some more water into his glass, lifted it up to his mouth, smelled at it nervously, drank slowly, put the glass down on the tray again, wetted his lips, said: 'Now, that's the way Mr McCabe got his gentleman's agreement – but what he forgot to get was the lady's agreement – the lady in question being Miss Ray. It was like this: when Jensen left the club Miss Ray went with him to have a look at his etchings. So you see it was not only chicken-heartedness that made Jensen switch off the light when he first heard Mr McCabe ring the bell. When Mr McCabe bumped into Jensen's flat Miss Ray was still there. As a matter of fact she watched the whole show from the bedroom. The door was ajar and Mr McCabe did not even trouble to search the place. So the next mine that blows up is Miss Ray telling Mr McCabe she knows

Jensen killed Estella which means that Mr McCabe has to break his gentleman's agreement for the lady's sake. Promptly next morning at eleven o'clock Mr McCabe comes along to Scotland Yard and tells me he has found the film. I ask him whether he could leave me the film and he says: 'I'd rather not.' So we arrange to show it at seven o'clock that night. All of you with the notable exception of Mr Müller were present. After we had shown the film I had a very interesting interview with Miss Ray and Mr McCabe. We got a lot of contradictory statements – a lot of fun – and nothing that made sense. The same night Mr Christensen who is Mr Jensen's best friend sends a wire to Jensen's hiding-place, a little place called Aardals in the south of Norway. Jensen is furious about the break of Mr McCabe's gentleman's agreement. He's so furious that he gets the idea into his head to go back to England with the single purpose of bumping off Mr McCabe to get revenge for Mr McCabe's double-crossing. Like all vengeance racketeers he first sends a telegram to his intended victim. That telegram, in Jensen's case, had a lovely wording: "Two timer caught tripping. Wait and see." As you will clearly remark, the film language as it is spoken is humbug Americanese. Mr McCabe burns the telegram. The next morning Jensen arrives in England. He comes by 'plane and lands on the private aerodrome of his flying-club where they know him without knowing anything about the Estella case. We issued orders for Jensen's arrest to all Customs and frontiers officials but we never carried the case into the papers. So once he had dodged our frontier people he could land without danger and hide in London in a small furnished house in Delilah Square. He gave a false name and a wrong address. The one thing he was longing for was to get Mr McCabe to Delilah Square. To do that he used a simple device – too good really to be true. He sent Mr McCabe a letter he himself had once received from Miss Ray – "My love – will you come to see me Monday night – I feel lonely and blue – help to get me out of the dumps!" – this sort of thing. He cut off the date and typed on a little slip of paper: "Changed my address. New address: 69 Delilah Square, Abbey Road. Come and let us have a midnight bed-warming party for two." Now that's the kind of invitation Mr McCabe wouldn't refuse for anything in the world. So he goes to Delilah Square, rings the bell and meets Jensen instead of the fairy. Diabolus ex machina. Well, you all know Mr McCabe. Any normal person would bang the door in Jensen's face, turn round and beat it. Things are different with Mr McCabe. He has his own code of honour. And Jensen knows that and builds on it. So when he asks Mr McCabe to step in and have a little quiet conversation Mr

McCabe says: "All right, proceed." They walk up to Jensen's bedroom which is the furthest away from the housekeeper's flat. It isn't long before the trouble begins. It's Jensen who starts kicking up a row, flying from one rage into another, threatening Mr McCabe with his gun, only to be disarmed by Mr McCabe and finally winding up in a blue funk with a heart attack and a nervous breakdown. Mr McCabe picks him up and puts him to bed, looks into the medicine box, finds a sleeping draught, puts some few drops into a glass and is about to put the glass up to Jensen's lips when he suddenly realizes how deep he is in this mess, up to his eyes, and if he doesn't soon do something about it he knows the mess is going to get the better of him. So the one thing to do is to get rid of Jensen, now and for good and for always and ever – and at that moment he remembers everything – his dislike of Jensen's pansy mannerisms, Jensen's vanity, Jensen's superficiality, Jensen driving Estella into her suicide, Jensen getting tired of Estella and trying to make Maria, Jensen and Maria, Jensen finally off to Norway, Jensen out of the way, and now Jensen back again and all the trouble with him starting all over again. And at that moment with the bottle of a poisonous sleeping draught in his hand Mr McCabe remembers one other thing which has no direct connection with Jensen –'

Smith stopped again, halting, building up tension and suspense to increase the effect of his climax. Everybody looked at him, all mannerisms had disappeared, all faces were tense, expectant, alive with an emotion which went deeper than they would admit later when the emotion itself would have disappeared leaving nothing but a headache, a hangover and a shade of a shade of shame, perhaps. And the memory of it, of course. But the memory wouldn't matter so much after all.

Smith looked around: cool, critical, sceptical, more intelligent than a minute ago, no longer triumphant, no longer smiling, no longer jeering – said: 'The thing Mr McCabe remembers at that moment is the Johnson-Myers case. The report of the case has been given to Mr McCabe under rather peculiar circumstances – which makes the memory of it even more forceful now. The other day I realized that only two of you who are now present here in this room remember the case. To refresh your memory: the Johnson-Myers case was just another triangle story with a different angle only in the execution of the climax – we've had two triangle stories in our own case here – now here it pops up the third time. Johnson puts Myers's gun in his wife's hand after he's dropped a sleeping draught into her tea to make her unconscious. Then he tells Myers he's found his wife dead, shot with Myers's gun. Johnson thinks that'll terrify Myers so much that he'll run away and leave his wife alone – from now on to be enjoyed only by himself, her husband. A rather silly idea. It didn't come off, of course. But anyway here we have two ideas at once – both settle down in the background of Mr McCabe's memory. First there is a scheme for chasing a rival away by frightening him with a murder charge. Then there is another fine scheme for dressing up a murder as a suicide. Mr McCabe has already made use of the first scheme – now he remembers the second scheme and makes use of it too. He puts the whole bottle of that sleeping draught into a glass and pours it down Jensen's throat. Jensen, too weak and too tired to resist, swallows it, thinking that it is a sedative. He is soon unconscious. But Mr McCabe, watching him, is suspicious. He must be sure of his success. He can't risk a second disappointment with Jensen cutting in between Miss Ray and himself. Besides, he can't get rid of the memory of that fine possibility first realized but never fully used in the Johnson-Myers case. If I were a novel writer I would probably mention here a lot of other things too – things which matter in the commission of a crime – though they can never be used for the solution of a crime. Those things which happen in the criminal's mind at the moment of committing a crime – or before or even afterwards – ideas, plans, obsessions, emotions, thoughts, wishes, longings – never uttered and perhaps not even known to the man himself – combinations of facts, things, persons, names – Johnson and Jensen sound much the same and Myers and McCabe both begin with the same letter – all those things come together, pour down on the man, don't leave him much freedom to remain his own master – and so Mr McCabe puts his gloves on again, washes the glasses clean of all traces of the poison, puts the bottle back into the medicine box, picks up Jensen's gun from the floor where it has dropped during the struggle, puts it into Jensen's hand, closes his fingers round, puts Jensen's index finger against the trigger, aims the gun carefully at Jensen's temple and pulls the trigger. He is lucky here as in everything else: it's a silent gun. Nobody hears the shot – or, to be more exact, Mr McCabe thinks nobody has heard it – and so he walks down the stairs quietly and leaves through the back entrance. It's too perfect to come off. It's the nearest approach to the perfect crime I've ever encountered. It almost sounds like a movie story. As our friend Müller remarked so strikingly: "It's the best picture I've seen for years." It's really admirable. It clicks from whichever angle you may like to look at it. Think it over: Jensen kills Estella because he is fed up with her troubling him about Maria. After the murder he escapes. But after some few days – as all good criminals do – he comes back to London, mysteriously drawn back to the place of the crime, and shoots himself – suicide out of remorse. A perfect case. Only – the poison killed Jensen before the bullet was fired. And a dead man – unfortunately – can't shoot himself. Which means that Ian Jensen was murdered – in cold blood, with malice aforethought – and the murderer, Mr McCabe, is you.'

He pointed his finger at me and raised his voice, finishing his sentence with a fine booming 'you', thunder in his voice and lightning in his eyes. Everybody was deeply impressed. Nobody dared to breathe or to speak. Eyes looked with awe and terror alternately at Smith and at me. But the distribution of awe and terror between Smith and me was not ethically correct: a lot of awe went to my account and a lot of terror went to Smith's. But when I laughed they thought me mad and everything went in perfect order as it should be amongst civilized Western Europeans: all the terror became concentrated on me and what there was left of awe was showered upon Smith.

It was a beautiful scene, moving, touching and righteous to the bone: a toast to law and order with the certain hope of deserved punishment throwing a shining aura of justice round Smith's head and a black shadow of depravity upon the face of the sinner who was I, Cameron McCabe, thirty-eight years of age, born in the city of Glasgow, grown up in the stone towns of the New Land Beyond the Seas, a worker working on a work that does not help to make the world better, a Christian without belief and without unbelief, neither good nor bad, neither rich nor poor, neither happy nor unhappy, both native and stranger, host and guest – a murderer now, a slayer of human blood and soul, an enemy of our civilized society of industrious and law-abiding citizens, a shame to my mother's memory, a disgrace to my father's name, a boil on the body of this Empire, a disease soon to be eliminated.

I laughed.

'Thank you, Smith,' I said. 'That was a noble effort. I'll have to try hard if I want to top it at the trial.'

He said nothing.

I did not stop laughing when the two plain-clothes men took me out.

Twenty-three

But the trial did not come yet. First they locked me up for one night, then they brought me to the Marylebone Police Court and asked me a lot of questions. I said: 'I have nothing to say, I reserve my defence.' So they sent me to Brixton Prison and gave me a nice quiet cell which was fun for the first hours and hell ever after. But at least I could read. I asked them whether I would be allowed to read some law books and they brought me two. Both were written by two authors each, which was quite proper if you considered that the one had 607 pages and the other one 1,622. One was called *Principles and Practice of the Criminal Law*, by Seymour F. Harris, B.C.L., M.A. (Oxon), and A. M. Wilshere, M.A., LL.B. The other one, the bigger one, was *Archbold's Criminal Pleading, Evidence, and Practice*, by Robert Ernest Ross, of the Middle Temple, Barrister-at-law, Chief Clerk in the Court of Criminal Appeal, and Theobald Richard Fitzwalter Butler, of the Inner Temple, Barrister-at-law, Midland Circuit. They were good books, both of them, and by consulting the one where I couldn't follow the other I got on quite well and at the end I found I liked them both and I had learned a lot.

I learned that whether I'd done it or not did not really matter. What did matter was for them to build up a case against their suspect – I being the suspect – then to take care that all details in their case fitted well within the frame of the law, afterwards to pronounce judgement upon me and finally to proceed with the punishment which would probably be death if they could build up a case for murder, or lifelong penal servitude if they couldn't build anything better than just a cheap case of manslaughter. On my part I was neither asked nor allowed to build up a case of my own and make it stick and put it against their case and let the jury decide which of the two cases was the better one – an arrangement which would have been only fair once they had dropped all pretensions to tell and prove the things that had really happened. It is unfair competition to let the counsel for the prosecution, a professional, build up a case against you, a mere amateur. And even if you buy a professional to fight for you, the fight in the court would still be a foul one because the counsel for the prosecution is allowed to build up a case of his own while your counsel, instead of being allowed to build up a counter-case for you, is only allowed to hit out against the other guy's case. It is unfair because it gives your opponent a chance to choose his weapons and because it forces you to fight him on a basis which suits him best. Archbold says on page 875: 'The defendant has to prove, either that the murder was not committed by him, or that the offence actually committed does not amount to murder.' Though on page 349 he says: '... the prosecutor is obliged to prove at the trial every fact or circumstance stated in the indictment ... The general rule is that, apart from any provision to the contrary, the burden of proof of guilt lies upon the prosecution, and it is not for the defence to prove innocence.' Now here the thing that mattered appeared to lie in the line about 'apart from any provision to the contrary'. It seemed that an allegation of murder was one of the 'provisions to the contrary' which gave the prosecutor a holiday and left you all the work to do. Though a case in which 'the prosecutor is obliged to prove at the trial every fact or circumstance stated in the indictment' seemed rather unfair to the prosecutor. It was more or less a reversal of the proceedings at a murder trial – just as unfair to the prosecution as the murder trial was unfair to the defence. Why the hell couldn't they let both fight each other on a fair and sportsmanlike basis, without handicap and without drawing up rules which were made applicable only to the one competitor and not to the other?

Now one could object, of course, that this wasn't supposed to be a fair fight but a trial in which a criminal was to be judged and sentenced according to his being guilty or not guilty. But that was obviously a ridiculous objection considering the situation in which you could find yourself at any time. Smith had built up a case against me and the counsel for the prosecution would take it up from him and if I could I had to prove that the charges against me were wrong. Now that showed you clearly that the outcome of this trial – gallows or no gallows – was merely a question of my own intelligence: whether I could or could not break down the case

Smith had built up against me. Or it could also be a question of money: whether I had or had not enough money to hire the best lawyer, to buy his intelligence and let him break down the case they had built up. Nobody cared a damn whether I had actually killed Jensen. And in order to provide against any judge or any member of the jury failing to realize that he must not care about the human being in his power he was most safely tied up by the law to guard him from mixing up private sentiments with his official function of judge or juror. This was law and not sentiment. And so I would have to hang unless I could blow up Smith's case.

And after I'd had a careful look at the laws which governed a murder trial I found that this case Smith had against me was quite admirable with a fair chance to get me hanged on the strength of it.

Smith was going to prove the killing by circumstantial evidence, 'being evidence of facts, from which the fact of the crime may be inferred as a natural or very probable solution'. Harris on page 393 gives an example: '. . . if the witness proves that the prisoner was seen going to B's house at four o'clock, that there was no other person in the house at the time, that at 4.15 B's throat was found cut, and that a bllod-stained knife was found concealed in the prisoner's locked box, the evidence is circumstantial.' Now that was a fine and delicate example of how a murder should be first committed and afterwards proved by circumstantial evidence. The murder Smith charged me with was not quite so fine and certainly not half as delicate as Harris's example. But the circumstantial evidence Smith alleged he had against me was just as good as in Harris's example, no doubt about it. He said he had seen me go into Jensen's house at midnight – had not heard any shot as it was a silent gun I was supposed to have used – had seen me leave the house at half-past twelve – and the landlady had found the dead body the next morning. And though it had first appeared to be suicide it had soon been proved that it was murder, and deliberate cold-blooded murder at that – for, he argued, 'only a deliberate murderer would poison a man and put the victim's gun in his hand and make it look like suicide'. The *malice aforethought*, moreover, 'was clearly apparent in my first actions of charging Jensen with the murder of Estella while I knew all the time that Estella had committed suicide' – so he argued. There was no need for him to prove it – for, as Archbold said on page 873: '. . . the prosecutor is not bound to prove malice, or any facts or circumstances besides the homicide, from which the jury may presume it; and it is for the defendant to give in evidence such facts and circumstances as may prove the homicide to be justifiable or excusable, or that at most it amounted to manslaughter.' And finally there was this to be considered, that 'of all forms of death by which human nature may be overcome the most detestable is that of poison; because it can of all others be the least prevented either by manhood or forethought' (3 Co. Inst. 48).

Now once I had realized that there wasn't over-much hope of getting the indictment quashed there wasn't much else to do but to try and make the best of the charge as it stood. If I had to end up in a rat-trap I would at least choose one of the type that merely keeps you in a cage and not one of the ugly type that cuts your head off. So if I couldn't quash the murder charge I would at least have to try to get away with a verdict of manslaughter. The difference between murder and manslaughter was in the point of malice. Which meant that the first thing to do was to smash up all support Smith had for his thesis that the Estella business proved the presence of malice aforethought in my behaviour towards Jensen. That in its turn meant again going back to the beginning of the case, back to the first day and the first hour and the first minute and the first second of the show.

Of course, I could waste all my money and hire a fine criminal lawyer. But Harris said on page 343: '. . . on an indictment for murder, a man cannot plead that the killing was done in his own defence against a burglar; he must plead the general issue – not guilty – and give the special matter in evidence.' This meant that if I had no chance to build up a case of my own I had to turn the tables upon the prosecution. I had to smash up the whole system of proceedings and turn all rules upside-down. No lawyer was going to do it for me. They would think I was crazy – a layman's idea of our noble profession – and they would smile.

I'd got about as far as that when the door opened and the warder brought Smith in.

'Official or not?' I asked.

He said: 'Semi.'

'Don't give yourself away,' I suggested.

'Oh, thank you, don't bother,' he said with a rather friendly and pacifying smile.

'Now look, brother,' I said, 'our pleasant co-operation is about to be broken up by a lot of outsiders who don't know the first thing about how it was done. You've finished your job and I'm about to see others relieving me of the effort of finishing mine for me. Now what about us establishing a last co-operation to clear up some few things I know and you don't and another few you know and I don't.'

He smiled.

I said: 'There isn't really so much cause for your sadness. You got your case in order. You can't lose anything by my telling you things and not even by your telling me things.'

'All right,' he said, 'all right. I don't mind, I rather like it, you know. I appreciate you a lot and I like to listen to you. It's you I'm thinking of. What about you losing by telling me too many things?'

'Thank you, don't bother,' I said.

'I always appreciate the honour of being quoted,' he said. Then, without pause, in the same tone, 'What did Estella's death mean to you? Any sentiment such as normal human beings feel in those situations or just the usual William Powell effect of "a laugh in every morgue" – that kind of thing?'

'I'll tell you what I felt,' I said. 'I felt so fed up with Jensen I could have cried. I liked Estella very much. Probably because I never had an affair with her – you know you can only like a girl as long as you haven't slept with her – because then it can only become either love or disgust – and both those noble feelings are mixed up with a lot of dirty sentiments. No, Smith, believe me, I did like Estella and by God it was more than just jealousy that made me kick Jensen out of this town.'

I meant it when I said it. But then when I thought of the effect it would have on him I added: 'Don't believe it, brother. I just wanted to soften your case. Don't take any notice.'

'All right, I won't,' he said. 'But will you explain what you thought you were doing when you bumped into Bloom's office the morning after the killing, knocking at the door but not waiting for Bloom's come-in, behaving like an Old Testamentarian Angel of Vengeance, asking Bloom why he wanted to blot out the Estella girl, asking him why he wanted to cut her out of her picture, why he wanted to cut her out of the chance of her life, asking him: "What was the exact reason for killing Estella Lamare?" Will you explain that, Mr McCabe? At that time you were the only one who knew that Estella had killed herself. And just you, of all people, had to accuse Bloom of murder. It's a rather difficult thing to understand, Mr McCabe. I'm asking you now as a private person. Your answer won't change anything at all, neither in your favour nor in your disfavour. Now will you tell me without any obligation what you felt when you performed that show for us?'

'I'll tell you with or without obligation. I did it for the very reason that I knew it was suicide and not murder. But if anyone is morally guilty of killing Estella it's Bloom. Jensen was a little louse without importance. Estella could have fallen in love with him just as well as with anyone else. He can't help being the sap he is – or was. But Bloom knew what he was doing. He could have given her a chance – but for some damned reason he asked me to cut her out of the film. If she had had success, work, a career, she would never have thought of taking her love disappointment to heart as she did. I'm not talking through my hat – I *knew* Estella. She wouldn't grieve about anything as long as she felt she was getting on in her career. But she would kick up a row about anything and everything as soon as she had the smallest professional setback. And that's why I was fed up with Bloom, and I swear it, Smith, I *was* fed up with Bloom because I did like Estella . . .' I paused because I saw he was smiling and I knew that I was making a fool of myself.

'Yes, thank you,' he said, 'and now it's your turn.'

'It is, sure enough,' I said. 'And as we are just about it, tell me now, if you know it, what was Bloom's reason for ordering me to cut Estella out of her picture and what made him confess he had killed Estella when he hadn't?'

'You know both answers,' he said. 'You told me the first, I told you the second: Bloom tried to make her and got a cold shoulder. And another company was making almost exactly the same triangle story as you did. So Bloom had to change it into a "honeymoon for two" – that's your formulation, isn't it? Now the second question . . .'

'Wait a minute. That doesn't make sense. I told you before that Bloom wouldn't waste the money for script changes and re-takes just because he couldn't get a girl he wanted. And neither would he change a picture just because somebody else was shooting a similar story. No, he would not even change it if somebody else were producing exactly the same story with another cast. It's the cast that makes box-office, not the story.'

'You're a highbrow miser,' he said. 'There is protest in your voice.'

'Maybe, but neither the one nor the other of your reasons, Smith, would make Bloom do what he did.'

'Right you are,' he said. 'Neither the one nor the other – but both together. And that's the truth.'

'It doesn't click,' I said. 'It sounds too damned much like a Hollywood melodrama.'

'You're not only a miser, McCabe, you're an idealist, too. And that's a bad mixture. You're a Hollywood man yourself and you complain about Hollywood. And besides this isn't a detective story where things have to click. They only do in bad stories anyway. This is a thing that *happened*. Detective stories are puzzles – chess played with figures that look like human beings – but they only look like humans: they aren't. You must decide what you want to do – write a detective story and make things fit fine and dandy so that your readers in Walla Walla, Tooting Broadway and Kansas City Suburb like it – in which case you must cut out the human element and concentrate on the machinery – or you work with more or less normal human beings under more or less normal circumstances – which is real life as it is: more or less normal and far from the perfect machinery of that fine detective story that you want to make out of our case here, brother Mac.'

'All right,' I said.

'All right,' said Smith, 'and I haven't forgotten your second question. Bloom confessed to the murder of Estella because I told him to do so. When you bumped into the office I was almost dead sure that you had killed Estella. It was a hell of a come-down when I learned that she had killed herself. When I told Bloom to confess I meant to provoke a reaction from you that would give me an idea of what kind of man you were.'

Now that was good for me. He'd let me have a look into his cards. That gave me quite a new idea about a lot of things. If that was his method of work then I'd been the sap and not he. Then I had to discount a lot of certainty from all those points I'd always thought dead certain.

'Did you arrange Chris's confession too?' I asked him. 'Now I come to think of it I wonder whether you didn't arrange the whole game including one suicide, one murder, five suspicions and one gallows in the background.'

'I didn't,' he said. 'You did that. And some players in the game even arranged their own parts. Chris was one of them. He confessed because he had a perfect alibi for the night of Estella's death.'

'That's a fine reason for a confession,' I said. 'I think that's the only sound reason I've ever heard.'

'It is,' he said. 'Chris knew that Jensen had an affair with Estella –'

'Who didn't?' I asked him. 'Mrs Cohen in Brest-Litovsk knew it as well as you did and I did.'

'I didn't,' he said.

'That proves something – only I don't know what,' I told him.

'It proves that I don't care a damn what Mr Jensen does with Miss Lamare at any time of day or night,' he said.

'You're a fine detective. You'll learn a lot that way,' I said.

'Enough,' he said. 'But Chris learned more the other way. He learned almost everything there was to be learnt about Jensen and Estella. He learned so much that Jensen was never sure what he knew and what he didn't. So he'd made it a habit to tell Chris everything rather than let him find it out for himself. It was more or less a game and they both enjoyed it – they were the best of pals. Now the only man whom Jensen ever told anything about the Estella affair was Chris. Jensen rang Chris in his last eighty minutes in London, ten minutes after you had left, five minutes after Miss Ray had left, ten minutes before he himself left his flat, seventy minutes before he left London on his way home to Mother Norway. He told Chris the whole story as he thought it had happened – you know he believed himself that he had killed Estella – and so Chris had the fine idea of confessing the murder in order to cover Jensen's retreat. He knew that as long as we had one ace-suspect who more-over confessed to having committed the murder we wouldn't be interested in things of such minor importance as Jensen's contract-breaking departure. He was wrong, alas, but he gave us the first clues as to what had actually happened in Mr Robertson's room. So even your film didn't come to us as such a surprise –'

'Us,' I said, 'Majesty's plural.'

' "Us" is the police, Scotland Yard, the case for the Crown, Mr McCabe. Let me inform you that I'm not a private detective playing a game of my own.'

'It looks too damned much like it was a game of your own. If I make a mistake I can't be the only one who's responsible for it. You do cause illusions, Smith.'

'Sure,' he said. 'That's part of the game.'

'As long as we keep the rules – may I ask another one?'

'Come on, do,' he said jovially. 'This is your party. I haven't much to ask anyway. I know enough. And my case stands – even you were kind enough to admit that. And I have nothing to hide, brother, nothing on earth. So you go on asking and I'll tell you all you want to know.'

I wondered whether he really believed I was so dumb as not to realize that even if he had really had nothing to hide he wouldn't have let me ask him questions. I saw soon that his case was not half as strong as it seemed to him. He thought that by letting me ask him questions he would find out all weak points in my case – all those things I didn't know and wanted to know – all those things he

151

needed to build up his case to that perfection which it finally attained at the trial when I tried to smash it in the cross-examination.

He thought I was too damned silly. I left him in the belief and I asked him everything I wanted to know. It took a long time and we spent a pleasant afternoon. At the end we said goodbye and we were both satisfied with the afternoon's work.

Twenty-four

For the first two hours after curtain-rise the trial ran smoothly and decorously as all good trials should. Once you agree to the custom of making a fancy dress ball out of a meeting that is to decide whether a man is to be sent to the gallows or not, you cannot take much objection to those people talking a language that is quite as pompous and almost as venerable as their wardrobe: which is also quite as it should be: responsible adults who dress up in robes and wigs that come from another age can hardly be expected to speak the language of this age without creating the impression that they are trying to make fun of themselves. So they talked as they dressed and left it at that.

There weren't any surprises, and after the first impression of pomp and décor had worn off, there was nothing left but the shabbiness of routine and the sordidness of hard and fast rules.

The examining justices at Marylebone Police Court had come to the conclusion that the evidence raised a strong or at least possible presumption against me and so they committed me for trial. And so here we were.

After the court had been opened – in the usual way by the crier making proclamation – the indictment was read.

It was not very exciting.

The King v. Cameron McCabe (that seemed most flattering). *Central Criminal Court. Cameron McCabe is charged with the following offences* (followed various counts, the most important one being plain and bi-syllabic: *Murder*). Then *Particulars of offence: Cameron McCabe, on the 3rd day of December 1935 in the county of London, murdered Ian Jensen.*

The Clerk of Assize asked: 'How say you, are you guilty or not guilty?'

I said: 'Not guilty.'

The Clerk of Assize said: 'Prisoner, these good men that you shall now hear called are the jurors who are to pass between our sovereign lord the King and you upon your life and death; if, therefore, you will challenge them as they come to the Book to be sworn, and before they are sworn, you shall be heard.'

Then he said to them: 'You good men, who are returned and impanelled to try the issue joined between our sovereign lord the King and the prisoner at the bar, answer to your names and save your fines.'

He called one name after another.

They appeared in single file as they were called. It was very much like a fashion parade.

So I should challenge them, should I? But they all looked alike, and I knew none, so why should I?

I didn't.

They were sworn. 'I swear by Almighty God that I will well and truly try, and true deliverance make, between our sovereign lord the King and the prisoner at the bar, whom I shall have in charge, and a true verdict give according to the evidence.'

Two of them swore differently. The one said: 'I do solemnly and truly declare and affirm that . . .' The other one said: 'I, being one of the people called Quakers, do solemnly, sincerely and truly declare and affirm that . . .' The remainder, in both cases, was the same.

Now this was quite thrilling and unforeseen: one atheist and one Quaker in a jury to try me.

I took it as a compliment.

Then the crier said: 'If any one can inform my lords the King's justices, the King's attorney-general, or the King's serjeant, ere this inquest be taken between our sovereign lord the King and the prisoner at the bar, of any treason, murder, felony or misdemeanour, committed or done by him, let him come forth, and he shall be heard, for the prisoner stands at the bar upon his deliverance.'

The Clerk of the Court then called me to the bar and said to the jury: 'Members of the Jury, the prisoner stands indicted by the name of Cameron McCabe, for that he on the . . .' (followed the substance of the offences charged in the indictment). 'To this indictment he has pleaded that he is not guilty; your charge, therefore, is to inquire whether he be guilty or not guilty, and to hearken to the evidence.'

Then finally the senior counsel for the prosecution popped up and opened his case.

'May it please your Lordship, Gentlemen of the Jury . . .' he started, and then he went on describing Jensen and his life up to his first meeting with me. In this first part of his speech there were some few things that were new to me but they were all of minor importance. The whole centre part was an almost exact, only more polite, replica of Smith's story, different only in the presentation, not in the ingredients, the whole told in the very effective coquettishly archaic style of the profession, delicately spiced with epigrams and puns of a smart home-made brand, dished up with a well-blended dressing of irony and fine scepticism – the whole to be consumed with relish and consideration.

Only the last part gave me any news. I gained a good insight into the way Smith had prepared the case and an even better outlook on the way the prosecutor was going to dish it up.

He finished with a well-sounding, pleasantly involved technical phrase.

The first witness he called was Smith.

That was interesting. It showed that he was going to work the case backwards, starting with the death of Estella and working all the way up to Jensen's death. This was unusual, though it was in correct chronological order: it meant that he started with the minor counts on the indictment instead of beginning with the chief charge of the murder of Jensen.

Smith was sworn: 'I swear by Almighty God that the evidence I shall give to the Court and jury sworn between our sovereign lord the King and the prisoner at the bar shall be the truth, the whole truth and nothing but the truth.'

To see Smith lift his hand and to hear him repeat those words in that language was the finest bit of unconscious humour I had encountered so far in my poor thirty-eight years of vegetation.

Then it started off. After Smith had explained his position as the official sleuth of the case the prosecutor asked him straightforward questions.

The thing as it finally appeared through examination, cross-examination and re-examination, amounted to about this:

They had first called Smith into the case on the morning of Friday, the twenty-ninth day of November, one thousand nine hundred and thirty-five, when the body of Estella had been found by Robertson in his room, and Robertson had rung the police before telling anyone anything.

Now the district police who arrived didn't like the look of it at all. So they in their turn rang Scotland Yard. And Scotland Yard sent Smith.

So here is Smith now, faced with the treble task of finding out whether this is a plain simple suicide, or plain simple homicide, or a cross between both – one of those things that disturb all plain and simple calculations. And no doubt it *is* one of those pleasantly unpleasant things where nothing is plain and everything anything but simple. He finds that out soon after he has asked Bloom some questions about Estella. 'Can you possibly give me any suggestion as to what may have driven Miss Lamare to her death?' is his standard question at this first stage of his examination. And most unexpectedly he gets an answer from Bloom that seems at once to solve the mystery – or what there is of a mystery. But soon he sees that things aren't quite so simple.

'I killed her,' says Bloom.

'You mean you murdered her, or you killed her by accident, or you killed her in self-defence?' asks Smith.

'No – as you said first – I drove her to her suicide. I . . .' and then he tells Smith of his attempts to make her and of her showing him a cold shoulder and of his fury and rage and finally of his petty revenge: ordering me to cut her out of the picture – the face on the cutting-room floor.

Cornered by Smith, Bloom cracks up wildly and that gives Smith something like a *carte-blanche* for his further investigation.

When Smith is just about to finish his interview with Bloom the door opens and I come in without introduction, looking rather a mess, shouting at Bloom 'Why did you want to blot out the Estella girl?' and finally asking him straightforwardly why he killed Estella Lamare.

Now though Smith has already learnt the story from Bloom himself he is somewhat surprised by my peculiar behaviour. So he says goodbye to Bloom and decides to have a little talk with me. But before he comes he prepares his entrance. He is a careful man. He spends the whole day interviewing people, not only asking them the simple questions he asked Bloom, but adding now some very cautious questions about Bloom and about me.

From the answers he gets it appears that the only man who has a genuine alibi for the whole of Thursday, Thursday night and Friday morning is Robertson. Besides, Robertson seems the most intelligent man of the lot. So Smith decides to collaborate with Robertson – to collaborate carefully, cautiously and circumspectly, for it is a most delicate business for a sleuth to depend on an unofficial collaborator. Anyway he comes to terms with Robertson and after he has interviewed everyone else he has a final talk with Robertson and then he sends him down to the cutting-room to let him question me. Robertson accomplishes his task so well that I tell him quite a lot. The most peculiar bit of evidence he gets from me is the bit about my two attempts to get his room on the telephone – first getting no reply, then finding the line engaged, then finding the door of his room open, the camera still warm, and finally finding the door locked at my return a few minutes later.

At first Smith thinks that I am telling lies in order to shield myself – then he finds that I am telling the truth; the switchboard operator of the studio telephone exchange supports my statement. She says there were various telephone calls from Robertson's room after four fifteen – the time Robertson alleged that he had left his room and locked the door. But she could not identify the voice because, naturally, she did not pay any attention to it.

Now Smith is in a sad dilemma. Shall he believe me or Robertson? He gets out of the dilemma by believing both of us. That introduces an unknown factor: what happened between four fifteen and six forty-five in Robertson's room? who unlocked the door after Robertson had locked it? who telephoned from Robertson's room after four fifteen? who locked the door between six forty and six forty-five? and who unlocked it again so that Robertson found the door open when he came in the next morning? It is more than likely that the person who answers to these questions is the man who knows something about Estella Lamare's death. If, however, Estella killed herself or was killed between four fifteen and six twenty-five – how was it possible, then, that I did not find her when I entered Robertson's room at about six thirty-five? If I told Smith the truth – and he has no real reason to doubt that I did – then Estella's death must have taken place after six forty-five: after I had come back and found the door locked.

Now these are a lot of hard questions.

And it is not even the end of the questionnaire. There is a lot more to come. Robertson tells him that when he left the studio that afternoon at four fifteen he had his automatic camera loaded, fixed and connected with the door in order to test it: if it worked all right it should have taken a film of him when he entered the room the next morning. Now when he does enter the next morning he not only finds the body of Estella on the floor but also the spool of his camera empty: no film.

He tells Smith about it and after conferring with him Smith advises him to go and tell me about it and find out what I have to say.

Of course I smell a rat when John comes and asks me questions though at that time I don't know yet that he is acting on

Smith's behalf. Anyway, when he asks me I ask back: 'You mean it was not suicide? She has not done it herself?' and Robertson says: 'I don't know. Maybe she has. But somebody else has been in there. Either together with her or afterwards.'

Now all this is no news for Smith. He has been listening to our conversation from outside – stage-detective-like – and when Robertson unexpectedly opens the door and finds him there at the keyhole he is so flabbergasted that he almost gives the show away.

But then he only says: 'But you mustn't listen at doors – only stage detectives do . . .'

Smith says nothing, Robertson goes out, Smith comes in.

Instead of answering his questions I tell him all about Bloom's request to cut Estella out of the picture. Smith is bored to death: he knows all that. But he mustn't show it. So I begin to nag him by just talking away and offering him silly puns and all the time talking about anything except the thing he wants most urgently to talk about. I talk him out of his guardedness, I keep on talking until he gets so tired of me and so fed up with my pretentious petty jokes that he can't hold it back any longer and comes out with what he has to say. I drive him from the defence into the attack – out into the open – trip him then and there.

He tells me Bloom tried to make Estella. I laugh at him though I know he is telling me the truth.

My untimely humour works him up so much that he really can't hold it any longer and he blabs: 'I almost forgot. Isador Bloom says it was he who killed Estella. He is pleading guilty.' Then he goes out, bowing first to Dinah and then to me.

Now there I had Smith's début – a rather typical performance which gave me quite a good idea of his methods. First method: to spring quick surprises at people to test their reaction before they are able to control themselves – that was his quick one about Bloom having confessed to the murder of Estella. Second method: to sow discord between people in order to make them testify against one another – that was his bowing first to Dinah and then to me: it was to flatter her and to annoy me. Quite a good method: only he didn't succeed with Dinah until much later – not before he had made her believe that I killed Jensen. Then of course she was willing to say everything she knew. But I did not realize that until much later.

I did not realize any of these things until much later. I had to squeeze it all out of him in the course of the cross-examination. He was mad like hell. He wouldn't give me any chance to learn things he knew and I didn't. He was afraid I would use them to smash his case at the last moment. And he was right – right as ever. But he couldn't very well refuse to answer my questions in court – though, of course, he had the perfect right not to answer any question that might incriminate him. But he knew that the whole case for the prosecution was dependent on his testimony and if he wanted to save his case he had to reply.

Then came Christensen's confession. They tried to dodge any questions about it. But I asked a lot – not in order to learn new facts about it: there weren't any left to be learnt: we both knew all about it by now – but merely in order to weaken the case for the prosecution by showing the jury that there was a fair amount of dirty business going on amongst the prosecution's chief witnesses – for Chris, of course, was one of their chief witnesses, quite as important as John, Dinah, Maria, Müller, Bloom and the house-keeper at 69 Delilah Square.

I, for one, found that the array of his witnesses was really the most admirable proof of the excellence of the job he had done. From the first minute onwards he had concentrated on getting witnesses, had specialized his work in this one direction, working for this one aim of sowing discord between all his potential witnesses so that at the end everyone would be willing to testify against everyone else. The finest job in this line was, of course, the one he had put up on me: how he had made them leave me, all of them, Robertson first, then Maria, Chris, Bloom, Dinah and finally Müller who was the last one of all those who could have testified for me instead of now testifying for him.

So now Chris testified to what he called my extraordinary behaviour towards him. That I had stopped him from telephoning the police after he had told me that he had killed Estella. That I had seized him by the collar of his shirt and forced him down on his chair (another count: assault and battery) – 'all against my own will', which sounded quite funny when he said it.

Smith, in his turn, testified that this story of my curious behaviour towards Chris had again strengthened his suspicion against me. My behaviour allowed only one interpretation: that I feared Chris's confession and that I used physical force in order to extract from Chris all he had to say before he could say it to the police.

All this means more support for Smith's suspicion against me. He goes all the way back, examining everyone all over again, and now not only examining studio people but also people from outside: the housekeepers of the various suspects like myself, Bloom, Chris and others: their relatives (Estella's mother later on was one of them): then the people who had only loose connections with Estella: her dressmaker, her hairdresser, her chauffeur: and there he comes across some unexpected results.

Now this was news even for me: when he questioned the people at the garage they couldn't tell him much about Estella but Max told him something about me. He said (and he testified to that effect now at the trial) that he had seen my car stop at the corner of King's Cross Road at half-past one that night, twenty-eighth to twenty-ninth November – the night Estella was killed. He stated that he had seen me leave the car and walk towards the studio. He had followed me because he thought I might want to put the car in the garage. So he had seen me enter the house and walk up to the janitor's box, then stop there for a moment, probably wondering why the janitor wasn't in the box (the janitor explained his absence later with the simple excuse that he had been to the lavatory – which was probably the truth). Then I had walked up the stairs and Max, seeing that I apparently didn't need him, had gone back to his garage. He stood there, looking back at the studio, aimlessly, when he suddenly saw a light go on in the darkness. It's a light in a window on the third floor, the second window from the left. After a couple of minutes the light was switched off again and a flicker of a more whitish light could be seen. That lasted another few minutes, then the light, the normal yellow light, was switched on again, and after a minute or so, switched off again. Another minute afterwards he saw me leave the studio, jump into my car and drive off.

Max had soon forgotten all about it – late nightwork in the studio was nothing unusual and the flicker of a film being projected in one of the rooms was an even less unusual sight. Neither does Smith think much of it when he first hears of it. But then, when he checks up on Max's statement he finds that the second window on the third floor, on the left side of the studio front if you look at it from the garage, is the window of room 126, Robertson's room.

And now there he has something to gloat about. Here is a fact, a fine clear tangible fact, one fact that combines with another fact to result in a perfect complex of circumstantial evidence: A sees B enter the house, a few minutes later the light goes on (I see the body of Estella on the floor, see the camera, take out the film), the light is switched off again (I put the film into the projector), the white flicker begins (I project the film), the light is switched on again (I have seen the film, take it out of the projector, put the spool into my pocket), the light is switched off (I leave the room, walk down the stairs), Max sees me come out of the house, jump into the car and drive off.

Of course Smith does not yet develop this theory of my

having pinched the film. He merely jots down the facts and instead of trying to deduce some theory from the facts – as the traditional detective of the Sherlock Holmes type would have done – he tries to make other people tell him so much about it that he needn't deduce anything at all. This is almost Prussian pedantry: Smith never guesses unless there is absolutely no other way out – he prefers to get definite testimonies from eye-witnesses – his task is not to guess but to find the witnesses and to make them tell him all they know: the detective's work becomes transformed from detection to psychology: the purely psychological task of making people talk more than they intend to talk – and, of course, to find the right people to do the talking.

But he cannot always stick to his favourite methods: Scotland Yard has different ideas and Smith is not an independent man. So he realizes that there may be one or two means of escape from his fine tight ring of circumstantial evidence and if he wants to keep his job he must first get rid of those. He has to have another careful look at Robertson's room to find some definite proof that I have actually been up there – and, looking about, he finds the most definite and most primitive proof not only of my having been in Robertson's room but also of my having touched the camera: there are clear fingerprints on the gearbox – and they check up with mine.

Now his case is slowly growing into shape. Not too slowly – for luck is with him: the next morning, Saturday the thirtieth and last day of November, after he has just been interviewing the sound-engineer in his booth and the sound-man has just begun explaining to him the mechanism of sound recording, the boom is being lowered from the crane on to the floor and the mike already switched on and the noise from Stage B already becoming audible in the loudspeaker, and suddenly Smith hears a voice he knows and another one he doesn't know. The one he doesn't know says: 'You're the cutting chief, you're the man what made the boss own up.' Then he knows whose voice the other one is: it's mine. He hears me say: 'Just a moment – you'd better clean your teeth before you start talking. That dirty talk is going to do us a lot of good.' And the other voice replying quickly: 'Well, what's the good word? Ain't yer got enough on that guy to make sure of nailin' 'im all right?' Then my voice after a second of hesitation: 'You stay here. What are you getting at?' And the other voice replying without excitement: 'No good talkin' this close to the mike.'

Now that sounds almost too good: like an Elstree attempt at a Hollywood gangster film.

Smith says goodbye to the sound-man, walks out on to the floor, sees me up there on the gallery over Stage B. He hides, sees me walk down and talk to Vic, then he hears Vic calling Happy, then when Happy speaks Smith recognizes the voice he heard through the microphone in the sound-booth. Now here is a good old detective game. He follows Happy and me up to my room and listens to our conversation without understanding more than I myself did when I listened to Happy that morning. 'Bloom's in a tough spot right now. Sock 'im on the boko or you'll be sunk.' Then: 'The thing's no good if Chris is wriggling out from under. You gotta give 'im the works.' And again: 'It's all up with your case against Bloom if you don't keep that fella Chris from stirring things up.' And again about Bloom: 'What kind of job did you put up on rosy-cheeked friend Bloom?' Now that didn't express much respect for Bloom. And not much for me either. Then Happy comes out with the cause of his disrespect – or at least with an intimation of it: 'The day before yesterday, sometime after seven fifteen, the Estella girl was pooped. It's a pipe somebody knows something about that afternoon. It's gonna raise a stink ... you're smoked ... lay low ... you ain't got the right temper ... you'll fly off the handle.'

Smith tries to make sense of that. It seems that Happy

(a) does not like Bloom;

(b) thinks that I tried to frame Bloom;

(c) thinks there is a danger of Chris interfering (probably through his confession);

(d) thinks (or knows) that Estella was killed on Thursday afternoon some time after seven fifteen.

Now Smith has to find out:

(a) why does Happy dislike Bloom?

(b) why does he think I framed Bloom?

(c) how did Happy learn of Chris's confession?

(d) what does the new figure seven fifteen indicate?

They are the same questions I asked myself after Happy had left me that Saturday morning. The difference was that Smith had found the answer and I hadn't. Now at the trial when I cornered him he finally had to tell me all about it. He tried to dodge it again because he naturally liked to keep his case clean – and Happy, he knew, was a dirty spot in it. Everybody in court tries to make his witnesses sound as honest and sincere as possible. So the prosecution didn't like my drawing Happy into it. They fought with all the professional means of protesting against my questions, calling them irrelevant, inadmissible, leading. But they couldn't pull it off. And it came out better than I could ever have hoped.

It came out like this:

Smith has Happy watched day and night. He pulls all strings at Scotland Yard. The whole machinery gets moving. And with success.

They find that Happy entered Robertson's room Thursday afternoon at four twenty, not more than five minutes after Robertson left. They find that Happy sketched the camera, worked it, copied every detail carefully; in short, the good old gag of the secret service yarn: industrial espionage.

Robertson's camera was a fine job and John guarded it well. I should have known that he wouldn't have left his room without carefully locking the door. Well, someone (the name was never mentioned at the trial and it didn't really matter) paid Happy to slip into the studio crowd, get a job as grips on the floor and copy the camera at the first opportunity.

The first opportunity came on Thursday afternoon when Robertson left at four fifteen. Happy did his job well but could not quite finish it because he had to rush away when he heard me at six thirty-five, but he came back and locked the door after I had gone away so that I found the door locked when I came back at six forty-five.

Happy, like all nosey-parkers of his kind, could never get away from the vanity of boasting with the knowledge of dirty facts he acquired in the course of his snooping. So he learned of my clash with Bloom and, knowing Bloom well enough to know that Bloom could never have killed Estella, he naturally concluded that I was framing Bloom when I accused Bloom of the murder.

The death of Estella and the arrival of Smith were most unfortunate events for Happy: they disturbed him in the task he had to accomplish. Now there was not only Robertson but also Smith to be watched – every new fact Smith learned about Thursday afternoon brought him into more dangerously close contact with Happy's activities on that afternoon. So Happy had to keep track of the progress of Smith's work. Keeping an eye and more than one ear on Smith he learned about Chris's confession before anyone else – except myself – came to hear of it.

So he could not help boasting about it – knowing – or at least believing – that I, in my own interest, could not risk giving him up. He could tell me frankly that the killing could not have happened before seven fifteen, for he himself had watched the door till seven fifteen, but realizing that it was too dangerous to make a second attempt at entering and sketching the camera he had given it up. So he knew that the killing must have taken place after seven fifteen and he told me so.

And just like his boasting was his behaviour on the job he had to do: he had to telephone from Robertson's room – not because he had any urgent news to transmit (later they found out that it was his little tart whom he had rung) but just because he liked the feeling of danger: the same pride which makes the matador work close to the bull and the gangster close to the police: leaving a note for the police is another gag of the same kind.

(In the course of time Smith got quite fond of Happy: they were so much alike.)

And, of course, Happy didn't like Bloom because Bloom had caught him once snooping about – though he didn't know anything about Happy's actual designs.

Now after his adventure in the sound-booth, after his snooping on my conversation with Happy, Smith is prepared to watch me more carefully than ever. So when I leave the studio Saturday afternoon at six o'clock to join Dick Flaherty he even follows me up to Hampstead, is disappointed when I don't do anything more exciting than just playing drums with the orchestra, is bored by the whole recording session, is glad when he sees me leave, is annoyed again when he discovers that I am merely going to feed, is furious about the price of the dinner at Simpson's, dislikes the atmosphere of the Café Royal, is happy when he hears me ring up Maria, follows me to Mecklenburg Square, bribes the maid with his police badge, hears Maria telling me she had been in Jensen's bedroom when I had shown Jensen the film of the murder, hears how Maria blackmails me into breaking my agreement with Jensen, gloats again and does not even take the trouble to pretend surprise when I bring him the film the next morning. Teasing me to provoke an outburst – one of the methods he has in common with me – he asks me whether I wouldn't like to leave him the film. And – as he has expected – I tell him I'd rather not. Stagily chewing the sides of his lower lip he makes an appointment for seven o'clock that evening to view the film.

When he sees the film he is surprised: here is perfect evidence that Jensen killed Estella – Jensen, a man he never considered as a suspect – a mere outsider so to speak. Smith has asked Bloom, Chris, Maria, Robertson – all his suspects – to come and see the film. He originally wanted to test their reactions but now this is a disappointment – he does not need them any longer: the early stage of suspecting people is finished: here is proof now – proof almost too conclusive to be true – proof so amazingly conclusive that Smith begins to suspect dirt again: so he tries to launch another quick one at the audience. 'Gentlemen,' he says, 'you are at liberty to leave the room. Thank you, gentlemen.' Maria, brought up to the nearest thing there is to hysteria, bursts into slightly cranky laughter because she thinks Smith has forgotten all about her important female presence in this room, addressing the audience as 'Gentlemen' and forgetting the lonely lady. But Bloom, by now well enough acquainted with Smith's methods, tells her to shut up ('You don't understand . . . you never do') not realizing that Maria understands only too well.

Smith sees his opportunity, of course. 'But she *does* understand,' he tells them, 'she understands *perfectly*. I want to have a talk with her. *Alone*, if you don't mind, gentlemen.' This is the kind of situation Smith likes: first concocting a surprise for his audience to test their reaction, then shocking the others and flattering Maria at the same time – a fine preparation for the examination to come – and finally trying to catch me by teasing Maria. And he sure does catch me. 'I'm staying,' I say. And that's what he expected. He knows that it is too big a risk for me to let him talk with Maria alone – she may make a mistake and up flies the whole shop. Of course, Smith could have me thrown out. But he doesn't want to: this double examination is much more profitable for him. First he begins by teasing me: '. . . pity they didn't put up a reward. Otherwise you would get it.' Then he tries to land another quick one: 'How did you find the film?' Now he knows there's a shock for me. After having left Maria last night in such an uncertain position I don't know now whether she will play the game or blow up. So I look at her, trying to force her eyes on me to make her realize the urge to answer one definite thing and only that. Smith watches and sees and feels amused when she gives me her sign with her eyes and when I tell him: 'I found the film in Jensen's flat in Guilford Street.' Smith drives me into a corner, showing me how ridiculous it would be if Jensen had left the most incriminating piece of evidence behind him in his flat. It's quite a bad corner for me. And there, just at the right moment, Maria intervenes, telling Smith *she* pinched the film from Robertson's room after Jensen had come to her to tell her he had killed Estella. Now that makes it a corner for Smith. He knows that I can always make a fine impression by telling anyone that I said what I said in order to shield Maria, a thing I actually said to Müller later on. Alas, Maria makes one mistake: she tells him she ran the film through her own projector – a pardonable mistake in consideration of the fact that she actually did see the film through someone's own projector – only it was Jensen's and not hers. And Smith soon finds out that she never had a projector of her own. There's his chance to trip her. And he does trip her and then he has her as far as he needs her to make her confess all she knows.

And here was Maria now at the trial as witness for the prosecution. Another score for Smith. His case was getting on fine. It was an aesthetic pleasure to see it grow slowly, definitely, irresistibly.

And at this stage, after he had already scored well enough with his shrapnels, he fired his big trench mortars.

After Maria and I had left on Sunday night he had another talk with Robertson. He showed Robertson the film and asked him whether he thought that this actually was a film taken with his camera. Robertson looked at it, tested it, was about to say yes, hesitated, looked at Smith, said: 'Yes, it's sure enough taken with my camera but it isn't the film that is missing.' 'Why not?' asks Smith. 'Because the camera took a thousand feet and the meter showed that a thousand feet were exposed. But this bit here can't be more than five hundred feet.'

Now Smith thinks that this begins to look rather dirty again. And right he is. Robertson has another look at the film and finally he admits: 'It may be the film we are looking for but if it is it's only half of it. Somebody must have cut off the last bit.'

That makes it a clear-cut puzzle. Smith knows now what it is all about. So he asks Robertson to give me a ring in the middle of the night, some time about four o'clock. He is using his old strategics of springing quick surprises at his victims to test their reactions before they can get themselves under control. Robertson rings me Sunday night at four, asks me whether I found the film loose or wound up on the spool and breaks off with a mysterious intimation. Unfortunately that doesn't go down with me.

But things get better for Smith when he learns that next morning I received a telegram from Aardals, Norway: 'Two timer caught tripping. Wait and see.' I burn the telegram – which is some more proof for Smith that I have some dirty business to hide. There is a fake sender stated on the telegram – but Smith has no doubt the sender's name is Ian Jensen.

He sends Vic to provoke me with his good old-fashioned blundering tactless remarks: no success. He tries to make Maria work against me: no success. He tries Dinah: in vain. He has to fall back on Robertson.

And there his difficulties begin again: by some kind of accident Smith has found out that Robertson knows much more about Estella than he has ever told him. That looks bad for John and confusing for Smith.

Smith goes and frisks Robertson's place. There he finds a map of Norway with a circle round a place by the name of Aardals: sure evidence that Robertson knows something about the telegram I received the other day.

So Smith begins to check up on Robertson's moves. Investigating into John's past he finds John's old Oxford affair with Edna Lenore, a young woman-about-Oxford-town whose original name was Esther Lammer and who died under the name of Estella Lamare. He smells a mystery. But he finds it is only a harmless vanity, this play with names.

Checking up on John and Estella, Smith soon discovers the whole familiar family story: early undergraduate affair, firework passion, marriage opposed by John's Society dad, approved by Estella's old crazy Whitechapel mom, marriage plans soon dissolving into a nice little affair without hope of, or wish for, marriage – a thing which, however, has to be presented to Estella's mother as a good legal marriage – until Estella finally advances from the crowds to the extra-ranks and from extra to feature-player. When she has got so far she is fed up with her dirty screwy old West India Dock Road parents. So she tells her mother that she married John and went to the States. As Mrs Lammer never reads newspapers she doesn't learn anything about Estella's career. The only thing she knows is Estella's new name and she adopts it and adds some ornaments: 'Annamaria de la Santa Bellina . . .' Nice foreign sounds.

In those days Smith used me against John and John against me. So on our way back from our memorable Whitechapel excursion he shoots that classical question at me: 'Do you know Norway?' and I answer just as quick: 'Aardals, Southern Norway, Df, page 80,' which is the spot marked on Robertson's map. First Smith thinks that I have been searching John's place just as well as he has done it and he gets mad with me for holding things back. But then, later, John asserts that the map was smuggled into his place and now at the trial the prosecution is holding it against me, trying to prove that I planted it to John's flat to plant suspicion against John.

Another good stone to help build up the case against me.

Then the first anonymous letters arrive. Smith isn't interested until he gets the idea that maybe Jensen is back in town, up to some kind of mischief. In those letters there is talk about an agreement broken, an injustice to be avenged, a Mr M to be punished for his infidelity. Now M could be McCabe but only a foreigner would use M as an abbreviation for McC.

However that may be, Smith, with his Prussian pedantry, follows me wherever I go:

(a) to find what I am doing,

(b) to trace Jensen.

So on Monday night after our return from West India Dock Road he says goodbye to me when we get to Scotland Yard but after he has said goodbye he gets himself one of those lovely little black Hillman police cars and goes on following me. It doesn't disturb him much that he sees me go home: he knows I must go out again: he has caught and opened Maria's letter with the invitation to meet her that night at twelve o'clock at 69 Delilah Square. Actually, of course, this is not a letter from Maria but from Jensen. But at that time Smith does not know more about that than I do: so he follows me to 69 Delilah Square but doesn't go in because there is nothing new he could learn from Maria. Half an hour later he sees me come out again, thinks I must have quarrelled with Maria (good for him), sees me drive home, is satisfied that I'm actually going to bed, posts a copper outside my house and goes to bed too – justly tired after a day's hard work – so he tells us at the trial.

At half-past eight the next morning he gets a message that a man has been found shot at 69 Delilah Square. This is a hell of a mess. He finds Jensen and it looks like suicide. He arranges a meeting of his suspects to find out whether anyone reacts in any way peculiar to the sight of the body. No success.

Then the autopsy shows the curious result that Jensen was dead before the shot that was supposed to have killed him had been fired.

Now Smith is in a pet. Something has got to be done. Things are getting tough. So he starts gagging again. He begins with a fake arrest of John to make me feel free and easy – so free and easy that perhaps I may trip myself in the overjoy of getting out of the tongs.

He makes John's sister May ring me up on Wednesday morning to tell me that John has been arrested for the murder of Jensen and that I had better beat it if I had something to do with the killing. Now Smith thinks if I *had* something to do with it I would gladly take her advice and beat it. And in the course of my running away he would intervene and catch me. He had his people posted outside my house already before he had May Robertson ring me.

Alas, I messed up the plan. Instead of running away I stayed at home, had my morning bath in peace and quiet and took such a long time over it that Smith lost his patience and came up to find out what had happened to me. He finds me in the pink of condition, is slightly disappointed without admitting it even to himself, lets me put my clothes on, throws me into a Black Maria and takes me for a ride to 69 Delilah Square to stage the fine reconstruction of the murder with John as the mysterious Mr X (or Mr M, as you like it), and myself as Jensen.

At the murder reconstruction – as a parting shot – Smith fires his best ammunition: 'You'd better put Mr McCabe in charge of the reconstruction. He remembers the Myers-Johnson case better than I do.' Smith knows that Jensen's murderer must have learned a good deal from the Myers-Johnson case – and he has little doubt that he's addressing the right man when he is talking to me.

The only two things he wants now are:

    (a) proof of my having been deeply influenced by the Myers-Johnson case;

    (b) a method of using Dinah's film as a means to make me either confess or trip myself.

He has me trailed wherever I go and he is quite amazed when he finds how well his plan works. Troubled by Smith's remark about the Myers-Johnson trial I go out to find Müller and get his assurance that he won't testify against me in case it ever comes to a charge against me. And there it is what Smith has been looking for: a proof of my having been deeply influenced by Müller's story of the Myers-Johnson case.

Smith is more than just lucky about Müller.

Müller is an amateur sleuth, and to prove his sleuthing ability he makes use of the story I tell him. Comparing my version of the events with the version Smith has given him over the telephone twenty minutes ago, he finds:

    (a) that I leave out certain vital events;

    (b) that I change certain other events;

    (c) that I tell certain things which are not at all to be found in Smith's, the official version.

He finds that I leave out Happy, the finding of the film, Maria's hysteria at the first showing of the film, Robertson's telephone call about the spool and Smith's story about my car in front of Maria's house with its effect on Dinah.

He tells Smith about my funny little Freudian mistake: 'Can they really prove that the poison killed him before the bullet did?' and Smith agrees with him that that's really a good one.

But the greatest support for Smith's theory comes when Müller tells him what I said to him about Chris's confession: 'He told the story almost exactly as it had actually happened.' Müller replied: 'Well, probably he saw the film before you found it.' But I denied it sternly: 'No, he didn't.' Now Müller argues that I could only state that so definitely if I'd had the film in my possession all the time: which is exactly what Smith wants to prove.

Then there is my insistence on having Robertson locked up.

Finally there are the three express questions I asked Müller that Wednesday afternoon:

1. Why did Bloom say that he had killed Estella?
2. Why did Chris say that he had killed Estella?
3. What is the connection between Estella's death and Jensen's death?

Müller argues that only Jensen's murderer would pick out exactly these three questions. Only a man who definitely knew that neither Bloom nor Chris had anything to do with Estella's death would ask why they confessed that they had killed her. And in the same way only a man who knew the connection between Estella's and Jensen's deaths would ask what the connection was. And who else but Jensen's murderer could possibly know these three things?

Smith does not like this argumentation, but all together it makes enough sense to let Smith develop his final plan of convicting me.

He invites me under the false pretence of a final party of reconciliation, makes me show the film – the whole film including Dinah's last part – and expects that I'll betray my guilt by stopping the film when it comes to that critical moment which shows that Estella was not killed by Jensen but killed herself. And the plan works: I actually do stop the projector and now here I am, charged with the murder of Ian Jensen, not to speak of the whole long list of minor offences.

It had been lovely to see the counsel for the prosecution build up his case with Smith's support and with Smith as chief witness. It had been like a curve swinging up to a well-planned climax; mathematically correct but also humanly moving and sentimentally touching with its good sound basis of well-established morals and ethics.

But I think it was just as lovely to see me now break down the case again. I believe I can give myself the right of judging it – indeed, I sincerely believe that I can judge it better than anyone else – for I had the objectivity to see Smith's and the prosecutor's point of view and I didn't mind them building a case against me – I realized that this was their job and I enjoyed seeing them at work because they worked well – it was a pleasure to see them work – even if they worked against me. But I could also judge my own case, knowing all the details of it and seeing the effect it had on the Court. I knew when I wanted to get an effect and I knew what that effect should look like if it succeeded. And I admit it was a kind of creator's pride to see how I got the effects exactly as I had planned them.

Smith and the prosecutor led up to a fine climax. But I first led them down again to an anticlimax which was even lower below par than their climax was high above par. And after that I led them up to a second climax, *my* climax, that stood higher than theirs.

I had no lawyer – things had happened exactly as I thought they would happen: when I told my prospective lawyers that I intended to use the prosecutor's case for my own purposes, that I was going to use his attack for my defence – well, the noble professionals just smiled. Then, when I told them that I was going to play Smith off, play him off so much that it would be as if he was the accused and I the accuser – then they laughed outright.

But I had known from the beginning that I couldn't build up my own case and that therefore I had to make the other one's case my own. And I did it.

I started with the cross-examination. I asked all the questions I wanted to ask. From Harris I had learned that there were a good number of questions that were not allowed. Not only irrelevant questions but also a good number of others. I knew that the prosecutor had the right and even the duty to interpose and object to the question before the witness had time to answer it. And I realized that I could use this very right as a method to smash their case. I knew that in the case of a leading question – and not only in that case – the protest would be ineffectual inasmuch as I had done the mischief by the suggestion alone – and by protesting the prosecutor would only make himself ridiculous – and in a certain way it would weaken his case.

So I asked all the questions I wanted to ask. The prosecutor kept on protesting. I didn't give him time to sit down between two protests. He had to pop up again and again. That was what I wanted. Protests repeated to such an extent gave the jury the impression that there were a lot of things the prosecution didn't want to have pulled out into the daylight.

And I had a fine excuse for doing that. I was not a professional – no lawyer – no counsel for the defence but just a layman conducting his own defence. I did not know the rules. I could not possibly know them. And then I was fighting for my life, for my own life: this was different from a barrister conducting the defence for his client – even if that client's life was in danger.

Those were fundamentals – reasons that made the judge forgive me for the continuous 'mistakes' I made.

But the whole thing was unusual, for the judge as well as for the jury. Much more for the jury, of course. They had to watch the proceedings with much more than normal attention. Questions and answers were so confusing that their *professional attention* slowly and almost imperceptibly changed into a kind of *personal and sentimental interest*.

They saw this was a fight. And they took sides for and against – a thing they should never have done and *would* never have done if there had been normal proceedings at a normal trial. But the proceedings were so un-normal that they even forgot this *was* a trial. The only thing they realized after it had continued for some hours was that it was a *fight*. And they were English. It appealed to their sportsmanship. They forgot that they were jurors, supposed to be models of impartiality. They forgot all about it. Later on they would feel ashamed of it. But that didn't matter now.

It got them because it overthrew all their routine business. If you had asked them they would never have admitted that they were fed up with the stiff, cold, dead system of conducting a trial as it was normally conducted – restricted by hard and fast rules, everybody's, even the judge's, rights retrenched, curtailed, limited. They would never have admitted it even secretly to themselves. But that didn't matter either. What did matter was the effect. And I got the effect.

I got the effect on the prosecutor, on the jury and even on the judge. None of them was used to what I did with the rules of a British trial at the Central Criminal Court.

The prosecutor got confused. He repeated himself. He asked questions he wasn't allowed to ask. The judge had to warn him because with him things were different: he was a professional. He had to give me a good example of how a witness should be cross-examined. But he couldn't fight back with his methods against mine. He had to adopt my methods if he wanted to win the case. And adopting my methods was the very thing the judge would not pass.

I had five lines of defence to fall back on:

(1) In case the prosecution should attack through their witnesses: deny everything, say: 'No, I did not do it, I was not there, the witness must be mistaken': *prove* that the witness is mistaken.

(2) In case Smith should be able to build up some kind of

evidence to prove that I was the only possible person to have killed Jensen: say: 'If I am supposed to have killed Jensen, then you must admit that he was the attacker and I *could* only have acted in self-defence: the anonymous letters to the police – aren't they the strongest proof that Jensen lured me into the house with the intention of killing me?'

(3) In case they should use the argument that Jensen had already died from poisoning when the shot was fired: say: 'Maybe that was what happened. But I did not poison him. He must have put the poison into my drink to poison me and must have mixed up the glasses afterwards. When he dropped down I thought he had a nervous breakdown. He had threatened me with his gun before and he still had the gun in his hand when he broke down. I put him on his bed, opened his shirt, poured some water down his throat, was going to take the gun out of his hand when it went off. Perhaps it was a final convulsion, perhaps the final rigor, perhaps even my own clumsiness – but it certainly was not murder. And anyway, the very arguments of the defence that Jensen was dead when the shot was fired shows that I could not possibly have shot him: if he was dead when the shot was fired I cannot possibly have murdered him. In British law there is no paragraph against shooting a dead man – except the moral law against the desecration or mutilation of dead bodies, and, perhaps, the Firearms Act against discharging a loaded firearm in an inhabited place.'

And finally, if they should dress up some kind of evidence to the effect that I changed the glasses wilfully and deliberately to make Jensen himself drink the concoction which he had intended for me: say: 'I did not administer poison wilfully and deliberately. If I changed the glasses wilfully and deliberately, as you are trying to prove, even then I would not have administered poison wilfully and deliberately – I would merely have administered something which I thought to be a sleeping draught though it actually may have been poison; and even if the administering of it was wilful and deliberate it can only amount to manslaughter.' For I had learned from Archbold that 'if a person while in the act of committing a felony . . . kills another without having the intention of so doing, the killing is murder'. If, however, 'the act is unlawful but does not amount to felony, the killing is manslaughter'. Now the changing of the glasses did most certainly not amount to felony, and consequently the killing of Jensen could not possibly amount to murder.

If they should ask: 'How can you prove that you did not know that the drug you saw Jensen pour into your glass was poison?'

I would reply: '*I* need not prove the fact for the very reason that you yourself already proved it: the very argument on which you build up this line of attack disproves your theory: nobody, not even I, would be so mad as to shoot a dead man. If I had tried to kill him deliberately and wilfully, as you try to prove, then I would have been glad of the opportunity of having him killed by his own poison: I would most certainly not have endangered myself by shooting him after I knew he was already dead enough to satisfy all my purposes.'

But it never came to any argumentation as detailed as that. I knew that they could convict me of quite a good deal of offences but most certainly not of murder. And that knowledge that my life was never in danger made the trial a child's play for me.

I showed them that the whole case was dependent on Smith's testimony. And then I started to attack Smith from every possible angle. I quoted Archbold: 'The credibility of a witness depends upon his knowledge of the fact he testifies, his disinterestedness, his integrity, his veracity . . .' and there was no disqualification I did not ascribe to Smith.

First I showed them his methods – the methods he had used to build up this case against me. I showed them how he had thrown up animosity between me and my best friends. I appealed to their sentiments, giving them little details like his bowing first to Dinah, then to me; like his attempt to make Dinah jealous by telling her how he had found my car in front of Maria's house. I showed them how he had used and misused all his witnesses – John, Maria, Dinah, Bloom. I underlined the irresponsibility of instigating Bloom to make a false confession and the unreliability of Chris as a witness. I gave them examples of Smith's tactlessness and injudiciousness: how he had kept on referring to Maria's and my friendship with little remarks like: 'I know, I know, and there was another girl in it, Maria Beam or Maria Flash or something like that.' His remark: 'Pity they didn't put up a reward; otherwise you would get it' – this at a time when he had nothing at all against me. Then his constant corrections: 'Miss Ray, please' or 'Miss Lee, please' every time I mentioned Maria or Dinah by their first names. I gave them a vivid description of the outcome of his attempt to arrange a reconstruction of the murder in his style. Then I showed them, and I made them believe it, that Smith had misused my gullibility by making me believe that he wanted me to work with him side by side as his assistant: how he had asked me 'How much does she know?' pointing at Maria, talking to me as if I was his colleague-at-arms. How he had said to me: 'You got the right sort of eyes to look at things and see what is behind them.' How he had taken me with him to Estella's mother and how I had helped him to get anything at all out of her.

Then when I had finished with the milk and honey business I switched them straight over to the hard facts, smashing their case in every detail, starting with Max's testimony that he had seen me enter the studio shortly after half-past one on the night of Estella's death – that he had a few minutes later seen the light in Robertson's room – and that about half an hour later he had seen me leave the studio and that next morning Estella's body had been found in John's room. I showed them that this was a poor example of circumstantial evidence. I quoted Harris's example as a good specimen: '. . . *the witness proves that the prisoner was seen going to B's house at four o'clock, that there was no other person in the house at the time, that at 4.15 B's throat was found cut, and that a blood-stained knife was found concealed in the prisoner's locked box . . .*' I showed them that the difference between the two cases was:

(*a*) that there were a lot of other persons at the studio – not *no other person* as in Harris's example;

(*b*) that Estella's dead body had not been found before the next morning – which left a sufficiently large margin of time for the commission of the murder by practically anyone at any time between two o'clock and nine o'clock the next morning when Robertson found the body;

(*c*) that there was no proof whatsoever that I had ever been in Robertson's room that night: nothing of the character of a *blood-stained knife in a locked box* had been found in my possession: anyone could have been in Robertson's room while I was in the studio. The fact that the light was switched on shortly after I had entered the studio and that it was switched off again shortly before I left proved nothing at all.

The judge smiled.

I said: 'The witness for the prosecution states that he found fingerprints on the gearbox, and he deigns to conclude therefrom that I have not only been in Mr Robertson's room that night but moreover that I touched the camera, the fact which the prosecution wants to establish. Now may I inform the learned counsel for the prosecution that I do not deny the fact that I did touch the camera.' (Great commotion.) 'May I remind the learned counsel that I never denied the fact? I stated – spontaneously, without having been asked any question – that I went to Mr Robertson's room Thursday afternoon at six thirty-five, that I touched the camera and found the gearbox warm. No wonder the witness for the prosecution found my fingerprints on it. If he had only asked me I could have saved him the trouble of having to look for the fingerprints: I could have shown him the exact spot where to find them.' (Laughter.)

I used their applause to show them that all those things I was supposed to have done in Jensen's room that night could not be proved. And once I had established the fact that the prosecution worked with conjecture instead of having real watertight evidence at their disposal, once I had shattered the credibility of the prosecution's evidence, the rest was fairly easy.

I said: 'The next witness cited by the learned counsel for the prosecution to support his case was the witness Maria Ray who stated that she spent the night from Thursday the 28th November to Friday the 29th with the so unhappily deceased Ian Jensen, a fact which enabled her to watch from the bedroom those scenes which the prosecution alleges to have taken place between Mr Jensen and myself.

'My Lord, Gentlemen of the Jury, I believe I need not trespass on your patience to outline and sketch the fact that the testimony of a woman who herself admits frankly – though she was not judicially compelled to make the admission – that she spent the night with a man to whom she was not legally married, has to be received with some reservation.

'I do not wish to pass with silence over the allegation made by the prosecution against me that I am guilty of the same moral laxity. The chief witness for the prosecution testified to the effect that I spent the night from Saturday the 30th November to Sunday the 1st December with the witness Maria Ray. This testimony is only supported by the witness Maria Ray herself. Now my Lord, Gentlemen of the Jury, I could easily try to attack the testimony of the chief witness for the prosecution whose so-called evidence in more than one previous incident has proved to be conjecture of the vaguest and most irresponsible kind. But I refuse to descend to those depths of argument which have been used by the prosecution against me. I only desire to point out the full meaning of the testimony given by the witness Maria Ray. I understand – and I ask the learned and honourable counsel for the prosecution kindly to interrupt me if I misunderstand or misinterpret the facts – that the witness claims to have spent the night from the 28th to the 29th with Ian Jensen and the night from the 30th to the 1st December with another man, to wit, with myself. This confession – I trust the counsel for the prosecution will grant me the privilege to call this amazing admission a confession – means that a woman admits – nay, *claims* – to have allowed two different men, to neither of whom she was married – to have carnal knowledge of her on two alternate nights – a truly amazing state of affairs. I can only admire the courage of the learned counsel for the prosecution who dared to quote these admissions as support for his case instead of trying to do all there was in his power to hide these disgusting details of the private life of those persons on whose testimony he has to fall back for evidence.

'But I refuse to dwell on these facts. I think it beneath the dignity of this Court to attempt to sway the opinion of the jury with appeals to their moral conscience. I have enough cold, clear, unsentimental arguments at my hand to disprove the case for the prosecution on a different basis – the secure and approved classical basis of hard facts.

'Now if I remember the proceedings correctly, it was the witness Dinah Lee who was called by the learned counsel for the prosecution to establish the next point in his theory that I had entered the studio at night-time to steal the film of Estella Lamare's suicide, to cut it into two parts, using the first to blackmail Ian Jensen and losing the other on my doormat.

'My Lord, Gentlemen of the Jury – you have seen the lamentable collapse of the first part of this allegation. May I now proceed to show you the almost insulting attempt of the prosecution to make you believe that a man who is supposed to have done those evil deeds which the prosecution alleges against me, would be so careless as to leave the most vital piece of evidence of his crime on his doormat? I beg to be allowed to quote the words which the chief witness for the prosecution addressed to me when I stated that I found the film – the first part of the film – in Mr Jensen's flat. I admit that my statement then was untrue, but though untrue it was a statement made in defence of a lady – a lady whose true character was never revealed to me before today –'

I lowered my voice and made it sound broken – the commotion grew – I realized it with satisfaction and continued with a new note of 'well-let's-drop-it-there-are-more-important-matters-at-stake' in my voice.

'What the chief witness for the prosecution said when I insulted his intelligence in the same way which the counsel for the prosecution is using now against me, was this: "And then you went up to the flat, told the housekeeper a nice story, or bribed him, searched every corner of the place and finally found the one piece of incriminating evidence which the perpetrator had fortunately left behind at the free disposal of the police." '

Smith jumped up and shouted: 'And do you also remember what you replied? You said . . .'

The judge hammered on his desk and shouted: 'Silence, please – remove the witness.'

Smith was taken out. There was a huge commotion. The prosecutor bit his lip. He was afraid for his case. Smith had made a very bad impression.

I said: 'My Lord, Gentlemen of the Jury – I feel deeply sorry for the deplorable interruption. May I assure you that I had no intention to provoke it and that no one can deplore it more than I do. But I beg you to grant me permission to reply to the interrupter's question – unwarranted as it was. Yes, I do remember what I said in reply to the gentleman's remark. I said: "There's something wrong with coppers. You can't punch them in the jaw when you want to." ' (Great commotion.) 'I am sorry, my Lord, Gentlemen of the Jury, that I have to draw this kind of language into this solemn and dignified place. But my moral conscience and my duty as prisoner at the bar demands of me that I furnish the Court with all information I may be able to give. The triumphant course of justice is the only aim of this trial – my own little self is nothing but one cog of many in the wheelwork of the carriage of justice. And so in the interest of justice I merely wish to point out the absurdity of the allegation that a criminal would be so careless as to leave the most important proof of his crime at the free disposal of anyone whom it might concern.

'Before we go on to the most important issue, the death of Ian Jensen, I must take the liberty to stretch your patience for another few minutes in order to point out the remaining mistakes in the case for the prosecution – those mistakes which enable the learned counsel for the prosecution to find a connection between the death of Estella Lamare and the death of Ian Jensen.

'The witness Dinah Lee testified that she saw a lady leave my house, Thursday night at four o'clock, when she claims to have found the film which the prosecution deigns to hold as evidence of my guilt.

'May I first point out the extreme improbability of the situation: a young lady pays a visit to a gentleman's flat at the highly unconventional hour of four o'clock in the morning. The young lady has no latchkey to the front door but just in order to help her the gods send her another lady who leaves the house at the very moment when the first young lady wants to enter. We have already pointed out the absurdity of the film on the doormat – now let us consider the absurdity of this young lady's intended visit which never came to the actual realization of the intention. The young lady goes away again without giving a sign of her presence to the gentleman, without even letting him know that she attempted to visit him that night.

'My Lord, Gentlemen of the Jury – I could again attack the witness's testimony – I could have proved her errors in the cross-examination – but I refrained from doing so in order to give the prosecution that chance which the prosecution never gave me. Let us now suppose that the testimony of the witness Dinah Lee be correct – let us believe her that she actually paid a visit to my house that night, that her good fairy sent her the dark, mysterious lady to open the door for her at exactly the right moment – let us even believe that the witness actually found the film on my doormat – let me ask you then, my Lord, Gentlemen of the Jury, is there any proof in this testimony that I must have lost the film on my doormat? Or even that I must have known of its existence?

'My Lord, Gentlemen of the Jury, I leave the answer for you to decide in your verdict. The mysterious lady who, may I remind you, has not been introduced by the defence but by the prosecution, is she not the most probable suspect? She came down the very staircase where only a minute later the witness Dinah Lee found the film. My Lord, Gentlemen of the Jury, I repeat my humble request: may Justice herself decide about this first stage of the charge that has been launched by irresponsible hands against me!

'Let us now proceed to the testimony of the witness Müller who declared that I had given him a report of the events which differed in many points from the official version given to him by Detective Inspector Smith.

'I wish to point out three facts in connection with this testimony:

'(1) That the testimony of the witness is correct: there was a discrepancy between my version of the events and the version given to the witness by Detective Inspector Smith.

'(2) Detective Inspector Smith's statements have so far proved unsatisfactory in practically every way. Therefore we cannot wonder that his version did not correspond to the actual and true facts as they were related by me to the witness Müller.

'(3) I allege that Detective Inspector Smith's version was indeed wilfully distorted and can therefore not be considered as the official version. This means that the testimony of the witness Müller that there was a discrepancy between my version and the "official" version can only be considered as evidence for the defence and not as evidence for the prosecution.

'Another important point which has to be cleared up before

we come to the final issues is the testimony of the witness for the prosecution, John Robertson.

'The prosecution alleges that I smuggled a map of Norway with the name of Ian Jensen's hiding-place underlined into Mr John Robertson's flat – an allegation that is supposed to prove my guilt. "Only a guilty man would attempt to guide suspicion on another man in that way," was the prosecutor's argument. I do not doubt the possible correctness of this logic. But I understood that the learned counsel for the prosecution was prepared to disprove my statement that I did not smuggle the map into Mr Robertson's flat. Meanwhile I had to discover to my great disappointment that the prosecution thought it satisfactory merely to point out the argument aforementioned and the discrepancy between their argument and my statement. I believe this astonishing way of trying to build up a case for the prosecution shows conclusively that the prosecution does not see fit to establish the truth of the charge that is made against me.' (Big commotion.)

'We now come to the vital point of the death of Ian Jensen. You will realize, my Lord, Gentlemen of the Jury, that I deliberately refrain from using the word "Murder" for the death of Ian Jensen – though I realize as clearly as you do that the evidence which has been produced seems to leave no doubt about the sad fact that the deceased's life ended in a violent death. But the case for the prosecution has so far proved invalid in so many aspects that I believe I can say without danger of exaggerating or of committing myself that in this trial every allegation made by the prosecution has to be weighed with more than normal caution.'

(Protest – commotion – the judge interrupts and warns me – then quiet again.)

I continued: 'Now we come to the final issues. Only a few minutes ago I had to refer to these final issues as *vital* issues. I cannot continue to do this any longer. The fact which made this final issue of Ian Jensen's death so extremely important was the allegation of the prosecution that there was a connection between the first and the second case of death. All the issues mentioned so far were not only minor counts in the indictment against me but also at the same time alleged *motives* for me to kill Ian Jensen. Now as we have disproved the first allegations there is no motive left which could have possibly given me any cause to kill Ian Jensen. So I believe I can declare with satisfaction that the case for the prosecution has broken down already at this early stage.'

(Commotion – interruption – warning – quiet again.)

'I could now finish my defence at this point: there is clearly no case against me! I could ask the Court to realize that there is no case against me. But I prefer to repeat instead my sincere conviction that the issue at stake is not the verdict on me but the correct judgement upon those dark issues connected with the two cases of death the mystery of which has to be solved – if not in the course of this trial, then in the course of another one. But whatever the next developments may be – this trial here will form the basis of any further jurisdiction upon the case.

'Therefore, my Lord, Gentlemen of the Jury, I beg you to lend me your ears for another few minutes so that I may point out all those matters known to me which might help to clear up the mystery of this case.

'First I wish to point out how strange it seems to me that nothing about this case has ever been said in any newspaper.'

(Laughter.)

'Normally the police are quite eager to avail themselves of the services of the Press which are at their disposal. Nothing of the kind has happened in this case. Is it a far-fetched question to ask why the police have never done so? Is it not very natural to wonder whether – perhaps – the police did not feel quite sure of their case – not sure enough, perhaps, to carry it into the papers?'

(Slight commotion.)

'This is another question which I leave for the jury to answer.

'Another point which seems extremely strange is Ian Jensen's return to England. The chief witness for the prosecution stated in the cross-examination that only the frontier officials like immigration officers were furnished with orders to detain Jensen. It seems strange that Jensen should have known this fact so well that he could choose the one possible way which would not bring him into contact with any frontier officials: the way of travelling by air and landing on the private aerodrome of his flying-club where nobody would betray his arrival – one of those conveniences which make flying-clubs so popular.'

There was a slight stir, but no protest.

I waited a moment and continued: 'And so we finally come to those issues which form – or rather *formed* – the chief charge against me: the charge of the murder of Ian Jensen.

'The only support for this fantastic theory is the testimony of the witness – Smith.'

I hesitated, suddenly realizing that I did not know his first name. It was my only hesitation in the course of the whole trial.

Later on when I came to think about it I realized how much they would have liked it in Vienna.

The judge passed it. I said: 'The witness testified that he saw me enter Ian Jensen's house Thursday night at twelve o'clock and leave it half an hour later. The housekeeper found Jensen's dead body the next morning.

'My Lord, Gentlemen of the Jury – need I point out the extreme flimsiness of this supposed "evidence". I have asked you before to treat the testimony given by this particular witness with the greatest care. I do not wish to repeat myself but may I also point out the extreme resemblance which this evidence bears to the evidence submitted by the garage man? If you look at those two statements which were made by these two witnesses for the prosecution you will realize, however, that it is not the defence but the prosecution which repeats itself, thereby forcing the defence to follow in its tracks. In both cases the witnesses testified:

'(a) that they saw me enter the house at a specified time;
'(b) that they saw me leave the house at a specified time;
'(c) that the dead body was found in the house more than seven hours later.

'May I again inform the prosecution that these testimonies are inadmissible as circumstantial evidence, because the prosecution failed to prove that there was no other person in the house during the whole period of time between my entrance and the discovery of the body. Anybody else could have committed the crime at any time between my exit and the discovery of the body. The witness declared explicitly that he ceased watching Ian Jensen's house when I left it and that he followed me back to Bennett Street and went home after he had assured himself that I was asleep.

'But not only could the crime have been committed at any time between my exit from Ian Jensen's house and the discovery of the body the next morning – it could also have been committed even during the time of my presence in the house: the witness for the prosecution utterly failed to give any information as to my actions in Ian Jensen's house between twelve o'clock and twelve thirty.

'Considering these facts it seems very strange to me that the witness who at an earlier date gave me an exact report of the scene that was supposed to have taken place between Ian Jensen and me, should not have been able to establish any of his carefully detailed statements here in the witness-box. I can only conclude that either the statement made by the witness at an earlier date or his testimony given here in front of this Court must be false or at least strangely careless.'

(Commotion, growing hostility against the prosecution, growing applause for me, the judge orders silence and I proceed.)

'Though the witness at this earlier date saw his way to repeat even bits of my alleged conversation with Ian Jensen he stated today that he did not even know the fact that 69 Delilah Square was Ian Jensen's house.

'If we believe the latter statement – and I am rather inclined to take this course – then we have here more proof of the extreme unreliability of this witness on whose testimony my life depends. May I now come back to my first point: the strange similarity between the evidence given by the garage man and the evidence given by the chief witness for the prosecution. May I draw your attention to the significant fact that not only is the argument equally flimsy in both cases but also that the designs of the two statements are so amazingly similar that a strange suspicion might enter even the unsuspecting onlooker's mind – the suspicion that both statements were deliberately manufactured at the same source.'

The counsel for the prosecution jumped up. 'My Lord, this is an outrage! I protest,' he shouted.

I said: 'I am sorry, my Lord; I promised to point out all those matters known to me which might help to throw light upon the dark issues at stake. The whole case for the prosecution is faulty in every point, up to the last detail of my act of stopping the projector when the film came to the critical point: every innocent person would have done the same. There is no more evidence of my guilt in this last allegation than there was in any other allegation made against me. There is no case at all against me. This is the end of the defence. With your leave, my Lord, Gentlemen of the Jury, I wish to thank you for your patience and kind attention. I do not wish to finish with a plea. I think the case is clear enough; let the law take its course. I can but pray that the verdict be a just one.'

There was enormous applause from the audience. The judge ordered silence. The silence was even more tensely excited than the commotions had been before.

The counsel for the prosecution had sweat on his face. He looked like Bloom after too many pastries. He could not reply. If I had had a lawyer he would have had a right to reply.

I was glad I had no lawyer.

The judge began the summing-up. He explained the law as I had learned it from Harris: as it was applicable to the case. He marshalled the evidence so that it might more readily understood and remembered by the jury. He first stated to them the substance of the charge against me – which was murder; he explained to them the law upon the subject of murder; he referred to the evidence which had been adduced in support of the charge and could not hide his disappointment that he found it as poor as I had found it; he made some observations to connect the evidence, to apply it to the charge and to render the whole plain and intelligible – which was not easy and I did not envy him. Then he stated my defence and did it well. And so he came to the conclusion, telling the jury that, if upon considering the whole of the evidence, they entertained a fair and reasonable doubt of the guilt of the prisoner, they should give the prisoner the benefit of that doubt and acquit him.

They did entertain a fair and reasonable doubt of the guilt of the prisoner and they did give the prisoner the benefit of that doubt and they acquitted me.

The verdict was delivered by the foreman of the jury. He was the Quaker. He had pink cheeks and gold teeth and wore a pince-nez.

The Clerk of Assize had hardly addressed him with: 'How say you, do you find Cameron McCabe guilty or not guilty?' when he replied 'Not guilty' and the fun broke loose.

It was a general verdict: not guilty on the whole charge.

I was discharged without any comment.

It was an acquittal with flags flying. The audience kicked up a devil of a row – but it was a pleasant row: shouts, laughter and applause – the picture-snatchers worked like hell – the news-hawks smashed the telephone cells – the judge tried to smile but gave it up soon – the jury came to shake hands with me – the prosecutor laughed embarrassedly and said he had enjoyed it – Smith had disappeared – I saw none of the others.

The crowd carried me out on their shoulders. An old woman wept and a girl put her visiting card into my hand.

She looked pretty and she smelled good.

When I got home I rang Maria.

She was there and rang off when she heard my voice.

I rang Dinah.

She was not there. I left a message for her to ring me during the next hour or two.

She did not ring.

I took the visiting card out of my pocket. Her name was Miriam Pascal. A good name. She lived in Highgate Village.

I phoned her.

She said yes.

I took the car out of the garage and drove out into the fog.

It was colder today. Winter had finally begun. There was cold white wet thin snow in the fog.

Twenty-five

The morning was black with fog and later on still dark without colour but finally dull yellow when the sun came out. And all the time it was wet and colder than ice with the wind cutting across the car when I slid down from Highgate Hill to the Archway. And I felt my clothes all over wet and clammy and spongy like mud but colder and more queasy.

I felt dead empty. I felt so empty it hurt in all limbs. I heard an alarm clock in the quiet mist. It was not loud. There was a window between and it stopped soon. A stray dog started across the street and I had to brake sharply. At the Nag's Head I met another car and for some time I followed it till it turned off to the left into a dark turning. I was on the rails and I did not expect a street-car. But then a Number 7 car came up Caledonian Road and I swung into a right turning where it was even quieter than on the road and I said:

'But what becometh of my honeymoon
When all the honey turneth stale so soon?'

I said it again and again with the vibrations of the car. But it was not till long afterwards that I realized I had said anything.

I felt so empty, no man ever felt empty like that.

Three kids, arms interlocked, marched along King's Cross Road and sang. They should have been in bed.

After I had put the car in the garage I walked up to Bennett Street to change.

I had opened the front door and was walking up the stairs when somebody got up in front of me. He had been sleeping there on the stairs.

I said: 'Hallo, Smith, I didn't expect you so early.'

'Early!' he said. 'When I came it was late.'

'Last night?' I asked.

'Sure,' he said.

'You had a pleasant night?' I inquired politely.

'I was going to show you that it was possible to get in without a key,' he said.

I said: 'I never doubted it.'

He said: 'You didn't say so at the trial.'

'Would you like to get yourself hanged?' I asked him.

'Would you like to lose your job?' he asked back.

'So they finally threw you overboard?'

I could not help saying it. I did not try to hide it that I felt glad he too had now made the acquaintance of that feeling I had carried with me for more than four weeks. I had not felt well, by God, I had not.

I said: 'All players lose. Why did you play? If you don't want to risk it, don't play. But don't tell me afterwards I didn't play fair. You didn't either. And fairness between two means that they use the same methods, not one worse methods than the other. But when they are both bad it makes them even and the game becomes fair and balanced again.'

'Yeah,' he said, 'that's what you say. But I don't like it. You wouldn't like it either if you were in my place. Not only that you wouldn't say it – you would not even think it; it's winner's wisdom. You think it now 'cause you think you've won. But you haven't. You only think you have. You haven't won as far as I'm concerned. Not as long as it makes me the loser. No sir, that's a joke; I'm not going to take it.'

He was quite white in his face and you could see he meant what he said and he felt it. He was quite impressive as he stood there and I got some kind of respect for him. He did exactly what I would have done in his place and I understood him and I liked him better than ever before.

'So what are you going to do about it?' I asked him and even before I had begun talking I knew what I had to expect.

'I'm going to finish you off,' he said. 'A copper's job doesn't seem to have much sense if a louse like you can get away with it and make fun of the law afterwards.'

'That's a fine twist,' I said. 'It kind of tops my humble efforts.'

'It sure does,' he said without vanity.

'Yes,' I said, 'it tops it so much that it'll bring you close enough to the top of the gallows. It's as good a look-out as any. You'll have a fine view of us poor lice who can't get higher than on people's heads.'

'Sure,' he said, 'but you first had a fine time wallowing in the filth. I didn't even have that. Seems kind of not quite right, somehow.'

'Wallowing in the filth,' I thought. Digging up the mud. Playing underground trains. Two children in King's Cross Road one rainy afternoon long long ago. Lost and gone. Now Smith.

'All right,' I said. 'Let's get to business. You going to shoot me in the back or poison me with ratsbane or hang me from the chandelier or knock me on the head with two feet of rubber hose or what? May I choose or are you going to do the job of picking out the most suitable method for me?'

'I'm a fairly adequate shot, McCabe. I'm leaving all the other methods to you. I don't like trespassing on other people's territory.'

'I appreciate that all right. Is there anything I can do for you before you bump me off and get yourself hanged for murder?'

I did not expect an answer but he said: 'Yes, there is. You can tell me whether you killed Jensen or whether you didn't.'

That was a hell of a surprise for me. I had never doubted that he had known it all along.

'I killed him,' I said.

'I knew it,' he said.

'And I don't feel sorry about it,' I said. 'He was a damned sucker and he wasn't fit to live as life should be lived.' And then I added: 'And you aren't fit for it either.'

He looked at me with cold hopeless humourless eyes. 'But my theory was correct, wasn't it?' he said.

'It was,' I said. 'Every part of it. Only you didn't have enough to lose. So you couldn't win your case. And Jensen was a supernumerary. So I threw him overboard, the same as I did with your charge against me.'

'Yes,' he said, 'and you are a supernumerary now and I'm throwing you overboard.'

'Sure,' I said, 'and then someone will find you are a supernumerary and he'll throw you overboard. And you can go on with that for quite a long time. We're getting along fine.'

'You can't blame a pig for wallowing in the mire. You can't blame a parasite for sponging upon others. You can't blame a poison snake for killing you when it bites you. What you can do is wipe it out, get rid of it, render it harmless that way.'

'That sounds like a Hyde Park Corner speech on capital punishment,' I said.

'It's more,' he said. 'It's an incitement to take justice into your own hands when the net of official jurisdiction has got so loose that the fish get out of it as easily as they get in.'

'And there you said more than you know, brother Smith. Take the law into your own hands, first as individuals and call it outlawry, then as nations and call it war. A fine way of justifying the come-back of medievalism. Bribing, protection-racketeering, gangsterizing the government: call it gangsterism in the States and fascism in the Old Country. All right and that's a fine prologue for heaven or hell, whichever it may be. All right, don't say anything, brother, don't talk, do something. It isn't much good here anyway with people like me preaching and people like you gunning. But if you give me a couple of minutes I'll be happy about it. I want to get my things in order. It's the pedant in me, forgive me. I'm writing it down as it happens, there isn't much left beside that. This thing has a funny smell but if you remember it and put it down and let others read it and if they see it again and feel it again and hear it tick and smell its funny insistent smell again and maybe like it and maybe don't but smell it as it is and always was and always will be after all the changes have come and gone – if you try to do it and get it done and feel that it was worth doing then you've done what you could do and it's no use trying to find out whether it was really worth it and whether the others found it was worth it and whether it did what it set out to do: whether it did change what it set out to change. I've written it down as it is and was and came along and there are still some few pages left to be filled with what is happening now. Sit down, brother, and give me a few minutes.'

'I'll wait next door,' he said. 'The telephone is cut off. If you open the window I shoot. If you shout I shoot. When you call me I'll come in.'

'The same old blunderer to the end,' I said. 'You won't learn it, brother. You're too damned hopeless. I don't want to phone and I don't want to jump out of the window and I don't want to kick up a row. I want to write. If I wanted I could have blown you out half an hour ago,' and I took my gun out of my pocket and held it out to him.

'Give it to me,' he said.

I laughed.

'All right,' I said. 'It's hopeless, brother. You won't ever learn it. It's good they are going to hang you after this,' and I gave him the gun.

When he took it his skin was so white you could have thought he had died a long time ago. His hand, when I touched it, was colder than the gun. His mouth was yellow, hard, hopeless – the most desperate mouth I'd ever seen. His eyes, too, had died a long time ago and the skin around his eyes had sunk so deep that the apple of the eye stood out more than half an inch. There was black sweat in the rings all round his eyes and his teeth ground the flesh of his lips inside.

He said nothing and walked out without looking back. But when he opened the door he shivered and turned his coat up.

I sat down and lit a cigarette and took out the paper and wrote the last pages from where I had left them last night before I had gone up to Miriam Pascal till now as I am sitting here writing this.

I don't feel sorry that I've killed Jensen and I don't feel sorry that Smith is going to kill me now but I do feel sorry that it has all been so damned futile. Of course, I can try to convince myself that I have killed Jensen because he was no good – just like Smith is trying now to convince himself that he is killing me because I am no good. But I won't try to fool myself that way. I killed Jensen because he came between Maria and me and as I couldn't live without Maria there was nothing to do but to get Jensen out of the way. So he had to go. Of course I also remembered that 'Thou shalt not kill.' Oh, the hypocrisy of it! They killed one another in war time and on the barricades under one pretext or another, and often it was not a question of life and death. But if you can't live without a woman and a man comes between you and the woman then it's a matter of life and death between you and him. And I wouldn't have said to Jensen, 'Thou shalt not kill,' if he had tried to kill me for the same reason. I would have seen his point just as I had seen the prosecutor's point during the trial and as I am now seeing Smith's point. But I wouldn't have allowed Jensen to kill me just as I hadn't allowed the prosecutor to get me sentenced for murder. Yet I don't mind Smith now. It is as good an end as any and better than a lot of other endings that might have happened to me.

I had fought the prosecutor as long as I had believed that Maria would be there at the end of the trial. But now the trial was finished and I had seen that Maria was no longer there and so there was not much sense in fighting Smith any longer.

All right then, this was the end of the fight. It had been a good fight as long as it had lasted. It had been a fight even before I had known that it was going to be one. It had opened that way with Müller's report of the Grainger-Bennett fight, given at King's

Cross tube station in the middle of clerks and typists rushing home, one late afternoon in November with the feel of July or August and the sky orange and heavy on top of you, but red and lighter in the west. I remembered the smell of the evening with too many things in the air, the chimneys and the exhausts and the perfume of powder and lipstick and hair oil and sweat and Müller in the middle of it, introducing himself without introduction and telling the story of the Grainger-Bennett fight without comment and his face pink and his hair brownish grey like gunmetal.

'It was no murder story, no detective story, no thriller, but a plain good fight.' Müller would insist on that even now if he could see how it was to end.

He was the only one who knew. He had known it from the beginning on. He had known it before I had known it myself.

Hair like gunmetal. 'It was a fight, a battle, a war . . .' he would say.

'All right,' I would say.

'All right for you,' he would say. 'But I'm German: we've lost the war and that makes it different with us.'

'We've lost it too,' I would tell him. 'We've all lost the war. In a war you can't do anything else but lose.'

He wouldn't believe it. He would insist: 'It's all very well for you to say: you're American – you've won the last war . . .'

'Yeah, that's what they'll tell our kids at school,' I would say. 'It's all wrong. We haven't won the war any more than you have. Nobody has won the war. Not those who made it to make a profit out of it and not even those who made the profit. Nobody has ever won any war. You can't win a war. You just can't do anything but lose. You lose if you fight and you lose if you don't. You lose if you fight against fighting and you lose if you let them fight as they please. You lose when you're the victor and you lose when you're the defeated. A fight is no game, but all fighters lose as all gamblers and all players always lose. Smith lost – he lost his job and now he's losing the fight because I'm not fighting any longer and soon he's going to lose all he has to lose, just like Estella did and Jensen did.'

I knew now what it must feel like to lose as Estella had lost when she had stood there, looking after Jensen who wouldn't come back, looking after him who had gone, finding that it wasn't worth it: she was alone. I knew it now as she had known it then. They always catch you. There's no way out for you. No way out for a woman once a man has got hold of her. No way out for a man once a woman has got hold of him. Fight it – and it won't fight back. One night in December five nights after Müller had told me the story of the fight, one Tuesday night in the docks I had known it. Fight it – and it won't fight back. Try to dodge it – and it will kill you from behind. Run away – and it won't follow you. But it will get you in the end.

And it has sure got me in the end. No reply from Maria, no reply from Dinah. Oh Lord! What had I killed Jensen for if Maria wouldn't reply afterwards? She would fight with Dinah, but she wouldn't be there in the end when I wanted her. She would flirt with Jensen and sleep with him – but she wouldn't cry after he'd gone. She would help me to cheat Smith – but she would testify for him in the end. She would say 'Mac, one of these days I'll fly off the handle and give you what's coming to you' because she didn't like me flirting with Dinah – but she wouldn't mind herself sleeping with Jensen. And in the end she would go.

Smith double-crossed Robertson but Robertson stuck to Smith. I did not double-cross Maria but she thought I did – and she would not stick to me. And Smith thought I had double-crossed him – and he would stick to his childish ideas about law and order and private justice. And would not know all the time that he was merely feeling sick about losing his job and would never admit that he had only himself to blame for it.

I could not do much except writing it down as it came along and Müller would read and say: 'How funny, those modern he-mannerisms: telling important things in a trifling way and trifles with an important air, saying things you don't think and thinking things you don't say. If you would even say the opposite of what you think and do the opposite of what you say – then you could make good writing of it. But as it is . . .'

'It isn't good writing,' I would tell him. 'It's a story for Maria. But she's too damned dumb to read it. So it's a story for you.'

'It isn't,' he would say. 'Things are different with me. As I grow older and as I learn to understand things the things convince me more and more that the art of story-telling – like all arts – is nothing so mysteriously undefinable as I have always been told to believe. If you follow the line of art which was art when it was made and remained art after the man who made it had gone back to the earth he came from, you will soon see that only that is art which enables you to find in it what you are able to see – to find all that you are able to see and nothing more and nothing less and damned little else – you'll find it's always so simple that the simplest of you can understand and appreciate and enjoy it but the man who made it had to put in so much that those of you who have learned to see can see anything their eyes will take in and more than that: all they'll ever want to see, and they'll see it as well as the poorer ones see all they are able to get into their poor eyes.'

'I know,' I would say.

'If you know why don't you write it that way?' he would ask.

'I'll try it next time,' I would tell him.

All right, now the time is up. I'll send it off as it is.

I have written out the envelope and addressed it to Müller.

Maybe he'll know what to do with it. If he doesn't it won't matter. The things that matter aren't said in detective stories anyway.

All right, now I call Smith.

An Epilogue
by A. B. C. Müller
as Epitaph for
Cameron McCabe

I

My name is A. B. C. Müller. I want to say how sorry I feel for the alphabet of my initials. They stand for Adolf Benito Comrade. Originally Comrade was Conrad. But to balance the allied powers of Adolf and Benito I felt obliged to introduce some left-wing appeal.

This is all I can say about myself. Everything else that could possibly be of any interest to the readers of Mr McCabe's book has been said by Mr McCabe himself.

I can only add that I would very much like to apologize for this unwarranted intrusion into Mr McCabe's story. I humbly wish to apologize for the inexcusable officiousness of adding my unauthoritative comments to another person's work. I humbly wish to apologize for every word of this commentary, but, alas, I am not at liberty to do as I wish. By force of Mr McCabe's last will I appear to have become foster-father to this literary child of his. Watching myself in the mirror of my vanity I see a rather unwilling father, his heart throbbing with a somewhat unbalanced alloy of surprise, mystification, faint anger and greatly dominating awe.

Awe because I feel that Mr McCabe did his best, and anger because I find that Mr McCabe had prejudiced his readers against me, that he has introduced me into his story and thus deprived me of the right to introduce myself and to apologize for the intrusion. I am not even allowed to speak of my officiousness; Mr McCabe would protestingly point out my damned duty, as his brainchild's foster-father, to take care of it in the most officious manner possible.

No restitution can be made – a state of affairs which I

welcome because it allows me to come right to the point which the perusal of Mr McCabe's book urges me to make.

II

I received Mr McCabe's last letter, the manuscript of this book, six hours after his death, a bundle of notes tied together with a lady's silk stocking which on inquiry proved to be Miss Ray's property.

I read the notes in the course of the next six hours, utterly at a loss what to make of them. Every normal man in Mr McCabe's place would have written a diary. I was almost shocked when I found a novel instead – or, rather, a story that read like a novel, was built on a definite literary pattern, had plot and construction and outline of character, and was yet nothing but the autography of a man's last few days before his death.

It was not till I had finished the last line of the last page that I realized McCabe was no longer alive. I rang McCabe's flat and got no reply: Smith had already left to give himself up. On his way to his own department in Scotland Yard he had posted McCabe's last letter, the notes to *The Face on the Cutting-Room Floor*, addressed to me.

An ironic comment on an ironic situation.

The *Observer* said on 6th December, when it reviewed the first edition of Mr McCabe's book: 'Open confession may be good for the soul: it certainly makes for more sensational writing than does the consuming of one's own smoke. This wide-open confession, while verging occasionally on the sentimental, will be either devoured by the reader or fastidiously eschewed.' I had no possibility to eschew the confession. And I did devour it. But not because of its literary merits: it was the closeness of the real living drama that made me read it.

And the propinquity of the events is affecting us still now, many months afterwards; the trial of Inspector Smith is still in everyone's memory; the violent death of Mr McCabe and the nation-wide publicity which followed the trial are still lending a curiously malicious poignancy to a basically simple case; the painful sharpness of those last hours of the trial, the strange perversity of that pleasantly piquant attraction which the case seemed to hold even for the sober-minded spectators, even for the readers who followed the trial in the papers, even for the listeners at the wireless – all of it is still affecting all of us. And it will have to be seen whether McCabe's story, as a work of literature, will be able to exist on its own merits; whether its oddly pungent effect was not merely a reflection of the trial; whether the book – as a book – will still have the power to affect us after the smoke and thunder of the case will be forgotten, leaving dead and waxen what was once living and warm under our touch, leaving only waxworks where life was once so strongly lived, waxworks in fine clothes, but the fine clothes also soon decaying, the gold and purple rotting, the splendour putrefying, the pomp of the poor earthly raiment falling to shreds, then to dust, finally leaving the waxen flesh cold, nude and tainted in the green light of the last morning.

III

The tests of a story like this are manifold. As Mr McCabe's trustee, holding this literary heritage in trust for him, I can but try to clarify the exact properties of this somewhat unusual legacy, its credits and debits.

I find my task eased by time. Now, more than twelve months after the trial and more than six months after the first serial publication of the story, I have the reports and reviews, the comments and remarks of the book critics and reviewers at my disposal and it is indeed a very comprehensive picture of public opinion which we obtain by studying their comments, by comparing their opinions, by testing protagonist against antagonist, hammer against anvil. Most of the critics, following the established rules of their trade, abstained wisely from taking the actual facts of the case into account and concentrated on the merely literary merits or shortcomings of the story, as if it were a work of fiction. Very few chose to inquire into Mr McCabe's analysis of the historic and social background of the case. I remember Mr Gerald Gould's review, which was published in the London *Observer* on 20th September, 1936. It contained a most excellent sentence which characterized the situation quite admirably.

'Now I, as a novel-reviewer,' says Mr Gould, 'have nothing whatever to do with whether this analysis is historically or sociologically correct: the sole question I have here to ask myself is whether Mr McCabe does or does not succeed in absorbing me into the world he takes for granted.'

I might be excused if I beg to differ. As a participant in the case – a minor participant, it is true, but nevertheless one who, just because of his lesser degree of participation, could steer free of partisanship, without, however, missing any detail of the actual events – I might be permitted to state my conviction most emphatically that in the case of Mr McCabe it was the correctness of the historical and sociological analysis which helped him to give a true picture of certain events, and it was the absence of a correct analysis in other parts of the book which caused his failure to give a true picture of certain other events. The reason for this is that in Mr McCabe's book – as in every book that is based on actual events – it is the historical and social background of the characters which explains them both to the author and to the reader.

The forces which move the characters originate from their historical and social background. And both pattern and plot of the story originate from this movement of the characters.

Every writer knows this. And every writer likes to forget it: it is less difficult to invent motives for one's characters than to analyse and describe the motives which would have moved them if they had been actual people. He likes to forget that both pattern and plot of his story reflect the forces which have influenced him, the author, himself: they reflect his whole mental inheritance, which is a filtrate of all his ancestors' collected experiences; all his own experiences, which are a filtrate of the combined influences of the men with whom he has come into important contact; parents, relatives, friends, schoolteachers, superiors, subordinates. The direct influence of propaganda, publicity and agitation; newspapers, books, posters; radio and cinema; exchange of gossip and argument; the office, the factory, the farmhouse, the pub, the club, the trade union, the employment exchange: in short, the influence of society on the individual: his *historical* and *sociological* background.

Mr McCabe was a typical twentieth-century big-city middle-class man, especially post-war in his attitude towards that present-day structure of society which he himself helped to build, therefore both creator and creation, unwilling creator and unwitting victim of that social development which began in the eighteenth century, grew up during the nineteenth century, ripened, flowered and showed plainly evident signs of early decay at the beginning of our age and is now fighting a last desperate and losing struggle against odds of its own creation.

This development, the growing concentration of capital in fewer hands, cannot fail to influence the psychological outlook of the individual. A pressing need, ever growing in urgency of pressure, to earn increasingly more money so as not to sink into a relative pauperization forces his standard of values to undergo a profound change: the so-called 'eternal' values disappear and are replaced by values of the moment: the mercenary aspect becomes

dominating: the individu[...]
a growing disregard for th[...]
become purchasable and m[...]

Considered from this p[...]
Room Floor is not the story of [...]
the autobiography of a rather aver[...]
of our age who became a murd[...]
innate criminal tendencies but me[...]
certain typical present-day tendencie[...]
in almost every contemporary big-city [...]

McCabe is, even at the beginnir[...]
young man who shows the normal marks [...]
certain innate toughness of the 'dour Sc[...] [...]ound
support and amplification in that modern Am[...], ashamed
of its pioneer toughness, produced a first reac[...] [...]owards a curiously sugary sentimentality and a second reaction towards a synthetic and romantic modern toughness which is typified by writers
like Hemingway, Hammett, Cain, McCoy, Fessier and, to a certain
extent, by the O'Hara of *Appointment in Samarra*.

It is a long dialectic history which leads up to this latest
stage. The Pioneer-Western-Red-Indian-Gold-Digger toughness
formed the basic thesis which found its antithesis as soon as the
men settled down and required their women.

The scarcity of women enhanced their value. All rare goods
are expensive. Caviare is treated with more reverence than pork.
Champagne is not only more expensive than Coca-Cola, but it is
also of a greater sentimental value – not because it tastes better but
simply because it is more rare.

Women, therefore, attained a greater sentimental value in
Pioneer America than in Old Europe.

Sentimental attachments breed like rabbits. That curious
sentiment commercially known as 'love' would never have
attained its present-day face value if people had not talked so much
about it. It's like abroad: no one would want to go there if they
hadn't been told it existed, as Evelyn Waugh says. People who have
to work hard don't talk about love. They are in love, but they don't
make any fuss of it. Only idle people and people without partners
of the other sex talk about love. And once the talk has started it
never stops. It is an infectious disease. The uninfected ones become
sceptic: there must be something in it if it catches on like this. So
they put their nose into it. And already they have caught it.

America was dangerously ill with the disease. This could
not remain without reaction. The new thesis of aggressive

d. And soon it absorbed the earlier
formed a new synthesis – new only in the
ot in its ingredients – another egg laid into the
American nest by that funny bird History.

rtain peculiarities of the new egg became soon evident:
de it seemed hard-boiled but inside it proved soft: 'Hard-
boiled but soft-hearted.'

To hide the soft interior the thing produced a fine weather-
proof shell of nonchalance. Nothing mattered, nothing held any
surprise, nothing caused embarrassment, nothing was good,
nothing bad, everything was accepted as a matter of course.

It looked like cynicism, like superhuman detachment, like
perfect stoicism.

All is not dirt that does not glitter: there was a core of mild-
heartedness in these young men and women. But their hearts were
in their heels: the mild-heartedness was their Achilles heel, their
vulnerable spot, their weak point to be carefully hidden, their
innermost secret, their well of shame.

IV

McCabe was deeply in love with Maria Ray. His flirt with Dinah
Lee was passing, pleasant, but not sincere. It was of importance to
Dinah Lee, not to McCabe.

There can be no doubt that McCabe really loved Maria
Ray: 'I knew that I didn't give a damn for Dinah Lee and I knew
that there was Maria Ray and I knew that I would never be able to
get away from Maria Ray and now I knew it for certain.' Or, in the
eighth chapter: '. . . she smiled. The smile brought me down on my
knees and made me kiss her. Through the roughness of the sheets I
felt the softness of her body on my lips and the touch made me faint
with love.'

In *The Times Literary Supplement* of 9th May a reviewer
doubts whether this might rightly be called love. Whether it is not
merely physical passion or even plain vulgarity: 'Maria lends herself
very easily to her part in a relationship that is erotic without the full
dignity of passion. So far as the minor sensualities of looking and
touching are concerned, the two were evidently made for each other;
and this quality, which for lack of a less harsh term must be called
vulgarity . . .' etc.

I cannot reply to this sort of criticism. But I want to let *The
Times Literary Supplement*'s mother journal speak for me. In *The*

Times book column of 27th October we find the following sentences: 'In the fever of city life infatuations are apt to grow like mushrooms. The noise, the hurry and the sensation of being one alone among millions of unknown and therefore exciting people, make for a curious instability in those who live on what may be called the fringe of the artistic world. What they conceive to be love becomes with them an obsession and the whole of experience.'

Here is the key to McCabe's whole story, to his crime, to his curious love story, to McCabe himself, to Maria, to their interrelation and to McCabe's account of it.

I tried to show Mr McCabe's dependence on the age, class and environment from which he came: twentieth-century, middle-class and big-city, a product of the pressing need 'to earn increasingly more money so as not to sink into a relative pauperization'. This pressure produced a void, which is normally filled – and filled it must be – with the primitive essentials of human requirements: food and the other sex. Parts of the void are filled with various kinds of dope: with the last fragments of nineteenth-century religion, with nineteenth- and twentieth-century bogus politics, with pseudo-science, pseudo-art and other substitutional products of modern civilization. The result: 'a growing disregard for those human qualities which have not yet become purchasable and marketable merchandise'.

'*The fever of city life* – noise – hurry – the sensation of being one alone among millions of unknown and therefore exciting people': all of it breaks through McCabe's account in almost every line. McCabe in Soho, McCabe in the docks, McCabe in a traffic block on the way home from Whitechapel, McCabe in a Negro night-club – there is no getting away from it.

Here '*infatuations are apt to grow like mushrooms*'. 'Sentimental attachments breed like rabbits': what the inhabitants of this world 'conceive to be love becomes with them an obsession and the whole of experience': it fills the great void.

But once an infatuation becomes 'an obsession and the whole of experience', what else is it then but love? A peculiar kind of love, it is true, a post-war, big-city kind of love, but *love* nevertheless, love so strong and complete that it 'fills the whole of experience'.

And if it fills the whole of experience then there is simply nothing else left. Nothing else matters, neither the rules of society nor the code of morals, neither the law external nor the law internal. Even murder is no longer a crime – it is simply a means to an end, a natural and necessary means to an all-justifying end: 'There's no way out for you ... No way out for a man once a woman has got hold of him.'

Maria becomes an obsession, the whole of experience. But Jensen is about to take her away. The whole of existence is in danger. Therefore Jensen must be got out of the way. First by cunning and trickery, then, both having failed, by force.

V

But the crime does not come off. Not because McCabe is detected as the murderer, but because Maria leaves him in spite of the murder. To be exact: just because of the murder. Which is only natural.

So we find McCabe in the end bemoaning the ultimate futility of all things: 'Oh Lord! what had I killed Jensen for, if Maria wouldn't reply afterwards.'

Reason begins to work again after a long time of utter confusion of all senses.

This can be clearly followed in McCabe's own words.

In the beginning his brain works very well. He realizes the social futility of his work: '. . . a worker working on a work that does not help to make the world better . . .'

He comes to realize even the dilemma of society and its influence on his own crime.

At the beginning of chapter nineteen he meditates on this: 'It makes you think and once you start thinking you see it's all messed up. And if you try to clear up the mess you get a kick in the pants. They like to keep it muddled up as it is. It's better for them. They get more out of it.'

Now if I understand this correctly, I must assume that 'they' is meant to stand for the rulers of present-day society, in short, to use the Marxist term, the *ruling class*.

Then we must accept Mr McCabe as a rather extremist social critic, in fact that type of social critic which is liable to coin slogans like 'Exploit the Exploiters' or 'Don't produce any surplus value by working. Only Mugs work. The Wide people enjoy the fruits of the Mugs' labour.'

This type of social-parasite-turned-social-critic is bound to develop convictions like this uttered by Mr McCabe in a later paragraph of the same chapter nineteen:

'If a guy allows you to make a sap of him you'd better take your hat and go away. It's better to be welshed on and know it than to welsh on another guy and get away with it': *fascist heroism*: there is honour between gangsters.

And again a few lines later:

'Get your food before the other one gets it: he is also hungry. Hit him on the jaw when he tries to be quicker': *fascist economics*.

This gangster-cum-fascist philosophy shows its plainly hysterical character as it reaches its final stage which can be found in sentences like: 'Never let a bad man down: the good ones will follow you. But there are few good ones left. The penitence is long but the deed was short enough.'

Here one can clearly discover the way of a diseased mind, working from a sound analysis of society into a complete intellectual and moral muddle, a muddle that is a direct product and an exact image of the muddle of society itself.

VI

The muddle of society, reflected in McCabe's brain, is naturally re-reflected in his actions and views. These are reflected in the third power by his book, both in plot and pattern. The *plot* is merely an account of the actual events which were, however, nothing else but McCabe's actions and reactions towards the other 'characters'.

The *pattern* of construction of Mr McCabe's book is the *circulus vitiosus*. Like the degenerating society which he represents McCabe tries to prove one proposition from another that depends on the first for proof.

McCabe gained his acquittal by pointing out the irregularities in Smith's conduct of the investigations. Smith, therefore, was directly responsible for McCabe's acquittal. McCabe's acquittal, however, caused Smith to kill McCabe. And so Smith was hanged because he helped – against his own will – to get McCabe acquitted.

A plain vicious circle of events for which McCabe is responsible and which forms, at the same time, the plot of his book.

The pattern follows the plot: McCabe tells and retells the same story over and over again – not because he aims consciously at a literary pattern but because he is incapable of writing the story in any other way: the pattern of the story, with its constant repetitions which lead always back to the start, reflects the same vicious circle which we find in the plot and which we will later find for the third time in the style of writing which McCabe adopts to transmit plot and pattern of his book to his readers.

In the first nineteen chapters we get the story told in the first form by McCabe. Then in the twentieth chapter we get it all retold by Smith. In the twenty-first chapter we get it for the third time in the special version which McCabe makes up for my benefit. In the twenty-second chapter we get it served up for the fourth time – this time again told by Smith. In the twenty-third chapter you have that conversation between Smith and McCabe which begins like 'the famous solution dinner that should occur at the end of every good detective story'. It begins like that, but it ends in disaster and repetition: you get the story warmed up for the fifth time. Then, in the twenty-fourth chapter you get the counsel for the prosecution innocently telling you the same thing for the sixth time. When the prosecutor has finished McCabe gets up and starts his defence, in the course of which all good things become seven. McCabe is acquitted, spends the night in Highgate Village, comes back the next morning and finds Smith on his doorstep. So you get the conversation between the two which brings the number of repetitions up to eight. And it is not the end yet. Not even McCabe's death ends it. He writes a last will and makes me tell you the story now again for the ninth time.

It is true that every time the story is retold you learn more about it, new clues are discovered, new facts are disclosed, you see the thing from a new angle.

A dialectic method; things are built up only in order to be broken down again: evidence is discovered in one version of the story only to be discovered as worthless in the next one. First the mere facts are described, but no explanation is given. Then you get the explanation, but a few lines later you learn that the explanation was all wrong. And Mr McCabe proceeds to give you some new information which changes everything completely. In the next chapter, however, the same thing starts all over again. The old explanations are recanted and new information is given. This is again recanted in the next chapter and so it goes on and on: uncertainty and instability govern. Nothing is firmly fixed, nothing steadfast, nothing solidly established. Everything is in the process of change, demolition, destruction, decay: an exact picture of the man and his age.

McCabe, morally uprooted, is fascinated by everything unstable, uncertain, ambiguous, equivocal, multifarious. It is, therefore, not surprising to find him adopting a method of writing which has all these qualities.

McCabe has probably never read those writers whom he imitates. Probably he has not even heard their names. Yet unconsciously he follows the pull of their lines.

This is merely natural. Picasso painted abstract designs long before anyone ever mentioned the name of cubism. Hundreds of young painters, congenial minds, soon followed: they did not copy Picasso. Some of them did not even know there was a man by the name of Picasso who had first painted in that style, which they had adopted as their own.

A certain style is born at a certain moment when time is ripe for it. Ten years later you can discover traces of it even in places as far removed from it as commercial art and industrial design: Picasso in the 'London Transport' posters, in the 'Shell' placards, in newspaper advertisements, James Joyce and Ernest Hemingway in the daily newspapers, in *Esquire*, in the *Evening Standard*.

Joyce wrote *Ulysses* 1914–21. The first edition of 1,000 copies was published in 1922. The second printing came out in October of the same year – 2,000 copies, of which 500 were burned by New York Post Office Authorities. Of the third printing which came out January 1923 in 500 numbered copies, 499 were seized by the Customs Authorities, Folkestone.

This means that until January 1924, when the fourth printing appeared in Paris, only 2,501 copies of *Ulysses* were circulating; yet already in 1923 hundreds of books, essays, short stories had appeared which were incontestably written in the style of *Ulysses*.

The same with Hemingway, the second of the two authors who have influenced Anglo-Saxon post-war literature more than any others. At present hardly any good American short story is published that does not smell of Hemingway. The whole 'Esquire' school of writers, *Fully Dressed and in his Right Mind*, *They Shoot Horses, Don't They?*, *The Postman Always Rings Twice* – Hemingway, the whole Hemingway, nothing but Hemingway.

In what lies the success of Messrs Picasso, Joyce, Hemingway? Evidently in their close affinity to their age: the same complexity of structure, the same dialectic of pattern, the same method of multifariousness to reproduce the instability of post-war life.

Edmund Wilson, in his excellent essay on Joyce (*Axel's Castle*, Chas Scribner, New York, 1934), says: 'A single one of Joyce's sentences, therefore, will combine two or three different meanings – two or three different sets of symbols; a single word may combine two or three ... The style he has invented for this purpose works on the principle of a palimpsest: one meaning, one set of images, is written over another.'

Mr Wilson criticizes Joyce for going too far in this direction: viewing *Ulysses* in retrospect he finds that 'beyond the ostensible subject and, as it were, beneath the surface of the narrative, too many other subjects and too many different orders of subjects were being proposed to our attention'.

The same, though in a much more primitive form, can be found in Mr McCabe's book: in the thirteenth chapter, for instance, he quotes Smith as saying: 'To clear up a murder you must do your own killing.'

Basically, of course, this is a mere realistic account of what the man says. But at the same time it has another function: though primarily intended as a matter-of-fact statement which helps to develop the plot, it also contains a dark, but for the reader not yet intelligible, implication, which attains its meaning only in the last chapter, when the reader learns that Smith is about to kill McCabe.

The trouble with this kind of technique is that the reader, instead of 'hearing the bell reverberate later in his mind when he reaches the solution', has meanwhile completely forgotten the first ring of the bell. Tocsin becomes knell.

Instead of being '*not yet* intelligible' for the reader, the implication has become simply *un*-intelligible.

McCabe is fascinated by the possibilities of this method, adopts it instinctively, refuses to see its disadvantages, and uses it wherever he can.

In the third chapter the words of the 'St Louis Blues' are definitely used as a set of implications: they fulfil a multiple purpose. They are not only part of the realistic description of the night-club, they are not only used to depict the atmosphere of the place: they are interblended with McCabe's thoughts about Jensen, and, as verse and thought are interlaced, the first gives rise to the second and thus creates a 'feeling of impending doom', a 'foretaste of the imminent loss of all that was dear'.

> I hate to see
> That evenin' sun go down,
> 'Cause my baby
> She done left this town.

Maria is going to leave McCabe, Dinah is going to leave McCabe, Jensen is going to leave Estella, Estella is going to leave this town for good, Jensen is to follow, then McCabe himself, finally Smith.

So already here, in one of the first chapters of his book, McCabe is pulling the famous 'bell that is to reverberate later in the reader's mind'. Unknown to the reader, yet forcing him to realize something which he cannot yet analyse exactly, McCabe writes here already of the end – 'the end of love, the end of life, the end of hope, the end of all'.

> Got the St Louis Blues
> Just as blue as I can be.
> That man's got a heart
> Like a rock cast in the sea.

The shock of the first verse is over. The man is considered separately from the woman. His heart is again strong and hard 'like a rock cast in the sea'. The storm has swept the sea, but the rock still stands. Only mild waves are left. And even 'the low mild-looking wave has passed, leaving nothing but a swell, but somewhere at the shore it will turn into a fierce surf'. And it will catch the rock and carry it for a moment, floating, suspending, balancing, but it will smash it in the end.

> If I'm feelin' tomorrow
> Like I'm feelin' today,
> I'm gonna pack my troubles
> And make my get-away.

But we know he *will* feel tomorrow just like he feels today, and we feel that Mr McCabe will have to pack his troubles and make his get-away – in spite of his assurance that 'he enjoyed the night with the white teeth of the Negroes and their fine and graceful bodies' and 'the band playing blues and rumbas in turn'.

The difference between this sort of technique and the normal straightforward technique of both the academic and the popular story, is merely one of a different social purpose.

'The typical American story with a plot like those of Aldrich, O. Henry and others may be compared to a box of surprises, to a thrilling chess game with an intriguing opening, a tense mid-play and a brilliant and unexpected end-play,' says J. Kashkeen.

'We are sure to see their denouement, for *the social function of this sort of story is to captivate, divert and lull to sleep, whether by admiration or pity, by genuine harmony or by harmony that is false.*'

Stories of the Hemingway kind, on the other hand, are, in Mr Kashkeen's words, 'rather like chess problems – the chessmen being practically brought up to the decisive point but the problem ending in what looks like a stalemate. Actually, however, they imply a mate and in most cases the mate to the hero is so well prepared dialectically that any trifle can supply the decisive impetus and once the impetus is given and things have been set in motion, the mate is inevitable at whatever move the author stops the game.'

'*The social function of such stories is not to solve or even to set any questions but rather to evoke them in the reader's mind.*'

This explains clearly how the theory of expressive suggestions or implication leads the author 'to project the denouement of his stories into the future as if expecting the reader himself to supply the end'.

Vide *The Face on the Cutting-Room Floor*: at the end McCabe remains alone, 'nothing discovered, all well', to use Mr Howard Spring's words.

'Unlike the traditional murder story this tale has no apparent ending although the end is clearly foreseen,' says Mr Kashkeen.

Is McCabe ever going to be punished for the murder? Mr McCabe does not supply us with an explicit answer.

'And this,' to quote Mr Kashkeen again, 'is certainly not the right thing to offer to bored readers ... the natural question for them to ask is, "And what then?"'

On hearing one of Mr Hemingway's stories an old Spanish lady once dropped the disappointed remark: 'And is that all of the story? Is there not to be what we called in my youth a wow at the end?'

'Ah, madame,' replies Hemingway, 'it is years since I added the wow to the end of a story. Are you sure you are unhappy if the wow is omitted?'

Naturally the old lady is unhappy. She prefers Aldrich and O. Henry, whose stories will 'captivate, divert and lull to sleep'. She strictly refuses to have any questions evoked in her mind.

For the old lady Mr McCabe's book therefore ends in a stalemate. Actually, however, it is a mate which is inevitable at whatever move the author wants to stop the game. Though the denouement is projected into the future as if the reader himself were to supply the solution, the actual end-play of the game is to be found in the last chapter: though the tale has no apparent ending its end is clearly foreseen when McCabe says: ' . . . now the trial was finished and I had seen that Maria was no longer there and so there was not much sense in fighting Smith any longer. I didn't mind Smith now. It was as good an end as any and better than a lot of other endings that might have happened to me.'

Mr McCabe has no literary programme. He is not interested in the social function of his story. He wants neither to solve any questions nor to set them or to evoke them in his readers' minds. But he cannot help setting questions, he cannot avoid evoking problems.

We find the problem even in his style, his vocabulary, his language.

'Torquemada' of the *Observer* complains that McCabe 'has learnt most of his trade in the United States' and that 'he has not yet quite decided which language to use'.

Various other reviewers complained that all characters talked that same half-half language, that they were neither recognizable nor differentiated by use of an individual vocabulary.

This is one of my own objections to *The Face on the Cutting-Room Floor*, though I know McCabe's reasons for refusing to differentiate his characters by their vocabulary, the reasons for his insistence on that curious semi-American lingo which all his characters talk.

'I'll tell you a story,' he once said to me.

'What about?' I asked him.

'About films and philology,' he said. 'Ph and F, Philms and Filology. Here it is: an old lady of repute and name came to see us on the set. She wanted to know something about film production. We introduced her to one of these strangely well-educated young men who are kept by all film studios to save their reputation. Before the old lady could introduce herself to the young man, shooting began. The new assistant director shouted, "Quiet everybody," and Vic shouted, "Action, dead quiet, please," and they started shooting. But she soon got courage and whispered: "Who is the man with the frightful western accent? Why do you keep so many Americans in your film studios, sir?"

'"He is no American, madame. His name is John Robertson and he is a college boy from Oxford."

'"He should know better," said the old lady.

'"Should he?" asked the young man politely. "Madame, some years ago Robert Peter Tristram Coffin, a native of Maine, U.S.A., was, while in Oxford, selected as the most typical Englishman there. Times have not changed basically since then – merely the extremes have changed places – the balance is still the old one."

'"Perhaps you are right," said the old lady. "But who is the fat little man with spectacles? He surely is an American, though there might be some German in it; Pennsylvania, I should think."

'"No, madame. I am inconsolable but he also is far from being American. His name is Bloom, but this is merely the name he chose when he was made a British citizen. He actually comes from somewhere in the East, somewhere between Poland and the Balkans and here he is and his Americanese, I admit it, madame, is pure, like Mr Mencken's."

'They finished shooting and one of the scene-shifters by the name of Happy said something and the old lady said: "But I know what *he* is, sir. He is a good Englishman but he also speaks American. He does it, however, with a Cockney accent and that betrays him. Am I right for once, sir?"

'"Perhaps you are, madame. Perhaps you are not. For – I am sad to have to confess it – I know nothing about the gentleman in question."

'And the old lady, never to be discouraged, went on asking questions and the polite young man kept on replying politely. They all spoke American though some had an American vocabulary but a Bulgarian, Dutch, French, Norwegian accent. Some had a Cockney or Yorkshire or Scotch or Welsh or Irish vocabulary but their American pronunciation was perfect. And the old lady asked many questions and the young man gave many answers and the old lady asked yet another and still another question. "But why," she asked, "why do they all talk American? They may be German or Greek or Armenian or Monégasque or Liechtensteinese – but they all, all talk this dreadful, awful, disgusting American language. Why is this?"

'"Madame," said the young man, "there is one reason only, and it is a very simple reason: they are all film people. And their language as she is spoke, is American, madame!"'

A typical McCabe story: facetious, prolix, unfunny. Yet the facts are true: film people actually talk like that. Smith said it once – and McCabe quotes it in the twenty-second chapter: 'The film language as it is spoken is humbug Americanese.' But Smith himself talks the same language. 'He's got an overseas accent but he doesn't talk genuine Americanese. He's too English to be American and too American to be English.' (Chapter twenty-one.) Here we find what Mencken prophesied ten years ago: the typical post-war Anglo-American language, a product of the new means of communication. And it would not be of any interest to analyse this language if it were not for the extraordinary use which McCabe makes of it.

He picks out all the words without colour, like *put*, *take*, *have*, *is*, *said*; phrases like *he said*, *there is*, *here is*, *we are*, *we have*. He combines these by means of contrast, parallel, parable, allegory, simile, metaphor, symbol. This is dialectic writing, a method evident in Hemingway's short stories and in all those old Russian films of Eisenstein, Pudovkin and Dovzhenko.

Pudovkin says: 'To the poet or writer separate words are as raw material. They have the widest and most variable meanings which only begin to become precise through their position in the sentence; to that extent to which the word is an integral part of the composed phrase, to that extent is its effect and meaning variable until it is fixed in position, in the arranged artistic form . . . the single word is only the raw skeleton of a meaning, so to speak, a concept without essence or precision. Only in conjunction with other words, set in the frame of a complex form, does art endow it with life and reality.'

It is evident that McCabe, a film man, would at once realize the importance of this. 'The single word is only the raw skeleton of a meaning . . . a concept without essence or precision' – therefore Mr McCabe rejects the pretentious word, chooses the bare, cold, short word and puts all his trust in construction: 'Only in conjunction with other words, set in the name of a complex form, does art endow it with life.'

Hemingway says: 'Prose is architecture, not interior decoration, and the Baroque is over.'

McCabe, instinctively adopting this, rejects all colourful word-ornaments in favour of colourless word-bricks. Even the number of slang terms is comparatively small. And thus the resulting style becomes a reflection of the man's hopeless state of mind, his despair, his disillusion, his utter desolation. It is a picture of a man who has arrived in the last depth of pain and there is no way out except that eternal back door which leads into crime.

C. Day Lewis speaks about a 'jargon which is not only picturesque in itself, but – by its general resemblance to the slang of "backward" schoolboys – gives a remarkable impression of the arrested development of the criminal mind'.

McCabe cannot help writing like this: it is his only language. We have to forgive him for this just as we have to forgive him for the terribly Hemingwayish chapter nineteen – McCabe felt it perhaps as he wrote it. But things are different when it comes to McCabe's catalogue mania – see the endless enumeration of machinery which McCabe gives in the second chapter when he enters Robertson's studio.

'Anything in the nature of a catalogue is apt to attract Mr McCabe, for it provides him with possibilities for the exercise of rhetoric; and rhetorical his art nearly always is,' says L. P. Hartley in the *Observer*.

McCabe will insist on saying things like: 'The coloured managers changed.' The reader cannot help asking: Changed what? Changed colour?

Here it becomes evident that an amateur is writing.

But generally the amateur represents a more typical case than the professional. And it is only the typical case, not the individual exception, which is of historical interest.

VII

Basic qualities become amplified when required. If pursued, a man runs faster than he would under normal circumstances. In McCabe's case the innate Scotch dourness, amplified by his American education towards toughness, becomes further amplified in the crisis of crime and pursuit. His carefully studied nonchalance becomes genuine coolness, unexcitedness, indifference. The new American stoicism, so far only partially assimilated, becomes now actual part of the man. The result: McCabe begins to look at the murder as if someone else had committed it, as if he were an interested but non-participating spectator, sometimes even as if he were the judge in charge of the proceedings.

A typical example of this can be found in McCabe's description of his reaction when he finds himself finally charged with the murder. 'Everybody was deeply impressed. Nobody dared to breathe or to speak. Eyes looked with awe and terror alternately at Smith and at me. But the distribution of awe and terror between Smith and me was not ethically correct: a lot of awe went to my account and a lot of terror went to Smith's.'

It is a long way from the McCabe of the first chapter to this McCabe, obsessed with his own superhuman detachment. It begins quite normal and pleasant. But slowly McCabe's attempts to dodge Smith and Smith's attempts to catch him attain for him the meaning of a kind of game. And as the game approaches its climax it undergoes a second metamorphosis: it becomes a 'fight' – but a fight that is fought with rules as definite as those of the game in the beginning.

It is a game of skill, a battle of wits, a thing that has no connection with any standard of good and bad, right and wrong, allowed and forbidden.

This is again a direct product and an exact reflection of that social development which we described before: the standard of values undergoes a profound change: 'The eternal values disappear and are replaced by values of the moment: the individual shows – and can hardly help showing – a growing disregard for those human qualities which have not yet become purchasable and marketable merchandise.'

The muddle in society becomes exemplified by the muddle in McCabe's mind. And as the 'game' turned into the 'fight', so does the 'fight' now turn into the central issue of McCabe's life: it is no longer a fight for life; it has already become a fight for fighting's sake. Even Maria, the object of the fight, has dropped into the background: the outcome of the fight no longer matters – only the fight itself does matter. And the man is only disappointed when the fight goes stale, when it is no longer a 'game': 'It had been a good game at the beginning but now it was just a fag-end.'

So finally, when McCabe gains the better of Smith, he does not rejoice in the happiness of having dodged and escaped the law, but complains that the 'fun of the game' has gone: this is McCabe's objectivity *ad absurdam*: detachment has turned into indifference: the man has become oblivious of his own fate: the instinct of self-preservation has become ineffectual: nature lets the parasite kill itself.

The debilitation of the instinct for self-preservation concurs with the curious detachment and objectivity which the crisis has developed in him, and both together produce a very curious re-action: McCabe begins to cede to others the same right which he claims for himself – the right to do wrong.

The whole complex structure is explained by McCabe himself when he looks back in the last chapter:

'I didn't feel sorry that I'd killed Jensen and I didn't feel sorry that Smith was going to kill me now but I did feel sorry that it had all been so damned futile. I could try to convince myself that I had killed Jensen because he was no good – just like Smith was trying now to convince himself that he was killing me because I was no good. But I wouldn't try to fool myself that way. I killed Jensen because he came between Maria and me. And as I couldn't live without Maria, there was nothing to do but to get Jensen out of the way . . . I wouldn't have said to Jensen, "Thou shalt not kill", if he had tried to kill me for the same reason. I would have seen his point just as I had seen the prosecutor's point during the trial and as I now saw Smith's point. But I wouldn't have allowed Jensen to kill me just as I hadn't allowed the prosecutor to get me sentenced for murder. Yet I didn't mind Smith now. It was as good an end as any and better than a lot of other endings that might have happened to me.'

Despairing, he confesses in the end: 'A fight is no game, but all fighters lose as all gamblers and all players always lose.'

Like Hemingway, 'the prophet of the lost generation', McCabe, another typical member of those who got caught in the machinery of that society which they refuse to change, comes to see the world as a sordid arena in which even the winner takes nothing: 'Unlike all other forms of lutte or combat the conditions are that the winner shall take nothing; neither his ease nor his pleasure, nor any notions of glory; nor, if he win far enough, shall there be any reward within himself.'

VIII

Throughout the book we can follow McCabe's peculiar objectivity from its earliest stage of brilliant analysis to its doomed end in utter confusion.

But two products of this same objectivity remain constant throughout the book, in spite of all changes and developments. *Firstly*, the methods which McCabe uses to dodge Smith: they have the calmness and ingenuity of a man completely undisturbed by the enemy's possible superiority. *Secondly*, his perfectly objective and impartial way of describing both his own and the enemy's actions: Smith gets off neither better nor worse than McCabe himself: the two enemies are on the same footing.

Yet it is not only McCabe's objectivity – though that is without doubt – but also a natural equality between the two opponents which helps McCabe to portray the fight with fairness: it is easier to be fair to a fight between equals than to a cat-and-mouse play.

A similar attitude requires a similar strategy. And that strategy, used by both, is *provocation* – provocation both with words and with deeds, but, especially in McCabe's case, talk is preferred to action.

This makes the combat a natural drama – like a stage drama it is fought not with swords but with words.

The *technique* of provocation is, in both cases, *teasing* or *bantering* in the new style of the American tough school – the only style of which both Smith and McCabe have a certain command.

Mr McCabe describes in chapter thirteen Smith's extraordinarily tactless talk to Robertson about Estella Lamare: '... she lived at Pembroke Street, St Aldate's, Oxford. Mr Robertson could tell us more about that epoch in the deceased lady's life ... Now, ladies and gentlemen, is the appropriate moment to show the cards. It is now the time when no secret can remain concealed. Gentlemen, Mr John Robertson will tell us now the story of the once so glamorous Miss Estella Lamare.'

Here you can plainly recognize the extraordinary resemblance between Smith's remarks and McCabe's various banters: the use of the address 'Ladies and gentlemen', the deliberately stilted tone and the use of the word 'glamorous', to mention only a few affinities.

Various reviewers have complained about this fact of too great a likeness between Smith's and McCabe's methods.

The answer to any criticism of this kind must naturally be this: if they had not been so much alike they could not have fought on such an equal footing: instead of a fight we would have got a cat-and-mouse play. The public would have missed the sensations of the two trials and the book readers would have missed the clash of forces and its outcome, which seems sometimes to approach true tragedy.

Doreen Wallace, in her *Sunday Times* review, which was published on 21st June, maintains, however, that 'true tragedy' can never be the clash of right against wrong but only of right against right.

I am quite willing to agree with Miss Wallace. But Mr McCabe – and this is most characteristic – holds that true tragedy is simply the clash of equal forces, whether right or wrong, which involves the inevitable defeat of one of the two opponents: ' . . . fairness between two means that they use the same methods, not one worse method than the other. But when they are both bad it makes them even and the game becomes fair and balanced again.'

Thus, in Mr McCabe's distorted view, the 'fight' becomes 'fair', because the two opponents use the same methods, both methods being 'bad' – but *equally* bad and therefore 'equal', 'even', 'fair' and 'balanced'.

IX

It is the same dialectic process – objectivity turned into distortion – which makes McCabe, the chronicler, try so desperately hard to be fair to his chronicle – to the events and persons depicted as well as to his readers.

Where he is unjust to either – and there are enough examples of this – he is unjust by accident and not by intention. McCabe simply misunderstood – he did not distort.

He is often quite unjust where I am concerned. Unjust not only to me, but also to himself and to his readers.

In the twenty-second chapter he describes, for instance, how Smith rang him up at my place. But he does not realize how very odd it is that Smith should ring him there. Normally Smith could not know where McCabe was. He could not know me at all, he could not know that McCabe was staying with me, and he could not know my telephone number. McCabe goes on telling us how he went back to the studio, how Smith took him up to Robertson's room, how Robertson inserted the film into the projector and how Smith suggested that he, McCabe, should work the projector. He tells us then how he stopped the projector involuntarily when he discovered that Smith had found and affixed the second part of the film and, finally, how I entered at that very moment, how I asked Smith 'You are Inspector Smith, I presume?' and how Smith answered in the affirmative and proceeded with the third showing of the film.

McCabe fails to report what had happened between his leaving my flat and my entering Robertson's studio. He failed to record it because he knew nothing about it. He fails even in the twenty-fourth chapter, when he tries to explain the link between Smith and me: 'Müller is an amateur sleuth, and to prove his sleuthing ability he makes use of the story I tell him. Comparing my version of the events with the version Smith has given him over the telephone twenty minutes ago, he finds . . . ' etc. – follows an account of my attempts at deducting the true facts of the McCabe-Jensen-Estella case.

What McCabe does not know – and could not possibly know – is this:

I had known Estella Lamare for quite a long time. I had met her in Oxford. We remained in touch till the Jensen affair began. I knew all about it. She had told me of her dilemma. I knew that something was going to happen. It was inevitable. So I watched out, thinking that perhaps I might be able to prevent the worst. I watched her; I watched Jensen. I watched Maria Ray. Watching Maria Ray I came across McCabe.

That evening at King's Cross tube station I cornered him. The same night Estella was killed.

This was Thursday night. Six days later, Wednesday, 4th December, Smith's policeman, who was trailing McCabe, followed him to the *Evening Express* and overheard our conversation. He informed Smith and Smith approached me with the request to help him. I obliged him only too gladly.

We arranged a meeting. I missed him. But he had my phone number and he gave me a ring to tell me all there was to be told about the case. But he had never met me personally, which explains his enigmatic answer to my question whether he was Inspector

Smith. I am asking him: 'You are Inspector Smith, I presume?' and he answers: 'Yes, you met the right one this time. And your name is Müller – "u" with two dots, if I didn't misunderstand you on the telephone.'

I rang Smith again when McCabe was on his way to the studio, so that at McCabe's arrival Smith was already informed of the result of my talk with McCabe.

Yet, these very few blunders excepted, McCabe understood his opponents amazingly well, and – which is more important – made no attempt to deceive himself about their superiority in many stages of the 'fight'.

X

But 'superiority' in this kind of 'fight' means only greater ruthlessness, less consideration for the normal rules set up for normal members of a normal human society.

We, the normal members of this society, take it for granted that a criminal will do everything in his power to escape the law. We do not forgive him, we hunt him, we punish him, we try to make him innocuous. But to a certain extent we understand him. We are not surprised when he develops the conviction that the end justifies all means – the end being the defence of his life against the forces of the law which threaten to convict him.

But we cannot forgive the law if it uses the same methods against the criminal which the criminal uses against the law: the judge does not pull out a woman's hair if the woman is charged with having pulled out her neighbour's hair.

The outlaw has his own laws. But the policeman who fights the outlaw has to fight him within the boundaries of the approved laws. Therefore, theoretically, McCabe is defensible, Smith is not. McCabe can be forgiven for the methods he used against Smith, but Smith cannot be forgiven for the methods which he used against McCabe. Smith – just as McCabe did – believed that the end justified all means. It is this belief that led to the extraordinary similarity between their methods.

Each used the peculiar methods of the other for his own ends.

Both lost.

It is evident that McCabe only gained his acquittal in court by a sytematic – and wholly hypocritical – attack on Smith's methods. Thus the argument could be brought forward that Smith was directly responsible for McCabe's acquittal.

Yet it remains doubtful whether any evidence against McCabe could ever have been collected by any methods other than those which Smith used.

Smith's methods were so unconventional, his whole behaviour so extraordinary, that the first readers of Mr McCabe's book – those who did not know yet that Smith was a real person – rightly refused to believe that there could possibly be a detective as unconventional and unscrupulous as Smith.

The critics, therefore, attacked McCabe, the author, for having invented such an unbelievable character, instead of attacking Smith, the man, for being what he was.

'Torquemada' in the *Observer* said: 'I am beginning to be anxious about Inspector Smith's pension. His contempt for Police Regulations, to say nothing of his contempt for Judge's Rules, must, I feel, involve him sooner or later in an unpleasant interview with the Commissioner, if he continues his career on his chosen lines . . .'

And Mr McCabe is made responsible for this behaviour of his 'character' Smith: ' . . . I could wish that he (Mr McCabe) had studied police methods more carefully . . . In this book it is clear that he has little knowledge of the nature of evidence or of criminal procedure, but equally clear that he possesses a penetrant understanding of the human mind.'

Now never mind the penetrant understanding of the human mind, but concentrate a little on the lack of knowledge of Police Methods, Police Regulations, Judge's Rules, Criminal Procedure and the Nature of Evidence.

If a book reviewer, and one of the very best at that, condemns a book in those harsh terms, accepting as fiction what was offered to him as fiction, how much more condemning must be the verdict of public opinion when it learns that all those events which the intelligent man rightly refuses to believe even when they are offered to him as fiction, were actually based on fact, were, indeed, parts of an actual account of actual events.

This got McCabe into a dilemma. Realizing that he could only be either true to the facts or convincing to his readers, he decided to take the first course.

McCabe is true to the facts even in that most difficult case of all, the case of Maria Ray.

The British libel laws prevent me from stating my exact opinion of her. But I think that in spite of his deep infatuation with her, McCabe kept his head clear enough to see her faults and shortcomings. In the last chapter of his book he freely admits his disappointment in her – an unjustified disappointment. For who could expect a woman to keep faith with a man whom she knows to be a murderer? But Mr McCabe has his own code of morals – we mentioned it at the beginning of these notes – and so it is not surprising to find him complaining in the last chapter: 'She would fight with Dinah, but she wouldn't be there in the end when I wanted her. She would flirt with Jensen and sleep with him – but she wouldn't cry after he'd gone . . .'

So Mr McCabe realized both her hopelessly promiscuous sexual tendencies and her ultimate indifference towards the partners of her various bed-affairs. From this it appears so much more surprising that he – who is generally willing to cede to others the same rights which he claims for himself – complains in one sentence that she left him and in the next that she would not cry after Jensen.

If she did not cry after Jensen, why should she cry after McCabe?

He never asked himself that question.

John Brophy, in the *Daily Telegraph*, comments on this situation: ' . . . this is what I consider the most interesting aspect of *The Face on the Cutting-Room Floor* – it is all about a most undeserving young woman. Very often in fiction, as in real life [*sic*], one is appalled by the kind of female that men choose to lavish their affections upon, but this love-'em-and-blame-'em Maria is a prize specimen. McCabe – not an entirely estimable character himself – perceives many of her faults, and develops towards the end a sense of injustice, but he never ceases to love her and never seems to question her right to his love.'

Yet at the beginning McCabe ceded Jensen the same rights which he claimed for himself. Only later, when the position became intolerable, did he begin to fight Jensen.

And no one can blame him for it. He hated Jensen with the sound hatred of a jealous lover. He never hid either sentiment, neither his hate nor his jealousy. In the third chapter he says to Miss Ray: 'I don't like that young man of yours.' In the twenty-first chapter, to me: 'I . . . I didn't like Jensen.' In the twenty-second chapter, to Smith: ' . . . I won't tell you, Smith, that I'm sorry he got bumped off. I never liked him and I'm glad he's gone.' In the twenty-third chapter, again to Smith: 'Jensen was a little louse without importance.' But a few lines later: 'He can't help being the sap he is – or was.'

Or, about his jealousy, in the third chapter: 'And there was Maria with that man Jensen with his face like a Copenhagen hairdresser. Couldn't she have found anybody else to take her out? Just that pink-faced dummy . . . And Maria on his arm. Go over and punch him in that sweet pinkish face of his. Knock it to pieces. Knock it flat. Bed Bug. Getting some thousand quid for nothing. Ruddocks for riff-raff. And now with Maria on his arm. Just that dirty brick-presser.'

But a few minutes later his extraordinary objectivity breaks through – that extraordinary detachment which allows him to grant Jensen the same rights which he would demand for himself if he were in Jensen's place: 'The man is all right. He earns his living like you and me. Right. Let him have his fun. Maybe she likes him. Why shouldn't she? Sure she likes him. Right. Give him a chance.'

This is not the usual jealous lover speaking. This is a strangely sublimated kind of jealousy, the product of a genuine love, certainly not of mere passion, surely not of 'plain vulgarity'.

But I can quite understand any objection that might be made against conversations like this one in the eighteenth chapter:

Dinah: 'Oh, Mr McCabe, how wonderful, how tough you are. I adore big, silent men.'

McCabe: 'All right . . . come on, let's go to bed.'

John Brophy, already annoyed with Maria, gets very angry when confronted with this sort of thing, and complains to his readers that 'things are discussed and described in novels nowadays which not only would have made the hair of our Victorian and Edwardian forefathers stand on end, but would have had the same effect on our own hair had we read the novels of 1936 ten years ago. Sometimes this "frankness" is mere vulgarity [sic!] that has slipped the rein, for bad taste does not change its nature simply because it is able to claim that it is "advanced".'

In the end Mr Brophy comes to the conclusion that 'It is a book of faulty but admirable achievement, stored with a rare, not always pleasant emotional intensity.'

Horace Horsnell in the *Observer* agrees with Mr Brophy and calls it 'a love lyric in the carnal mode', a Passion-play of passion in which 'the growth, flowering and death of passion are passionately reviewed ... Psychology and physiology are equally frank [sic!]. The curve of this tragic affair (see Doreen Wallace about "true tragedy") is traced against an opulent background ... It is a remarkable and also an embarrassing document. Not because it is outspoken but because it tempts the reader to say "Serves you right!"'

The harmony of opinion is awe-inspiring.

About 'vulgarity':

The Times Literary Supplement: ' ... must be called vulgarity ...'

John Brophy: ' ... is mere vulgarity ...'

About 'frankness':

John Brophy: ' ... this "frankness" ...'

Horace Horsnell: ' ... psychology and physiology are equally frank ...' Later: ' ... it is outspoken ...'

About 'passion':

The Times Literary Supplement: ' ... the full dignity of passion ...'

Horace Horsnell: ' ... the growth, flowering and death of passion are passionately reviewed ...'

Milward Kennedy in the *Sunday Times* of 5th July: ' ... there is plenty of physical passionateness ...'

Note here also the insistence on the *physical aspect* of the affair:

Horace Horsnell: ' ... psychology *and physiology* ...'

The Times Literary Supplement: ' ... the minor *sensualities of looking and touching* ...'

Horsnell again: '... a love lyric in the *carnal* mode ...'

'Remarkable' and *'admirable'* but *'embarrassing'* and *'unpleasant'*:

Horace Horsnell: '... it is a remarkable and also an embarrassing document.'

John Brophy: ' ... it is a book of faulty but admirable achievement, stored with a rare, not always pleasant emotional intensity ...'

And about Maria:

The Times Literary Supplement: ' ... lends herself very easily to her part in a relationship that is erotic without ...' etc.

John Brophy: ' ... a most undeserving young woman ...'

Horace Horsnell: ' ... was no inexperienced lover. Before she met McCabe and fell for him she had done pretty well, even by her own standards ...' This 'should have warned her that passion can be both treacherous and fleeting ...'

But 'Torquemada' in the *Observer* comes to an utterly different conclusion: ' . . . so entirely skilful is the unfolding of the hero's personality, that we feel that here is merely a youth working off a grievance against the other sex.'

True.

And 'anyhow McCabe tries to be tough and a one with the ladies': Mr Connolly speaking again.

And truthfully spoken, too, Mr Connolly.

XII

Mr McCabe's is by nature a provocative mind. He does not always want it, but he can never help it. He tries to be fair to Smith, but he succeeds only in becoming provocative. He tries to treat his readers as fairly as he tried to treat Smith. But, just as in Smith's case, he succeeds only in becoming provocative.

He provokes criticism. Instead of keeping his mouth shut he insists on telling us all about his case. That is vanity. He may be forgiven for that. But then, instead of writing a straightforward account of the events, he writes a novel. That is pretentiousness: he provokes criticism. And in that novel which gives him the first chance to distort things in his favour, he gives an objective account of his crime, tries to be objective to his enemies, tries to be fair to his readers: that provokes opposition. Finally he comes to the end of his story and in the last but one sentence he says: 'The things that matter aren't said in detective stories anyway.'

That provokes the question: is it a detective story? An 'account of actual events', a murderer's 'autography', a 'story', a 'novel', a 'pattern', a 'plot' – and now a *detective story*?

We found at the beginning that 'most of the critics, following the established rules of their trade, abstained wisely from taking the actual facts of the case into account and concentrated on the merely literary merits or shortcomings of the story, as if it were a work of fiction'.

Every critic who read the words '*detective story*' therefore picked it up eagerly: there was a justification for not considering the actual events, a good reason for considering the book as a mere work of fiction, a work of 'detective fiction' to be exact; a good reason, in short, for concentrating on the merely literary merits or shortcomings.

Other critics wrote their reviews at a time when it had not yet become known that the book was a documentary story. These latter critics are justified. We will, therefore, only consider the views of this latter group.

Milward Kennedy in the *Sunday Times* said: 'Admittedly, a writer of good detective stories is not necessarily a good detective. For there is a world of difference between controlling your clues and interpreting those left by other people, and often, moreover, inadequately reported by third parties.'

Or, inversely, a good detective is not necessarily a writer of good detective stories. And a criminal is not necessarily a writer of good crime stories.

Mr Kennedy thus gives us a good analysis of Mr McCabe's dilemma, which is even more complicated by the fact that 'there is almost inevitably a weakness in a crime story narrated in the first person; the narrator must be presumed to write under the influence of the natural climax, and, therefore, it is unnatural that his narrative should work up to the climax which it inspires'.

Correct, Mr Kennedy.

Fact and fiction are constantly fighting one another. Fairness to his characters and fairness to his readers are expected of the author. And once he has claimed to have written a detective story, strictest adherence to the rules of detective fiction is demanded of him.

But, as Smith said in the twenty-third chapter, 'This isn't a detective story where things have to click. They only do in bad stories anyway. This is a thing that *happened*. Detective stories are puzzles – chess played with figures that look like human beings – but they only look like humans: they aren't. You must decide what you want to do – write a detective story and make things fit fine and dandy so that your readers in Walla Walla, Tooting Broadway and Kansas City Suburb like it – in which case you must cut out the human element and concentrate on the machinery – or you work with more or less normal human beings under more or less normal circumstances – which is real life as it is: more or less normal and far from the perfect machinery of that fine detective story that you want to make out of our case here, brother Mac.'

Smith is right so long as he is a participant in the case. He is wrong as soon as he becomes a character in the story. Once McCabe sets out to write a detective story – be it fiction or based on fact – he has to keep to the rules.

And the rules of detective fiction are very strict indeed – so strict that the real bibliophile feels hurt in his most democratic feelings: he feels threatened by a dictatorship of rules and retreats to the wide open spaces of fine literature.

The detective-story adherent, shocked by this faithlessness, feels attacked and begins to entrench himself: Miss Dorothy Sayers writes a defence of the detective story which appears as introduction to Messrs Dent's lovely *Tales of Detection*.

Mr Howard Spring, for the opposition, replies: 'For myself I find this High Priestess attitude as amusing as that of the earnest advertising agents who can't put a toilet roll on the market without an obeisance to Service.'

What was it in Miss Sayers's learned defence of detective stories that caused such an outburst from Mr Spring's usually so peaceful pen?

The cause, as usual, was Miss Sayers's attempt to consider the historical backgrounds of her subject. In the course of her research she had come across traces of her subject in the most sacred places: in Oriental folk-tales, in the Apocryphal Books of the Old Testament, in the play scene in *Hamlet*, in Aristotle's *Poetics* . . .

But what, we ask impatiently, has become of the detective story since then?

Cyril Connolly says:

'The more one investigates the condition of the detective story today the more one discovers something stagnant and fatigued about it, in particular a complete lack of excitement.

'In none of these modern books does one really long to know what happens next, and if a detective story can't make one, there is no hope for it. Most of the best detective stories, like most of the best jazz, were written in the 1920s when life was more gay and adventurous, and there was less sense of ominous responsibility. The 1930s have given us three good detective stories: *Malice Aforethought*, *A Question of Proof*, and *Murder of My Aunt*.

'The great period of the detective story seems to me to begin with *The Cask*, by Freeman Wills Crofts (1918), and to end with Francis Iles's *Malice Aforethought* in England, and Dashiell Hammett's *The Glass Key* in America in 1931. It includes the best of Inspectors French, Poynter, Poole, and Wilson, the activities of Colonels Gore and Gethryn, of Philo Vance and Peter Wimsey before they became parodies of themselves, and of Roger Sheringham, Hercule Poirot, Dr Thorndyke, and the efficient but essentially unlikeable Sir Clinton Driffield.

'Who has taken their place? What figures have succeeded those businesslike, painstaking inspectors, with their passion for chops and scenery, or those brilliant amateurs, each devoted to a special make of car, each with innocuous hobbies and harmless vanities, yet as ruthless in the identification of a murderer as in that of a dubious bottle from one of their excellent cellars?

'Who now enjoys the famous solution-dinner that should occur at the end of every good detective story, when the Doctor Watson of the case is given a detailed spread ("Have a little more of the Biscuit Dubouché 65, Wiggins." I needed no pressing, but it was not till we had lit our Rockefeller Coronas (1920) that he consented to begin. "Now the first thing that struck me as a little curious . . .")? Who pays for them? Who takes two seats at the opera, like Vance, or starts mugging up useful quotations from Plato for the next crime, like Ellery Queen?'

Certainly not Mr McCabe. But, Mr Connolly says, 'reading detective stories is usually a recurrent habit. For months, sometimes for years, one does not read them at all; then an illness or a visit or a trip abroad sends one back to them, and it seems for a time inconceivable that one should want to read anything else.' But every time they are forced on you, by the paucity of other fiction, 'it is interesting, if disappointing, to see how badly they stand up, those books which would seem such a godsend if found among the back numbers of engineering papers in the salon of a Mediterranean hotel when one is on the way up for a siesta.

'It is not only because one is not in the right mood, however, that they disappoint, but because the detective story itself is in a dilemma. It is a vein which is in danger of being worked out, the demand is constant, the powers of supply variable, and the reader, with each one he absorbs, grows a little more sophisticated and harder to please, while the novelist, after each one he writes, becomes a little more exhausted.'

Now what is this all about? What is this 'detective fiction' which seems to have such exact rules of its own?

Milward Kennedy, in the *Sunday Times* of 5th July, says:

'There is heresy abroad. An eminent critic declares it useless for his kind to draw distinctions between the various types of crime stories. To the public, he says, any book containing a crime capable of logical solution (by the reader) is a detective story; and then, since this would hardly make a book like *Malice Aforethought* a detective story, as he holds it to be, he adds another criterion – a book is a detective story if it provokes the question "Will the villain escape?"'

'Surely "thriller" is the undiscriminating word still in general use; surely it is increasingly recognized that it is too undiscriminating?

'The question "Will the villain escape?" is often a subsidiary interest in books like *Malice Aforethought*. Indeed, it is often left unanswered, as it is in *The Face on the Cutting-Room Floor*, a story "after" Mr Francis Iles.

'It will be gathered that, to my mind, Mr McCabe's is not a "detective story". Nor is it a book for children or for squeamish adults. It is an outspoken study of deliberate murder; its theme and interest are the murderer's psychology.'

So to Mr Kennedy's mind *Malice Aforethought* is not a 'detective story'. Neither is *The Face on the Cutting-Room Floor*, 'a story after Mr Francis Iles', a detective story. 'Thriller' is a word which could be applied to both books. Yet 'it is increasingly recognized that it is too undiscriminating'.

The eminent critic quoted by Mr Kennedy declares, however, that it is useless to discriminate between the various types of crime stories. There is the first contradiction between two eminent critics of detective stories.

Now Mr Connolly says: 'The 1930s have given us three good detective stories.' And as the first of the three he names *Malice Aforethought*.

So *Malice Aforethought* is, at least to Mr Connolly's mind, not only a detective story but one of the very best detective stories.

Mr Kennedy, however, refuses to call it a detective story.

Mr Kennedy's 'eminent critic' holds that to the public any book containing a crime capable of logical solution (by the reader) is a detective story; and then, since this would hardly make a book like *Malice Aforethought* a detective story, as he holds it to be, he adds another criterion: a book is a detective story if it provokes the question, 'Will the villain escape?'

Mr Kennedy, on the other hand, holds that 'the question "Will the villain escape?" is often a subsidiary interest in books like *Malice Aforethought*'.

So now we have three eminent critics disagreeing about an agreed classic of a certain type of fiction that is called detective fiction by only two of the three – with an additional difference between these two, who disagree about the definition of detective fiction.

Mr W. H. Auden in the *Daily Telegraph* tries his hand at a co-ordination of so many divergent views. 'I have forgotten how many possible plots there are said to be, but they are few,' is his thesis. He then develops the argument that 'under the stimulus of competition the detective story has developed many mutations, of which at least two are now as important as the original parental stock. These, to borrow a terminology from the film studio [sic] are the "Documentary Murder" and the "Murder on Location". A characteristic feature of both is that the main interest of the story does not lie in the detection of the murderer.'

Now this is very curious. If the main interest of the story does not lie in detection, why then call it a 'detective story'?

So even Mr Auden cannot help us solve the problem. For, instead of explaining his statement, he subdivides it: ' "Documentary Murder", of which Mr Francis Iles is the recognized master [sic!], is the realistic study of the characters involved in a murder, frequently of the murderer himself, the actual murder being only the crisis which reveals the characters of the actors. In "Murder on Location", which most people will associate at once with Miss Dorothy Sayers [sic], the murder provides an excuse for the investigation of some unusual and interesting activity or form of social life.'

Before we can discuss this statement we must note how the same names are always mentioned in connection with the same problem: Mr Francis Iles and Miss Dorothy Sayers.

It certainly is 'the realistic study of the characters involved in a murder', a study 'of the murderer himself'. Remember Mr Kennedy's analysis of *The Face on the Cutting-Room Floor*: 'It is an outspoken study of deliberate murder; its theme and interest are the murderer's psychology.' It is, therefore, a detective story of the 'Documentary Murder' type.

Yet 'the actual murder' is far from 'being only the crisis which reveals the characters of the actors'. As a matter of fact, the murder is not described at all. There are three murders – two (Estella's and Jensen's) actual, and one (McCabe's) implied, but not a single one reveals the character of any of the actors. The revealing of character – if any – is done as the tale goes along. It stops completely when a murder happens – this simply because the murder is not described.

So *The Face on the Cutting-Room Floor* is only half a 'Documentary Murder'. It is, however, a complete 'Murder on Location': 'the murder provides an excuse for the investigation of some unusual and interesting activity or form of social life' – namely, of the life in a modern English film studio.

According to Mr Kennedy's anonymous but eminent critic of detective fiction, the criterion of a detective story was the question *Will the villain escape?*

Now does Mr McCabe's book provoke the question?

The answer is *no*. This for the very simple reason that the reader has no idea who the villain is. He can guess, if he wants to, but he receives no statement from the author. It is only in the last chapter that McCabe states plainly that he killed Jensen. Up to that point various charges were made against him. But not a single one was proved. Moreover Smith, the detective, was often suspected of being the criminal, while McCabe, the criminal, often acted as detective.

A complete confusion of even the simplest rules of detective fiction was the result. The detective as criminal and the criminal as detective. The criminal as hero and the detective as villain.

Will the villain escape? The reader cannot answer the question, because he does not know the villain. Therefore, according to Mr Kennedy's 'eminent critic', this is no detective story. Point against Mr McCabe.

But in the next round McCabe gains a couple of points: *The Times Literary Supplement* of 14th November admits that Jensen 'is mildly antisocial; his murder, therefore, conforms to one dictate of detective fiction'.

And McCabe himself is certainly more than merely 'mildly' antisocial: his murder, therefore, conforms to the same dictate of detective fiction.

How pleasant to see even reality follow the rules of fiction!

And Estella? Certainly a very antisocial young lady from every point of view.

Three points for Mr McCabe.

Mr Francis Iles, author of *Malice Aforethought*, that much-discussed classic of crime fiction, gives his own opinion about Mr McCabe in a *Daily Telegraph* article of 22nd May 1936.

'Mr McCabe,' he says, 'comes at times perilously near to breaking that golden rule of the first-class detective-story writer, that no vital information known to the detective shall be withheld from the reader.'

True. But Mr McCabe had to write his book in the first person. He could, therefore, hardly avoid withholding information known to the detective – this again for the very simple reason that he himself did not know what information the detective had. Mr Iles's hero of *Malice Aforethought* had the same difficulties (though he had no need to tell the story in the first person). According to the author of *Malice Aforethought*, *Malice Aforethought* is, therefore, no more a detective story than *The Face on the Cutting-Room Floor*.

Mr Iles does not assert, however, that Mr McCabe actually broke the 'golden rule of the first-class detective-story writer, that no vital information known to the detective shall be withheld from the reader'. He merely states – and states correctly – that Mr McCabe 'comes at times periously *near* to breaking' the rule.

Other critics, less cautious, accused McCabe of giving the reader no chance to solve the problem. 'The reader cannot possibly know that McCabe killed Jensen,' says a very famous critic. And another one, equally famous, asserts that the reader has no chance to realize that McCabe went to the studio and found Estella's body after he had left the 'Haunt' on Thursday night, 28th November 1935.

Both allegations are true to a certain extent. The reader cannot possibly *know* that McCabe killed Jensen – but he can *suspect* it: Mr McCabe, who attains his effects – if any – rather by intimation than by exact statement, can hardly be expected to change this technique where murder and its deduction are concerned.

And indeed, though there might be a lack of exact statement, yet there is an abundance of intimation and implication, which attains quite often the effect of direct statement.

There is an obvious break between the sixteenth and seventeenth chapters – a break which, to my mind, hints clearly at what has happened in between. Moreover, the first sentence of the seventeenth chapter informs the reader that McCabe did not sleep that night: 'The rain ceased for some hours after midnight but it began again in the early dawn . . .'

Not satisfied with this, Mr McCabe gives the reader another chance in the twentieth chapter, when he views the line of suspects (suspects from the reader's point of view), and remarks: 'Even if one of them was the murderer, he should have been able to control himself.'

Even if: this is a plain statement – though in an indirect form – that none of them was the murderer. All the suspects are present (except Happy, who is soon cleared of any suspicion). The careful reader knows, therefore, already in the twentieth chapter (if not before) that McCabe is the murderer of Jensen.

In the case of Estella the same method is being used: the same hiatus of time (which indicates that an important event has happened) can be found between the third and fourth chapter.

Moreover, McCabe hints at it by asking Dinah to keep Robertson at the 'Haunt' for at least two hours. He goes so far as even to say exactly what his suspicions are, where he is going and what he is going to do.

He tells his readers that his curiosity was first roused when Robertson said that he left the studio at a quarter past four. The reader, knowing, just as McCabe does, that Robertson's telephone was engaged between six thirty and six thirty-five that afternoon, more than two hours after the time at which Robertson now asserts to have left his room, knows, therefore, what McCabe's suspicions are, and is able to imagine what he is going to do. Even the exact nature of McCabe's suspicions is explained when McCabe says: 'Jesus Christ – the face on the cutting-room floor.'

The reader is prepared for this by the title of the book. It is true that he cannot yet understand the exact importance which the phrase is to attain, later, in the case of Estella; yet it is not long till the meaning is explained to him: already in the next chapter follows the conversation with Smith, in the course of which the reader learns all there is to know about the 'face on the cutting-room floor'.

And the fourth chapter begins with the sentence: 'The next morning when I arrived at the studio the crowds were *already* there' – the *already* is a clear hint.

All this shows us that McCabe's story conforms to certain dictates of the detective story critics, but fails in certain others. The critics, however, contradict each other so often that no unmistakable definition can be found of what a detective story ought to be. All dictates thus become mere matters of taste.

Certain critics, probably realizing this dilemma, abstained, therefore, from passing any criticisms other than those dictated by their own likes and dislikes.

The Times Literary Supplement of 29th August speaks about 'the atrocious pun in the title', comments on 'a desire to be modern and outspoken', tries to justify its comments by saying that Mr McCabe 'tempts discussion of the origins of his work in this way because he fills it out with so many of his own ideas of life and the world in general, whether in digressions or through the mouths of his characters' and states finally that 'the result is a book in which the setting is tiresome, the problem lacking in elaboration or development and the detective too long over a dull job'.

Well, it seems as if *The Times Literary Supplement* does not like Mr McCabe overmuch.

Cyril Connolly, so often quoted before, complains that McCabe 'tries to be funny and is only facetious', yet admits that it is 'an averagely readable and competent detective story all the same ... something in the line of Dashiell Hammett, but without his talent. If you saw *The Thin Man* on the screen you will know what this line is.' (About Dashiell Hammett see earlier quotation from Cyril Connolly: ' ... the great period of the detective story seems to me ... to end with ... Dashiell Hammett's *The Glass Key* in

America in 1931 . . .') '*The Face on the Cutting-Room Floor*', continues Mr Connolly, has, therefore, 'all the faults of the talkie novel style, its sentimentality, insistence on virility, bad grammar and unnecessary close-ups of passion'.

The Times Literary Supplement of 20th June agrees with Mr Connolly: 'The story might be more intelligible on the screen than in a book: the characters live in the world of the American film-thriller.'

Note here the repeated references to the cinema: Mr W. H. Auden borrowed his terminology from the *film studio*, 'the *Documentary* Murder' and 'the Murder *on location*'. Mr Connolly borrows his comparison from the *screen* (*The Thin Man*), and speaks about '*close-ups*' of passion and about the '*talkie*' novel style. *The Times Literary Supplement* finds that 'the story might be more intelligible on the *screen*' and that 'the characters live in the world of the American *film* thriller'.

Smith himself says in the twenty-second chapter: 'It almost sounds like a movie story.' I find myself quoted by Mr McCabe as saying: 'It's the best picture I've seen for years.'

And Mr Maurice L. Richardson coins a fine phrase by complaining that he finds Mr McCabe's story rather 'on the Wardour side of the street'.

Well, that is where it belongs.

The Face on the Cutting-Room Floor was written by a man who came from the 'Wardour side of the street'. It is hardly surprising, therefore, to find that it is a much closer approach to a film story than to a novel. It is a novelized film story – a reversal of the usual procedure of filming a novel. Filmed, it would possibly turn out to be the normal Hollywood version of crime and punishment. A detective story in fancy dress.

I said at the beginning that only an analysis of McCabe's own sociological background can help us, the readers and critics, to understand the reason for his failure.

A film man will always write a film story. It may be a good novel at the same time. But it will always be more suitable for filming than for printing.

It is, therefore, not surprising at all to find *The Times Literary Supplement* adding to Mr Connolly's complaint of 'facetiousness' that of garrulousness, prolixity, verbosity, complicacy of plot and excess of characters: 'The complications of the plot are increased by an army of subsidiary characters introduced to keep it moving . . . That all of them are indispensable to the story is perhaps questionable. But it is certain that some of them are far too fond of the sound of their voices.'

Now there is not much left of Mr McCabe. Impossible to count all blows. Count him out. Have mercy.

All right, gong.

Mr Connolly wins: the whole species is no good. Mr McCabe is only a victim: the detective story as such is to blame.

'We are tired of books in which the criminal tells the story,' says Mr Connolly. 'Tired of "the psychological crime"; tired of the Van Dine five-card trick, in which each suspect is made to seem guilty, and one must guess at the right moment; tired of the Bradshaw and tide-table alibi, of the murder that is really an accident, of the detective story that is really a novel, of the words-of-one-syllable crime of violence (and then I knew I had to kill the old man. It was the only way to get her. And I knew she knew we had to. And I guess he knew too.)'

This could almost make you think that Mr Connolly is tired. But it is merely an optical illusion. Mr Connolly has some suggestions to make.

'What can be done for the detective story?' he asks.

'One of the things, I think, is for crime writers to concentrate once more on evoking horror, not by a succession of murders, which defeats its object, but by keeping the murderer on the stage long enough for the reader to get fond of him. Or by choosing sympathetic types – not enough children, for instance, are murdered. Another variation would be to make the police really crooked for once; the most sophisticated readers would be startled by a story in which the detective battles with all the resources of a corrupt headquarters. Or even by one which broke all the unwritten laws, refused to disclose clues, introduced magic freely, and did not, on the other hand, introduce the murderer till the last page, with an ending like:

'"John Hanbury was killed by a Mr Grogblossom, you say – but how? Why? I've never even heard of him! Besides, the motive?" The great detective shrugged his shoulders. "We shall never know," he murmured.'

That sounds pleasant. 'Not enough children are murdered' – Mr Connolly is a philanthropist.

'What about it, Mr McCabe? Why take notice of the laws if a fine chap like Mr Connolly proposes to break all unwritten laws, to refuse to disclose clues, to introduce magic freely and not to introduce the murderer till the last page?'

'All right, Mr Müller.'

'Who said that? Who said "All right, Mr Müller"? Who's there?'

'Knock knock, Mr Müller. This is McCabe.'

'But Jesus, man, you're supposed to be dead. Now I've written all those pages about you and there you pop up afterwards. All the epitaph in vain. Why don't you stay dead? Don't you feel ashamed?'

'Well, Mr Müller, it's about all these critics. Mr Connolly wants you to introduce magic freely. So here I am. Something'd gotta be done. So I've come along to show them.'

'Show them what?'

'Well, you see they're all mistaken. You too.'

'Oh, am I?'

'Yes. You are.'

'I don't believe it. Come on and prove me wrong, if you can!'

'All right. Tell me why did Jensen run away to Norway?'

'Because he thought he'd murdered Estella.'

'Had he?'

'Of course not. But he thought he had.'

'How could he? He tried to save her. She threatened to kill herself.'

'Well . . .'

'Well? Who's crackers now?'

'Well . . . look here, Mr McCabe, you can't do this sort of thing. You wrote a nice story and I explained it all nicely and then you come along and upset everything. It just isn't done. And besides you're dead anyway.'

'But what about those critics who don't even leave a dead man in peace? Come on, and let me rewrite the story the way Mr Connolly likes it.'

'Oh, stop talking about Mr Connolly, McCabe. I'm telling you that you just can't do it with your public. They won't like it. No one likes to be made a fool of and a guy what likes reading detective stories likes least of all them bastards what dislike any deviation from a scheme they've got used to.'

'But remember, Mr Müller, what Mr Connolly said. You mustn't get tough with your readers. Don't call them bastards. The thing to do for a writer is not self-consciously to introduce himself like Michael Arlen and not to get tough with him like Hemingway. That's what Mr Connolly said in the last June issue of the *Daily Telegraph*.'

'Oh, shut up, McCabe. Go to hell.'

'That's where I come from, Mr Müller.'

Pause for veneration.

'Now look here, McCabe, I'll tell you something. Once in Berlin I saw a picture that was called *Die zwölf verfluchten Herren – the Twelve Confounded Gentlemen*, if you want me to translate it into your lingo. It was all about twelve guys who got themselves bumped off one after the other; there was a hell of a mess of red juice in that picture, and the people in the picture house were waiting for the climax of it all, 'cause the thing was kind of hot and they knew it would have to get still a damned lot hotter towards the end. They were waiting for a fine blood-bath to top all the previous killings. But then it came to the end and what you think it was?'

'A close-up, I suggest, brother Müller; Boy gets Girl.'

'The hell he did. It was all a gag. They were all alive in the end, the whole dirty dozen, all alive and kicking, see?'

'No, brother, that beats me.'

'That's what I told you. It beat all of us. Though it was well done. Clever. Really a fine gag, a lovely finish, quite a new story, and what you think the audience did?'

'They enjoyed it, huh?'

'Like hell they did. They whistled! Lord, they did whistle. Now, you know that whistling in Germany is a sign of disapproval. It used to be, anyway, till Hitler came. Now it's all different, of course. There's no disapproval left. They've abolished it officially. You sure can't hear them whistle nowadays. But in those days you could. Jesus. I never heard whistling like that in all my life. They disapproved. And they didn't hide it. They felt they were being made fools of. And they didn't like it a damned bit. They whistled like the Pied Piper of Hamelin plus all his gang of Musical Mice. If you haven't heard a Berlin audience whistle you don't know what whistling means. They whistled on door keys and on two fingers and on anything they could lay their hands on. Don't ask me what they did lay their hands on. They kicked up the damn biggest hell of a row I ever heard. Yessir, they sure did. And what's that to you? You've got to stick to the rules! Don't try anything new. Do as you're told. Supply your reader with a traditional happy end. Or a traditionally unhappy one. But for sweet Jesus' sake don't try to make saps of your readers. You won't keep many if you do. What you say, McCabe?'

'What I told you before. You can change a story. But you can't change things after they've happened. And you don't even know what happened. Who killed Jensen?'

'Now, you wouldn't try to fool me, would you? Why, you killed him of course.'

'You think so? What about Maria?'

'Why should she have done it?'

'Disgust and jealousy. You like quoting me. Remember what I said in chapter ten?'

'I don't. What was it about?'

'About the film. When she sees it for the second time. At the Yard. I said: "I saw Maria's face, how her lids got slowly weary and sank down and how the lips grew flaccid and how all features gave way until she suddenly pulled herself together and how now weakness and disappointment changed slowly into something I didn't like to watch." What do you think that something was in her face?'

'How should I know? Make yourself clear.'

'It was murder. She killed Jensen.'

Second pause for veneration.

'I don't believe it, McCabe. It doesn't make sense. Who dropped the film on your doormat? You know the second part of the film, the one you cut off and held back, the one which Dinah found on your doormat.'

'I never cut it off. The girl did.'

'Which girl?'

'The one whom Dinah met on the way up to my flat when she found the film.'

'Well, that beats me again. Ask me some more.'

'All right. Who killed Jensen?'

'Well . . . Maria did. You just told me so, didn't you?'

'I didn't. Do you know who really killed him?'

'No, I wouldn't dream of trying to figure them out any longer. Who killed him anyway?'

'Robertson did.'

'So he did. And why, if I may ask a little question?'

'Because he loved Estella. Jealousy.'

'Well, I'll be damned. Next you'll tell me I killed him.'

'Well, to tell you the truth, you did.'

'I thought so. Now you have made everything quite clear. Tell me, anyway, what reason I should have had to kill Jensen. I hardly knew him.'

'You had a bet with Smith, for a good sum of dough. He was sure that I had killed Jensen. You said I hadn't. You were so sure of it that you offered him a bet on it. He accepted. To win the bet you killed Jensen.'

'Yes. Now I see it quite clearly, I killed Jensen, you killed Jensen, Maria killed Jensen – we all killed Jensen. Who else killed him and why did they all kill him? Haven't they got any work to do? Must they all stalk about, all killing the same poor old geezer?'

'That's history, Mr Müller. You can't change it. Look here: the girl whom Dinah saw coming out of my street door, she killed him. And then Smith, of course. He killed Jensen to win his bet with you. To get me convicted for it. And then everyone else killed him. You'll hardly be able to find a human being that couldn't have killed him. That's circumstantial evidence. Thank you for your kind attention, Mr Müller, Goodbye, Mr Müller. See you later.'

'I hope not. I guess I'll book a room at another hotel.'

Exit Mr McCabe.

Well, that would have been a fine ending for Mr Connolly: 'The most sophisticated reader would be startled by a story . . . which broke all the unwritten laws . . .'

Our ending did certainly break more laws than were ever unwritten. Thank you, Mr Connolly.

The possibilities for alternative endings to *any* detective story are *infinite*.

There is not even a need to have anyone murdered at all: neither Estella, nor Jensen, nor McCabe, nor Smith: they could all have committed suicide, or they could have been killed by accident or in self-defence.

But in that case the book might have had to share the fate of Cecil Champain Lowis's *Prodigal Portion*, on which *The Times Literary Supplement* remarked: 'The publishers admit that, though this is the nature of a detective story, "the mystery has no reality and no crime has been committed", which leaves the reader faintly dissatisfied.'

The climax of all slapstick comedy is the smashing of something – smashing crockery is very effective – but smashing a man's skull is the real stuff.

The reader remains faintly dissatisfied if he finds in the end that the skull was merely cracked.

Death is the thing.

And McCabe gave us death, not only in fiction, but in fact. What wonderful sacrifice for an ideal! Self-sacrifice, self-denial and blind devotion, exemplarily blind and, therefore, worthy of the widest imitation.

Mass action is required.

Yesterday afternoon I met Maria Ray. I was on my way to the publishers to return the first corrected galley proofs of *The Face on the Cutting-Room Floor*. The proofs in my satchel, the satchel under my arm, my hands in my pockets, I was walking down Bond Street, studying the varieties of the Mayfair femininalities in the windows of the dress-shops, when the door of one opened and Maria, black furred, tan skinned, platinum haired, rushed out, ran into me, knocked down the portfolio, apologized hurriedly and was already about to step into her car when her eyes, cast down with faint embarrassment, went back and met the portfolio which had opened and spilled its contents over the pavement. She saw the front page of the book, read Cameron McCabe's name, startled, stopped, looked again at the paper and from there up at me, recognized me finally and with surprise, said 'Hallo, hallo . . .' and hesitated again, unable to remember my name.

'Müller,' I succoured. 'U with two dots.'

'How are you?' she asked, still somewhat affected by the shock of sudden unpleasant memory.

'All right, thank you,' I muttered.

'What about picking up those things,' she suggested, pointing awkwardly at the scattered pages on the ground.

I bent down, picked up the satchel, saw her eyes following me, saw them resting on the page with McCabe's name, and murmured, 'Poor Mr McCabe.'

It had slipped out before I could prevent it.

'What did you say?' she cut in unbelievingly. 'Did I really hear you saying poor Mr McCabe? Well, honest to God, you are a crazy feller. Why don't you save your pity for poor Mr Smith? He needs it more up in his tiresome heaven than Mr McCabe making whoopee with the younger generation of the more susceptible she-devils.'

'I wouldn't be too sure they aren't sharing the same boarding-house,' I mumbled.

'Anyway, reserve your pity for the better man.' She looked seriously outraged.

'Well,' I stammered, 'I can't help feeling more with the victim than with the murderer. Maybe it's just stupid sentimentality. I reckon it's only my upbringing . . .'

'What do you mean by victim and murderer?' she interrupted angrily. 'Who is the victim and who the murderer?'

'Well . . .' I stuttered, 'if you start that way . . .'

'Which way?' she shouted so loudly that some passers-by turned their heads. 'There are no two ways, you little hair-splitting schoolmaster! I heard of the sermon you have written to deface McCabe's book. Tell me, little preacher, which way am I starting? There's only one, and we have all started on it and we'll all end on it, like Estella and Jensen and McCabe and Smith, and I'll follow and you won't be spared.'

'I know, I know . . .' I pleaded, 'but please don't shout.'

'All right,' she grumbled. 'Come into my car. I'm not allowed to park here, anyway.'

She opened the door of the car and I stepped in, rather against my better judgement.

'Now,' she ejaculated, when we had started down Bond Street, 'if you can't help feeling more with the victim than with the murderer, why don't you pray for Smith instead of writing a silly epilogue to McCabe's bundle of lies!'

'Yes, of course,' I tried to pacify her, 'yes, you're right about McCabe, of course. He is a murderer himself, of course, but so is Smith. And McCabe is the victim.'

She turned into a side street and stopped the car. Then she turned her head slowly and looked at me for a long time without speaking. Then she said: 'Well, now, are you really as silly as you pretend, master? Do you really believe all that tripe? Can you really imagine Smith murdering anyone?'

I began to regret having let myself in with this. She became quite embarrassing with her obsessed big eyes.

'Please,' I implored, 'please don't excite yourself, it's all over, really . . . it's too late now. You can't change anything . . .'

'Can't I?' she shouted, throwing her arms up so that her hands hit the top of the car. 'Can't I really, can't I?'

Then suddenly she changed and became quite quiet. 'Well, I suppose you're right, I can't. It's too late, it can't be changed. I don't want to change it anyway . . .' Then, after a little time, she added: 'But I want to tell you a few things, you wise old man. Just a few things, so that you won't go on walking about with that omniscient air on your benign bishop's face.'

She halted again and then she said: 'Smith never killed McCabe. McCabe killed himself to get Smith convicted for murder.'

'Lord have mercy,' I said. 'O Good God in Heaven have mercy on us.'

I had not said that for more than forty years; it was a strange feeling to hear oneself praying for the first time in a man's life.

'Oh shut up,' she cried. 'For Heavenly Lord's sake shut your bloody gate.'

It was quiet for a time. Then a policeman came walking over to the car.

She started the engine again.

Then when we were driving again, she said: 'You see you can kill a man in this island but you can't park your car in a dead empty street.' And after another few minutes she continued: '. . . but you know that was a fine revenge to kill himself in order to get Smith killed by the law.'

'Revenge . . .' I stammered, '. . . revenge for what? McCabe got acquitted . . . And Smith was only doing his job, anyway . . . he didn't wish him any harm . . .'

'Oh no, no,' she screamed. 'No harm at all! He was just in love with me, that's all . . . All there is . . . just in love with me . . . love, you know . . . love your neighbour . . . but not your neighbour's wife . . .'

'But what about the book?' I asked her. 'Why did he say Smith was going to kill him?'

'Isn't that evident? Must you ask that?'

'You mean he wrote it to implicate Smith?'

She nodded.

'But why didn't Smith defend himself? Why didn't he tell the truth?'

'He knew it wouldn't help. No one would believe him. He went to McCabe to tell him that he was in love with me. That's what they really talked about that last morning. Smith didn't want to sneak in between McCabe and me as Jensen had done. Besides, he didn't want to get himself killed from behind by McCabe.'

'But McCabe never mentioned in his book that Smith ever showed even the slightest interest in you.'

'You *are* a quickwit! What would have been the use of the book if he told the truth in it?'

'Yes,' I admitted. 'You are right as can be . . . But how do you know all this? How did you learn it?'

'Smith didn't go straight over to Scotland Yard after McCabe had shot himself. He came over to see me first. And he told me.'

'But if that is so, why . . . why didn't you tell the truth in court, why didn't you defend Smith?'

She looked in front of her, straight, cold, stubborn.

'Why should I defend him?' she asked.

'Didn't you love him?'

'No!' she shouted.

'And it didn't matter to him that you didn't love him?'

'Do you know what Dickens says?'

'No.'

'If every man had to wait until some woman loved him there would be an awful lot of celibates. And, after all, would it be fair to ask for something and give nothing in return?'

'No,' I admitted, 'I suppose it wouldn't.'

I looked out. We had left the West End. I did not know the streets we were passing.

'Where are you going?' I asked her.

'Out of town,' she said.

'I must go back,' I said. 'Will you please put me down somewhere?'

'You can get out here,' she said. 'Take a taxi.'

'Thank you very much for telling me everything,' I said.

'It was a pleasure,' she said. 'Put it into your epilogue.'

'I can't very well,' I said. 'It would make life very hard for you.'

'Do it,' she said. 'Don't put your nose into other people's affairs. I can manage my own.'

'All right,' I said.

But I thought it is not all right at all, there is a question unanswered: why did Smith not defend himself?

She made you believe she had answered the question. It sounded all perfect as she said it. But it was the way she said it. Not what she said.

I repeated her words in my mind till I arrived at the question:

'Would it be fair to ask for something and give nothing in return?'

That was the question unanswered.

And the answer was *no*.

No voice was loud enough to shout no. For fair was a wrong word. The right word was murder. That was the answer.

I was looking at her and I found she was looking at me. Her eyes opened widely and rapidly into mine, then closed slowly. Then I found I had been wrong about it. I thought that perhaps she would marry me despite my age. I was going to ask her when I saw the gun in her hand and before she could aim at me I took it away and shot her dead.

ENVOI

'As for attempts being made by malevolent persons to fix crimes upon innocent men, of course it is constantly happening. It's a marked feature, for instance, of all systems of rule by coercion . . . if the police cannot get hold of a man they think dangerous by fair means, they do it by foul.'

E. C. BENTLEY
Trent's Last Case

APOLOGIES

Some of the quotations of book reviews in the epilogue had to be altered. The name of the reviewer, the name of the paper which published the review, and the date of publication are correct in each case. Sometimes altered were, however, the name of the author, the title of his book and the names of the characters therein. These are replaced, respectively, by *Cameron McCabe*, by *The Face on the Cutting-Room Floor* and by the *names of the characters therefrom*.

Intended was neither an attack on, nor a criticism of, the reviews and reviewers which were thus quoted.

A list of quotations with their sources is appended.

LIST OF QUOTATIONS

Book Reviews

M. L. RICHARDSON, *Observer*, 8th November 1936, *By Greta Bridge*, LOUIS GOODRICH.

GERALD GOULD, *Observer*, 20th September 1936, *Major Operation*, JAMES BARKE.

L. P. HARTLEY, *Observer*, 13th December 1936, *Inhale and Exhale*, WILLIAM SAROYAN.

HORACE HORSNELL, *Observer*, 6th December 1936, *Duet in Discord*, ELIZABETH GARNER.

'TORQUEMADA', *Observer*, 17th May 1936, *Tragedy at Wembley*, CECIL F. GREGG.

'TORQUEMADA', *Observer*, 28th June 1936, *So I Killed Her*, L. O. MOSLEY.

'TORQUEMADA', *Observer*, 28th June 1936, *On the Night of the 18th*, LAURENCE W. MEYNELL.

DOREEN WALLACE, *Sunday Times*, 21st June 1936, *We in Captivity*, KATHLEEN PAWLE.

MILWARD KENNEDY, *Sunday Times*, 5th July 1936, *So I Killed Her*, L. O. MOSLEY.

MILWARD KENNEDY, *Sunday Times*, 6th December 1936, *The Anatomy of Murder*, ANTHOLOGY.

HOWARD SPRING, *Evening Standard*, 14th May 1936, *I'd Do It Again*, FRANK TILSLEY.

HOWARD SPRING, *Evening Standard*, 15th May 1936, *Tales of Detection*, ANTHOLOGY.

JOHN BROPHY, *Daily Telegraph*, n.d., *Duet in Discord*, ELIZABETH GARNER.

C. DAY LEWIS, *Daily Telegraph*, 10th July 1936, *The Gilt Kid*, JAMES CURTIS.

CYRIL CONNOLLY, *Daily Telegraph*, 16th June 1936, *The Sutton Place Murders*, ROBERT G. DEAN.

CYRIL CONNOLLY, *Daily Telegraph*, 16th June 1936, Introduction to Book Column.

CYRIL CONNOLLY, *Daily Telegraph*, 30th June 1936, *Mr Loveday's Little Outing*, EVELYN WAUGH.

CYRIL CONNOLLY, *Daily Telegraph*, 12th July 1936, Introduction to Book Column.

FRANCIS ILES, *Daily Telegraph*, 2nd May 1936, *Trent's Own Case*, BENTLEY and ALLEN.

W. H. AUDEN, *Daily Telegraph*, 5th January 1937, *Murder in the Family*, JAMES RONALD.

ANONYMOUS, *The Times*, 27th October, 1936, *Of Mortal Love*, WILLIAM GERHARDI.

ANONYMOUS, *The Times Literary Supplement*, 9th May 1936, *Gulls Against the Sky*, MICHAEL COPELAND.

ANONYMOUS, *The Times Literary Supplement*, 16th May 1936, *Trent's Own Case*, BENTLEY and ALLEN.

ANONYMOUS, *The Times Literary Supplement*, 20th June 1936, *The Stuffed Men*, ANTHONY A. NEWNES.

ANONYMOUS, *The Times Literary Supplement*, 4th July 1936, *Prodigal Portion*, CECIL C. LOWIS.

ANONYMOUS, *The Times Literary Supplement*, 9th August 1936, *Belt of Suspicion*, M. RUSSELL WAKEFIELD.

ANONYMOUS, *The Times Literary Supplement*, 14th November 1936, *Death of a Dog*, LEONORA EYLES.

Books

V. I. PUDOVKIN, *Film Technique* (G. Newnes, London, 1933).

EDMUND WILSON, *Axel's Castle* (Chas Scribner, New York, 1934).

ERNEST HEMINGWAY, *Death in the Afternoon* (Jonathan Cape, London, 1932).

ERNEST HEMINGWAY, *Winner Take Nothing* (Jonathan Cape, London, 1934).

C. STAFFORD DICKENS, 'Day In Day Out' (Manuscript).

OTTO LUDWIG, 'Editing' in *The World Film Encyclopedia*.

Periodicals

J. KASHKEEN, *International Literature No. 5* (Moscow, 1935).

A. V. McCANN, *Time, Vol. XXVII, No. 21* (Chicago, 1936).

Afterword

A DOSSIER ON A VANISHED AUTHOR AND A VANISHED BOOK BY THE EDITORS*

During the long hot summer of 1937 there appeared in London, wrapped in the shocking yellow cover of the House of Gollancz, studded with aggressive black and violet typography, a book with the weird title *The Face on the Cutting-Room Floor*. The author appeared to be a certain Cameron McCabe who wrote the tale in the first person singular. But half-way through the book the author died or was killed or killed himself, and the action continued with an *Epilogue by A.B.C. Müller as Epitaph for Cameron McCabe*. Once you had read the *Epilogue*, you were no wiser, for now there followed a *List of Quotations* which were not quotations and an *Apology* that was no apology. The whole thing was a box of tricks and left a bad taste in many a wry mouth. Traditionalists of the crime story felt themselves cheated. But the prominent critics of the era rather liked it.

Milward Kennedy, the then doyen of the British crime critics, wrote in the *Sunday Times*: 'If you are jaded from a surfeit of conventional detective stories or if you are persuaded that all detective stories are made to a conventional pattern, make haste to read *The Face on the Cutting-Room Floor*; and if you are neither, make haste to read it . . . I have found it difficult to give any idea of it without spoiling it, and I would not do that for worlds.'

E. R. Punshon, another one of the popes of crime criticism of the 1930s, wrote in the *Manchester Guardian*: 'The book contains

---

* A version of this Afterword first appeared in the edition of *The Face on the Cutting-Room Floor* published by Gregg Press (a division of G. K. Hall & Co.), Boston, 1981.

a great deal of very clever writing . . . and may be enjoyed . . . for its purely literary qualities . . . [it] displays itself as being as up to date as could be desired.' Ross McLaren, one of the forgotten masters of the realistic crime novel, wrote in *Punch*: 'This unusual tale . . . is cleverly and elaborately constructed, and the epilogue (over fifty pages) is really ingenious and, as regards detective stories, more than a little informing.'

Sir Herbert Read, the most famous art critic of his day and one who had never deigned to write about crime fiction before, reviewed the book for *Night and Day* (a kind of British *New Yorker*, edited in those days by Graham Greene) and said: 'This thriller is cunningly constructed on the formula of the Hegelian triad – thesis, antithesis and synthesis – . . . a complete philosophy of life . . . a more than ordinary thriller, giving distinction in a literary sphere where distinction is rare.'

The *Evening News*, then one of London's two evening papers and now amalgamated with the *Evening Standard*, wrote under a heading which till then had not been applied to crime stories, *Novels You Should Read*: 'The ingenuity of some authors takes the breath away. A reading of Cameron McCabe's book leaves one helpless with astonishment and amazement that a detective story could be so very, very good. But it is not only the fact that a new kind of story has been told that so pleases the mind of the reader, it is the fact that the author so clearly wants to make detectives of us all: indeed, to obtain the fullest enjoyment from the book one has to be constantly on the alert.'

Reynolds News, a trade union paper, wrote under the title *Starred Selection*: 'Strange breathless story of murder in, and around, a film studio whose curious staccato life is smartly put over . . . to those who like something thoroughly unusual in treatment this is emphatically not to be missed.'

The *Edinburgh Evening News* said: 'The reader is carried to the end on wave after wave of new interest and excitement. This is a detective story with a difference!'

Even the journals of the distant parts of Empire reacted in the same way. *The Dominion* wrote: 'Printed on the familiar yellow jacket is the legend, "Something very special in detective stories". This is very true, for *The Face on the Cutting-Room Floor* is one of the most unusual novels of its kind that has appeared this year. It is the story of a murder in an English studio, told from a new angle, and one which is exceedingly well negotiated . . . and provides opportunity for racy and interesting descriptions in an ingenious manner . . . a tale for discriminating detective-story enthusiasts.'

And the *Cape Times*, then South Africa's only daily with a claim to literary distinction, said: 'It presents a problem in deduction; it moves on a shifting plane; it has finite construction, a sometimes elliptical but always robust idiom and a solution which leaves one provoked.'

The book was twice chosen as the Book of the Week, twice as the reviewer's double starred selection, and once as the best novel of the year. It appeared in French and German translations, was reprinted eight times in various English pocket editions – but was never issued in the United States. During the 1960s, Ordean A. Hagen rediscovered it and praised it in his Who's Who of crime fiction, *Who Done It?*, as one of the milestones of crime fiction. A decade later, the distinguished British novelist Julian Symons wrote a history of crime fiction under the title *Bloody Murder* ★ (published in 1972 in the U.S. under the title *Mortal Consequences*). On p. 223 of the U.S. paperback edition he refers to *The Face on the Cutting-Room Floor* as 'the detective story to end detective stories . . . a dazzling and perhaps fortunately unrepeatable box of tricks'. In April 1974, he added in the *New Review* that the book had become such a rarity as to be 'worth getting hold of at almost any price'.

Two months later, in June 1974, probably encouraged by Ordean Hagen and Julian Symons, Victor Gollancz published a facsimile reprint of the 1937 edition. Since the publishers did not know the real author they advertised for his heirs and placed the royalties in a trust fund for them. In July 1974, Symons reviewed the reissue in the *New Review*: 'A couple of months ago I said that Cameron McCabe's *The Face on the Cutting-Room Floor* was a curiosity worth getting hold of at almost any price. The price, it turns out, is £2.25, in the reissue just published by Gollancz . . . A final word about the author, who is deeply involved in the story, and of whose identity his publishers seem unaware. His name was (perhaps is) Ernst Wilhelm Julius Bornemann, he worked in films, probably as a cameraman, and he wrote at least two other books neither of which I've read. More information from readers would be welcome.'

Fredric J. Warburg, founder and late senior partner of the distinguished London publishing house Martin Secker & Warburg, replied in one of the next numbers of the *New Review*: 'Sir, – About Ernest Borneman, the author of *The Face on the Cutting-Room Floor*, referred to by Julian Symons in his article on "Criminal Activities", he was a friend of mine and a charming

---

★ A revised edition of *Bloody Murder* is available in Penguin.

individual. He fled from Nazi Germany in the 1930s as a Leftist likely to be unpopular with the regime. He did work in films, as Julian Symons remarks, and indeed made one, I believe, for the Canadian official film unit. As an Aryan German, he was arrested in May 1940, at the time of the great scare of invasion, and shipped off to Canada to an internment camp. An important Home Office official, who had known him quite well before his arrest, saw him quite by chance when inspecting the camp and secured his release. He returned to England and wrote other books, though I don't think they were published over here at the time. He returned to Germany a good many years after the war and has there written a number of books of considerable importance . . .'

Meanwhile another long review of the reissued *Face on the Cutting-Room Floor* by the British novelist and screen writer Frederic Raphael had appeared in the *Sunday Times* of 25 August 1974, which ended with the words: 'The last quarter of the book consists of a critique of the reviewers and what they will have to say about his story. Connolly, Iles, Milward Kennedy, Torquemada, Day Lewis, the whole galère, are literally taken personally by the dead and deadly author who substitutes his own name and his book's title for those in recent reviews by the aforesaid gentlemen and then demolishes their objections. This section is positively Nabokovian in its piqued, captious elegance; its far from pale fire is worth the price of admission on its own. He's an insolent, bitchy bastard, McCabe, and in the literary sense at least, he gets away with murder.

'Who is he? Who was he? No one seems to know; he is indeed a mystery author. (I should like to think that he is the scapegrace brother of the great Stan McCabe, caught thrillingly lowdown by a substitute flinging himself to the left in the Trent Bridge Test not more than a year or two before publication.) Since the hero of the book bears its author's name and is killed three-quarters of the way through, it is perhaps not surprising that his début was also his swansong.'

In the *Sunday Times* of 1 September 1974, Brian Doyle replied: 'Sir – In his interesting review of Cameron McCabe's detective story *The Face on the Cutting-Room Floor*, first published in 1937, Frederic Raphael asks: "Who is Cameron McCabe? Who was he? No one seems to know; he is indeed a mystery author." He also goes on to imply that "His debut was also his swansong". – "Cameron McCabe" was in fact a pen-name of Ernst Wilhelm Julius Bornemann, and he published at least two other books – *Face the Music* (for which I cannot trace a date) and *Tremolo* (published by Harper's, New York, 1948).'

After the Gollancz edition of 1974 was distributed in the U.S. by Doubleday, Derrick Murdoch reviewed it in *The New York Review of Books*: 'This freakish prewar classic has been described by critic Julian Symons as the detective story to end detective stories. Though it didn't, it might have. For it proclaimed an anarchic gospel: "The possibilities for alternative endings to any detective story are infinite." But in 1937 not enough people read it for the message to be widely received. And in any case, even if this was a truth sly authors admitted to themselves, the idea was too disturbing to be believed by a tidy minded public with an abiding trust in shipshape plots. So the book went out of print without ever seeing a second edition or American publication, and has lain dormant through the years. Today uncertainty exists about the author's real identity, and whether he wrote anything before or after. The pseudonym Cameron McCabe has been borrowed from one of the fiction narrators in the book. Symons flatly states the author was Ernst Wilhelm Julius Bornemann, but this is booby-trapped territory, and conceivably Symons is putting us on.'

Well, we, the editors of Penguin Books, can assure Mr Murdoch that Julian Symons was *not* putting him on, for we've discovered 'Cameron McCabe' spry and alive as a well-known Austrian university professor, teaching sexology at Salzburg University and living on a huge farm in Upper Austria. He is now seventy-one, has guest professorships at three other universities (Marburg, Bremen, and Klagenfurt), is President of the Austrian Society for Research in Sexology and author of about twenty books – but only one of them under the tricky pen-name Cameron McCabe. We have even discovered that the scholarly American periodical *Maledicta* (published, of all . places, in Waukesha, Wisconsin) had dedicated a *Festschrift* to him on his sixty-fifth birthday (*Maledicta*, vol. III, Number 1, Summer 1979).

We quote the following passages from the three-hour tape of an interview in which the *Maledicta* editor, Reinhold Aman, questioned Borneman on the story of his extraordinary life. The published version of this tape was slightly shorter and considerably re-edited. We quote directly from a verbatim transcript:

Aman: Ernest, you've led a completely lunatic life. Do you think you are a success?

Borneman: No.

A: Why not?

B: Because I got bored every time I was successful at something.

A: And turned to something else?

B: Yes.

A: You've been a very successful novelist, a famous film maker, a jazz musician of some standing, a leading journalist who has written for just about every major periodical in England and the U.S., a stage author with a number of well-known plays to your credit – why in the world do you live now in a tiny village in Austria – so small that you don't even need an address for letters to find you: just A-4612 Scharten, Austria?

B: I like it here. It's peaceful and quiet. The air is good. The view is pleasant. I have a working day of eighteen hours. I couldn't manage that in the noise and stink of New York, Paris, London, or Rome.

A: What do you do during those eighteen hours?

B: Half of it I spend reading, the rest writing. I have a private library here that is a good deal larger than some university libraries. And I could never afford a house large enough for my books if I lived in a city.

A: I've seen the library, it's larger than most people's complete apartment, but I never checked exactly what kind of books you keep there.

B: Roughly a third are left-overs from earlier parts of my life – fiction, poetry, literary criticism, aesthetics, cinema, stage plays, jazz, other forms of music and musical history. But the greater part is what I work on now – the borderland between anthropology, psychoanalysis and sexology. I teach at two universities – Salzburg in Austria and Marburg in Germany – Libido Theory in Salzburg and Sexual Psychology in Marburg. The books are my main sources. But of course you can't do research by just reading books. So in fact I only spend four days per week at home, one day in Salzburg, one day in Marburg and the rest with my children.

A: Your children? As far as I know you've got only one son who is an art dealer in London. Are all the others illegitimate?

B: I mean the children I work with. For the last nineteen years we've been running the largest project so far undertaken in any country to find out something about children's sexuality. So far we've interviewed roughly 5,000 children.

A: What kind of children are they? How does the whole thing work?

B: My training analyst gave me the idea to check up if children's rhymes, children's games, children's songs and children's riddles confirmed or refuted Freud's theory of five stages of development—oral, anal, phallic, genital, with a latency phase between the third and fourth. If you could find out when precisely the majority of children became fascinated with a certain rhyme and then got bored with it, you could perhaps ascertain at what precise age they got bored with oral patterns and moved on to anal ones.

A: And did it confirm Freud?

B: Not quite. First of all, everything happens roughly eighteen months later. We think this is because children learn to speak at the age of twelve to eighteen months, and this has a delaying effect on the verbalization of libido phases. Secondly we found relatively little evidence of penis envy, but a lot of evidence of bosom envy. We also found that Freud's equation of male with active, and female with passive, doesn't work any longer with Austrian, Swiss, and German children. Nowadays it's always the little girl who takes the initiative. The little boy likes to be courted. The girls do the courting. Old rhymes and songs where the boy acts the active part and the girl the passive one are being altered everywhere in the German language area so that the girls can take the active one and the boys the passive one. You see the same reversal in traditional children's games.

A: What conclusions do you draw?

B: The obvious ones. Gradual extinction of patriarchy as a social institution.

A: You've written a famous book of nearly a thousand pages that bears the title *Patriarchy* and for some mysterious reason has never been translated into English. What's it all about?

B: Actually I wrote it in English, but the manuscript got lost during a postal strike in England on the way to my typist. By then I had moved to Germany, so I had to reconstruct it all in German. The most horrible job I ever did in my life. Took nearly ten years. It's a history of pre-patriarchic societies in Europe. Everything we know about matrilineal, matrilocal, matrilateral cultures of the palaeolithic, mesolithic and early neolithic. I excerpted roughly 40,000 sources in the course of forty years. I thought the book would become the bible of the feminists, but since it was written by a man they rejected it – and plagiarized it. There's hardly a feminist work written in any tongue that hasn't pinched whole chapters, pages, paragraphs. Nearly every American publisher rejected it – not because they disliked it but because it's far too long for the American market and would drive every translator mad – so they say.

A: What caused you to devote yourself to two projects so different as children's sexuality and prehistoric society?

B: They aren't that different. My academic career was influenced by half a dozen teachers: Wilhelm Reich in Germany, Bronislaw Malinowski and George Thomson in England, Vere Gordon Childe in Scotland, Géza Róheim and Melville J. Herskovits in the U.S. Now Malinowski and Herskovits were anthropologists. Reich and Róheim were psychoanalysts. Childe was a prehistoric archaeologist and Thomson a scholar of Greek with a strong leaning to pre-Greek cultures on the Balkan Peninsula. All six of them, however, were united in that they took an uncommonly strong interest in sexuality. This caused me to consider the common denominator of their work – sexual research – as my own destiny, a sort of moral obligation to carry on where they had left off and to cultivate the territory they had in common.

A: You became important to us, the students and scholars of verbal aggression, because you wrote an enormous two-volume work on German sexual idioms which also contained a large number of terms of sexual insult. What caused you to turn your mind to these *Maledicta* activities?

B: I was born in Germany, emigrated to England as a boy of eighteen when Hitler came to power and was called back by the German Federal Government in 1960 to build up and head a Federal TV Network. By then I had forgotten to read and speak German. I had married an Englishwoman. I had become a British citizen and our son was born in Canada. I had been out of Germany for twenty-seven years when I received the call to come back. In order to learn German for the second time I used to make systematic notes of German idioms because that was my weakest side. Since there were no skilled TV specialists in Germany at that time, I couldn't find anyone to delegate my routine work to and therefore had to work till after midnight almost every day. Often, when I came out of the office at dawn, I found I hadn't eaten all day. So I asked a taxi driver one night where I could eat that time of night. He showed me two all-night restaurants which were cheap and had good food. I used to eat there almost every night and I used to make notes of everything idiomatic that was being said around me. For a budding sexologist I must have been uncommonly naive, but I swear that I didn't cotton on to the fact that these were street girls' joints till it dawned on me, while sorting out my notes, that I seemed to have a disproportionate number of sexual idioms. After the German Supreme Court in Karlsruhe had decided in 1961 that the Federal Government had no right to start a Federal TV Network and my own organization with some 600 employees that I had hired was dissolved, I decided to turn my notes on German idioms into a book on German sexual idioms. Having by accident effected good relations to the underworld, I began interviewing prostitutes and pimps all over Germany. I became quite well known in these circles and got introduced to highly specialized branches of the trade, for instance sadistic and masochistic varieties. Which helped to make my book pretty spicy.

A: Your children's books, too, contained a huge number of terms of aggression.

B: If you say 'children's books' you make it sound as if it had been books *for* children. Of course, they were books *about* children. They consisted of the transcribed tapes of the songs, rhymes, riddles and games that the kids had sung and spoken for me. Naturally, since these were big-city kids they also used a lot of slang terms, and since there is an enormous amount of aggression in these kids they used an enormous amount of terms of insult and aggression.

A: Is it true that you had some difficulties with parents, teachers, and other authorities?

B: Yes, only too true. It's impossible for a grown up to interview children without causing suspicion. And if the adults discover that some of the rhymes you collect aren't to their taste they can get very irritated. Four times I was arrested by the police and released again only by showing my credentials, my books and my academic record. It's hard to believe for most adults that someone who is heterosexual and without paedophilic leanings may still be interested in the sex life of children.

A: What about schoolteachers?

B: Well, many teachers offered me their help but I always rejected it because I discovered that the kids don't trust you any longer if you approach them through 'official' channels. Each year, during the school vacations, I've been going from town to town, from school to school, in order to copy 'dirty' verses from lavatory walls and school desks. Here, too, the authorities were uncooperative because they felt themselves in some obscure way responsible for the kids' fantasies. Usually, the moment I'd gone they began to paint over or plane away what I had discovered – as if trying to erase their own bad conscience.

A: Who financed this project? It must have cost a great deal of money?

B: By the standards of university grants it was cheap – roughly $300,000 by now. I financed it entirely out of my own pocket. The Swiss publishers Walter – a highly specialized house that publishes C. G. Jung, Jacques Lacan, and Jean Piaget gave me

30,000 Swiss francs for the right to publish my findings. The remainder came out of my own savings.

A: How did you manage to save that much?

B: That's a long story. As I said, I studied social anthropology with Bronislaw Malinowski at the London School of Economics and then prehistoric archaeology with Vere Gordon Childe in Edinburgh. When the war broke out, I was interned by the British, although I had been denaturalized by the Germans in 1935 and had been a stateless subject since then. In 1940 I was deported to Canada and there I was released to work for John Grierson, the father of documentary films. I made a good many pictures about anthropological and ethnological subjects. When Grierson became head of the two most important UNESCO departments in Paris, Mass Communications and Information, he sent for me and made me acting head of the film section. This was in 1947. A year later I met Orson Welles in Paris who wanted to make a feature about Homeric Greece and was looking for a script writer with knowledge of pre-classical Greek. When he heard that I had known George Thomson whom he considered to be the greatest scholar of Homeric Greece, he hired me away from UNESCO at three times the salary I had earned till then. He asked me what I thought of the idea of filming the Odyssey. I said, 'Not big enough.' For a moment he seemed baffled, which is rare indeed with Orson, and then he smiled and asked, 'Well, what would *you* do?' I said, 'I'd do the Odyssey *and* the Iliad.' This seemed to fascinate him. He gave that great bellowing laughter of his and said, 'Yes, my boy. That's what we'll do. We'll do the Odyssey *and* the Iliad!'

A: And did you do it?

B: No, of course not. Orson insisted that a 'creative person' ought not to be without his wife and children and told my wife to come to Italy where Orson had a house. And to bring our young son with her. First-class passage paid, of course, The house was heavenly, Monte Porzio near Frascati. Six lavender-coloured bathrooms, five servants, love letters from Lea Padovani painted with lipstick on every mirror. Alas, Orson went broke a few weeks after I had set to work. He never came back. I finished the script nevertheless and he sold it to Carlo Ponti and Dino de Laurentiis who were partners that year, 1949/1950. It was shot in a totally altered version with Kirk Douglas as Odysseus and Silvana Mangano as Penelope. I had argued that Homer used the same adjectives for most of his women and that they should therefore be played by the same actress – Penelope, Circe, Nausicaa and all the others. I'd also argued that they weren't white but brown and should therefore be played by blacks. Orson found that funny but thought there weren't enough coloured actors who could do classical parts. I said I'd come across a talented black girl during my time as a jazz musician. She'd been dancing in the Katherine Dunham Show which was, in my opinion, the best Afro-American Ballet there's ever been. Orson went to see her in Paris where she was dancing and singing at the Carrousel and sent me a cable which read: DEAR ERNEST JUST MET THE MOST EXCITING WOMAN IN THE WORLD STOP THANK YOU STOP LOVE ORSON.

A: Eartha Kitt?

B: Yes, we used to call her Kitty because she was so cat-like. That was the beginning of her career. We never made the Odyssey or the Iliad with her, but Orson did Marlowe's *Faust* with Eartha as a black Gretchen – just to *épater le bourgeois*, for Gretchen doesn't appear at all in Marlowe's *Tragicall Historie of Dr Faustus*.

A: Did you ever get paid? We got on to this whole subject because I asked you how you managed to finance your research projects.

B: Yes, about ten years later, when we had a house in Chelsea, a pretty young woman rang the bell and brought us an attaché case full of pound notes. She said, 'Sign here', and passed me a voucher on which it said, 'Received from Mr Orson Welles £10,000.' I said, 'I'd like to count them, if you don't mind, before I sign this.' She said. 'Well, I'll admit, it's not all there, but most of it. If my clothes hadn't been on top they would have pinched more.' It appeared they'd been playing strip-poker and someone had raided the clothes. Then, while I was counting the bank notes, I noticed our local cop at the window. He was just standing there, a pink-faced young man with a yellow moustache, and grinning. I asked him in and said, 'You won't believe it, but this is neither a bank haul nor a counterfeit workshop. I merely got paid in cash for a film I wrote a decade ago.' My wife perked up and said, 'From Mr Orson Welles. He always pays in cash. Or not at all.' The policeman saluted and said, 'Sir, about Mr Orson Welles I believe almost anything.'

A: But your wife had a good reason to perk up. She got polio in Frascati, didn't she?

B: Yes, it turned out that the heavenly open house with the six lavender-coloured bathrooms and the five servants didn't belong to Orson at all. He hadn't paid the rent for ages. The servants hadn't been paid either and expected to be paid by us. The electricity works hadn't been paid, so they switched off the power. The water works hadn't been paid and cut off the water. We had plenty of wonderful wine in the cellar, barrels of wine. So we washed with wine and flushed the toilets with it. It seemed a kind of extravagant revenge for bringing us to Italy without paying us. But the one who paid the price in the end was my wife. She became partly paralysed as a result of the polio infection.

A: And then?

B: I took her to England to her mother, but her mother couldn't get on with our son, so I raised him. Which is the reason why I can talk about running a household and raising a child when I get into arguments with feminists these days. Having to support two households meant that I had to make money as fast as possible. As a university teacher I couldn't have done it. So I made a virtue of necessity and practised what Orson had taught me. I wrote five feature films and started directing. Between 1950 and 1960 I must have been writing, directing and producing close to a hundred radio and TV shows, also a good many serials and series. And since I lived very simply, I saved most of what I earned. This is what I've been living on since 1961, and this is what financed most of my research projects.

A: But surely, your books must have earned you a good deal of money, too. You've done seven novels in English, some of which have been bestsellers, and ten works of non-fiction which have also sold well.

B: I was paid $50,000 by New American Library in 1968 for the U.S. pocketbook rights of my last novel, *The Man Who Loved Women*. That was the largest single sum I ever received for any book. It's my experience that you can't live by writing books. Only if a novel gets filmed or is bought for TV do you begin to break even. My third novel, *Tremolo*, was bought by Hitchcock but never filmed. It was directed for CBS-New York by Yul Brynner. He still had hair then. Yul also played the lead in my last feature film, *The Long Duel*. My scientific books were – by the sales standards of scholarly works – quite successful, but they wouldn't have covered the repair costs of my house.

A: Well now, that's not quite fair, is it? You have a house that simply does require a lot of repairs. How old is it?

B: Probably fourteenth century. All we know for sure is that one half of it was burnt down during the peasant wars in 1594. It used to be one of those atrium farmsteads that they call *Vierkanthof* in upper Austria. They are on an average 50 yards by 50 on the outside, and 30 by 30 on the inside. We have thirty rooms and a library of 150 square yards.

A: How many books can you fit in?

B: When I bought the house, I thought I'd have enough room to expand till I die. Now it's already far too small again. I guess we must have between 20,000 and 30,000 books. Then, of course, complete back-numbers of many journals and magazines. I don't like working in libraries, it takes too much time to get there and back. So I buy every book that may be of conceivable interest to me in any of the projects on which I work. Which means between fifty and a hundred per month.

A: Perhaps that's the reason why you say you can't break even by writing books.

B: Perhaps. But I'm pretty frugal in every other regard. We haven't had a holiday in two decades, we haven't bought any new clothes in years, we rarely go out to restaurants, we run a cheap car, we're satisfied with what we have.

A: Is that really true? You are the only person I know who always says that he has no desires for anything that he hasn't already got.

B: It's true in every way but one. I'm a political animal and I don't like the state that our society finds itself in. So if I have urgent desires they concern me less than my fellow human beings.

A: We know from earlier discussions that we don't see eye to eye in these matters. So I won't try to argue with you. But just for our readers' information: are you politically active?

B: Of course, I was a socialist youth functionary when I was fourteen, I was twice fired from school for socialist activities. I had to go abroad temporarily when Hitler came to power, but I went back a number of times to do underground work and I'm now a local functionary of the Austrian Socialist Party. I edit all the local village newspapers that my Party issues, I speak to farmers and workers in our district on matters of education and information. The only thing I don't want to do is to become a paid functionary. I want to stay close to the people. I don't want to rise in the party hierarchy. Power corrupts socialists just as it corrupts everybody else. I doubt whether I shall want to be a socialist in a socialist *country*. But as long as there exists a socialist *opposition*, I'll be active in it.

A: Well, that's a little less painful than most other political views. I consider all politicians a pain in the ass.

B: I know, but we mean two different things by politics. Some people go into politics to make a career, others sacrifice their career to go into politics. With my political views you can't make a career. That's why I'm still at the lowest level of the academic establishment. People of my kind are as unpopular in the Austrian groves of Academe as in the American ones.

A: But you teach at two of the oldest and most distinguished universities in Europe. Isn't that enough?

B: I teach four hours per week in Marburg and two hours per week in Salzburg. But I have no chair of my own, no security, no permanence. I can be fired any time, and my political opponents do their damnedest to see that this happens soon.

A: In spite of the fact that you are considered a very good teacher?

B: Because of it. I have so many friends among students that the other professors get madly envious. Nothing makes them see so red as the fact that the reddest students rally around me each time I'm being attacked by the establishment. Also they work very hard for my lectures and they learn a great deal. I ask a lot of them, and this refutes the wicked rumour that 'left' professors just chat and don't work. Finally, I received my Ph.D. summa cum laude, and there are hardly any other professors teaching psychology today who did that well in their own exams.

A: But you completed your Ph.D. very late in life. Didn't that make it a little easier for you to get super grades?

B: On the contrary. I had to work very much harder. Since I had left Germany at the age of eighteen, a few months prior to my matric, I couldn't graduate in England. I was poor and couldn't afford to go to crammers to do an English matric. Which meant that I had to earn money first of all, then do my matric at an age when many other people are about to retire, then my state exams (what you would call B.A. and M.A.), and then my Ph.D. (or the German equivalent of it which is a little more demanding). Only in 1977 did I finally get my professorship.

A: I fear that some of our readers may get so muddled by now that we'll have to try and get some chronology into it.

B: All right, I'll try. I was born during the second year of the first world war in Berlin. I've always been grateful to have been born there. Berlin is as different from the rest of Germany as New York from the rest of the U.S. – or *was* that different, anyway. To be born a German is a terrible fate. It's the most unhappy nation I know. But to be born a Berliner is great luck. It's one of the most relaxed, sane, open, cosmopolitan cities in the world. Was, I should say once more. Berlin between 1900 and 1930 was an education by itself. If you had your five senses and nothing else you could learn more by just living there than with the best of brains in any other German city. We were sexually mature at fourteen, politically mature at fifteen, intellectually mature between fourteen and sixteen. We played the blues when others still played ragtime. We sang *cante hondo* when others still thought Ravel's *Bolero* was Spanish folk music. We had recognized Joyce as the greatest writer in the English tongue since Shakespeare at a time when the English still raved about Galsworthy and the Irish about Yeats. We had read Proust before the French had accepted him and we'd recognized d'Annunzio for the fool he was when the Italians still thought him a genius. We'd recognized Mark Twain as a genius when the Americans still thought him a clown. It was quite a city, then.

A: About yourself?

B: My parents were the happiest couple I have ever known. I was raised in a climate of such affection and security that nothing, not even Hitler or the soviet invasion of Hungary and the ČSSR could ever shake me out of it. My father is still alive at ninety, very spry and charming as ever. The only thing he never liked was work. My mother did everything. They had a store for baby and children's wear. My father pretended to run it. My mother ran it. She had a quiet strength, a wisdom and a warmth that has shaped my attitude toward women. I feel now, have always felt and do not repent feeling that women are in every way superior to men.

A: Did that determine your interest in matrilineal cultures?

B: Certainly. But most of all it determined my interest in women. I don't know any man who is more dependent on women than I am. I can do without men, but I feel completely frustrated without women. Not that I want to go to bed with every one. On the contrary, I've never been able to develop any interest in any woman who wasn't interested in me. Which made it easy to avoid rejection. But I simply need female company the way other human beings need food and drink and air and sleep.

A: Is that what caused you to become a sexologist?

B: I don't think so. Almost all sexologists I know turned to sexology because they belonged to some sexual minority or other. More than half are homosexuals and therefore know more about heterosexuality than the heterosexuals. As for me, I remember that even as a child I was asked questions about sex matters by most of my friends, even the older ones. For some reason they seemed to believe that I had an answer. But what really got me interested in sexology as a science was my acquaintance with Wilhelm Reich. I met him through the socialist physician Max Hodann who was a friend of our family doctor. Reich had started a clinic for working-class people and had engaged some of us in the socialist youth movement to help him look after working-class children. Many of the questions they asked dealt with masturbation, contraception, abortion, and venereal disease. By the time I was seventeen, I knew more about these matters than many general practitioners learn in a lifetime. In 1933, the clinic was raided by storm-troopers acting as auxiliary police. The staff list fell into their hands. When two other socialist organizations that I worked for were raided in the same way during June and July 1933, I became No. 1 on the Nazi black list of socialist youth leaders in Berlin and was smuggled out to London by the Party.

A: When did you write your first novel?

B: Two years after I'd arrived in England. I learned English very fast and very easily. My main interest, then as now, was in idiomatics and slang. When my first two novels, *The Face on the Cutting-Room Floor* and *Love Story* (both titles have later been plagiarized by other novelists) came out, Eric Partridge thought them a mine of information for current English slang and published whole pages of them in his various lexica. In all my later novels, especially in *The Compromisers, Tomorrow Is Now* and *The Man Who Loved Women* (another title that got plagiarized as a film in France), I tried to characterize my cast by the way they spoke and tried to avoid all other explanations as to who they were, where they stemmed from, what region, what social class, what occupation they belonged to. Since you can't do that in a country like Western Germany where everybody tries to speak a synthetic language by the name of *hochdeutsch*, I've never written a novel in German.

A: Apart from playing jazz and writing novels, what else did you do to earn your living during these years in England?

B: I drove in rallies for a firm of hand-made sports cars called A.C. The first American racing cars built by Ford used their chassis. And I worked as a volunteer for the BBC. Without salary, but it helped me to pay my expenses and it also helped me to sell my first radio and TV scripts.

A: You told me once, I believe, that the day you were interned as an 'enemy alien', one of your first radio scripts was being broadcast.

B: Yes, that's true. It came out of the loudspeaker of the police bus that took us to the internment camp. I asked the policeman if he recognized the voice. 'He has a German accent,' he said. 'Yes,' I said. 'Kind of funny to arrest someone who's just entertaining the British public, isn't it?' He just shrugged.

A: How long were you interned?

B: From 17 May 1940 to 10 July 1941.

A: Was it bad?

B: Not at all. Better than to kill and get killed. The only problem was the lack of women.

A: And how did you finally manage to get out?

B: By one of those miracles that have ruled my entire life. Of 40 million Englishmen the British picked just the one man who knew me when they sent someone to Canada to sort the chaff from the wheat – Sir Alexander Paterson, Her Majesty's Commissioner for Prisons. I'd been interpreting for him in England. When he saw me, he said, 'My God, Ernest, what are *you* doing here?' And I said, 'Well, Alec, I might ask the same question.' So he said, 'Well, we must get you out of here, mustn't we?' And I said, 'Fine, but I've already made myself as unpopular as usual. I've protested against every damn folly, and they got mad and classified me as unreleasable. Which means I'll never get out before the war is over.' So he asked me if I couldn't do anything useful 'for the war effort', and I said, 'Well, Alec, you know, all I've learnt is something about social anthropology and prehistory. That won't exactly help us to defeat Adolf Hitler, will it?' Then I had an idea and added, 'But I learnt a little at the BBC about making films and I just read in the newspaper that John Grierson has come to Canada to start a film unit, the National Film Board. The paper said he was urgently looking for personnel. I've met him once at a party. Why don't you two Scots get together and break a bottle of Scotch and decide what you're going to do with me.'

A: And what did they do?

B: Well, I hadn't expected for one moment that Paterson would have time to do anything. After all, there were a few thousand other internees in Canada. But that extraordinary man got on to the night train and went to Ottawa. Next morning he went to see Grierson in the converted saw-mill which was the Film Board's first office and told him he had a German in one of his internment camps who'd told him he'd met him once at a party. Grierson said, 'Borneman? Borneman? Never heard of the man.' Paterson said, 'Well, I didn't really think you would have. The man is impossible, anyway. A born troublemaker. He'll never get out.' Grierson, who was at his best when he had to do with the restrictive tendencies of the state, perked up and said, 'Well, if he'll *never* get out, it's high time that we'll get him out *now*, isn't it?' And Paterson said, 'Yes, that's about what I had in mind when I came here.' That dialogue, of course, is apocryphal, but I've heard both Paterson's and Grierson's versions a number of times and they were pretty similar. So I got out and began to make films. The RCMP said to Grierson, I wasn't to go out after seven in the evening. Security reasons.

Grierson laughed and said, 'Well, if Borneman isn't allowed in the street after seven, we'll send him where there are no streets.' So he gave me a camera and lots of film and sent me up north into the great pre-cambrian shield where I survived the war among Eskimos and Indians.

A: And then?

B: Then I came back and made films with a radio announcer from CBC Toronto. He made his way, too – Lorne Green. One of the films we made was *Blitzkrieg Tactics*, the first training film for the Canadian Tank Corps. He was the voice of Canada, I was the voice of Germany. Grierson had told me to make a training film for armoured warfare. I said, 'But Grierson, I'm the most peaceful man in the world, I've never even *seen* a tank in all my life.' Grierson said, 'Nonsense, all Germans know how to make war. Go and make a war film.' I was flabbergasted. Then I began to read up on armoured warfare. There wasn't much in those years. I found a German book by a fellow named Guderian, and I found a French one by an unknown young officer named Charles de Gaulle. So you had the paradoxical situation that an enemy alien who wasn't even allowed out at night was commissioned to write and direct and speak the official training film that prepared the Canadian Tank Corps for the invasion of Europe.

A: À propos de la bataille de l'Europe – you once told me a story about another film of yours that made history.

B: That was *Zero Hour*, the film about the Normandy Beach battle. We had it in every American movie theatre within twenty hours after the first news of the invasion was broadcast. The Americans never understood how we did it and accused us of having received secret pre-information. But we hadn't. I had the idea that the invasion was coming, but it could come from seven different points. So I asked Norman McLaren, the most brilliant man the Film Board had, a genius at animating films, to make me some animated maps for each of the possible routes of invasion. Then I intercut all the footage we had of allied manoeuvres (some pretty drastic stuff with genuine casualties) with German footage of the war in France. Perhaps I should say – by now it's no longer a secret – that we got every German war film within a few days after it had been made. How it worked, I don't know. But I had something like twelve hours of battle footage to select from. So I edited up the goriest passages of landing under fire, aerial support, infantry duels, artillery fire against landing troops on beaches, and so on. I edited seven versions of twenty minutes each, all with precise maps as to where the action took place. Then I appointed a round the clock team to listen for news of any possible invasion. One night, at about three in the morning, they rang me and said, 'It's happened, it's Normandy.' I phoned Lorne Green and he got on to a plane in Toronto at four in the morning. We recorded from five to six. Grierson had arranged with the RCAF to fly out the negatives and dupe negatives to every large American film lab. That night our film was in every cinema from Alaska to Tijuana. Grierson said, 'Well, what did I say? It always takes a German to make a war or a war film.'

A: What other films did you make?

B: Oh, I don't want to talk about it. It's another part of my life. Oh yes, I made a little animated picture about war bonds with a little Canadian kid who played piano. He also made good – Oscar Peterson. That was his first recording.

A: Who else did you play with in the jazz world?

B: Mostly with English musicians who aren't awfully well-known. I was a poor musician. I never wanted to play anything but blues. Like Mezzrow. I played a lot with Mezzrow. And with Bechet in his tailor-shop in Brooklyn. In Paris, later, I became friendly with Panassié, the jazz pope, and his ex-friend, later his enemy, Charles Delaunay. I saw a lot of Boris Vian who didn't only write novels and plays but also played quite competent trumpet.

A: Then you got hired away from UNESCO by Orson Welles and went to live in his house in Italy. Then back to England after your wife's polio?

B: Berlin 1915–33, London 1933–40, Canada 1940–7, Paris 1947–9, Italy 1949–50, England 1950–60. That was the time I wrote my five feature films and began directing TV plays. The best was a jazz opera called *Four O'Clock in the Morning Blues*, a story told partly in dance, partly in dialogue, partly in music, partly in song. With Cleo Laine and the Johnny Dankworth Orchestra. And with Pamela Charles who later played the lead in the New York version of *My Fair Lady*. I was head of script department of three British TV networks. Then the British Film Institute hired me as Programme Officer. We started the London Film Festival, the first festival to work without a jury. Then, in 1959, a German TV commission came to England and asked Cecil McGivern, head of BBC-TV, if he didn't know anyone who spoke German and could be hired away for a short time to help build up a German Federal TV-Network. Cecil recommended me, and in 1960 I went back for the first time in twenty-seven years to work in my 'fatherland' as head of programming and head of production – a joint operation that was unique in the history of television and gave me a power I had never dreamt of. I had discussed the offer for a long time with friends in the Labour Party, and they had said, 'Do it. If you don't, someone else will.' Well, I thought I would go back as a sort of socialist Goebbels and pay those bastards back in their own coin. I hired only emigrants and ex-emigrants, Austrians and Swiss, next to no Germans. Almost everybody stood left of the middle in his politics. It was the most advanced T V operation in history. But West Germany, like the U.S., is a Federal Republic, and the individual states felt themselves threatened by the prospect of a federal television network. So they sued, claiming that only the federal states had the right to indulge in cultural activities. The Supreme Court in Karlsruhe decided that the Federal Government had the right of emission through the post office transmitters, while the states had the right to decide *what* was being transmitted. Result: our organization was dissolved, 600 people were fired, and a new organization called ZDF (Second German Television) was founded. Enormous waste. Since the majority of the German states are and were conservative, the left-wing employees of my own organization were not rehired. But they couldn't get around buying the films and the taped shows that we had produced. So they broadcast all those where they could delete the name of our production company, *Freies Fernsehen*, and put their own company's name in its place. All productions where that was impossible were never shown. Millions of marks down the drain. That browned me off once and for ever with television. I had told my wife for close to a decade that I was tired of the whole T V and film world. Sham and waste and incompetence and kowtowing to the boys and girls with money and power. I wanted to go back to writing and to research. The only question was whether we could afford it. She had left her post with one of the largest British publishing houses, Oxford University Press, to join me in Germany. Our son had gone to a pretty expensive school, Salem, since no other German school would accept him because of his lacking German. I had no idea how long our savings would last and how much I would earn. She said not to worry. She'd take a job if necessary. So we started advertising for a house of our specifications - old, open view, preferably fruit trees, and at least one room large enough for our books. We would have gone anywhere, including the U.S. or the Seychelles, but it so happened that we found what we wanted in Upper Austria.

A: That was when?

B: 1970. We were ten years in Germany, 1960–70, and we've now been nearly ten years in Austria. I wrote eight books in these nineteen years, including a four-volume encyclopedia of sexology, and I edited two, one of which has been translated – alas very poorly – into English: *Psychoanalysis of Money*. Even the title is horrible. It should have been called *Money: A Psychoanalytic Study*. You can say *Psychoanalyse des Geldes* in German, it sounds just right. But you can't say *Psychoanalysis of Money* in English. It's clumsy. It's a Germanism. But you try and explain this to a translator who has no sense for style, rhythm and lingual melody.

A: Well, now we're back to *Maledicta*. Do you believe that you learned something about idiomatics, perhaps even about verbal aggression, from your contact with the jazz world?

B: Less from jazz than from the black musicians. I'll always be grateful for the chance I had to learn something from them about minority problems, about social oppression and about the psychological terror that a majority can carry out against a minority. I began to understand minority problems only after I had been playing jazz with black musicians. I began to understand the problems that Jews have with Gentiles and Gentiles with Jews. If a black man hears a white man use the work 'black', he at once thinks it's a racial insult. If a Jew hears a non-Jew use the word 'Jew', he at once thinks it's an anti-Semitic remark. A black man can say lovingly to his woman, 'You sweet black bitch,' but let a white man say that to his black girl friend and hell on earth will burst open. Rightly so, too.

A: I think we've forgotten one point – Brecht.

B: I met Brecht when I was at school. He had written a 'school-opera', *Der Jasager*, and was looking for children with good singing voices and a bit of stage experience. I was one of those selected to take part. He asked us what we thought of the plot. We said unanimously that we found it unconvincing. He promised to alter it according to our views. But with typically Brechtian deviousness he published our negative comments, didn't alter a word in the script – and wrote a second school-opera, *Der Neinsager*, based on our opinions. That taught me a lot not only about tactics. He needed it later when he started his own theatre in East Berlin. As far as I can make out, he is the only writer who ever managed to survive without compromise in a communist country. Brilliant. I could tell you a lot about Brecht. But not in public.

A: But you liked him?

B: I admired him enormously. I still think he is the greatest poet Germany has had in centuries. But to *like* Brecht is impossible. I don't think anyone ever liked him, not even his own mother. His women may have *loved* him, but no one ever *liked* him.

    A: And yet you worked with him a number of times later in life?

    B: I adored working with him, just as I adored working with Orson. It's wonderful to see a really brilliant mind at work. What a consolation after all the dwarfs one has to cope with in films and TV – *crippled* dwarfs, at that. I played a boy in the beggars' street procession during the first three months in the first stage version of the *Dreigroschenoper*, I worked under his direction in our school version of *Die Rundköpfe und die Spitzköpfe*. I rewrote the English translation of his *Dreigroschenroman* for him, and he helped me in exchange to write my first stage play, *The Windows of Heaven*, a piece about the German peasant wars. It reads more like a Brecht original than any English translation of any Brecht play.

    A: I heard it's a very good play. Why wasn't it ever staged?

    B: Because I didn't want to finish it without Brecht's help. After his death I developed some kind of psychological impediment *vis-à-vis* that play. Only this year did I put the last touches to it. It can only be played in English – all attempts to translate it into German have failed. Erich Fried will try it now. He's the only one alive who could do it. I can't. I hope he will.

    A: Last question: do you ever want to come back to the U.S.? You've visited the country often. Would you like to come here for a while as a guest professor?

    B: Certainly. If it's the right university and the right subject.

So for the taped interview with 'Cameron McCabe' by Reinhold Aman in 1979. We have asked Ernest Borneman to add a few words on the history of *The Face on the Cutting-Room Floor*. He sent us, in addition to his short comment at the end of this dossier, copies of letters from Julian Symons and Frederic Raphael, the two men primarily responsible for the rediscovery of the book:

37 Albert Bridge Road London SW11 4PX
01-622 3981

8 September 1974

Dear Mr Borneman

    Do forgive me for not answering your letter before today. I've been out of England for a couple of weeks.

    Delighted to hear from you, although the whole thing leaves me reddish with embarrassment about my ignorance. First Philip Oakes of the *Sunday Times* rang me up to say: 'But this must be *the* Ernest Borneman who . . .', and then somebody wrote from Paris to say: 'I suppose you must mean the Ernest Borneman who is famous for . . .' Well, there you are, I'm ignorant.

You've seen, I hope and expect, the piece by Freddie Raphael in the *Sunday Times*, which can have done no harm at all. Perhaps Gollancz will be moved to a reprint. I hope so. And I hope also that you'll forgive my ignorance, and give me a minim of credit as the first person in recent years to raise a hurrah for *The Face*, not in the *New Review*, but a little while further back in a history of the crime story called *Bloody Murder*. Was *The Face* your only detective story? From that short fascinating personal history I assume that it was, and that Cameron McCabe never came back from the dead.

Thank you once again for taking the trouble to write. And, again, forgive me for being so ignorant in the first place.

Yours sincerely
Julian Symons

The Wick, Langham, Essex
Dedham 2108.

9th September 1974

Ernest Borneman Esq.,
Ebohaus,
A-4612 Scharten,
Austria.

Dear Mr Borneman,

I do not know whether you saw my notice of the reissue of *The Face on the Cutting-Room Floor* but it may amuse you to know that you are far from forgotten in this country. My suggestion that nobody knew who you were prompted several reminiscing letters from various parts of the country. I am delighted to discover that you are, as one of my correspondents says, 'alive and well and living in Austria'. *The Face on the Cutting-Room Floor* has lost little of its sharpness and your not-so-remote neighbour, Mr Nabokov, who lives in Switzerland, might have been proud of several of the shafts directed at critics and rivals.

With best wishes,
Yours sincerely,
Frederic Raphael.

To conclude this dossier, we publish a letter from Ernest Borneman, written during the first week of 1981 at his farm in Scharten, Upper Austria.

January 1981

Dear Mr Peacock, dear Mr Penzler,

I am delighted, though baffled, at the continued interest in my first-born book. I was nineteen when I wrote it, had just arrived in England as a penniless political refugee, could barely speak English and had started writing because it was the only activity *not* forbidden by the British authorities. They didn't want foreigners to take jobs away from British citizens.

The authors who fascinated me at the time were Proust, Joyce, Dos Passos, Hemingway, Hammett and Aldous Huxley. *The Face on the Cutting-Room Floor* was meant to be no more than a finger exercise on the keyboard of a new language. It had no message and wasn't meant as a spoof on the great masters of the crime story. I simply wanted to know if my English was good enough to let me earn money with my pen.

Half-way through the book I received my first labour permit and my first job – as script reader with Douglas Fairbanks Jr in a movie company called Criterion Films. I wrote the first draft in my office at Worton Hall, a movie studio near London. Almost everything that happens in the book – except the crime plot – was copied straight from life, including many of the dialogues. Almost everybody had a living counterpart and was described as I saw him in the studio. Bloom's prototype, apart from the name which stemmed of course from Joyce, was Marcel Hellman, my boss and Doug's partner. Since some of the others are still alive, I won't name them.

During the spring of 1935 my friend Jim Harris, now head of the New Zealand Government Film Unit, left me with a tent, a kayak, and a ton of tinned food on the beach of Archirondel Bay in Jersey, one of the Channel Islands, and went off to the Moscow Film Festival. During the summer, my girl friend Eva, for close to forty years now my wife, came to visit me, which made life on the beach much more pleasant and the writing of the book much easier.

After Eva had typed the book I took it under my arm and went to see Victor Gollancz in his converted store opposite Covent Garden, London's fruit market. It was the first publisher's office I'd ever been in and it remains the dingiest. I had never met Victor Gollancz, but as a socialist I admired the orange-covered volumes of the Left Book Club which he had been publishing for some years. I had no idea whether he had ever published crime fiction and I wasn't even aware that I had written a kind of detective story. But with the preposterous optimism which has governed my life I assumed that Gollancz would read the book, publish it, and pay me.

Oddly enough, that's just what happened. I didn't know that you had to make an appointment to see a famous publisher, that he would probably pass you on to some minor editor or script reader, that the book would probably never be read and would most likely be returned to me half a year later with a printed rejection slip. But since I didn't know any of this, Gollancz, with a green reading screen over his eyes, came out of his tiny office at the end of the dark store, listened to me without interrupting me, promised to read the book, read it, sent me a contract, and paid me. Proverbially mean as he was, he paid me very little. But he paid me promptly and I've been grateful to him ever since.

In the course of the next thirty years I became quite a good novelist. The critics were kind to me. I was praised as one of the British fathers of the *roman nouveau* (for my novel *The Compromisers*, published in 1962 by André Deutsch in London), but the best of my books, *Tomorrow Is Now*, came out during a newspaper strike and was lost – literally. Only years later, when the book had long gone out of print (only 500 copies had been found till then), we discovered the remaining 9500 copies in a deserted warehouse. They were never sent to the wholesalers and retailers. The book was dead.

I shall never know why *The Face on the Cutting-Room Floor*, which seems mannered and puerile to me now, has been reissued so often, while *The Compromisers* and *Tomorrow Is Now* have never been published in the U.S. at all. True, two of my other books have been issued in the U.S. – but both of them under very odd circumstances. My mystery story *Tremolo* was published by Harpers in 1948 – but by a freak of publishing history the first draft, not the finished one, was printed. It had less than half the length of the final version published by Jarrolds in London.

My last novel, *Landscape with Nudes*, was published by Coward McCann in 1968 under the idiotic title *The Man Who Loved Women*. Three motion picture companies paid advances on the screen rights – and forgot about production. Peacefully, the book went out of print in 1970. Hardly had that happened when a few critics began to lament the unlamented death of a masterpiece. It was about the same as with *The Face*.

I seem to collect nostalgia the way other relics collect dust. Happy 1981!

ERNEST BORNEMAN

Footnote by the Editors

Borneman's adventures with Orson Welles have been described in great detail by Peter Noble in *The Fabulous Orson Welles* (Hutchinson, London and New York, 1956, pp. 194–229). The story of the German refugees interned in Canada and their later fate is told by Eric Koch in *Deemed Suspect*, Toronto, Methuen, 1980 (references to Borneman, pp. 5, 72, 92, 139, 140, 187, 188, 210, 211).